Sandra Van der Merwe has a BA in Sociology, an MBA and a doctorate in Marketing. In her distinguished career in marketing she has taught and consulted worldwide. She is the author of a number of academic books and articles, although *Skin Deep* is her first novel. She lives with her husband and two daughters in Geneva.

D0674770

Skin Deep

SANDRA VAN DER MERWE

Futura

A Futura Book

Copyright © Exectra Management Consultants Ltd 1986

First published in Great Britain in 1986
by Macdonald & Co (Publishers) Ltd
London & Sydney

This Futura edition published in 1987

*All characters in this publication are fictitious
and any resemblance to real persons, living or dead,
is purely coincidental.*

All rights reserved.
No part of this publication may be reproduced,
stored in a retrieval system, or transmitted, in any
form or by any means without the prior
permission in writing of the publisher, nor be
otherwise circulated in any form of binding or
cover other than that in which it is published and
without a similar condition including this
condition being imposed on the subsequent
purchaser.

ISBN 0 7088 3371 3

Reproduced, printed and bound in Great Britain by
Hazell Watson & Viney Limited,
Member of the BPCC Group,
Aylesbury, Bucks

Futura Publications
A Division of
Macdonald & Co (Publishers) Ltd
Greater London House
Hampstead Road
London NW1 7QX
A BPCC plc Company

I have a husband who loves me
two divine daughters
two poodles
a great dane
two siamese
one tabby
and a handful of family
and friends

Who could ask for more?

This book is dedicated to them

I gratefully acknowledge the imput of the individuals who contributed invaluably to this book in various ways.

PRELUDE

She was no longer afraid of flying. Frances smiled as the thought flickered across her mind, flung up briefly from among the turmoil within her. At least that was one thing she had gained – even if she had lost everything else.

Then, with a whistling roar of power, the twin Rolls Royce engines of the Airbus lifted one hundred and thirty-two tons of metal, fuel and humanity off the ground.

The half-light for take off in the first-class cabin was comforting. It gave Frances a feeling of anonymity, but she knew the sense of security was false. As she had boarded, she had seen her own face, or a version of it, looking out from the front pages of a dozen or so newspapers.

It was a remarkably childlike face for a woman of almost forty-three, finely moulded around a strong but delicate nose, and a hint of high cheekbones. Wide and free was the smile, the eyes both calm and powerful, and alive with expression.

She'd seen several newspapers dip, and felt the stares, before her fellow travellers compared her pale, strained features with those of the photographs, and read the story of betrayal and disaster printed alongside.

She would have to get used to it. The dividing line between fame and notoriety is very thin, she thought. And you, Frances Sarah Kline, have been pushed across it.

But why did they seem to *loathe* her so? She had arrived at Orly at 7 am, while the brief sleep of Paris was ending under a sky stained with crushed mulberry on a belly of low-lying cloud. Waiting, they were already there - like jackals, acrylic teeth gnawing at her raw fresh wounds, seeking blood to smear on their newspage pulp.

A barrage of flashgun flack and babble of questions - the distorted images danced round in her mind. Frances had fought to preserve her carefully created public image: the calm, collected businesswoman, never at a loss for an answer. But this time she had no answers.

She felt an unfamiliar ache, conscious of her fragility as a woman alone, and grateful that she had accepted Gray Barnard's offer to drive her to Orly. Because now she needed the man's pure masculinity, his God-given bulk, to shield her and to shoulder aside the throng.

She had already had to endure the first day's headlines. THE GREAT REJUVENATION RIP-OFF, blared the *Sun*. PREMATURE DEATH OF ETERNAL LIFE the *New York Times* scoffed; the *Financial Times* front-page report was crisp and crippling. KLINE TOPPLED. Momentarily, Frances wondered how many of the reports of her sudden and dramatic downfall had been written by the same people who had praised her so unstintingly when her revolutionary new rejuvenation drug had been announced.

Then, they had called her 'Elixir Kline', and had ecstatically dubbed PS-21 the 'balm of youth'. The Paris correspondent of *Fortune* had written of her almost sycophantically, as 'a one-woman business revolution', and 'probably the only really beautiful, Jewish, New York *wunderkind* we'll ever see.' He'd described her as a woman who had confounded international critics, who had built an unassailable financial empire, and who was poised on the brink of success so great that it would make her career so far pale by comparison.

When she had stepped from the low-slung Citroen taxi, with Gray Barnard trying to fend off the reporters, she had seen the same writer, as eager as the rest to attack and destroy her.

'You short-circuited safety tests on PS-21; is it true?'

'Did you falsify medical data to beat the Japanese competition?'

'Is it true that PS-21 has made human guinea-pigs go blind?'

'Are you running away to . . . ?'

Madness, lunacy! Until she had made it to the departure lounge in mind-numbing agony; and then the automatic process of boarding her aircraft, where at last she could re-focus on the thing that was troubling and baffling her the most – the role that David had played in the conspiracy.

David. Her son. Who was implicated in – had perhaps engineered – the break in. David, who had fled from Paris and who she was following now, with a ticket to Athens and directions to an obscure archaeological dig on the island of Samothraki.

She had to know the truth. Had he betrayed her? Or was he also a victim? She just couldn't bring herself to believe that he was part of it. If he was a fellow victim, then she needed to share with him their mutual vulnerability, and prove that their bond was strong enough to survive.

In the end they were all victims, she thought. They who worshipped and served the corporation. Without the human beings that orchestrated it, there was no corporation. Yet as an enemy, it was a monolith. Heartless and faceless, rigid and unyielding like some massive block of stone.

Again and again she had gone through it all in her mind, trying to piece it together like some deadly jigsaw.

She knew now that PS-21, her gift to the world, had been deliberately destroyed. Tragically. Now the human race would never have the benefit of a drug that could still offer them so much. They would never trust it again.

She even knew part of how it had been done.

What she couldn't understand was *why*. And how did the savage murder in New York just one floor above her own office fit in?

'*Madame . . . café, thé, citron pressé?*' The Air France stewardess broke into her thoughts. She could see behind the lipstick-

9

bright smile that the girl was very well aware of who Frances Kline was.

'Perrier water, please,' she said, using her dark glasses as camouflage from behind which to examine the taut skin and flawless coiffure. Quite suddenly, Frances felt a burst of unexpected envy of this girl, and her simple life of hairdos and wake-up calls, and rendezvous with men.

But she could see the irony, that this girl would a short time before have envied Frances Kline, the feminine tycoon. She'd have been jealous of the billion-dollar power of her decisions, and her care and responsibility for the future of thousands of employees.

How frail her protection had proved, under the assault of an enemy she could neither identify nor understand.

She leaned back and stared through the porthole again. She could see the wing tips flex up and down as the aircraft added resilience to its miraculous equation of flight. The engineers had thought of every possible strain, and made everything twice as strong as need be. Frances' own business success had been built on just such an approach – an ability to foresee future problems, and to be more than ready for them.

That had been at the core of her downfall, she realized now – the sheer unpredictability of it all. Never before in her meteoric business career had Frances had to contend with such an unexpected rival. The disaster of the sabotage had been impossible to predict. It was beyond bad planning, bad management, or bad luck.

It was as though a shadowy enemy was moving just beyond the periphery of her vision, a spectre that slipped swiftly out of sight if she glanced over her shoulder. She shuddered as a half-remembered poem by TS Eliot came to her mind – about Scott's fatal expedition to the South Pole, where in his last doomed days, he had been aware of a presence that he could not see. She wondered from where came her own silent and invisible companion of misfortune . . . and of what more it had in store for her.

The Airbus had by now shrugged off the layer of ground-hugging winter cloud, and was suspended in a blue dome, clear and sparkling. They were flying almost straight towards a low, distant sun, which picked up the cicatrices of jet vapour against the azure ceiling – scars in the sky left by other travellers. Frances wondered how many of them were like her – on a mission so important that it transcended even the need for her to pick up the pieces of her shattered career.

The hostess interrupted Frances' whirling thoughts. '*Madame, petit dèjeuner?*' Brioche and pale, unsalted butter from Holland. Absently, Frances broke the thin crust, and spread the butter and jam. But then she pushed the food away untasted.

The decision to fly to Athens had been the most clear and certain one she had ever taken in her life. With the journey now irrevocably under way, she was alone for the first time in twenty-four hours. Instead of being able to think clearly, as she had hoped, her mind was still racing . . .

The Chairman of the Cranston Group, Maxwell J Bennis, had been insistent. 'Kline, you'd better get your ass back here,' he had bellowed over the trans-Atlantic phone line. 'The Board is meeting next Friday – and I want you here before then. We want an explanation of just what happened to the millions of dollars you've spent on your wonder-drug.'

It gave her less than one week to get back to New York – and instead she was heading in the opposite direction.

She wondered if Bennis could hold the Board off until her return; whether her track record as one of the most successful Divisional Presidents in the Cranston group would be enough to secure support. When he had called her two days earlier with the news of the murder, he had said: 'Kline, you've never been as close to a Board appointment as this.' But that had been before he'd heard about the sabotage of PS-21.

Her thoughts flipped back to Gray Barnard. She remembered his words: 'Franci, I will wait a week in Paris. If you are not back by Friday night, I'll know you've decided to go back to New York on your own.'

It hadn't been said like an ultimatum, but the remark had a finality about it.

Somehow, it seemed even Web had been involved in it. Webley Kline, her psychoanalyst husband, her backstop and her support system. He too had betrayed her . . . what had been driving him?

A flashback of memory came to her. 'Frances, you see things too simply,' Webley had told her. 'People aren't good or bad – they're a mixture of both. Your dearest friend can be your most dangerous enemy. If pushed too far.'

She was only now beginning to appreciate the sheer scale and complexity of it all.

She ordered strong, black coffee, and drew a crumpled newspaper cutting and a glossy tourist brochure from her handbag. She read about the archaeological significance of the island of Samothraki, then she glanced at the pictures of a dramatically scenic small island, steeped in mystical history.

The papers focussed her mind, and gave her a sense of perspective. Samothraki was her immediate goal, and only after she had been there could she return to the problem of PS-21.

The thought brought her a kind of peace, and as the gently humming cylinder of aluminium floated effortlessly over the Alps and down the Adriatic, Frances slept, crumpled in her seat, the big dark glasses untidily awry.

When she awoke, the Airbus was sweeping over Athens in a wide arc. The sun-baked hills with their slanting strata of red-ochre rock reminded her of the approach to Cape Town, and Gray Barnard. Then there was just enough time to assemble her thoughts and her hand luggage before she left the comparative security of the aircraft, and stepped alone and friendless onto Greek soil.

Two thousand years of history hung rich in the air, and the scent of wild thyme moved with the mist. The mysterious power dwarfed Frances, and made her feel as if the problems that had led her into the teeth of this wild, driving storm were suddenly insignificant. What, in an amphitheatre such as this, were mortal struggles?

She had awoken on her second day on Samothraki to see an improbably blue sky. The storm had been building up for two days, but now all was calm. By the time she reached the temple, the wind had howled itself up to full strength again, and she could see rain squalls sweeping in across the plains. Her search for David had so far proved frustrating. She had come to the temple as if drawn there. And now she felt she understood why. Because these ancient, lifeless stones were bringing her a kind of tranquility that she had feared she might never find again.

Down in the far corner of the site, a flash of yellow caught her eye. She turned down a staircase, the marble rounded by the tread of centuries. It looked like a bundle of clothes, shoved into a sheltered corner of a shattered niche.

No. It was a person, a man, asleep, huddled up and using a rucksack as a makeshift pillow.

But surely . . . Frances broke into a run . . . surely the set of those shoulders, that cloud of yellow hair . . . it was David.

Her mission was nearly over. Was she about to find out the truth?

When Frances woke him, he had looked confused. Then his expression changed, his fine features crumbling as silent sobs racked his body.

'Fran,' he said. 'I have done something that can never be undone.'

CHAPTER ONE

'I see.' Frances' eyes flashed. 'Jonathan, I don't think you understand the way we work.'

'We don't give in. And certainly not to people who snatch deals from under our noses. We fight for what we want.'

She strode across the penthouse suite high above the Edwardian splendour of the Hotel Frances and sat down at an exquisite eighteenth century desk. They matched perfectly, the antique and the petite woman sitting at it.

Silhouetted against a large picture overlooking the February bleakness of London's Hyde Park, she looked poised and calm, slightly fragile, with slender wrists and neck; her delicate face framed with a glow of fiery blonde hair.

If Jonathan Blake, manager of the Hotel Frances had known her better, he would have read the warning signals. Frances was in fact extremely angry. The signs were there; in the taut skin around deep green eyes that accentuated their feline slant and piercing look.

Combined with her innate sensuality, the effect was unwittingly and devastatingly sexual. She knew that anger enhanced her looks, and had turned this to her advantage more than once to win business battles without spilling any blood.

It had been a useful tool especially in her early days in the giant Cranston corporation, when she was desperately learning how to survive the in-house skirmishing that came along with the growth of her empire.

Frances had learnt well, so that Cranston's Leisure Division had grown from the insignificant section she had taken over to one of the biggest contributors to profit in the Group.

At first, her only desire had been to hold on to one of the most prestigious jobs any businesswoman could want. Then her success grew and so did her aspirations. Now what she was after was a senior seat on the Cranston board.

Naming this hotel after herself had been an act of pure vanity, a blatant celebration of her first international success since joining the New York based Cranston Group as the first woman president. Until now she had been glad to share that triumph with Blake whose suave Englishness had been a big asset in building The Frances into one of London's most exclusive hotels.

She had been prepared to overlook his languid approach to business. But he had let an important deal slip through his fingertips. Frances had set her heart on clinching this deal – the purchase of her second London hotel, the Marley.

Frances didn't look at the Englishman as she spoke. Instead, her gaze was level and distant, over the now-darkening park and the leafless trees with their gaunt outlines. Blake fingered his old school tie. It had been his contacts that had led her to the Marley Hotel; a family run tourist business in a quiet street close to the British Museum. Now he was telling her in his nonchalant way that the deal was off. That the Marleys had accepted a better offer.

'What happened, Jonathan? You told me that you and the Marleys had shaken on the deal.'

The Englishman smiled and shrugged. 'We were beaten. They had a better offer, and they took it. Can't blame them really. That's the way it goes.'

This bland acceptance was too much for Gerald Rule, Frances' vice-president and right-hand man who had been pacing the room in a lather of dyspeptic frustration.

'Goddammit! You shouldn't have ballsed it up! You should

16

have seen the signs. The Marley was the perfect place. We crossed the frigging Atlantic to sign the deal up!'

Rule took a Maalox pill from his jacket pocket and crushed it violently between his teeth.

At the marble fireplace, Frances held out her hands to the glow of the open coalite fire. She enjoyed cold weather. She'd spent her early life in California, and far from missing the endless West Coast summers when she moved to New York, she had quickly learned to love not only the contrast of seasons, but the actual cold as well.

She'd insisted on a real fire in the Hotel Frances penthouse which she had personally decorated for her own use, indulging in the cosiness of open hearths and the opulence of winter interiors.

This was one of the pleasures that she set against the heavy demands of the international travelling imposed by her career as President of the most global of divisions within the gigantic Cranston Group.

Paradoxically, she needed strong roots. Her frequent trips abroad were stimulating forays away from the comfortable security of her matrix made up of her husband Webley, her nine-year-old daughter Stacey, and her house overlooking Long Island Sound in Westchester County, north of New York.

The expansion into the luxury hotel business had been a turning point in her career, a deal she had pushed through alone. Frances had still been a fledgling executive then, but her suite at the top of the imposing hotel was a statement of pride and independence.

A huge picture hung over the fireplace. She always had to take a step backwards, simply because of the impact of the image. It was a horse. Nostrils flaring, eyes proud, the muscles rippling with life. A Marini horse, so perfectly captured that its power was a presence in the room.

'Okay. Who are these big spenders who have knocked the Cranston Group out of the running?' Frances wheeled around and aimed the question at Jonathan Blake.

'A property company, Bristol Developments,' he said, shooting his immaculate cuffs. 'I haven't come across them before, but it seems they have big plans for a multi-storey re-development. They're planning offices and luxury flats. Where they'll find the tenants I really don't know.'

The stress of the past weeks, showed clearly in Rule's 45-year-old face. Deep furrows of fatigue were etched from his nose to his mouth and Frances knew his ulcer would be giving him hell, as it always did when the pressure was on.

He knew just how important the Marley deal was to Frances. An important diversification. It was a key element in a new tourism initiative, itself a perfect example of what her husband, Web, called 'Kline-think': a swift insight into a gap in the market-place and a clever idea to fill that gap.

Rule had been Frances' Vice-President of Administration and Finance for four years now, and he was a man who liked to get things done. Frances had been careful not to become too reliant on Gerry Rule, for his immense knowledge of the business, his ability to delegate authority and an uncanny knack for getting accurate results quickly, would have made him a dangerous rival.

Not that Rule was in any way threatening. On the contrary, he made the perfect foil for Frances, happy to feed off her energy, vitality and breadth of vision. In return he gave her the detailed back-up that carried projects through successfully.

He took a neatly bound folder of computer print-outs from his briefcase and passed it to Frances.

'Here you are, boss-lady.'

She turned to him, ignoring Blake.

'Gerry, what's the Bristol's track record?'

'Profits down for the past three years,' he replied succinctly. 'They're obviously looking to improve their property portfolio. It's all in here.'

Frances Kline read rapidly, scanning the rows of figures and flipping back and forth to compare the various pages of the file. She would miss nothing. This he knew from long experience.

'Looking at this, it's hard to see how they can *afford* the

Marley, let alone any further development. Their cash flow is really weak,' she said, linking directly into his thoughts.

'Nevertheless, they have raised the capital.' Blake masked his embarrassment with a supercilious tone of voice.

'How much did they pay for the Marley?'

'Two-and-a-half million dollars. Sky high.' Rule's mouth was turned down at the corners. 'Bristol must have done one hell of a selling job to raise that kind of bucks.'

'Who owns Bristol?' Frances' mind was racing. She thrust her hands into the pockets of her slim, mustard, ankle-length, Calvin Klein suit and began to pace across the Persian carpet.

'The stock is all over the place,' replied Rule. 'Mainly small investors. There are no significant blocks of shares held by anyone from what I can tell. They never really attracted the heavyweights.'

'And what are they selling at?' asked Frances, stopping at the window, and turning back to face the room so that her golden hair picked up a halo from the pale wintery sun.

'They ran between seven and a half and three and a half dollars in the last year, and the last few deals have been as low as two and a half.'

'Are there many shares outstanding?'

'Two million,' replied Rule.

Frances leaned over Rule's shoulder to pick up Bristol Group's annual report in front of him. With lips pursed, and slim fingers caressing the pages, she leafed through it.

'Is this their complete portfolio?' she asked.

'Yeah. Apart from the Marley.'

Blake made an attempt to re-assert his presence. 'There's no real problem here, surely. We can use The Frances for the tours. It'll certainly help keep the hotel full.'

Frances turned on him.

'Yes, Jonathan. That's a solution. But the suggestion tells me you don't understand what we are trying to do. There's no way that I will let in cost-cutting tour groups to The Frances. This is an up-market luxury hotel, and it's going to stay that way!'

She turned abruptly and looked out of the window, across Park Lane, to the muffled, hurrying figures which emphasized the loneliness of London's greatest park in winter. The primer-grey sky reflected from the surface of the Serpentine, where flocks of migrant Canadian geese and exotic waterfowl patrolled the still waters.

The telephone shrilled loudly into the silence.

'I have a call for you, Mrs Kline.' The pert London accent, overlaid with tones of acquired gentility, annoyed Frances. In New York, Jo-Beth would have vetted the call before putting it through. Her irritation vanished when she heard her son's voice, and her mind switched instantly from the problems in hand.

'David! It's so good to hear your voice. Say, how would you like to take your diet-starved mother out to dinner?'

'Oh, Fran. I can't. I'm tied up tonight, doing a presentation. We're pitching for a big account. How long are you in London? How about lunch tomorrow?'

'Just fine,' said Frances. 'Why don't I come to the apartment. I can arrange a hot-and-cold hamper with the chef here, and bring lunch round with me.'

'Great,' replied her son. 'But don't bring food. Gaby will fix something up.'

Frances sat silently for a few moments after the line had been cut. The sound of David's voice filled her with sudden elation. He'd had that effect on her since the moment she'd felt him literally slip wide-eyed and shiny, from her shaking body, his eyes never leaving her, even as the doctor gently cut the cord and carefully wrapped him in a clean, white towel. Frances knew then that a new connection stronger than the physical, had been made. A blood bond.

She turned back to the two men in her office. 'You can go now Jonathan.'

When Blake had left, she motioned Rule close: 'Gerry, I've got a plan. I want a list of every shareholder in the Bristol Group. And I need it by tomorrow morning, early.'

'You don't want much, do you? What's the urgency?' He goggled at her, looking earnest.

'I want to buy them out.'

'That could take months.'

'It will take three weeks exactly. You can come home for weekends.'

Rule lifted his black-rimmed glasses, and looked at her cheerlessly. 'You have to win, don't you, Frances.'

She smiled. 'It's the only way to survive.'

Frances worked through until 6 pm, and then went through to her living quarters leading off the big office. Her dinner with David that had come to nothing left her feeling empty. She telephoned her home in New York anticipating the safe comfort of Web, and a few words with Stacey. No reply. No doubt Webley had taken the girl out to lunch.

The child was fed junk food whenever Frances was away – and to make matters worse, seemed to thrive on it. She felt very alone.

She had just lowered herself into the steaming hot bath, luxuriating in the way the water brushed between her thighs, and made the trim patch of golden-brown pubic hair stand on end, when the telephone rang. Without bothering with a towel, she padded wetly across the carpet to the instrument by the bed.

'Hello, Franci.' She recognized the deep voice, with its soft, slightly guttural accent immediately, and sat in surprised silence for what seemed like a full minute before he went on. 'This is Gray Barnard speaking.' She had never expected to hear from him again.

Her mind flicked back to their meeting. She had been in South Africa, where the Leisure Division had a safety-fuse factory and some mining interests – all acquired unintentionally along with other deals, but which Frances had worked hard to develop. Her flight to London had been delayed, and she was sitting in the departure lounge of Johannesburg's Jam Smuts airport.

At a loose end, she strolled off to examine the trinkets at the duty-free shops. As she rounded a corner, she was quite literally swept off her feet by an enormous man walking fast in the other direction. She had stumbled, and he had reached out an arm and caught her easily. She recalled being astonished by the sheer size of the man – six feet four, and firm and bronzed, without a hint of flab. The South African had been profuse in his apologies, and later, when she had returned to her seat in the first-class cocktail bar, he came over and joined her.

They sat and talked, idly at first, she with her Perrier water, he sipping a glass of old Cape brandy. Frances was preoccupied with her usual fear of flying, a feeling of helpless and nameless terror, that started as a low hum in her head, and gradually gained in pitch as take-off approached. When she was younger, she had often been sick shortly after take-off. Experience had taught her to concentrate on a distant mental image, and take plenty of Stelazine air-sickness pills. But like a malign presence inside her, the fear still remained.

She had been alarmed when she overheard Barnard arranging with the booking clerk that they should sit together. Oh God! she had thought. What if I throw up!

Then, as the Boeing 747 taxied out, he put his big hand firmly on her slim wrist, as she shook two Stelazine tablets out into her hand. 'For air-sickness,' she offered lamely.

'You don't need them.' His soft voice was so full of conviction that Frances wryly allowed him to put the two pills back in the vial, and then to put it in his pocket. 'You won't get sick. I'll talk to you until you sleep.'

Her abiding impression of him after the flight had been of the back of his enormous hands. Tanned, with thick, dark hairs, veins roping across determined sinews; hands that moved with assurance, or rested quietly in his lap. His hands, and that soft, powerful voice.

It was only in the limousine on the way to The Frances that she realized she hadn't felt sick at all on the flight, and she had felt very little fear. It was almost as though – she grinned at the

22

foolishness of the idea – as though Gray Barnard had made the flight safer by his presence; that somehow if the aircraft had floundered he would have kept it up in the sky.

'Gray. How did you find me?'

'I called your office in New York.' He must have produced a convincing story, Frances thought quickly, to get Jo-Beth to reveal her number. 'Are you free tonight, Franci?' He pronounced the name with the 'a' short and hard, to rhyme with 'fancy'.

His directness left her momentarily unbalanced. 'Yes . . . no . . . well . . . '

'Yes or no?' The tone was firm, but not threatening.

'Well, yes, I suppose.'

'Good, I'd like to see you.'

'Gray,' she began, half wishing she had lied. 'To tell the truth, I'm totally bushed. In fact, I was in the bath when you rang.' Then, suddenly aware of it, she added involuntarily, 'and now I'm wet and naked, and dripping all over my bed.'

'Well, finish your bath, I'll call for you later.'

'Gray, I'm swamped with paperwork, and I was really hoping for an early night. I . . . '

'Eight okay?'

She felt him take control. Again, she thought, and weakened. 'Okay. On one condition.'

'What's that?'

'I take you to my favourite restaurant.'

'Is it very smart?'

'No. Anything but.'

'Good. I don't feel like dressing up.'

'Don't. You'd only feel disappointed.'

'I doubt it.'

He had hung up before she had time to answer.

In another part of The Frances hotel, Gerald Rule lay on his bed. He had the heating turned up full, but still wore the loud check

23

sports jacket he had had on at the meeting earlier that day. He cradled the phone to his ear, and his eyes were closed in resignation.

'Well, you'll just have to tell the O'Rourkes another night. I can't make it tomorrow, because I've gotta stay in goddamn London, and there's nothing you or I or anyone else can do about it.'

He paused while the receiver squawked, then began again. 'I know, honey, I know. And I thought I would be home tonight. But the deal's fallen through.'

'Yes, dear,' his tone reassuring, 'honey, I've told you often. It won't always be this way. Just you relax and I'll call you in a day or so.'

After he rang off, Gerry Rule made one more telephone call to New York. Then he lay back on the bed, to stare pensively at the fake antique light fitting, and crunch antacid tablets as if they were sweets.

CHAPTER TWO

Gray Barnard was already at the desk in the lobby. Frances studied his broad back as she approached, and was again staggered by his sheer size. He towered over the other people in the lobby and the effect was to make her feel absurdly young and light-hearted. She almost skipped to his side, and touched his arm gently.

'Hi, Franci.' His casual greeting had an air of formality.

Frances grinned. 'I thought we'd take a cab,' and she steered him towards the door.

'Where are we going?' asked Gray.

'To Soho,' Frances replied, as they climbed into the back of a black London taxi. She gave the driver an address in Wardour Street.

Gray Barnard was chuckling gently – a low rumbling sound. '*Soho*! I haven't been there for years.'

'My favourite restaurant, remember.'

'But of course. Lead me to it.'

They watched the city pass in silence for a moment, then Gray Barnard turned to her, and said: 'For a woman who gets air-sick, you do an awful lot of travelling.'

'You know,' said Frances, 'your treatment actually worked. I've been across the Atlantic twice since we met, and I've been just fine. Thanks a lot. I wonder how long the cure will last.'

'For just as long as you remain my friend.' Barnard stared straight at her. 'What brings you to London this time?'

'Oh, just business,' said Frances, suddenly not wanting to talk about it, for fear of spoiling the moment, but doing so out of politeness. Briefly, she outlined the story of how she had bought and refurbished The Frances, and turned it into a success with the young jet-set crowd. 'We put in aggressive managers, and a top-rate French chef, spent plenty of money on public relations. It's doing pretty well, too. We've just got to keep it that way.'

The taxi finally ground round the jam of Piccadilly Circus, and pulled up at the kerb. Gray looked up doubtfully at the surroundings as Frances thrust a couple of notes to the taxi driver. Then she was pushing open a door to a room with windows obscured by condensation. It bore the legend 'Nicks Cafe' in flickering neon overhead, sandwiched between an all-night porn video parlour and an old-fashioned cobbler's shop. 'Your favourite restaurant?' he asked quizzically.

'My favourite food,' replied Frances, with a flippant laugh. She shouldered the door open, and pointed Gray towards a bare formica table in the corner. Two empty cans and a smouldering ashtray showed it had only just become vacant. All the other tables were full, mostly workmen in overalls or donkey-jackets. 'Grab that table, Gray. Leave the ordering to me.'

Two minutes later, she slid two plates onto the worn yellow formica of the table. 'Two hot beef on rye coming up! Double pickled cucumber, plenty of mustard, and the fat hasn't been cut off the meat.' She pulled out a chrome-framed plastic chair, and grinned across at him. 'When I'm tired,' she took her beef-on-rye in both hands, 'I get hungry. And when I'm tired *and* hungry, I couldn't give a damn about *nouvelle cuisine*, or about my diet.' She took a deep bite, and spoke with her mouth full. 'I just want to eat.'

Gray Barnard laughed. 'I can see that.'

'Nicks doesn't run to the luxury of table service.' A thick thread of mustard tracked between her fingers. 'If you'd like a drink, just ask me. The choice is tea or coffee.'

'When you've finished eating, I'd like a cup of tea.' He looked delighted with the sight of this sophisticated and cosmopolitan New York businesswoman burying her face in a mound of bread and meat.

As they ate, Frances studied his face surreptitiously. It was strong, seamed with deep lines, and touched with humour. Then she spoke. 'And why are *you* in London?'

'I've been to Riyadh to negotiate with the Saudi government.'

'Oh?'

'We have a joint venture deal. They're too heavily reliant on petroleum. So we're moving into fertilizer together, based on one of the by-products from the petro-chemical industry. We're building fertilizer factories around the world – in five years we'll have a factory on each continent.'

'That's big stuff.'

'I'm on my way to Paris.' How could he admit that he had deliberately stopped off in London to see her? that she hadn't been out of his head for weeks. 'Cosmetics. It's a sideline of mine, really. One of my interests back home is running a sort of growers' co-operative. We produce raw materials for the cosmetic industry, and I've managed to find a market here in the UK and in France to keep the experiment going.'

'Experiment?' queried Frances.

'The co-op. It's a sort of experiment; it's a multi-racial communal farming system.'

'You mean a kibbutz,' said Frances, using the Israeli word.

'Something like that. It's unique where I come from.'

After Frances had brought each of them a mug of the strong brewed tea, dyed a muddy light brown by a generous dollop of milk, they sat and relaxed at the table, enjoying the mixture of London accents ebbing and flowing around them in the busy café. Frances noticed that Gray didn't take sugar. Then, quite suddenly, she felt the need to move. 'Shall we go? Let's take a tube to Covent Garden, and just walk around. I haven't done that kind of thing for God knows how long.'

At Covent Garden, they strolled over cobbled paving stones towards the old fresh fruit-and-vegetable market, preserved in all its wrought-iron splendour, and now given over to exclusive boutiques, trendy sports-wear salons, and high-priced gift shops. They called into a pub, and Gray somehow inserted himself at the crowded counter, to get them two half-pints of dark ale from the wood. Then they strolled on, past smart burger joints and discreet tailors, and a cocktail bar that was a fashion parade of colour, fabric, and bizarre hairstyles.

Frances felt very small walking next to Gray, yet she was not uncomfortable. As they passed the parade of street life, he spoke, hesitantly at first.

He painted a vivid portrait of the land that he loved and the image enclosed him and Frances in a private shell.

He spoke of grey-purple rock pallisades serrating vast blue skies; of vineyards and orchards cupped in the giant hand of wild mountain ranges; of rock-baked crags brooding over a thick-walled farm homestead, black-thatched, with fresh whitewashed gables under a baking sun, and of the people. His voice evoked the sound of mixed-blood peasants toiling in the vineyards, laughing and singing among huge baskets of freshly plucked grapes. Frances, treading the hard winter pavements of London, was mesmerized by his descriptions of tiny fishing villages clinging to the edge of cliffs with leathery fishermen putting out

27

in their clinker-built boats at dawn; and of skies where vultures wheeled so high that they were invisible to the naked eye.

In a self-conscious Fifties-style coffee bar, they stopped, and sat facing one another drinking espresso coffee.

Suddenly, Gray leant forward. 'Your eyes are so green. Like emeralds.'

Frances loved the compliment, but dared not show any reaction. Why should she? She'd been told that before. A million times. He changed the subject. 'Do you make a lot of money?'

'Yes, but not just for me. For the Cranston Group.'

He laughed. 'That's the trouble with working for someone. Are you the token woman?'

He was teasing, she knew, but she answered seriously. 'I was once, but I'm through that now. When I first moved to New York over six years ago, I am sure that's what I was. I probably wouldn't have got the job if I hadn't been a woman. Then again, I would have got the job sooner if I'd been a man.' She laughed, and Gray echoed it with his deep rumbling chuckle.

'I started off as a sort of a mascot. Then my division started doing well, and the other executives became interested in me. When I started doing better than them, they stopped treating me like a little lady, and started giving me a harder time than any of the men.' The image of Milton Rae came unbidden to her mind.

'Being successful makes enemies,' he said. It was more a statement than a question.

'Yes, I know. The difficulty I have right now is knowing who my enemies are.'

'That's dangerous,' said Gray. 'What are you up to?'

'Something big.' Her eyes lit up and she spoke quickly. 'It's a new project I've been working on for four years. It's been expensive, but I know – I can feel it in my gut – my scientists are just a step away from the breakthrough we need to make production possible.'

'Production?'

'Of the product. Something every person in the world will want. A substance that will keep them young.'

For a second she hesitated, shocked at her instinctive trust of the imposing stranger: ' . . . Rejuvenation.'

'Sounds fascinating.'

'Yeah, it is. It's based on a drug called Prostaglandin-S. Very exciting stuff,' she broke off.

'And very lucrative.' His eyes were fixed on her.

'But it's more than just a commercial coup, Gray. It could eventually be the key to prolonged, if not eternal, life.'

'My God, doesn't it frighten you?'

'Often,' replied Frances. She felt the importance of his question.

'Are you ever frightened?' she asked gently.

'Yes. Of growing old. Of failing to find what I'm looking for, and of being too tired to go on looking. Of not fulfilling my destiny. Life is so short and the only answers I've found so far always end up as questions themselves.'

There was a second's pause, and then another of those quick changes of subject, that seemed to Frances to be a characteristic of the man, as though he was afraid to probe too deeply. 'I saw your picture in *Fortune*.'

'Oh, yeah.' Her tone was dubious.

'I was impressed. I would enjoy working with you, Frances.'

'But we couldn't.' She surprised even herself with the spontaneous outburst.

'You seem certain enough of that,' Gray laughed wryly.

'Well, I am – you're a boy and I'm a girl.'

'Surely you're used to that?' His face was amused at the thought of being called a 'boy'.

'Of course.' Frances felt herself flush. This man was getting to her. She hadn't felt tongue-tied like this for years. 'But you're sort of . . . different.'

'It's only because I'm big.' He drew himself up in his chair, and struck an exaggerated lantern-jawed pose. Frances couldn't

29

help laughing. His self-caricature was so close to the image of him in her mind. Then he touched her hand briefly, and went on speaking.

'It's tough being big, you know. Everyone assumes because you're large you must also be brave. It's hard to live up to expectations like that.'

'The same as Lexington,' said Frances.

'Who's Lexington?'

'My Great Dane lady. She's a harlequin-spotted monster, and she looks so powerful that everyone expects her to be a fighter. But she's so gentle. Sometimes she walks backwards, just to avoid trouble.' The light remark relieved the growing intensity of their mood, and they were laughing as they walked out again into the chill winter night.

'Do you often act this way?' she asked suddenly.

'Which way?'

'I mean do you . . . ' she searched for the right words.

He supplied them. 'Do I screw around?'

'Yes.' She stopped, and turned to face him directly.

'No. The truth is that most women bore me. I prefer my own company. I got used to it on the farm. You . . . you're different, Franci.'

She smiled.

'What's funny,' he asked.

'The "Franci", the way you say it.'

'Franci. Franci.' He repeated it softly.

'Why did you pick on me,' she said quietly, 'of all the people in the world?'

'I thought it was you that picked on me.'

She burst out laughing. 'Oh, you're kidding.'

'I suppose it just sort of happened, by chance.'

'These things don't just happen, Gray.' She was serious again. 'And if you didn't pick me, and I didn't pick you, who is pushing the buttons?'

'Same person who always does, I guess.'

Frances had no answer, so she took comfort from the hard

30

ground striking up through the soles of her feet, and in the reassurance of Gray's imposing presence by her side.

Then he stopped, and turned her towards him.

Incongruously, she registered the name of a shop sign behind his head. 'Frank and Friendly,' it read. 'Clothes for Men.' In the window, a dummy wore a baggy suit, made from parachute silk and hessian. Frances saw the price: £240.

Gray's eyes were on her, shadows hollowing his eye sockets, and sculpting his jaw-line. She could tell by the way he looked and moved his moist lips that he wanted her. She held his gaze, her heart was pounding at her ribs.

'I'm cold.' Frances heard herself say into the silence. 'Take me home, Gray.'

They shared a cab back to The Frances.

Back in the safety of her suite, with the memory of Gray's physical presence, she called Webley again. Already, she knew that if he asked, she wouldn't tell him where she'd been for dinner.

It was Stacey who answered the telephone, her immature voice chanting the telephone code and number.

'Hi, Stace. How's my baby?' She deliberately kept her tone light and casual. She was worried about the effect her frequent absences were having on her daughter now that she was growing older. 'Is your father spoiling you?'

'He bought me a chocolate eclair, with too much cream, and another one for later. An' we had cheese and pickle pizzas for lunch. Cheese an' pickle's my favourite.'

Frances couldn't help laughing in spite of herself. 'That's great honey. But don't you ever get tired of pizzas?'

'No way. And if I do, then Daddy gets me Mexican food instead. And you know what, Mom . . . ' Frances listened as her daughter skipped from one topic to the next, the inconsequential items crucial to the child's life. Hearing the happy high-pitched voice, like major-key scales on a piano, she wondered just how

31

much her daughter really did miss her. Stacey seemed to have grown quite used to her mother being away.

Web came on the line. She felt a great sense of relief wash over her. 'Hi, Fran.' He sounded perfectly casual and relaxed, just as usual. 'All okay?'

'Yeah. Fine. I'm just real tired.'

'Did you see David?'

'Not yet. Tomorrow. How's things with you?'

'Stacey was a bit ill last night, but she's okay now.'

'It must be that crap you feed her. Honestly, Web, must you keep her on an exclusive diet of junk food?'

'She *likes* the crap. Anyway, what's eating you?'

'Oh, I'm sorry. Just tired, I guess.' Their conversation carried on, dealing with daily trivia that made Frances feel oddly comforted. He seemed to have no curiosity as to how she had spent the evening.

'How's the book going?' she asked finally, a little reluctantly. It was the same question she had asked him for the past four years, ever since her earnings had comfortably outstripped his, and she knew she would get more or less the same old answer.

'Great. Just great. I had a marvellous new idea. I guess I'll be getting to work on it this evening.'

Later, just before she subsided into sleep, Frances thought again of Gray Barnard's hands. There was a warning sounding in her head.

That night, she dreamed of flocks of hideous vultures wheeling down out of a terrifyingly large sky, to pick at the corpse of a woman who had a face exactly like her own.

CHAPTER THREE

A delicious experience. The rhythm of her feet beating a light tattoo on tarmac. She felt almost weightless, aware of her muscles, her heart, her breathing. These were second nature to her now, part of the background music. London's Hyde Park contributed the damp smell of winter bark and frost-bruised leaves, mingling with horse manure fresh on the Rotten Row bridle path.

Her breath a plume of vapour, she quickened her pace, and turned alongside the still lake of the Serpentine. This was when she got her best thinking done.

A clutch of sparrows around some discarded scraps scattered as she pounded light-footed towards them. Distracted by the birds, she realized that for the past few minutes her racing thoughts had been concentrated on Gray Barnard. She was fascinated by the man – and now she was frightened of that. Deliberately, she switched the focus of her attention to her son David instead. She would be meeting him in a few hours. She wondered if she would find him much changed.

It had been a year since he had left New York, and two months since Frances had seen him. She missed him dreadfully. His need for independence was understandable. But at twenty-two he seemed too young to be so far from home. She kept reminding herself that at twenty, she had been a graduate, wife and mother. David's mother. Somehow that was different.

The trouble was her inner conviction that David had left New York to escape from her, that he had run away to get out from under her shadow.

She had been so determined that they would always stay close. Something had spoiled when he had become a man, and Frances was sure it was his unspoken fear of failing her, of not living up to her expectations.

David had been a serious child. He had excelled at school, and found time for a host of hobbies. He had green fingers; twigs that he stuck into the ground would miraculously sprout leaves and become healthy plants. As she ran, she smiled at the memory of a solemn twelve-year-old David creeping into her bedroom to awaken her, and lead her wordlessly to the back door to see the first blossoms of two apple trees he had grown from seed, bursting green-and-white in the dawn.

From his first semester at art school, David had started paying more attention to the commercials on television than to the programmes. They spent hours discussing her marketing projects, and pretty soon she discovered that many of his fireside ideas were better than those supplied at great expense by the advertising agencies.

When he had moved to London, she had helped him set up a creative workshop, a small, informal advertising agency employing freelance talent. In the year since then, a series of small jobs had kept his head above water, including an excellent campaign for The Frances which had quickly helped to establish the hotel as a place where the rich and famous like to be seen.

Frances glanced down at her watch. She was late. The lake was far behind her now, as she swung back towards Park Lane and the hotel. She loped easily towards a gate, and then paused to capture a last scent of the morning. But the air was befouled by the traffic, and she ran on through the subway and back to the hotel.

Frances walked into her penthouse office 45 minutes later, showered and crisply dressed in a black Halston suit over a raspberry silk blouse, clinched by a supple leather belt. Her breakfast was laid out on the desk – orange juice, brown wholewheat rolls and honey, and a small pitcher of fresh-brewed Blue Mountain coffee. Beside the tray was her mail and on the top of the pile a single, immaculate, red rose. She picked it up thoughtfully, sniffed its almost artificial aroma, then laid it to one side. When she lifted the first envelope, she noticed a small smear of blood. A single thorn on the rose's stem had made a pin-prick on her thumb.

In the envelope was a telex from Cranston Towers in New York. 'WILL PHONE 12.30 YOUR TIME RE BUDGETS – MAXWELL'

'Damn,' she thought. 'It'll make me late for David.'

Frances knew very well why the chairman was making these far-off grumbling sounds, and knew also just how potentially dangerous they were. Maxwell J Bennis had the power to kill her Prostaglandin-S project – the most exciting and important thing that Frances had ever done.

It had come to Frances as something of a gift. Milton Rae's company, Epipharm, had originally been working on the Prostaglandin biochemical family. Their interest was based on the drug's medical significance. It appeared to speed up the regeneration of mucus in the stomach and intestinal linings, a valuable property in the treatment of ulcers.

Frances vividly remembered the executive meeting four years before. Then it had been Milton Rae under pressure, because of cost over-runs on the research and development budget. 'This is an important drug, Max,' he had said. 'The costs are justified. We've now isolated the particular Prostaglandin we want, so we can drop Prostaglandin-S. It's been hellish expensive and as it turns out a blind alley. It has cell regeneration possibilities but nothing we'd be interested in.'

Frances had pricked up her ears. 'Cell regeneration. Surely that would have other possibilities? Cosmetics, perhaps?'

Milton took the opportunity to vent his frustration. 'Cosmetics.' The word was spat out scornfully. 'Epipharm is an ethical drug company. We make high-quality products that make sick people well. We don't make things that make people *look* better. If there are any cosmetic applications, then they'd be better off in your leisure division.'

Frances remained cool. 'If it's okay with you, Max, I think I would like to take Milton up on that.' Bennis looked gruffly down at her, his cigarette adding to the pile of ash that had already accumulated on his shirt-front and tie. He looked as if he were going to speak, but at the last minute he had merely nodded his head.

So Frances had taken Prostaglandin-S. Since then, the race had been on between her and Milton Rae to be the first to develop a marketable product based on Prostaglandin. Frances knew she was winning.

So did Milton Rae. She knew that it was his voice in Maxwell Bennis's ear, pointing out her overspent research and development budget; whispering that the money was being wasted; that the product would never see production. Funny, she thought, how Milton Rae's role in her life had changed. Six years before, when she had first arrived in New York, Rae had appointed himself her mentor as well as David's. She had been grateful, even felt honoured. Rae was not only President of Epipharm, a much bigger Cranston division than her own, he was also a senior board member, and it was assumed by everyone that he was next in line for the top job.

During her first week at Cranston Towers, while Frances and her family were still coming to terms with life in a new city, Milton Rae had been the first person to invite them to his home, a Long Island mansion with a sweeping lawn stretching to the water's edge.

Rae lived like a gentleman bachelor, surrounded by priceless antiques and a private art collection of Americana, including a minor Whistler and a gigantic portrait of General Custer, painted shortly before his last stand. David was captivated more by the small modern sculptures placed in careful and contrasting juxtaposition than with the more formal older works.

Rae had introduced them to a brisk middle-aged woman called Mrs Richardson, his housekeeper; had overloaded them with details of how to use and enjoy New York city, and had served them a memorable meal of salmon and grilled lobster followed by blueberry pie and thick cream.

Afterwards, he had produced charcoal and a sketch pad, and

36

had fascinated David by producing an impromptu sketch of Frances. Then he had given David a book of Escher drawings and often after that taken him to art exhibitions as far away as Chicago and to rural upstate New York to sketch birds in the reed-marshes and wild mountain forests.

Gradually, Frances had learned some of the story behind Rae's current isolation. Rae had been devoted to his wife, who had died nineteen years before, while giving birth to his son, Julian. The boy was desperately crippled and retarded, and required the constant attention of a trained nurse . . . the Mrs Richardson they had met.

Her relationship with Rae had soured in the years since then. As Frances' empire within the Cranston Group grew, so too did Rae's jealousy. He started to contradict her at executive meetings, and she knew that he didn't confine his opposition to the committee room, using his influence to undermine her whenever he could.

Now, with Bennis going into his customary flap as another Board meeting approached, Frances wondered how serious was the threat to cut the funding of her research. They would have a fight on their hands, if they tried to do that. Prostaglandin-S was about to become a viable commercial property. And Frances Kline wasn't going to give up now.

'Right, boss-lady. Here's your list of shareholders. I'm not gonna even say what it cost me, but that accounts for ninety-seven per cent of all issued stock.' Gerald Rule sat with his fist pressed firmly into his belly, and a wince set on his features as he watched Frances scan the list.

Frances pursed her lips as she scrutinized the document quickly. Investment houses, pension funds, a minor publishing trade union, and a string of small-time trusts and private investors. 'Nobody big,' thought Frances. 'Nobody dangerous. And nobody with a controlling interest.'

'Good work, Gerald. Now we must get moving. I want every

shareholder on this list to get a simultaneous offer for his shares. It must all happen at once. I don't want Bristol stirred up, and working on any counter-moves.'

Crunching another of his perpetual Maalox wafers, Rule grinned mirthlessly. 'And how am I going to do that?'

'Mail shot, three days from now . . . You can get David to help on the creative side.'

'What's our offer?'

'One and a half times the present market value, final acceptance date seven days after mailing.'

Rule's eyebrows did a double flip. 'D'ya know how much it'll *cost* if all of them accept.'

'Gerry, I've told you before. Leave the worrying to me. Anyway, they won't all accept. After that week, I want you to start buying selectively. You can negotiate any price up to three times current market value. Just keep buying until we hold fifty-one per cent of the stock.'

When Rule had recovered from his astonishment at the scale and audacity of Frances' plan, he changed the subject. 'I heard that the Japanese consortium are working on a rejuvenation product, along exactly the same lines as Prostaglandin-S. We're going to have to move like hell to beat them.'

Frances looked attentive. She knew scientists in Switzerland and Holland were working on rejuvenation, but this was the first she'd heard of the Japanese. Then she shook her head. 'The Japanese have no background in pharmaceuticals.'

Rule stood up with uncharacteristic verve. 'Frances, just look around you. Look what the Japanese did to cameras, watches and now even computers. If they decide to move in, they will.'

Frances cut him short. 'Gerry, relax. I know all that. But they won't invade the market with just one product. It's not their style. See what else your contacts come up with, but don't press the point too hard. We don't want to show our hand just yet, not until we get a breakthrough. And I'm not going to get panicked into rushing through research on the strength of rumours.' She couldn't help an uneasy feeling. Usually it was her arguing drastic action, while Rule advocated caution. This time, their roles had been reversed.

'Kline. Is that you?' Frances smiled. He always opened his conversation in exactly the same way.

Holding the in-car telephone she leaned back into the comfortable leather of the Daimler seat. From the window, Frances watched London change from elegant and fashionable to austere and businesslike and finally into a passable imitation of a modern slum – soulless high-rise flats dotted among dilapidated little Victorian terrace cottages as they passed beyond along a broad highway busy with heavy lorries.

'I guess it must be. How are things, Max?'

He skipped the formalities. 'Kline, I don't have to remind you that the Board is meeeting the day after tomorrow to review budgets. We've been looking through your figures. I've got a few suggestions to run past you, about ways of trimming costs.'

'What did you have in mind exactly, Maxwell?' Her voice was several degrees cooler. She knew that her profits were good, but that he would focus on her research and development or her promotional budget.

'Your R&D budget, Frances. It's sky high – running an average of twelve per cent over per month.'

'Yes, Maxwell. And you know the reason why. It's the Prostaglandin-S research that's costing more than we expected.'

'Kline, you know as well as anyone the knock some of our divisions took during the recession. Something has to be done about overspending.'

'Max. We've been through this before, and I'm not going to be sucked into it again. If something has to be done, let the culprits do it. I don't see why my division should have to suffer because some of the others were too slow on their feet to cope when the going got tough.'

'I've got a Board to face, Kline. I need your co-operation. I want those budgets cut.'

The car had stopped now, in a quiet cobbled street, hemmed in by tall and faceless warehouses, relics of the days when London's dockland had been thriving and prosperous. Her chauffeur had nosed the Daimler into an impossibly small parking spot, between a gleaming sports car, and a jaunty hand-painted Mini van. But Frances was oblivious to her surroundings, as she spoke vehemently into the handset.

'Goddammit, Max, if I cut back now, I lose all my competitive edge. I can't afford that, and neither can you.'

'I've been in informal session with the Board all morning. It's not easy Kline,' he said thinking wistfully of his retirement, just two years away.

'It never is, Maxwell. Just hold on a bit longer. What I have is a product that will make the present overspend look like cookie-jar money. I guarantee it's worth waiting for.'

David's flat was on the top floor of the warehouse immediately opposite. Frances rang the bell, and he buzzed the door open. She was halfway up the second flight of narrow concrete stairs when he rounded the corner of the landing above her.

'Hi, Fran. So glad you could make it. Come on up – Gaby's in the kitchen.'

He looked more handsome than ever. His clear green eyes and narrow, chiselled nose were exact replicas of her own; he had inherited the strong jaw and cleft chin from Webley. His bright blonde hair was straight, and worn simply cut. She wished he would run up and fling his arms around her.

But he greeted her with a dignified kiss on each cheek.

Gaby appeared at the top of the stairs, and she and Frances hugged across the big bunch of daffodils Frances had carried from the car. The two women had become friends in New York, and Frances had been pleased when Gaby had joined David in London. She seemed to have grown more beautiful, as if her ebony black skin had taken a deeper and more lustrous polish.

She was a successful model, tall and poised, with tightly curled black hair that danced about her head in beaded strands. Her lissome body, with young breasts uncupped, moved with an easy grace. She was used to being looked at, and even barefoot in a track-suit, she was an object to be admired. 'Claude gave me two days off,' she said, 'before I go to Milan to show off his summer collection. So I hope you can stay on for the afternoon, Frances. Can I get you something to drink?'

'Just some Perrier, please,' said Frances. 'But first, I want to see your new apartment.' David had joined the creative migration to the side of the Thames, among the old warehouses and disused quaysides. The apartment he had created himself, leaving the huge top floor of the warehouse open, but making separate living areas using screens and furniture. A tall shelf of archaeology books – his latest passion – separated his studio area from the bedroom, and the bed hung from the rafters on four long chains. Frances prowled fascinated among the ornaments of her son's new life, picking up and caressing a small marble nude that she had never seen before, studying the titles of the books, and his small collection of prehistoric hand-worked stone tools.

Then she looked from the big picture window, over the river, where wintering swans swam among the once-busy jetties. This was not a beautiful part of London, but had a charm all of its own. On one side, she could see the Prospect of Whitby, one of London's oldest riverside pubs, crowded with tourists; on the other she could catch a glimpse of Tower Bridge.

Then she turned back into the large room, where a bow-legged coal stove formed the centre of the living area. 'Stacey sent you this,' she said, handing David a letter covered in childish hearts, flowers and birds in coloured crayon. A dime was scotch-taped next to his name. 'She said to tell you to buy something!'

'Thanks, Frances. I'll write to her. Don't worry.' And with a slight edge in his voice, 'So what has my hard-working old mother been up to?'

'Oh, the usual jetting around. A bit more than usual, I guess. Hardly been home in the past fortnight. I was in South Africa again last week.'

'Oh God, Fran. Not still . . . '

'Still what?'

'South Africa. You're not still stuck there, are you?'

'David, darling. I'm not stuck there. It was my decision to stay there.'

'But why? Shit Fran, why?'

'Because I'm a businesswoman, my darling,' Frances replied gently. She was about to go on, when David leapt in.

'You put money above everything.'

'It's not only a question of money. I do have responsibilities to my shareholders, but I also have responsibilities towards my employees and their families.'

'But what about your principles?'

'David. They're your principles.'

'Surely they should be everybody's principles. Otherwise you are saying that institutionalized racism – colour prejudice actually built into the system – is okay. And that it's also okay to enforce it with guns.' He was sitting forward on the edge of his seat now, eyes shining, face slightly flushed.

'David, please,' said Gabrielle, 'let's change the subject.'

'No, Gabs,' Frances insisted. 'Let's not. Why don't we talk it through. It's obviously bugging David.'

'Yeah, and it's bugging him because of me.' Her dark skin shone with indignation.

'All the more reason we three should be able to talk about it,' said Frances. She turned to her son.

'Leaving aside the fact that my returns in South Africa have persistently shown double those of any other investment, I still cannot find a good reason to leave. Not a reason I could justify to the people who work for me. If I pulled Cranston's investment out of South Africa, many of my staff would lose their jobs. It'd be their eyes I'd have to look into, David, not yours. Goddammit, I hate the system there too, but I'm dealing with real people here.'

'You talk about conscience and principles. My conscience tells me that I took two Canadian men and their wives and families to

South Africa when I moved the safety-valve operation there. They've done a damn fine job, for Cranston and for the workers. They've made themselves new lives.

'My conscience tells me I employ four thousand people in South Africa, three thousand of whom are black.

'My conscience tells me those people out there are relying on me. I have given them my word that I will stay, and I won't break it.'

'Listen, Fran. You do realize that if Gaby and I were to live together in South Africa the way we do here, we would be arrested. We'd be committing a crime. It's bloody unbelievable.'

Frances noticed the Englishness of her son's final remark. 'Yes. It's true.'

'What they've got is a fundamentally evil political system, and you're supporting it by being there. Did you hear what that Bishop with the crazy name said after he won the Nobel Peace Prize yesterday? Disinvestment, Frances. Every American business owes it to the nation to pull out of South Africa.'

Suddenly, Frances was weary of the conversation, tired of her son's hectoring. 'Listen, David. I'm a businesswoman, not a politician. Speaking personally, I abhor the system of apartheid. But at least I'm doing my bit to improve the quality of life for the people who have no choice but to live with it. I have seen the poverty. You, David, have not. I at least have helped to put food in the bellies of a few hungry kids. Believe me, it's something I've thought about long and hard. Maybe in time I'll decide differently. But right now, I stay.'

David spoke, with his mouth pinched and tense. 'Okay, Mom. Okay.'

Frances was piqued by his use of the word 'Mom'. It was something he reverted to whenever he was sulky. She swallowed her discomfort and tried to lighten the mood.

'Listen, can't we just agree to differ. I'm tired of having to account for my South African connections to the Board, to your father, and now to you. Please darling. I only have a couple of hours with you. Tell me about the studio. How's it going?'

43

'Okay,' he said. 'Well, not quite so okay. I'm making a living, but it's all one-off business. I need more regular clients, then we'd have the financial security to expand. As it is, I have to work all hours.'

'Regular work will come,' said Frances. 'When it does, you'll be ready. I've heard fantastic reports on your results, anyway.'

'Who from,' he shot back. Gaby was standing behind him, massaging his neck muscles.

'Oh, from the hotel. And on the grapevine.'

'I did a pitch for a big account last night. Cosmetics. A big fat deal.'

'Yeah? How did it go? Did you get it?'

'Oh, you never know. They seemed impressed by my presentation, but they're holding off their decision for a week or more. Thanks for the hotel work, by the way.'

'Oh don't thank me, you earned it.'

The rest of their time together was relaxed. David talked excitedly about some new archaeological find, and spoke with obvious pride about Gaby's success in the London modelling world. But Frances was concerned at the tension that showed around his eyes.

They ate a thick, rich bean soup, and Greek salad – crunchy lettuce acquired at great expense in mid-winter – and chewy-fresh Greek bread, broken in chunks from a large flat round loaf. And they drank rough Retsina, gathered around the glow of the coal stove, and talked on into the afternoon.

When Frances rose to go, she embraced them both. The three figures rocked in unison. On the stairs on the way down, he said: 'I'm sorry I shouted at you earlier, Fran. I'm a pig. It's frustrating going it alone.'

'I know,' she replied. 'But you'll make it.'

'With or without you?' he asked wryly.

'Yeah,' she answered with a laugh. 'With or without me.'

The girl gave a low moan of pleasure that was as artificial as a

44

painted smile. Her partner in what could only laughingly be described as the love act, accelerated his thrusting and then stopped. Lust had made his face ugly, and he looked every one of his fifty-two years and more, with beads of sweat making his pallid skin look pale and unhealthy. And a knot of grey hair usually trained carefully over his fast-balding pate, instead plumed ridiculously into the air.

They were in a large, luxurious office, with big picture windows looking out into the black New York night from thirty-seven storeys high; he standing on the deep-pile carpet, she sitting on the edge of the polished mahogany desk, her long legs twined around his back. A flimsy garment in lurid purple lay flung carelessly aside on the floor, and they were both quite naked. Beside the girl's left hand, thrown back onto the desk for support, was an up-ended sign. It read: 'Milton Rae – President, Cranston Pharmaceutical and Chemical Division.'

Leaning forward, Milton Rae whispered in the girl's ear. She nodded, and said, 'Gee honey, that'd be great. You're a tiger, huh?' But her eyes did not echo her enthusiasm, as she slipped her slender young body from around him, and flitted over to the leather couch facing the desk. There, she knelt, bent forward, so her head was in the cushions, and the firm twin orbs of her buttocks were thrust up in the air.

Milton Rae drank in the sight, then knelt behind her and entered her again. His one arm was around her, and his rhythmic pounding had pinned her against the side of the sofa. Without realizing it, she had allowed herself to be physically trapped.

He spoke again, and this time his voice was louder and harsher. She turned her head, helpless to move. 'No,' she hissed. 'No, you bastard. I never said you could do that.' Her eyes matched her voice now, and there was fear in both.

'Yes, you goddam will. It's what you're getting paid for, you slut.' And with a force she was powerless to resist, he plied himself into that other opening that she was involuntarily offering to him.

'Pain, you bitch. Scream.' Milton Rae was demented with the

power of the agony he was inflicting. The girl's whimpers were genuine now. Rae heard them as if from another world.

As he lurched his way towards an orgasm, the image of Frances Kline passed vividly through his mind.

CHAPTER FOUR

Twice that day, Milton Rae had felt the fury rise within him. It was a feeling he had grown to recognize. First, the migraine – half an hour of flickering vision. Then a rising tide of helpless frustration. So acute it was a physical ache in his joints, a taste like rust in his mouth, a prickling of his scalp. It was coming in waves, and had been going on for days now. His fevered sodomizing of the pretty young hooker in his office hadn't stilled the fury. It had sharpened it instead.

Post coitum, omne animal tristes est. After intercourse, all animals are sad. Well, it doesn't apply to me, thought Rae. It wasn't sadness that he felt, but revulsion – not at himself for his baseness – but at God who had twisted his life with a cruel indifference; making his child a stunted mockery of the joy of creation, and robbing Milton of the woman with whom he had chosen to grow old. A revulsion too that rapists feel for their victims, despising them for their vulnerability.

And a hatred of the normal world, for success and happiness, for all those contented people who know nothing of the subtleties of human despair.

'Look at them,' he thought. 'Ordinary people!' Through the windows of the big black Lincoln he saw the late afternoon throng of Fifth Avenue – window-shoppers, office-workers heading home, a sudden flash of a pretty young blonde girl throwing her head back in quick laughter, at some remark of her companion's. Milton Rae stamped viciously on the accelerator pedal, and the V8 engine gave a throbbing hiss as the wide, flat bonnet lifted up and the car accelerated away powerfully.

As he crossed the Brooklyn Bridge, and wheeled off the expressway into the mean streets, Milton felt the tension in his shoulders relax. He turned to his companion, a smooth-faced youth who was staring straight ahead, looking at the rows of seedy brownstone tenements, and the bright-lit street life at their feet. 'I think you're gonna like this, Jeremy,' he said, touching the young man playfully on the knee. 'I think you're gonna like working with me.'

Milton Rae had long since ceased to be surprised at his own depravity. This was his life now, a life he had coloured vividly with bold cacophony. Splashes, like the modern artists he admired and collected. Discord was something he could sympathize with.

As he nosed the limousine through the familiar side streets, he mused on the day that had just finished, and felt the temper rise in him again.

That fucking Cutler. Trying to bully him. When he didn't even know about, let alone understand, the scale of Rae's business problems. Bull-headed upstart.

Rae had spent an uncomfortable afternoon with Curt Cutler, his marketing vice-president for the past year. Cutler had turned up in Rae's office armed with a formidably well-researched document that unconsciously struck deep at Rae's own management of Epipharm. Mainly, it concerned Seditur, a 'hypnotic' tranquilliser that had been Epipharm's brand leader for years, in daily use by millions of frustrated housewives and bewildered business tycoons the world over. Ephipharm's patent was about to expire, opening the way for other drug houses to produce 'generic' drugs – formulations that could reproduce Seditur in everything except the use of the name.

Rae knew better than anyone the threat that this posed to Seditur, but he also knew that he had run blindly into a serious cash squeeze. The huge cost overrun on research and development of Epipharm's Prostaglandin-V, the 'Ulcer-Cure Project', had left them unable to afford the investment required to cash in on the generic boom.

Curt Cutler had repeated himself in his enthusiasm. 'Milt, the generic houses are already geared up. In six months, when the Seditur patent expires, they're gonna jump in on our back so fast we won't know what hit us.'

'Seditur has been market leader in hypnotics for the last six years. The name is known world-wide. Doctor's prescribing habits don't change overnight, Cutler. You know that as well as I do.'

'That's true. But Seditur is also widely known by its generic name, benzspirone. And once other benzspirone equivalents become available at a lower price, a large percentage of the medics are going to start prescribing them.'

'Sure, Epipharm's going to lose a slice, Curt,' Rae had said expansively. 'but we've taken that into account in our budgets, cut back production facilities in anticipation. At least we'll manage to maintain a healthy profit margin.'

It was then that Cutler had stood up, and started striding back and forth. The same Picasso that had witnessed Rae's buggery the night before was just as monocularly impassive at the ambitious young executive's impatience.

'But Milton, what I'm saying is that Epipharm can take a slice of the generic cake as well as maintaining Seditur. It's still not too late to produce a generic benzspirone of our own. Then we'll take a share in both markets. And believe me, generics is one hell of an enormous cake. Just one slice, like a Pentagon deal, or the hospitals for only one state, and we'll score every way. And I know my sales force can win a few institutional contracts.'

Rae knew the younger man was right. They both knew. What he could not tell Cutler was that there simply wasn't a budget available. He blustered, his voice authoritative. 'Curt, there's no way we can set aside facilities for benzspirone manufacture. The plant is at full capacity. We don't have the machinery, and we don't have the manpower.'

'We already have all we need,' insisted Cutler. 'It's only a question of reallocating resources. It's the same product, for God's sake, in a different box!'

'No, Curt. Generics are the cheap end of the market. Epipharm has a name for quality. That's how we'll keep the loyalty of our customers. Now drop it.'

Cutler had not said another word. He had picked up his papers, fastened his briefcase, and left, closing the door behind him with ostentatious caution. Before it shut completely, Rae could see him shaking his head.

Impudent pup. He thought it was all easy. He'd never taken any *real* responsibility in his life. Just had it all handed to him on a plate, because he had the right qualifications. And now he was telling Rae what to do!

Just like that bloody Kline bitch. He'd seen through her easy success. She was sly, that was all, clever at choosing areas of the market where the competition was weak. A knack for the quick profit. He'd fire Cutler if it weren't that Kline would snap him up.

And now she was about to make a bigger fool of him. He'd let the rejuvenation Prostaglandin go to her, sure that she would trip over her own feet. His own research scientists had all but written it off. Today, however, he had heard that her Leisure Division scientists had made good progress, while his own researchers were still struggling with the Ulcer-Cure Prostaglandin. Kline was almost finished with animal toxicology trials. Milton's Prostaglandin-V team would not be at that stage for another year, maybe longer.

Milton parked the big Lincoln out of sight in a side street, and then led Jeremy Farnsworth round the front to an entrance to a brownstone building identical to the others that lined the street. He rang the bell, muttered something softly into the voice-box, and then pushed the door open.

Inside, he followed the youth up the faded carpet of the stair. He reflected as he looked at those slim hips just how much like David Kline he was, but for the straight black hair where David's was blonde, and but for a confidence in the carriage that the Farnsworth boy lacked. They could easily have passed for brothers.

That was partly why he took him on. Not that he could really refuse old man Farnsworth the favour. Farnsworth Senior was head of the giant Chemex chain, the biggest chemical distributors in the US. He and Rae went back a long way in the business. Over the years, they had fallen into the habit of meeting regularly for lunch, and it had been at one of these lunches ten days before that Jim Farnsworth had first mentioned his young son.

'Jeremy's nineteen now. He's graduated, but I don't want him to join Chemex until he's had a bit of practical experience under his belt. He needs to learn the ropes, somewhere he won't suffer from being the boss's son,' Farnsworth had said.

Milton Rae had been quick to offer Jeremy a slot in his office, as his assistant. 'I'd be glad to help out,' he had said. 'In any case, he could be very useful to me.'

He had found the boy painfully shy, but receptive to his approaches. Talking over coffee one afternoon, Rae had discovered that Jeremy Farnsworth had never made love to a girl. 'A virgin! That's something we must correct at *once*,' he had said. And had arranged the trip to Brooklyn that same day.

When they had reached the second floor, he touched Farnsworth lightly on the shoulder. 'Just along here, Jeremy,' he said, moving past him to a black-painted door, and knocking three times.

The garish opulence of the apartment – crimson velvet, purple drapes with white fake fur lining, mirrors on the walls and ceilings – made the young man do a theatrical double-take, almost rocking back on his heels. The next thing he saw, in the pastel glow of the light, was more stunning still. It was the most desirable girl he had ever seen in his life. And she smiled at him invitingly.

Milton's partner, Mary-Lou, was a veteran at putting men at their ease. It had been her business for many years now, and though her looks now relied more on cosmetics than on her once-natural freshness of complexion, she was still a striking woman who took a pride in her appearance and in being an expert at her job. She led the conversation lightly from one inconsequential topic to the next – the latest movies, the crazy new fashions, the current political outrages of the day – as they ate roast duck Hawaii style, followed by figs, one of which she opened and licked expectantly, with a lascivious private wink to Milton. They were old travelling companions, these two, and Milton paid her handsomely to cater to his whims. Which tonight, he had instructed, were to provide a girl to deprive this trembling, faun-like man of his virginity.

After the older couple had left, Janelle went to work on Jeremy. Her pert looks, with tilted nose, a slender pointed chin, gossamer-fine hair of tawny bronze, and a cast in her light blue eyes, already had him spellbound. Now she got him talking about himself, moved with him to the sofa, and then – while she drank in his words with her eyes – she gently took his hand, lifted it to her full lips, and started licking the palm of it, moving her delicately pointed tongue in a circle that made him suddenly giddy with desire.

Expertly, she undressed him, then instructed his hands to do the same to her. When they were both naked, she led him to the bed, and laid him down, and started to caress him with hands and tongue, working up from his feet. When she got to the area of his groin, where his proud manhood stood disproportionately large in comparison to his slender hips, she whispered softly: 'Look in the mirror.' Beside the bed, their images were reflected, hers golden and smooth, his pale and trembling. She lifted her tresses of hair clear, so that he could see her face as she bent forwards and engulfed him with her bright red lips.

On the other side of the glass sat Milton Rae and Mary-Lou. 'Get an eyeful, Milt,' she said. 'She's expensive, but she's one of the best. And you know you always get good value from me.' Her fingers were busy in a copper bowl in her lap. Then she lifted a cigarette paper, expertly rolled into a cylinder, and licked the glue before a final deft twist.

51

Rae only grunted. His eyes were fixed on the one-way mirror, on the bodies that writhed together there. But it was something more than lust shining in his eyes. It was more like triumph.

Then he leaned back, took the paper cylinder from Mary-Lou, and drew deeply of the sweet-smelling, oily smoke. Time shifted gear as the marijuana reached his brain, and suddenly he was high, and didn't know how long ago it had happened. Then he gave a deep sigh of contentment and leaned back, as Mary-Lou's head dipped towards his lap.

Whores. Bitches. He hated them all.

Cranston Towers stood facing onto Fifth Avenue. As New York buildings go, it was not particularly tall, standing just forty storeys high. Yet in this city built by man to the scale of nature, it stood proud among giants, distinguished by the peculiarly rich grey-pink of the granite facing, that clad the bottom 30 storeys before the first of the terraces that provided roof-gardens for the executive floors above that. The stone came from Cranston's own quarries in South America. In the foyer downstairs, two Cranston executive cars flanked the fountain.

On the thirty-first storey, in an oak-panelled boardroom that opened onto one of the terraced gardens, with windows now closed against the chill, three men were gathered around the top of the long table. They were the Cranston Group's three executive Board members - Milton Rae of Pharmaceuticals, Yale Duke of Automotive, and Merill Lamb of Timber and Quarries.

At the head of the table, dressed in a rumpled suit sat Maxwell J Bennis, Chairman of the Board. He was the fourth full-time executive on the Board.

At sixty-three, Bennis had less than two years to serve before retirement, but he gave every appearance of trying not to live that long. He was heavily overweight, chronically ruddy from the consequent high blood pressure, and clumsily chain-smoked filter-tip cigarettes. For a man who had grown as tired of making decisions as Maxwell J Bennis, the approach of each board meeting was a very trying time.

That was why he had summoned his three executive colleagues today, for an 'informal status assessment meeting'. It was a habit all four of them had grown accustomed to, an inevitable prelude to full board meetings, when the five remaining board members – outsiders to the day-to-day running of Cranston's affairs – arrived in full force.

A reflective silence cloaked the group; Merill Lamb leaned the side of his jaw on a forefinger, Milton Rae looked steadily into space, Maxwell Bennis smoked messily, and a dowdy middle-aged woman – his secretary since she had been bright-eyed and beautiful – sat attentively, notepad on her knee. The only movement came from Yale Duke, sitting typically slouched back in his chair, forearms relaxed on the edge of the table. He flicked through his copy of the quarterly financial statement, the regular rattle of each page cracking the silence.

Finally, without changing his position, he looked up languidly and spoke. 'Quite a cost overrun on this Prostaglandin thing you've got going here, Milt.'

Rae knew that the laid-back tone was deceptive. Duke was a man who read balance sheets as others read detective novels, to whom figures spoke louder than words. His disarming manner belied a mind as sharp as a razor. He decided not to answer Duke directly; rather to defuse his questions by addressing Maxwell Bennis, who he knew would inevitably introduce a note of equivocation to the discussion.

'The animal toxicology studies should be through within the next twelve months. Then come human trials, and Federal Drug Administration registration approximately five years after that. It's a long haul, but eventually we'll show a healthy product. A cure for ulcers can hardly miss.'

'How long is Epipharm's patent on the drug?' asked Bennis, running a dimpled hand over the naked scalp.

'Total patent is for twenty years,' replied Rae.

'That gives the product an effective life-span on the market of about ten to twelve years,' observed Duke mildly.

Now Rae did turn to him. 'Epipharm will recoup all the R&D outlay in the first two years of marketing. Besides, when the patent expires, we'll carry on over into the generics market.'

'If that's your strategy for Prostaglandins,' Duke moved in on him, 'how come aren't you planning generic benzspirones as well. From what you've told us, Epipharm's patent on Seditur expires in six months.'

Rae turned to the chairman to defuse the attack. 'Only following policy, Maxwell, not to venture headlong into anything new without consolidating the areas where we already have a solid market. I decided that Epipharm would do better to put all resources into maintaining Seditur's name.

'I already have a big promotional campaign in hand to do that, aimed directly at the general practitioners. The idea is to book a whole wing at Caesar's Palace in Las Vegas, and then fly in selected doctors from all over the States in relays.' He was getting into his stride, thinking he had successfully diverted attention, talking about how each doctor would be given five hundred dollars in gambling chips, how they'd be a captive and receptive audience to the Epipharm marketing men, when Yale Duke cut across him.

'So,' he drawled lazily. 'Does that mean that Epipharm will never get into generics? You're going to do nothing while rival firms undercut you out of the market?'

Milton blustered, playing for time. 'I didn't get Epipharm where it is today by not knowing the market, you know. Of course we looked into the possibility of generics, but we decided on a no go.' Yale looked at him disbelievingly, and then pointedly re-opened the financial report.

This attack made Milton feel most uncomfortable. He wondered how much of his situation his fellow executive board members knew, and how much it affected his position as next Chairman of the Board, natural successor to Maxwell Bennis. That was something he must protect at all costs.

'It's all well in hand. After the Las Vegas relaunch, I plan a

54

continuous counter-strategy. Cutler is already working on it. Anyway, what's all this inquisition for? Your own figures aren't a lot better than mine. Seems as if I'm not the only one with problems. We're just coming out of a recession, don't forget.

'When my Ulcer Cure comes right, it's going to be the biggest ethical product to hit medical health care since the H-Two receptors back in 1980. What have you got coming up that can rival that, Duke? What has Automotive got in the future?' His voice was confident, but his face was white with emotion.

'Calm down, old man,' cut in Duke. 'You're getting pretty tense. We only want to find a way to help out, just like we always help one another. But if the outside Board members start asking awkward questions, we need to know what the others are going to be saying.

'I'd like to propose a motion, Maxwell,' he continued indolently. 'I vote we withdraw for a drink.'

'Good idea.' It was the first thing the Chairman had said for several minutes. He hated this sort of in-fighting. 'That will be all, Lilly,' he said to his faded bloom of a secretary. 'I'll call you if anything else comes up.'

They went through to an ante-room where a well-stocked mahogany bar reproduced the atmosphere of a gentlemen's club. Merrill Lamb poured drinks for all the men, as they settled on barstools, and then adroitly changed the subject. 'What's the latest on Cunningham's Korean offer, Max? I thought we'd agreed to keep things tight until we're sure the economy has lifted for good.' Lamb was the longest-serving of all them, and had reached where he was by a policy of keeping his head down whenever the going got tough.

'Cunningham really has his heart set on expanding the shipping division outside of the States. But I'm watching him carefully.' Bennis was grateful for the diversion. 'This worldwide expansion syndrome has gone crazy.' Maxwell cupped his hand beneath the precarious ash of his cigarette as he transferred it carefully to the nearest ashtray.

'I wish you could convince Kline of that,' said Rae. 'The woman seems hell bent on a global acquisition, and I'm afraid she's going to cost us a lot of money when she finally falls on her ass.'

'Do you think she will fall on her ass?' queried Yale Duke. 'Her results on paper are good, and getting better every month.'

Rae, the residue of the previous night's excesses still hammering softly at the top of his skull, drained his glass of Bourbon, and immediately refilled it, his nerves on edge. 'You obviously haven't seen her latest budgets then. Her Prosta-glandin R&D costs aren't far off mine . . . and it is highly questionable whether she'll even get hers into production. As you know, we rejected it.'

'Sure, Milt,' drawled Duke. 'But you can't deny that her performance so far has been impressive. She's no fool, and she means business.'

Rae exploded. 'She's an untrained upstart who got lucky, and now has too much ambition and too much power. You guys don't take her seriously enough. I've got a gut feeling about that woman, and I reckon we ought to clip her wings.'

'A gut feeling? As long as that's all you feel about her.' Duke tried to lighten the mood with a quip. Nobody laughed.

'Frances has her faults,' said Maxwell Bennis through a cloud of smoke. 'But failing to deliver is not one of them.'

'I still say,' said Rae sulkily, 'that she needs watching. If we give her too much rope, she's going to hang herself, and the Cranston Group as well.'

'But that's what we're here for,' said Bennis reassuringly. 'You know that, Milton.'

The group of Cranston executive directors began to break up soon after that. Merill Lamb was the first to go, Maxwell followed soon after him, sliding off the barstool in a crumpled pile. But the Chairman called into his office before leaving for home. He was concerned at what had been said about Frances Kline. Perhaps he had let her go too far, but her powers of persuasion were considerable. He would simply have to pull

56

rank. She must tighten her reins. He didn't need this pressure.

First thing in the morning, he'd see her.

Back in the boardroom, Milton Rae and Yale Duke were finishing their drinks. 'About what you said, Yale,' Rae leaned forward confidentially.

'What I said when, Milt?' came the laconic reply.

'About us all helping one another.'

'Yeah?'

'Well, you may think I'm overstating the case about Kline, but I am seriously worried. That woman is dangerous. She's over-ambitious.'

'It's a bit late to say that now, Milt.' Duke popped a pretzel into his mouth, and crunched it lazily, one bite at a time. 'There's no stopping her, when her results are so good. I'd say she's only a year or two away from a board appointment herself. Face facts: she's good at doing business.'

'At what cost?' Rae shot back, realizing too late that he'd overdone the belligerence.

'Wait up a minute there, Milt. You're overreacting.'

Milton leaned forward confidentially, the stale fumes of Bourbon making Duke wince involuntarily. 'Yale, you know me. I have Cranston's interests at heart. We have a responsibility to protect our good name. You get the point?'

Yale Duke said nothing for a while, but he gave a knowing smile that did nothing to make Rae feel more reassured. 'Sure, Milt,' he eventually said. 'I get the point.'

Milton Rae stopped off at his office before checking out of Cranston Towers. The suite was deserted, but for one desk, where a lone lamp picked out Jeremy Farnsworth's features in deep-etch contrast. He was puzzling over a pile of reports, making notes on a square-ruled pad.

'Not gone home yet, boy?' Rae asked kindly.

'I'm just trying to figure how these computer runs should be interpreted, Mr – er – Milton.'

'Leave that to the machines. It's decisions that count. I'll teach you in time, but get on home now.'

Then, becoming conspiratorial. 'Hope you had a good time last night, boy. Sorry I had to leave early.'

And Farnsworth Junior smiled shyly, and made an attempt at a macho gesture that sat uncomfortably on his willowy shoulders. 'Whew. She was some stuff, that Janelle,' little knowing that every detail of his expert defloration had been watched by Milton Rae.

After the boy had gone, Rae allowed the cordial expression to drain from his face. The heat would really be on him if Frances Kline's Prostaglandin product came good. He knew he could not count on support from his colleagues on the Board.

He must apply the pressure himself.

CHAPTER FIVE

The sky, a flat sheet rubbed with charcoal, was reluctantly giving way to the onset of another day as the Bell helicopter touched down on the helipad on the roof of Cranston Towers. The noise of the rotors was deafening, and Frances Kline tapped the pilot's shoulder and smiled her thanks, then stepped into the fine drizzle and hurried across the water-sheeted rough tarmac to the entrance on the far side of the roof.

In the mirrored elevator, she satisfied herself that the over-sized, canary yellow Valentino trousersuit she had travelled in was still presentable. At work, her rule was always to be impeccably groomed. At home, Frances preferred her oldest and most familiar gear.

On the flight, she had broken with her usual pattern. Generally, she would spend the first hour dozing, and the rest of the time catching up on paperwork. This time she had done neither. Instead, she had reclined her seat, closed her eyes, and spent the journey taking stock of her life, which up until a few days before had seemed so comfortably arranged.

She knew very well why. It was Gray Barnard. He had made an impact on her, and the ripples caused her comfortable image of her life to distort, magnifying all sorts of imperfections that she had never noticed before.

They all seemed to concern facets of her marriage that she thought she had come to terms with long before.

When Frances had met Webley Kline, she had been eighteen and he twenty-nine. He was practising as an analyst, though they met at college, where he was taking an undergraduate economics course, 'to find out about this weird money-making stuff'. She had envied and admired the breadth of his experience and the depth of his understanding, as he told the wide-eyed young girl of his experience in psychiatric hospitals. She'd always known that Web was a father figure; that her attraction to him was bound up with losing her own father when she was so young. Confused and alone, she had watched helpless, while her mother disintegrated emotionally, until all the feeble woman could do was hold on only long enough for Frances to finish high school. It left Frances determined never to rely on anyone; never to be trapped emotionally or financially. Never to repeat history.

For the first years, their marriage had been conventional. They had lived in the hills of Los Angeles, and David had been born after a year. He had been ten when Frances decided to hire Marita, their Mexican housekeeper, and get an MBA part-time. She went out to work and four years later, Stacey was born.

Web had been acquiescent, believing that Frances would get the urge to work out of her system. He had been wrong about that. With a combination of luck, good timing, and an innate talent for finding highly original solutions to problems, Frances had not only strived for success, but had achieved it.

Her progress up the ladder was remarkably swift. She had first found a job with a marketing consultancy, where her flair and freshness meant that she was rapidly snapped up to head the new in-house marketing department of a sports clothing factory. She had hardly begun to institute new procedures designed to develop an export market before the firm itself was acquired by a larger West Coast concern, and she initiated an expansion programme that saw the original small clothing factory expand into an organisation making branded leisure wear and sporting equipment sold all over the world.

Her salary moved upwards fast, and when she had overtaken Web, he had surprised her by responding with an announcement of his own; 'I've decided to quit full-time practice. There's no point in us both knocking ourselves out. There's a part-time post going; I think I'll take it. Stacey needs at least one parent around the house some of the time. I can see patients at home.'

When she had started working, it had been mornings only. By now she was engaged in a full-scale five-day week, and was finding it harder and harder to reconcile the demands of mother-hood and her burgeoning career.

As time passed, Frances had seen Web withdraw from active life. He had simply stopped initiating, and handed over to Frances.

The full realisation had left her scared.

But it was convenient, too. Once she had ventured into the work environment, she was hooked. Work and success filled a gap in her life. But in filling one emptiness, they had created another.

Then had come the greatest upheaval of all, the move to New York. Frances recalled the excitement she had felt when they arrived there six years before, how the thrill of the crowds of Fifth Avenue, and the inaudible but ever-present hum of power and dynamics within Cranston Towers had found an answering harmonic in her soul.

Frenetic and shamelessly avaricious, Manhattan was a complete antithesis to the laid-back West Coast, whose lifestyle had been infused into her system since childhood. New York gave her a sense of opportunity, to become exactly the sort of person she wanted to become. She loved the hugger-mugger of high-powered business life. To Frances Kline, at the age of thirty-seven, New York was like a rebirth, a first exposure to the whole vastness of human experience.

The move had been demanded entirely by her career. It was not planned for, but thrust upon them. Frances had by then become marketing VP of the international leisure wear division. Her plans to back a Japanese tennis player had born fruit, and sent sales of sports clothes and shoes sky high.

She was taken completely unawares when the president had called her at home one evening. 'Frances,' he had said. 'This is your ex-boss speaking.'

'What do you mean, Brad? What's happening?'

'We all work for a different corporation now, sweetheart. Or rather you do and I don't. It happens to the best of us, Frances. We get taken over. I've decided to take the money and run. I don't want a second coronary.'

'And Frances,' Brad continued, with triumph in his voice, 'I've done it.'

'Done what?'

'Got you the job.'

'What job, for Chrissakes Brad. Calm down and tell me what you've done.'

'The only thing they wanted to know is if you would move.'

'Move to where?'

'To New York.'

Her heart sank. Just when things seemed to have been smoothing out.

Brad Davis continued excitedly: 'I said of course you would. I gave you a big build-up, Fran. They want you. They want to open up a new leisure division.'

'Hold on,' said Frances. Just what had he gotten her into? 'They don't even know me.'

'The chairman, his name is Bennis, said did I know someone who could take over from me. I said: Yes. You. Then he said: What, a woman? And I . . .'

Frances butted in: 'I can't help that.'

'Listen, will you. He's not unhappy about the woman bit. In fact, he said a woman would look good in the business papers. It's a big break, Fran. They've got lots of plans for expansion, and Cranston is a really huge organization. They've got opportunities world-wide. If I didn't have this damn heart thing I'd take the job myself.'

'You're not a woman,' replied Frances tartly.

Web's reaction had been one of utter equanimity. 'It'll give me the perfect chance to get to work on that book I've been carrying around in my head for so long . . . ' So Frances had gone to New York to meet Maxwell J. Bennis, had impressed and charmed him, and had been offered the post of President of the newly formed Cranston Leisure Division. This comprised her own firm, recently taken over, as well as a mine in South Africa, and a safety-fuse manufacturing operation in Canada. She had no idea what these last two had to do with Leisure, but she had taken them on anyway. At last, she was building up her own empire.

Alone in her office, too early yet for her staff to be in, Frances savoured once again the overwhelming satisfaction she felt whenever she returned from a trip. She stood for several moments at the centre of her suite, and absorbed the brisk calm of the beige, black and white decor. The colour and contrasting textures of the drapes, carpet and furniture never failed to please her. If her suite at The Frances in London reflected the opulence of a bygone age, this office was very much that of a modern New York businesswoman – professional, classy, and not too brash.

Her taste in art was diverse – with a strong tendency towards supporting young unknown artists whose work appealed to her. The picture facing her desk was typical. It was 'graffiti art', derived from the spontaneous decoration of New York subway trains, and picked up cheap in a Greenwich Village gallery, before the style became fashionable.

She turned to the view of Central Park, through the plate glass running from ceiling to floor. From this height, the soft rain was turned to a cotton wool of mist settling in hollows, draping over the lattice-work of winter-naked trees. The moist haze softened the sharp edges of man-made concrete and steel to a more human blur. At times like these, Frances loved New York the most.

Then she walked across to the other plate-glass wall, that opened onto her section of the roof garden. Alone among the Cranston vice-presidents, she had taken control of this precious patch from the contracted office gardening firm, and had turned it into a bower of pot-grown trees, bare now of leaves, with a bench in a shady spot in the far corner where she could retreat in summer. In good weather, she would also invite selected members of her staff onto her patio for cocktails after work – making sure that everybody on her team was included at least once every six months. It suited her style of hands-on management, and they would enjoy the evening city lights puncturing through the early dusk as the setting sun painted the towering walls of Manhattan first rose-pink, then ochre, and finally purple.

Her mood was broken by Jo-Beth, fine young skin still rouged by the cold outdoors. Jo-Beth had been Frances's secretary since she had arrived at Cranston, a bright and efficient girl with a sunny disposition, who took pride in the achievements of her boss. She whooped out loud at the unexpected discovery of Frances at her desk.

'Hey, Frances. This is too much! We didn't expect you back until tomorrow morning.'

Frances grimaced. 'The Marley deal fell through. I left Gerry Rule to sort it out, and came on home. I could hardly wait to get back.'

'Well, that's just marvellous,' fussed Jo-Beth. 'How was the flight. Can I fix you some coffee?' Frances smiled as the crisp young blonde bustled about the room, her slender hands playing bird-like with the papers on Frances's desk, straightening and restraightening things which had already been perfectly arranged. Jo-Beth was another of the good things about New York – that great rarity of a secretary who was not merely willing to please, but had the intelligence and ability to match her enthusiasm.

'Sorry to spring such a surprise,' Frances teased the girl, idly envying the firm shelf her buttocks made, where they swelled from her slender back. 'But you'll be glad to know that I'm only planning a couple of hours here today. You can have your day off after all.'

'I guess you must be awful tired.'

Suddenly, Frances felt the weight of the travelling, of the dislocation of her internal clock, and of the emotions that had been playing through her mind over the past days. She closed her eyes, and leaned her head back. Jo-Beth had unwittingly made her feel very old. 'God. You're not wrong. Remind me not to do that sort of trip again in a hurry.'

Then, sitting up straight again: 'So what have you got for me marked "urgent". On second thoughts, make that "very urgent".'

'There's loads of stuff.'

'Well, let's just look at essentials. I've got a date with a little girl this evening. It's Stacey's school concert, and I want a long hot bath before I can face all the parents of her friends that she'll *insist* I meet afterwards.' With quick fingers, Frances scanned her mail, keeping a few items aside for immediate attention.

'By the way, did you manage to send her that good-luck posy I asked for?'

'Yeah,' Jo-Beth nodded, silken hair catching the light. 'Little pink daisies.'

'Thanks a lot. Any other feedback while I was away?'

'Nothing that can't wait,' said Jo-Beth. 'Oh, yeah, a call from South Africa yesterday.'

'Was it Malan at Athabasca?' She was expecting her mine manager to call. 'That can wait until tomorrow.'

'No. Not Malan. Same accent though,' said Jo-Beth

64

innocently. 'A guy called Barnard. Gray Barnard. He wouldn't leave a message.'

'Well, what happened? Did she buy it?'

The Trans-Atlantic line was as clear as if it was across the street rather than across the ocean. There was a moment's silence, then came the reply.

'We're not dealing with some turkey here. This is one bright lady.'

'Listen here,' came the reply from New York. 'Things are getting tight. There's not much time. So you can forget about me cooling my heels here while you pussyfoot about waiting for the timing to be right. You gotta get this scenario moving, and quick. Otherwise you're out of the deal, and your name's gonna be mud. You get me?'

'Don't worry.' The voice was nervous now.

Then, after he had rung off, he shuddered. This was getting serious. And with the thought came the realization just how far he had gone, and how much was at stake.

Oh God. He was in way over his head.

The sleek Mercedes Benz 450SLC coupé nosed through the overweight US cars that made up the downtown Manhattan traffic like a game fish among a crowd of well-fed carp. Like a shark among whales, thought Frances, as she enjoyed the precision of its responses, and the muted rustle of its fuel-injected V8 engine. On across the George Washington Bridge, then onto the New England Thruway, through Westchester County. Barely an hour later, she swung into the steep driveway of their house, parked the car, and braced herself for the welcoming rush of Lexington.

During the journey, her mood had shifted from the confusion of the morning to simple pleasure at the thought of seeing her family again. 'Damn Gray Barnard,' she had thought. 'Just as I succeed in getting him out of my mind, he pushes his way straight back in again.'

She had forbidden Jo-Beth from calling her home, to tell Web and Stacey that she was home a day early, that she would after all be able to attend Stacey's school concert. She wanted to surprise them both.

She pulled the coupé into the carport, alongside Webley's station wagon. He always scoffed at her indulgence in finely crafted European automobiles. 'They're just goddamn cars, for getting about in. Start getting fussy, and you're halfway to a king-size penis envy.'

Frances approached the front door undetected, and let herself in quietly. Where was the dog, she wondered? Where was Marita, the housekeeper? Now she really would surprise them together.

Web and Stacey were in the kitchen. She followed the rattle of knives and forks, towards the rich smell of garlic and cheese. He was feeding the child pizzas again!

'You'd better move it, Stace.' Web's voice was exaggeratedly urgent. 'We've only got an hour, and you're not even bathed yet.'

'Okay, Daddy. Just let me finish my pizza, willya?'

'And,' Web went on, 'I want to look my best so's I can show your friends your dad's not such a bad old guy.'

Stacey giggled. 'Daddy! You're not bad. You're just a little funny. That's all.'

'Well, thanks anyway. Now giddyup, and get yourself all clean and shiny. We don't want the star of the show to be late for her own concert.'

The sound of father and daughter's voices was like an age-old duet. Leaning against the wall, Frances realized that her test of spontaneity of affection had rebounded on her. She felt almost as though she had stumbled on an illicit love letter to her own lover from another. She could see so clearly how close they were, how they needed each other. She was envious.

Then Stacey saw her. 'Mom, Mom, Mom. You came. I knew you'd come.'

Frances hugged the little girl to her. 'How did you know, honey?' she said.

'I just knew. Thanks for the flowers.'

'They're for luck tonight. Did you give them some water?'

'Sure. They're next to my bed. Come and see.'

'Where's Marita?' she asked Web, over the top of Stacey's head.

'I gave her the week off. She wanted to visit her sister.'

'And Lexington?'

'Spending the night at the vets. She got a fried chicken bone stuck in her throat.'

His answer started a spurt of anger.

'Jesus, Web. Fried chicken? Can't you just look after things for a few days? I don't like a growing child to live on junk food. You know how bad it is for her.' Immediately, she hated herself for the outburst.

'Frances, as long as you go on hopping off on sudden and extended trips for your beloved Cranston Group, I will feed Stacey and myself on whatever it is that we enjoy.'

Soon, Frances was relaxing her nakedness in hot water, waiting for Web to join her before they dressed for Stacey's concert. As some couples never fail to hold one another before falling asleep, Frances and Webley always shared a bath, no matter what the friction between them. So she lay there and waited, submitting to the balm of the water, with her rosy-pink nipples just piercing the surface.

Web padded into the tiled steaminess. He was naked, and holding a cheese-and-salami bagel, which he placed delicately on top of the vanity shelf, next to the row of unguents and lotions.

'Web,' Frances chided. 'Do you really have to bring more food in here. You've just had a pizza, for Chrissakes.'

Her husband took no notice. Carefully, he selected a bath oil from the range on the shelf, and without a word unscrewed the bulbous head from the bottle.

'C'mon, Web. What're you doing now.'

His limp penis dangled to one side from a grey fernery. He

tilted the plastic bottle, and the oily contents dribbled over the triangular underwater shadow at the cleft of her thighs.

'You're out of your mind, Webley. That's too oily. You only need a teaspoonful.' She was laughing now, halfway between anger and surprise.

Webley Kline retrieved his bagel, and held it high as he stepped into the bath. Automatically, he put her between him and the faucets. It was something he had always done, because, as he had insisted early in their marriage, 'the extreme danger that domestic plumbing posed to male genitalia . . . '

'I have a patient who lost his penis in the bath,' he had told the young and credulous Frances. 'Strangled it with the bath chain, and it had to be cut off.'

She felt him settle in behind her, and then heard his mighty biting through the crust of the bagel. 'Jesus, Web. Do you really have to eat that thing in here.' She eddied the water up between her thighs. 'You really are a pig. If I find any crumbs floating round, you'll be out of this bath so fast . . . '

'Fran,' he teased her fondly. 'Just because you've got a hang-up about your weight doesn't mean you have the right to stop other people from eating. My advice to you would be to bring your lettuce leaf to the bath as well.' He broke off to bite another chunk, and continued with his mouth full. 'But since you're not my patient, it's not my job to give you advice.'

'Thank God for that,' she entered into the game. 'You are without doubt the shittiest analyst I've ever shared a bath with.'

'Now that I find strangely gratifying,' he said, reaching for her shoulders and pulling her back between his legs. 'It means I am ethically free to seduce you.'

'Take it easy there, Dr Kline.' She felt him hardening against the base of her spine. 'Just because you're sharing my bath oil doesn't mean you can take liberties.'

'Whether you like it or not,' he said, kneading her hardening nipples, 'your erogenous zones simply don't agree.'

'Mommy.' Stacey's voice intruded on them. Frances wondered how long she'd been standing there.

'What is it, honey?'

'I can't find my ribbon.'

'It's in the top right-hand drawer, Stace,' Web answered quickly.

'Thanks, Dad. D'ya want me to close the door.'

'Thanks, honey. You go get ready for the concert. We'll be down in a few minutes.'

As the door gently closed, Web resumed his finger play.

'Web.' Frances turned towards him. 'We haven't got time. We've got to leave in thirty minutes, and if you carry on like this, we're not going to make it.'

'Wanna bet?' He turned her head still further, and kissed her with forceful passion.

While the bath drained, she permitted him to explore her moistness with fingers that stopped just short of being rough.

Balancing herself within the empty but still warm enamel bath, she took in the comfort of his hardness.

Now, as she moved with him, she was able to forget all the guilt she had felt. His hard fingers were clawing at her buttocks, pulling her apart and searching for another orifice. To her surprise, Frances felt herself being driven towards a shuddering climax.

Web resettled in the cramped and uncomfortable chair, and gave Frances' knee a reassuring squeeze.

Then Stacey shuffled self-consciously onto the stage, wringing her hands in her nervousness. Halfway across, she suddenly spotted her parents in the audience. She stopped dead, causing the heavily costumed bumble bee following her to bump into her, and almost losing balance, before cuffing her crossly. Unconcerned, Stacey waved frantically, excitement lighting up her face.

Web turned to Frances, his face beaming with amusement and pride, his eyes glistening with tears.

But Frances was asleep.

CHAPTER SIX

By 7.15 the following morning, Frances Kline had braved the commuter traffic as far as Manhattan Island. Frances used the power of the Mercedes Benz skilfully, to cut through the raucously hooting melée, and twenty minutes later she had parked in her reserved bay in the Cranston Towers basement.

Heels echoing briskly off the concrete walls and pillars, she felt the pleasant tightness at the back of her thighs, and in the muscles deep in her buttocks, and wondered whether the comfortable ache was the result of her morning run, or the violent lovemaking in the tub with Webley. A fleeting grin crossed her face . . . what would her staff think of the dignified Frances Kline if they could have seen her then.

Running that morning had been particularly exhilarating. Her limbs had flexed and extended over the deserted beach under the taut grey of the still-dark sky, the water a drumskin picking up every nuance of light. The wet smells of larch-wood and humus were textures almost to be caressed; the underfoot hiss of sand saturated with seawater, and the steady elastic suppleness of muscles sliding against bone.

Frances had been jogging since before Stacey was born. It had begun as a vague desire to flatten up her stomach, and follow the 'Me Generation's' fashion for fitness, but it had rapidly become something much more important.

She had desperately wanted to share the pleasure with Webley, as she would a new-found delicacy or an enjoyable book. But he had turned it into an issue.

'Fran,' he said with a patronizing air. 'What do you need it for. Don't you realize how much damage it can do. Read the reports, for God's sake. You're gonna end up a wreck – fallen uterus, fallen arches, knees damaged by jarring, slipped discs, overstrained heart, and spavined joints. Doesn't seem worth it to me.'

'But,' she said, 'it just makes you feel so good. I get a glow that lasts all day. Anyway, it helps to keep my weight down.'

'Aha,' replied Web. 'There we have the real reason.'

'C'mon, cut the psychological crap. I just enjoy jogging, and I wish you'd come and try it, because I'm sure you'd enjoy it too.'

Frances had carried on running without Web.

One morning, she remembered, he had peered up at her from within his 6 am cocoon of blankets as she pulled on her track-suit and training shoes. 'It simply is not safe, you know. If I wasn't so liberated, I'd forbid you from going.

'It's not just my opinion. It's a genuine piece of information I'm giving you. I also read in *Time* magazine that joggers – especially female joggers – are the number one target for muggers.'

Frances had laughed. 'Well, they'll not get much out of me. I can run faster than any mugger this side of the Rockies. I also happen to carry a Gazapper.'

'What for chrissakes, is a Gazapper?'

'You squirt it in a mugger's face, and he goes blind and collapses.'

Undeterred by his scorn, she had continued jogging every day she could, covering three fluid miles, revelling in her body and also in the magnificent solitude of the early morning, and the unique opportunity it gave her to think without being interrupted. That morning's jog-topic had been the threat to the Prostaglandin-S project.

Her vivid purple twinset reflected in the automatic glass doors as she swept through – she'd had their reaction speed tuned up to maximum to suit her habitually rapid walking speed – heading for her office suite. She had already worked through the presentation she would give at that morning's executive management meeting.

Pleased to see Jo-Beth already at her desk and ready for action, she plucked a flower from the vase at her desk and drew in a deep breath. 'Got that report I left for you on the dictaphone?'

'The one on Prostaglandin for the executive meeting? I put ten copies on your desk.'

'Great. Take a break and grab us some coffee while I wade through that mail I didn't finish yesterday. Anything urgent?'

'Ed Potter wants to see you; something about a new hamburger mix for the south-west operations.'

'Tell him I'll see him tomorrow. And hold all calls, Jo-Beth. I need a bit of time to myself.'

Frances worked solidly for thirty minutes, then went into her private washroom to make sure she looked as sharp as she felt.

She was always careful not only to dress smartly, but to choose clothes that would fit the mood and image she wanted to project.

Her wardrobe was not so much extensive as exclusive. She bought carefully, saving time by sticking to famous-name designers, taking her pick from their wares in Milan, Paris, London and New York.

Today, she wore a classically cut dove-grey flannel skirt with a Jaeger twinset - perfectly expressed femininity - while a broad leather belt, added as an after-thought, lent a rakish, swashbuckling touch. At her throat, she wore a thick heavy-linked gold choker chain. Web had joked that it made her look like an expensive little poodle. 'Maybe,' Frances had replied, 'but poodles have sharp teeth.'

Then she took the lift up the chairman's office, smiling in reply to Lilly's greeting: 'Morning, Mrs Kline. Please go right in. Mr Bennis is expecting you.'

Maxwell J Bennis's den was the complete antithesis of her own crisp office. A lawyer all his professional life, his office carried a particular stamp; claustrophobically dark, hemmed in by massive pieces of once-fashionable furniture from the post-war era. There were shelves all around the walls, lined with heavy books with embossed leather spines, as well as an array of ornaments and memorabilia from around the world. One glass-fronted display cabinet in the corner was filled with golf trophies; the wall beside

it displayed photographs of Bennis posing with various person-
alities on numerous golf greens, the men grinning from under
long-peaked caps, Bennis invariably with a half-smoked cigar in
his hand, jaunty canopied caddy wagons parked in the background. The odour of too many cigarettes clung to the heavy
dark-brown drapes, and the office's sole occupant sat with a
plume of smoke rising from the gigantic carved soapstone
ashtray in front of him.

'That you, Kline? Take a seat.' He gestured to the heavy
leather-upholstered chair across his polished walnut desk. 'How
was the trip?'

'Very good. I got a lot done.'

'I hear you're buying up a property company, after your hotel
deal went wrong.'

Frances almost gave a start. He was surprisingly well-
informed. 'You been checking up on me, Max?'

'It's my function to keep a finger on the pulse of the Cranston
Group, Kline.'

'Yes, Max.' Frances did not want to get side-tracked onto this
particular battleground. After all, there was a war to be won. She
wondered when Maxwell Bennis would get to the point.

'It's all part of my plans for expansion into specialized tour
groups. I can't use The Frances. I need a new property. Believe
me, this is a damn good way of getting one.'

'Kline, the Board is on the brink of a major decision
concerning reinvestment, and it is particularly important at this
time to consolidate our existing resources.' His blustering tone,
Frances well knew, concealed an unwillingness to confront the
issue.

'Max – we've been "consolidating" ever since I joined
Cranston six years ago. The recession is over now, and those of
us who took advantage of it are away again.'

As a conservative professional Maxwell Bennis had been
chosen as Chairman of Cranston for his caution. He prided
himself on keeping costs and risks low, concentrating on safe
industries and predictable markets. The Cranston shareholders

got a relatively low return, but absolute security and a predictable dividend. No fireworks, but a good steady flame – that was the way Bennis liked it.

Frances abhorred this approach. She was always looking for new opportunities, finding ways to expand, to create new markets, and above all to maintain a leadership profile. Since she backed it up with an unsurpassed 'feel' for the market, and since she had been right so often in the past, Maxwell had learned to trust her instincts, and to like and admire her gusto and flair. At the same time, she frightened him.

'Kline, it's the Board that makes the decisions. I obey, and see that they are carried out. Profits have fallen in timber, drugs and shipping. And you know what autos have been through. Believe me, I can't justify buying up property development corporations all over the show. Surely you can see that?'

'Max, don't be short-sighted. The way to survive is to make sure we stay up front.'

'You may be right, Kline, but the Board is not going to agree. There's no maybe about that.'

'But Maxwell, surely you've got the clout. You're the goddamn Chairman. They're milking Cranston dry. They're sacrificing investment to show profits now. It's not on, Max. How is it all going to be in five years' time? My division is making profits, and ploughing them back into expansion. The hotel profit is twenty per cent up for the last quarter, and this quarter looks even healthier. We can afford to expand. Actually, we can't afford *not* to expand. And you want to take my investment to prop up other divisions. You're throwing good money after bad, Maxwell. If you want to cut costs, let the other divisions do it. Don't cripple mine.'

Maxwell frowned, a fold of jowl rolling over his collar. 'Kline, I don't deny that you've done very well. But you're not looking at the broad picture. You want a Board position, don't you? You have to play ball.'

Frances was outraged by the implied threat. 'There's no way, Max. The only way I get that place on the Board is if I show

74

results – and I can't do that if my hands are tied.'

Bennis paused significantly, leaning back and taking a deep draw from his cigarette.

'Okay. We can let the hotel thing roll for a while. I'm relying on you to recoup any investment quickly. Now the real cost problem you have is on this Prostaglandin thing you took over from Milton. How is it going?'

'It's going great,' she replied, trying to be cautious, but unable to prevent her eyes from shining with enthusiasm. Deliberately, her answer was terse and unembroidered.

Maxwell Bennis looked down at his notes, scrawled on a yellow legal pad. 'You'll need to cut back for the rest of the year, so you can stay within budget.'

'Max – couldn't we leave it until the meeting. I've prepared a full presentation, and it'd just be wasting your time now.'

'Kline,' he said, leaning his flaccid bulk across the desk at her, 'that's precisely why I called you in here before the meeting.' He paused to light another cigarette, his third since she came in, Frances noticed with distaste.

'I'm under a lot of pressure from the Board. You're going to have to stop spending. If necessary, you're going to have to can the project.'

Frances admired Maxwell J Bennis for many reasons, in spite of his fuzzy management techniques. But there was nothing vague about this.

'Maxwell, I can't believe what I'm hearing. I'm at a critical stage of development of Prostaglandin-S. We're on the verge of the final breakthrough. I will not be forced to give it up.'

'You may very easily have to.'

He was testing her. She could feel it.

'Max, do you have any idea how much we have already spent on Prostaglandin-S? How much time and effort? And how much money? If we quit now, all that will be wasted . . . '

'I know exactly how much,' he said. 'I have the figures right in front of me. But it happens all the time in the drug business, Kline. Eighty per cent of research is aborted. This is your

75

trouble . . . you're out of your depth here – and it's not even our usual pharmaceutical type of drug.'

'I know that. If it had been, Milton Rae would have handled it.'

Suddenly, with one of the bursts of disarming honesty that made her like him so much, Maxwell Bennis's faded gray eyes met Frances' direct green ones. 'And so he should have,' he said. They stared silently at each other.

The tension of the mood was broken by Lilly, bearing in a tray of silver and fine china, and pouring black tea with lemon for each of them.

'Maxwell,' Frances said, her tone subdued, 'I'm very grateful to you for warning me before the meeting.' He didn't dispute her assumption of his complicity. 'I want you to know that.'

'Frances,' he said, making rare use of her first name, 'you've more than proved yourself with the Cranston Group. Give yourself a break. You've done enough for the present. You have plenty more time.'

'If I give up now, I won't have done enough,' she said. 'Not for me, not for you, Max, and not for Cranston.'

She held his attention, forestalling interruption with her eyes. 'I've done my homework on Prostaglandin-S. It's a winner. Profits will easily offset development costs . . . it will outstrip anything we have ever done. But I must be allowed to carry the research to conclusion now. Otherwise we will lose everything.'

'We are not the only people working with cell rejuvenation. There is pure research under way in Switzerland, at least one other American corporation may be thinking along the same lines as us. And I believe the Japanese are well-advanced with their research. If we miss the opportunity now, it's gone forever.' She was sitting forward, on the edge of her chair, her hands thrust into her jacket pockets.

'How're things going in South Africa?'

Frances gave him a brief run-down, but it was clear that he wasn't listening.

When she cut her report short, he heaved himself to the

76

standing position, his rumpled suit hanging untidily round his buttocks. 'Okay, Kline, I'll see you at the executive meeting.' He walked stiffly across to the cocktail cabinet, extracted a crystal glass, and poured himself a small shot of neat bourbon.

'Maxwell,' Frances couldn't help herself. 'For chrissakes, it's 9.30 in the morning!'

'Yeah, I guess you're right.' He put the glass down untasted. 'It's this goddamn pressure. The Board meeting is going to be really tricky.'

'You shouldn't let it get to you. You can't run an operation like this without problems.'

'It's not just you,' said Bennis, confiding in her again. 'We've been lending heavily in the under-developed countries, at interest rates that are giving reverse returns.'

She replied gently, 'That's your fault, Max. It was a bad decision.'

'A necessary one, Kline, if you're thinking about investing in the future. I've told you before, you're bright, and you're beautiful. But you're not political enough.' He gave her an avuncular smile, and escorted her to the door.

On her way to the executive meeting, Frances called in to her office. The heat was on for Prostaglandin-S. She was so preoccupied that at first she did not notice an explosion of yellow on the corner of her desk. 'What's all this?' she asked Jo-Beth, who had followed her into the room to watch her reaction.

'A great big bunch of flowers, if you ask me. Just arrived by special messenger. There was no card. Just a delivery note with your name and address. You've got a secret admirer somewhere.' Jo-Beth's fresh young face was frankly inquisitive.

'God, they're unbelievable. Just smell that scent.' She pulled the vase over to her, and buried her face in the blooms. Then she smiled, searching her mind rapidly for some forgotten reason that might have prompted the gift. 'It must be Web,' she laughed. 'He's just a soppy romantic at heart. Jo-Beth, call him

77

for me. Ask him if he'd like to dine with his wife tonight. Just the two of us.'

'No,' said Frances Kline. 'We shouldn't let them get away with it. Why not make a bid for Zamachi ourselves? They're the world leaders in construction robots – and let's face it, it's a small step from manufacturing robots to construction robots.' She had cut across the discussion at the executive presidents' meeting. Now all seven men had stopped what they were saying and were looking at her, a petite, crisp figure with her eyes glowing with light. All her earlier despair had gone now, in the excitement and immediacy of the executive meeting in the boardroom. The grim faces staring at her, Milton Rae's prominent among them, did not frighten her. Rather they stimulated her to fresh mental agility.

Yale Duke was the first to speak, in his lazy manner. 'Exactly my thoughts, Frances. But we've got to face the reality of the costs.'

'It seems to me,' Frances replied, 'that it would work out in the long term. We could use robots ourselves, and sell them as fast as we could make them. It makes sense.' She was in her element now.

'Frances,' Rae intervened from across the expanse of polished redwood, 'don't you think robots are little out of your league?'

Frances Kline sat back and said nothing. She knew Rae was warming up for the argument to come about Prostaglandin-S, and she wouldn't allow herself to be drawn into a battlefield prematurely. Besides, the more corporate reserves that were allocated to other projects, the less would be available for her own division.

Her thoughts were broken by a sudden awareness of silence. As she refocussed her thoughts, she heard Maxwell Bennis speak. 'Can we move on? I think, Kline, we'd like to hear about the progress you're making on your Prostaglandin project.' She saw Rae stiffen slightly in his seat. He had been a fool to let her take Prostaglandin-S from Epipharm.

'I won't waste time going over ground we've covered in previous meetings. You all have a copy of my progress report. The status as of now is that animal toxicology trials have been successfully completed. The Federal Drug Administration here in the US and the MCC, their equivalent in France, have both okayed our bio-assay reports, and given us the go-ahead on human trials. That was just over a month ago.'

'The human trials will take at least another year then,' she heard Milton Rae interrupt.

'Not with this product, Milton. It's not the same as with your strictly ethical drugs. The requirements are not so stringent for over-the-counter products. And PS-21 will be sold over the counter in most countries.'

'PS-21?' queried Bennis.

'That's the tentative trade name I've given the product. I've already registered it, by the way. As a clinical cosmetic drug,' she continued, 'human trials are restricted to topical acceptability studies, skin reaction tests, and limited toxicological assessment. The trials will be completed in a fortnight, and full data will be available a fortnight after that. The results we have so far have been analyzed, and we haven't come up with any negatives.

'Our only problem is shelf life. Our researchers are looking for a stabilizing agent that will extend the life of the active Prostaglandin-S.' She didn't tell them that the present shelf life could be measured in minutes rather than hours, and that her team of scientists had been searching for a stabilizer for over twelve months now without success. That was her problem, not theirs. Instead, she hurried on, not leaving breathing space for anyone to ask questions.

'From today, I need a year to get the product on the market. Of course, it will be launched globally, so it's an enormous job. I am giving it top priority. As part of our agreement with Milton, we will use Epipharm's existing distribution facilities.'

She paused, and looked round the company. 'Because of the

intensely competitive nature of the ballgame we're in, I will be handling all the marketing myself. And I hardly need to remind you all of the need for the strictest security. We can't afford a leak.' She sat back, intertwined her long fingers, and laid them in front of her on the table.

'Gentlemen,' she spoke with quiet emphasis, 'rejuvenation via Prostaglandin-S will be marketed within the next year to eighteen months. With or without the Cranston Group. It appears that the Japanese are the furthest advanced of all the competitors, but there is work in progress in Europe as well. If we move quickly, we'll be in a position to beat them all.'

Milton Rae was the first to speak, with one of the questions she had hoped to forestall. 'What about your budgets?'

'What about them? You know better than anyone, Milton, how much this sort of research costs.'

'Do you know how much you've overspent?' It was Merill Lamb.

'Of course I do,' she replied, ignoring the obvious insult in the question.

'The Board won't like it.'

'I'm sure the Board will see the point, Merill.' She wanted to scream out loud. Almost half the goddamn Board was in the room.

Instead, she turned to Maxwell Bennis. 'Listen, Max. Surely we're all of us here fighting for the same thing? We want to see the Cranston Group maintain its leadership. We want to give our shareholders a good deal. And we each of us need to express ourselves through innovation, which means the creation of successful new products. That's all I'm trying to do, same as the rest of you.'

There was a silence across the room, broken by John C Cunningham of Shipping. 'A speech like that sounds like it's getting time to break for a drink,' he said, with a wry laugh.

The remark broke the tension, and gave the chairman the opening he sought. 'Gentlemen:' he addressed the whole group, not catching Frances' eye, 'I am going to suggest a compromise.'

Now he turned to her. 'Kline – you say you can get the product in the market within twelve months. That's too long for us to sit on your overspending. What's the absolute minimum time you need to get – er – PS-21 onto the shelves?'

She replied without even a moment's consideration. 'Six months,' feeling a surge of adrenalin course through her veins.

Around the table, several sets of eyebrows were raised spontaneously. Nobody made any comment, until Milton Rae broke the silence. He spoke directly to Maxwell. 'And if, at the end of six months it hasn't worked out for Frances and her . . . cosmetics,' the inflection on the word was full of scorn, 'what then?'

'Then,' Maxwell replied, 'then we'll take it to the Board.'

'Hcy there, Jo-Beth,' Frances floated into her office on a cloud. 'Come through to my office, please.' She felt high. The target she'd set herself was difficult, but she wouldn't accept that it was impossible. And thinking about cutting in half the time she had available to take PS-21 from embryo to adult made her feel excited rather than daunted.

'Any messages while I was out?'

She scanned the pile of letters and memoranda that Jo-Beth gave her, and signed them with a flourish. 'Gerry called from London; please would you call him as soon as possible.'

'Get him for me, please.'

Gerald Rule was his usual disgruntled self, and Frances smiled at the image she had of him scowling out of the window at the park he hated so much. They spoke about progress of the share takeover deal, then Frances said: 'Listen Gerry, you've got to get that done. I've just got us a deadline of six months to get PS-21 on the market, and I need you here.'

There was a short silence, and then Rule spoke. 'Christ, boss-lady. What have you got us into this time!'

'Gerry, don't worry. Just wrap up the Bristol deal as quick as you can, and get straight back to New York. That's what you want, isn't it?'

Frances' trans-Atlantic call had shared satellite space with another conversation which, if she had heard it, would have sent a shiver down her spine.

'About the Kline boy,' a strongly accented New York voice said. 'Are you ready?'

'Yeah. Don't worry, mate,' came the reply from London. 'It's all set up. We're ready to move right now.'

'Okay. Then give it to him.'

'The whole lot?'

'Yeah. The whole lot.'

Before Frances left, she sat quietly in her office for half an hour, making up a list of matters for urgent action on getting the PS-21 project moving. As she jotted down her thoughts, two things kept cropping up on her pad. One was the name of Professor Paul Rocher. The other was a question that she underlined three times, before she stood up in preparation for leaving.

It read: 'Factory – where?'

As she was about to close the door, her private telephone rang. She stepped quickly across the room, suddenly remembering with a curse that she was late, and she had wanted to spend an hour with Stacey before she and Web went out for dinner. Then she picked up the phone and heard the deep South African inflection of the voice that said 'Hullo.'

'Who is this?' she demanded, though she had realized the answer before she had even finished the question.

'I was saying that at this time of year, the roses are at their best in the Cape.'

'Gray. Where are you phoning from, for God's sake?'

'From home. Did you get the flowers?'

'Yes. But there was no card. I didn't realize . . . ' Again,

Frances found herself strangely flustered.

'I asked for yellow roses, so you could share my garden with me.'

The tensions of Frances' day were suddenly swept away by the easy confidence in his voice.

'They really are the most beautiful flowers. I wish I could see your garden.'

'I'd like that. Perhaps one day you will,' he said.

Neither of them spoke for a moment. Then Frances laughed. It was all so absurd. 'Perhaps,' she said lightly.

'Franci, I want to see you.'

She started to formulate a reply, but he went on. 'Say nothing, I'll call again.' And abruptly he had cut the connection.

Frances felt a strange inner glow as she walked from her office to the executive lift. Maxwell Bennis was already in it, and he smiled at her. 'So, Kline, what are you going to do next,' he said.

'I leave for Lausanne in the morning,' she said firmly, 'to see Paul Rocher.'

CHAPTER SEVEN

'Jesus, Fran. That's playing God!'

Webley Kline sat with a slice of fried brain poised quivering on a fork that had stopped halfway to his mouth. Opposite him, on the far side of a small red-checked tablecloth, sat Frances. They were in their favourite Italian restaurant, and she had just told him about Prostaglandin-S.

'That's real big. Why didn't you tell me about this thing before, for Chrissakes?'

'Web, I didn't think you'd be interested.'

'C'mon, kiddo. That's what husbands are for.'

Frances was sorry now she had arranged the dinner. Gray's call had made the occasion seem empty . . . just another goodbye. The tension had been simmering under Web's bluff bonhomie, as he had ordered *fritto misto alla Milanese*, indulging himself in four of his culinary passions at once – liver, brains, Italian cooking and huge helpings. Frances had ordered piccata al limone, and tomato salad with fresh basil, and a Perrier water.

Now partly to allay the coldness in him because of the unscheduled trip to Lausanne tomorrow, partly to answer his question: 'Why must *you* always go, Frances. Is there nobody else?'; and partly because she could no longer contain her excitement, now that the PS project was under way, Frances had told him all the details. She had explained about the Prostaglandin family, and how PS-21 would be a capsule, taken daily like contraceptive pills, which would retard skin and muscle ageing. Web had instantly jumped ahead to the broader implication.

'If you can retard ageing of skin, then the next step is to retard ageing, period! Fran, you're talking Eternal Life here. You're talking about replacing God with a little card of capsules. Jesus, you terrify me. You'll never get away with it, you know. You'll have every pillar of every establishment in the world crashing down on you. The drug companies, the medical profession, cosmetics, the government. And how do you think the goddamned church leaders will react?'

'Web, I've considered these matters,' said Frances, calmly biting into her tender milk-fed veal. 'I think you're getting carried away. After all, I'm dealing with the outside and not the inside of the human body.'

'My dear, power-crazed wife. People have enough hassles coping with life already. They look forward to getting older, to retiring, even to dying, when they're ready for it. What are you offering instead – a new race of superactive perpetual kids?'

'What's wrong with that. People look their best and perform their best between twenty-five and thirty. Add a decade of experi-

84

ence to continuing youth and vigour, and you have a pretty formidable human being. I can't see why that's a bad idea.'

Web shook his head, and finally transferred the fried brain to his mouth. He chewed for a while, and then spoke with his mouth full. 'The psychological trauma would be . . . atrocious.' A fleck of food arced across the table onto the basket of bread rolls as he said the last word. 'And what about the population explosion?'

'People will adjust,' Frances replied. 'Like they did to contraception, supermarkets, home computers. You know, the French quite happily buy wine in plastic bottles nowadays. Human beings adapt. That is what makes them human.'

'You will do what you want anyway, Fran,' he said with resignation. 'You always do. But must you be a missionary? Remember, the Indians killed the missionaries, and in Africa they used to eat them, too.' Significantly he sliced another piece of brain, and put it to his mouth.

Frances had continued talking about Prostaglandin-S, about how she had acquired it from Milton, how it had subsequently soured their relationship; about their difficulties in finding the breakthrough they needed to ensure stability and a reasonable shelf life, and about how the six-month deadline would mean she'd be working virtually day and night until then. It was when he broke in that she realized he hadn't really been listening.

'Had a helluva day. Goddamn book. My mind just froze. I sat and stared at a blank sheet of paper all damn day. Writing is not as easy as they make out.'

How he had changed, thought Frances. How different their relationship had become, over the years since she had met him as a naive and fresh-faced college junior. She often reflected on how her life would have gone if they had not sat next to one another in the first economics class of the term, and then it had not become a habit. They had exchanged casual greetings and small talk. Then came the day of their first big test. Frances confided in him as they sat down: 'I'm terrified. I just know I am going to fail.'

'You know what?' he replied. 'Me too. What do you say we play hooky? I mean, if we're both going to fail, we might as well enjoy it.'

He would hear nothing of her protests, and together they had sneaked out of the lecture hall and then run laughing across the campus fields down to the banks of the college stream. Then they really did talk, and he had listened to her avidly. After that lazy day in the sun, it hadn't been long before Frances had found herself falling in love.

What had happened since then? Frances asked herself. To bring them to this point; where she was sharing the most exciting thing that had ever happened in her career, and he was promptly changing the subject.

'So I told Schmidt he could take his course and stuff it,' Web's voice intruded on her thoughts.

'Why?' she said, trying to recall the thread of his conversation.

'Because I'll be damned if I'll stay on next semester if Schmidt expects me to handle undergraduates.' Then, noting the puzzlement on her face: 'Frances, you haven't been listening, for Chrissakes!' Angrily, he stabbed his fork into the last piece of liver on his plate.

'Sorry,' she said. 'I had my mind on other things.'

'Well if you're not interested in what I'm saying, I'll just shut up.'

'C'mon, Web. Don't be silly.'

'I mean,' he persisted, 'why should I waste my breath. I'll save it, as the saying goes, to cool my porridge. Or rather Stacey's and my porridge.' He stared sulkily away.

'Listen, Web,' she tried to re-establish a link. 'It's been so long since we did anything good together. I've got to leave for Lausanne in the morning. Why don't you come with me. I have some work, but then we can take a day or so to see if we can still ski, and maybe call in on David in London on the way back. How about it, Kline?' She reached across, and grabbed his hand, excited by the prospect.

He gave a perfunctory, dutiful squeeze in return, then pulled his hand away. 'No chance, kiddo. Forget it. The book is going really good, and I'm right into it. Besides, Stacey needs me to be with her.'

'Marita can look after her for a few days. They'd both love it. If you can't make Switzerland, why not just come and meet me in London. The first crocuses should be out in Hyde Park, and we can go shopping, and to the theatre. Come on, Kline, just this one time. Let's do it.'

'Let's not, Fran. Not this time. And now I need to take a leak.'

In his station wagon on the way home, she had stared ahead through the windscreen, watching the night traffic through the chill streets, buildings mere outlines in the enveloping mist. She was peripherally aware of his hands on the steering wheel, knuckles white with anger. Finally, unable to sustain the mood any longer, she looked across at him. His usually cheerful features were set hard, and he looked ugly. The neon street lighting reflected off a grim jaw, and eyes that stared straight ahead.

Without quite knowing why – perhaps for revenge? – Frances said: 'I have to go, Web.' She touched him lightly on the knee.

It was as though she had operated a switch. Webley Kline exploded. 'Crap, Frances!' He had lifted his hands off the wheel in anger, and the big Ford swerved. 'You don't have to do anything!'

Then after a minute of silence he turned and smiled at her. 'Forget it, Fran. Of course you have to go.'

She put his hand on her knee, and they drove the rest of the way home in silence. It accompanied them to bed. He fitted himself mechanically round her, to warm her as they fell asleep, but it lay between them under the sheets – a doughy mass of untold differences.

Frances sat cross-legged on the floor, sucking black olives noisily, in between chewing Greek cheese, onions, lettuce, and fat hothouse tomatoes. Outside her window, Lake Geneva lay

87

calm and still, and on the opposite side, great mountains disappeared into the low cloud, buttresses of rock hidden beneath the thick snows of a Swiss winter.

As she munched the incongruously Mediterranean salad, Frances worked her way methodically through the stack of papers beside her, the one on her left growing at the same pace as the one on her right was shrinking. These were the complete files of her Prostaglandin-S research, and she wanted to be word perfect when she met Professor Paul Rocher the next day.

Actually, Frances had meant to run through the papers on the flight from New York to Paris, but it seemed that her normal pattern of flying – air-sickness pills, and then furious concentration to distract herself from being humiliatingly sick – was broken. She had a packet of Stellazone tablets in her hand luggage, but she had resolutely declined to take them.

The night before with Web, she brooded over in the aircraft, had been disastrous. Her remorse at again leaving Stacey was coloured by annoyance at Webley's unbending refusal to understand why she had to see Professor Paul Rocher personally. Why wouldn't he accept the realities of her career? If only he had come to London . . .

Inevitably, these thoughts were interwoven with a new strand in her mind. The slow accented voice of Gray Barnard. She puzzled over her reaction to his call the day before. He was not the first man to send her flowers. He was not the first man to . . . yes, she realized, she had to use the word . . . try to seduce her. And she knew how to deal with that; how to deliver a polite but effective dismissal.

But Gray Barnard was the first who had brought out this special feeling in her. The man had an uncanny knack of taking over. Being there at precisely the correct moment. It wasn't as though she wanted an involvement. Had even considered it for that matter. Yet there was no doubt Gray had got into her space. And it excited her.

Now, she eliminated all this from her mind, and concentrated on the problems of PS-21, biting absently into a ripe peach as she admitted to herself that Professor Rocher represented her only real chance of meeting her six-month deadline. It was crucial that she should persuade him to join her team.

Professor Paul Rocher was a seventy-eight-year-old French Jew who had come to world prominence in 1976, when he had been awarded the Nobel Prize for Biochemistry, for his seminal work on the synthesis of a pituitary growth hormone.

After that, Rocher had withdrawn from public life, and had devoted himself to investigating the synthesis of Prostaglandins. Although his field of research was narrow, there was little doubt that he knew more about the Prostaglandin family than any other man alive.

This much she had established from Willem Rademeijer, the Dutch scientist who headed her own research team. He had studied under Rocher, and spoke of the old man with a respect that was tinged with awe.

Frances had first made contact with Professor Rocher when she took over Prostaglandin-S four years before. She had got as far as speaking with him on the telephone. She remembered the conversation vividly, and wondered whether the Professor remembered her. Probably not, she thought.

He had been quite obstinate, refusing to join the Cranston Group, or even to act in the capacity of consultant. Ever since the end of World War II, the Professor had been intensely private, even reclusive, and was violently opposed to commercialization of his work. Rademeijer had described him as a scientist steeped in his science, totally dedicated to research.

Rocher's published work confirmed Rademeijer's thesis, that Prostaglandin-S retarded deterioration of certain cells by up to seventy per cent.

Rademeijer had taken three years to prove his theory – that PS acted at a superficial level, to prolong the nuclear longevity of cutaneous cells. 'It acts directly on the skin and superficial muscles,' he had told Frances excitedly. 'It slows down their natural decay. That means no wrinkles and creases. It literally keeps the skin young.

'It is revolutionary,' he said, eyes shining.

Tests over a three-year period on rats, guinea pigs and primates had all been very positive. The human dosage would be lower, but could delay the onset of wrinkles by ten years or more, in an individual who started taking it at the age of twenty-one.

But Rademeijer's research had stalled. Unless momentum could be restored, the project would die of natural causes anyway. Not only had Maxwell Bennis's six-month deadline brought Frances to Switzerland.

Rademeijer's stumbling block was the short life of Prostaglandin-S. 'The compound crystalizes so quickly! Even in the space of a few hours, bio-availability is significantly reduced. I have tried everything I know, to find a catalyst that will increase its life. But I am no closer to a solution now than when I began,' he had confessed after months of increasingly desperate false optimism. It was an irony, thought Frances, that a substance which itself prolonged life required another substance to extend its own useful life.

Now, as she scanned for the hundredth time all the data and test results – chemical formulae, trial statistics, pH values, bio-availability studies, and absorption rates – she thought of all the work that would be wasted if she was forced to abort the PS project now.

She had to make Professor Rocher agree to help.

When Frances awoke the next morning, it was a brilliantly clear winter day. The sun was glittering off the snowclad peaks across Lake Geneva. Silenced by distance, a lake steamer scythed across a blueness colder than the pale sky. Icicles boot-buttoning the arthritic branches of an old apple tree captured the clear but feeble rays, and beyond that the snow-blanketed roofs of Lausanne terraced down to the waterfront. To her right, the spire and stubby turrets of the church of St Francois, to her left the sweeping arc of the lake shore.

The taxi drive from the Beau Rivage hotel to the new

Lausanne university campus was quicker than she expected – the diesel Opel swishing through light traffic on fresh-swept roads, past intimate little *patisseries*, and discreet merchant banks. Frances noted that a snow drift that yesterday evening had contained an empty bus – embedded and deserted like a giant coffin – was clear today. A few minutes outside Lausanne, they pulled into the campus, and the driver wordlessly accepted her tip. She was twenty minutes early for her meeting with Rocher.

Frances killed ten of those minutes by striding around the modern campus. Thick snow carpeted the ground and burdened the trees, and had she paused she would have seen squirrels and blue tits squabbling over scraps of food left on a table in front of the canteen, and milling students in their own winter plumage – scarves vivid at the throat, and capes, knitted and fringed with pom-poms, or sweeping and theatrical.

But Frances was too impatient to do more than register the imposing white-clad façade of the chemistry block before she stumped in the door, and summoned the best of her French to arouse the bundle of grey wool and grey hair sitting in a nest of newspapers tied up with string, behind the counter of the crisp modern vestibule.

'Dr Rocher? Room 2001.' She made a sparse gesture with her head to indicate the direction, and returned to her knitting as if she were quite alone. Then, after Frances had thanked her and set off, she called her back. 'If he's not there, look in the class-room or in the laboratory.' Frances saw that the folds beneath her chin quivered as she spoke, and that they were clad in an armoury of bristles.

Rocher wasn't in Room 2001, nor in the classrooms, nor the laboratory. Frances was back in the vestibule after ten minutes, and wearily propped both elbows on the desk. 'I'm lost,' she said. 'Dr Rocher is in none of the places you suggested, and now I am very late.'

Her exasperated smile failed to awaken any sympathy in the old lady. 'Don't worry about that. The Professor doesn't under-stand the meaning of time. Always late. Always lost.' She rose

91

heavily from her lair, wheezing as she fussed to find a place for her knitting among the bundles of *Le Monde* and *France Soir*. Then she led Frances along an echoing maze of lobbies and corridors, shuffling at a slow and halting pace that was somehow impossible for the younger woman to follow without having to stop every few steps. Finally, she stopped outside an unmarked door, knocked briskly, flung it open, and gestured Frances in.

Frances had been expecting a crotchety welcome. Rademeijer had spoken of a cantankerous old man. She was taken aback by the warmth that radiated from the figure that rose to his feet behind the desk.

'So this is the fierce young lady from New York.'

Professor Paul Rocher had a friendly face, set in a wispy floss of hair as white as the snow outside, with two thicker tufts of down over his ears. Age had taken his features and moved them downwards. Kindly brown eyes were set in pale oysters of flesh; his nose stood proud over two deep-etched furrows; and his lower lip pouted slightly. The effect was one of permanently wry amusement. But there was something more than that as well in the way those eyes were fixed on Frances' face. He seemed to be drinking in every detail, and in anyone else it might have been unnerving.

'Good morning, Professor,' she began in her hesitant French. 'I'm sorry if I'm late.'

'Late?' He seemed surprised at the idea. 'On the contrary, it is I who should have been awaiting you, in my office.' He spoke the precise English of one who has learned the language late in life, and learned it very well . . . without exaggerated accent, but slightly clipped. 'Come, let us go there at once.' He gestured her to the door, and again she felt warmth, as his eyes lingered again on hers. Intuition had led her to this man, and already she felt her instincts had been right.

Walking with him, Frances noticed fastidiously creased grey trousers, with old-fashioned turn-ups. His shirt-cuffs were frayed; his collar had been mended; and the colour had faded from the neatly knotted plain dove-grey tie. There was about him an air of growing old gracefully, in clothes that were being patched up to outlive their owner. She wondered who darned them so patiently, who had turned his collars, and polished the cracked leather of his shoes.

The office, lit by a small window, was lined with book-shelves, spilling over the manuscripts and arcane volumes. Bundles of books and papers spilled onto the floor – there was a narrow pathway cleared to his desk, and to a pair of ancient leather armchairs facing it.

Frances sank into the leather, supple with age. 'First of all, Professor, thank you for seeing me.'

'My dear,' he smiled, 'you were so eager. I knew it must be very important to you, after I had already refused you. And now I am curious. What is this matter that brings a young woman with such haste across the Atlantic to see an old man like me. It must be very important . . . a matter of life and death.'

'A matter of life, Professor. The extension of life, through the rejuvenation of cells. And I urgently need . . . '

'Now you are here, you do not have to rush. You must leave the urgency behind when you come to my office.'

His words, and his gesture across the leather top of his littered desk, stopped Frances in her stride. For what seemed like a full minute, his old eyes gazed at her, then he seemed to collect himself again.

'Now, quietly and slowly, tell me what it is about. We have time now.'

Briefly, Frances outlined her interest in Prostaglandin-S, the rejuvenation application she was planning, and the problems that Rademeijer had run up against with precipitation and crystalization of the unstable active compound. Rocher interrupted her practised flow.

'Ah, yes. Willi Rademeijer. A clever young man. If he can't solve it, then it must be a real problem. But, my dear, give him time. Give him time. You are working with a unique and revolutionary substance. You cannot rush the research in such new and difficult territory.'

'There, Professor, you touch on the problem. Time is the only thing that I do not have.' She gave Rocher a condensed account of the terms of the ultimatum given her by the Cranston Board, and of how she had just six months to make PS live or to see it die. She didn't even pause to wonder why she was telling this little old man so much, when just one hour before he had been a stranger. Rocher listened impassively, his gentle hands folded across his chest, a paper-thin corner of flesh by his eye reflecting the full grey light from the window. All the time she spoke, those eyes were fixed on her face. Then he rose to his feet, and walked over to the window.

'Now, my dear, there is something I must tell you about. I do not approve of the way a corporation such as the one you describe is always in a hurry – always needing to be the first to arrive. It thinks it can run faster than the human brain.'

'That's progress, I guess,' replied Frances. 'Without that kind of pressure and urgency, I'd never have got as far as I have with Prostaglandin-S.'

Rocher's crumpled face was looking stern. 'Corporations . . . big business! I have worked for them before. To tell you the honest truth, it was a suffering to me. A corporation is a monster without a face and without a heart.'

'I don't think the Cranston Group is quite as bad as that,' said Frances. 'We care for our employees, and we care about the quality of our products.'

Again the Professor took no notice. He was obviously following a familiar and well-rehearsed theme. 'Human beings create a business to make themselves rich. But soon they discover they have created a monster that consumes their own humanity. Trapped by dreams of wealth and comfort, they climb on the beast's back, like fleas. Then they become dependant on it . . . parasites that cannot live without their host. And then they find the positions are reversed. The corporation becomes the parasite – sucking a man dry of his knowledge, his skills, his abilities – and then casting the husk aside when the juices are drained.'

Frances remained silent, unwilling to argue the point, unsure of her ground in this foreign ivory tower. Then, quite suddenly, Rocher's face relaxed. The smile played again on his expressive lip, and the humour and warmth returned to his eyes.

'But you did not come all the way to Switzerland to hear an old man rant about the evils of free enterprise. In any case, there is something about the research involving your corporation that intrigues me. It is that I have had another call about you and your Prostaglandin product, from a man who would give me no name, but who said that you deserved my attention. It was a curious thing. That is another reason why I agreed to see you today.'

His eyes were on her as he spoke, and when he paused, Frances was again aware of how searching his gaze was, and that it went on for rather longer than was polite. 'How old are you?' he asked suddenly. And when she looked surprised, he said quickly, 'I am sorry. Pay no attention. Come, show me what it is in your attaché case that makes it weigh so heavily.'

Frances was relieved by his change of mood, but somehow not surprised. The urgency had left her now. In his presence, she felt an easing of pressure, and was content to let matters go at the pace Rocher preferred. 'In spite of all you say, I hope you will be able to look at the detailed research we have done to date. Then perhaps we could talk about solving Cranston's biochemical problems.'

She picked a sheaf of neatly bound notes, graphs and diagrams from her case. 'These are all our findings, right up to date. You will find the latest figures from Rademeijer were recorded two days ago.'

She flipped through the index cards of the file. 'Animal and early human trial results, bio-availability, manufacturing methodology . . . and the final problem. We cannot stabilize the finished compound for longer than a few hours. The active ingredient would not last long enough even to reach the shelves.'

'Let me have a look.' Threading a pair of rimless wire spectacles over his fleshy ears, he picked up the file and began to flick through it. 'This is Willem's alright. I would recognize his protocol anywhere. Oh me, but he does take time to get to the point.'

And then he read on, totally absorbed. For the second time that day, Frances felt in the unusual and uncomfortable position of being ignored. Then he glanced up over his round glasses, head still bent, and appeared to notice her again. 'My dear, forgive me. I need time to look at this. It is most interesting.'

'As long as you need, Professor. But I must tell you that those papers are absolutely top secret.'

'Mrs Kline, I may be old, but I am not a fool. I have worked on Prostaglandins for many years. You are not the first corporation to come and see me about them, although you are the most advanced in your research.' He returned to the file, marking sections of it, hurriedly making incomprehensibly exaggerated, scribbled notes on a square-ruled jotter pad. Without looking up, and with an air of finality, he dismissed her. 'Go for a walk, my dear, and come back in two hours. I'll be ready for you then.'

CHAPTER EIGHT

Frances walked the campus again. Then, after almost half an hour, still unable to relax, she finally persuaded the wheezing, old concièrge to order a cab for her. She instructed the driver to take her to a café, and to wait outside while she had fresh croissants and a huge mug of *café au lait* – half an inch of thick, chicory-flavoured coffee, filled up with steamed, sterilized milk. Like a weak caffein soup, reflected Frances as she watched the people strolling past the steamed windows of the Bally store opposite, overcoat collars turned up against the chill. After another half-an-hour, she left, and directed the cab driver to cruise around the steep and narrow streets of old Lausanne until two o'clock.

Despite the air of calm that enveloped the quiet, snow-bound old city, Frances could not rid herself of a growing sense of urgency. She was more and more agitated away from Rocher. She'd liked him instantly, and she could tell he was interested in the project, yet she sensed that he was disturbed by her. Perhaps not disturbed, more like unnerved.

She was convinced – a solid gut feeling – that Rocher would be able to supply the answer to the problem of crystalization. His answer was crucial, and as the time came closer for him to deliver it, the compelling nature of her trip was pressing in on her – the start, she knew, of a throbbing headache.

Back at the campus, she walked briskly to Rocher's office without greeting the surly concièrge. Let her be ignored for a change, she thought, and felt the old woman's beady eyes bore into her back as she clicked her way down the corridor.

'My dear Mrs Kline,' Rocher greeted her warmly. 'You have some excellent work here.' He tapped the file of documents, loosely restacked before him on the desk. 'But you've got a big problem.'

'The shelf life?'

'Exactly. The problem you have already identified. The crystalization of Prostaglandin-S renders it totally inert, and biochemically quite useless. You have isolated a compound that can only exist under strictly controlled laboratory conditions. It is going to be difficult for you to sell it in its present form, is it not?'

'Do you think we can overcome the problem?' Frances trod warily.

'Of course,' he chuckled, 'of course. But it is not going to be simple. You will have to alter the molecular configuration of the carbon rings without interfering with the compound's chemical activity. It will take time.'

'How long?'

'Who knows?' he shrugged. 'I'll give you some ideas to follow.

Here, I have made some notes . . . you can pass them on to Willem. Like most work of this nature, it is largely a matter of trial and error.'

'And what if we come to a dead end,' asked Frances, glad at least that Rocher was not going to send her away completely empty-handed.

'My dear, God willing, I will still be here. You can come back, and I will have another look at your problem.'

Frances rose from the old leather chair, and with her hands thrust into the pockets of the fur jacket she had not taken off when she returned, she prowled the floor. Deep in thought, she picked her way between the furniture and the piles of books and papers. Now was her moment. How best to phrase the crucial question to this man, whose eyes were following her around the room? She decided simply to be direct.

'Professor Rocher,' she stopped before the desk, and faced him, towering over his shrunken figure. 'Will you come to New York?' She saw him give a start, but before he could reply she went on.

'I understand your dislike for big corporations, and I'll ensure that you have no direct contact with the Cranston Group. You will work in my laboratory – on your own, or with whatever help and equipment you require.'

'Mrs Kline.' His voice had acquired a shade of formality it hadn't contained before. 'I am an old man. I love Lausanne, and I love my work here. And I'd prefer you to leave it like that.'

'But I know that you can solve my problem. You are the only man who can. But I need you to come to New York.'

'My dear, listen to what I am telling you. I am too old to travel, to uproot myself, even for a short time. Besides, I wish to complete my work here on the prostaglandin-pituitary axis.'

'But PS is part of that work. Indirectly, you'd be working in the same field of reasearch.' She was glad she'd done her home-work.

'Mrs Kline.' Now it was his turn to stand. 'Please do not try to

98

persuade me. I have told you. I have been impressed by your work, but I am not willing to go to America.'

'Professor,' Frances felt the imminent failure of her visit as if it were a blow in the stomach. 'I need you.'

'My dear, you certainly need no-one. Now let us go for a walk. Then we can part as friends.'

Leaving the campus buildings behind them, he led her to a small park along the road to Lausanne. Off the cleared pavement, crisp snow crunched beneath their feet on the pathway. Low down into their pockets they each shoved their hands, collars turned up around their ears. Rocher looked even more like a defiant refugee than ever, in an old-fashioned overcoat and a fur cap with earflaps to protect his thinly covered skull. The pine trees faded away in the mist, and the swishing of the occasional car was swallowed up as they walked deeper into the wooded park.

Soon it was quiet. The cushion of soft white isolated the incongruous couple, the youthful woman and the stooped figure of the old man. Nothing stirred in the hedges; only tiny track-marks in the crisp surface of the snow told of a nocturnal hurrying of hedgehogs and mice.

With his gloved hand, Rocher swept the snow off a bench beneath a frozen statue. 'This is where we shall rest. And this is what you and I should teach the world to enjoy. But first we must learn it ourselves – and we will not do so with tension and strife.'

Frances linked an arm with him. It seemed the most natural thing to do. They sat close together, cossetting their combined warmth.

'To absorb nature,' again he continued. 'The living world around us is so precious, and we spend so much time striving that we hardly see it. Striving. The word is derived from "strife". Trouble and strife. And all the while,' he waved his arm, 'life goes on at its eternal pace. The seasons control the pulse rate. Everything grows in its time, is fruitful. And then in

99

its time, it dies. A cruel world as well, perhaps. But no hurrying, no deadlines. Simply the rhythm of nature, at the pace ordained by a greater logic than any of our strivings can obtain.'

'True,' said Frances.

'How old are you?' His breath fumes rose thickly in the cold air.

'That's the second time you've asked.' Her expression was quizzical.

'I know. How tasteless of me. I really do apologize, but it's . . .'

'Forty-three. I'm forty-three,' she said too quickly, immediately sorry that she'd interrupted his sentence.

'I see.' The white sprigs of hair were escaping from under his cap as he turned to look at her full in the face. Again a stare – almost haunted.

'I know I have no right to ask your help. I don't even know whether I have the right to upset the settled order of human life with this new product.'

'My dear, you will do what you have to do. You must follow where your instincts lead you. As must I. We must each do it in our own way, according to our own lights.'

'But,' asked Frances, meeting his eyes, 'how can you ever be sure you are looking in the right direction?'

'Mrs Kline, I am afraid you will never know. That is one thing that experience has taught me. At any time, something can happen that can change your life so much that what was previously important suddenly fades; or a new light suddenly appears.

'It happened a long time ago,' he went on, oblivious to anything but his memories. 'You have reminded me of it.'

'What happened?'

'My light . . . it went out. My wife, she died and my daughter . . . well. She would be your age now. I lost them both.' His voice was matter of fact now, but Frances felt the frail body beside her's shudder. 'The war . . . ' He stopped without finishing the sentence.

For a full minute longer, they sat unmoving. Then Frances disengaged her arm from his, and put it round the old man's shoulder. He turned and spoke again. 'I have not talked about this for so many years. I never found out what happened to my daughter.'

Conscious of sharp snow crystals condensing on her cheek, Frances made soothing motions on his hand with her fingers.

'I don't know,' he said, his voice trembling. 'Perhaps she is still alive somewhere. If only I *knew*.'

'Don't talk now. It's okay. I understand.'

Her time with the old man had been short, and she was stunned at what had sprung up between them in such a brief time. Perhaps it was because of this that she did not feel his refusal was final. She knew she would see Rocher again, that this would not be their last meeting.

And he had apparently felt the same way. He had rapidly regained his poise, after his outburst in the park, but had clearly found the experience cathartic. After they had sat in silence for a while, she had asked him: 'Do you want to tell me more?'

'Yes,' he had replied. 'But not now. Not this time.'

So he too believed they would meet again. The thought was the most satisfying feeling she could remember for ages.

As they had walked back from the park, something had unfrozen between them. She chatted freely and he listened closely.

'I am aware of this much,' Frances had said. 'I can bring rejuvenation to the world. I'm not saying that if I succeed, it won't benefit me personally, but it will also be a real benefit to mankind.'

'Prostaglandin does promise eternal youth,' Rocher had replied. 'Or at least an illusion of eternal youth. In the wrong hands, that illusion could be a dangerous thing. It could cause so much damage to humanity, even psychological chaos.'

'But this is not a reason for you to stop. Neither you nor God can determine how mankind must use his gifts. But the gifts are not to be withheld, even so.'

'How do you see God?' The question was almost childlike, but she urgently needed to hear his reply. 'After what you've lived through?'

'This is what God is.' He stopped, and swept his eyes round the park. 'It is the trees, the plants, the energy that makes them grow. The micro-organisms which live in the earth, under our feet. It is you and I walking together.'

When they parted, she had said: 'Remember my offer. It will stay open for as long as possible.'

He had only smiled. 'We will see. We will see. But old men like me do not change their minds very often.'

Milton Rae sat at his desk. His abdomen felt bloated. A large bolus of gas was threatening to erupt, but he was not able to let it go. He had taken a glass of Alka-Seltzer, to no avail. The lunch he had eaten had been very rich, and he had drank far too much of the Rothschild.

Still, he enjoyed indulging himself at business luncheons, and he could always skip it tomorrow. He viewed these meals as essential to maintaining regular contact with customers, and lubricating his commercial relationships.

Take today, for instance. The meal had been one of his regular dates with Farnsworth Senior of Chemex, and he had been able to pass on confidentially and informally details of some formulation inconsistencies in one of the generic drugs that was slicing into Epipharm's market share. It was not strictly true, but there was no finer man with whom to place such a rumour – clever enough to understand all its implications, but too stupid to realize he was being duped.

They had also spoken about Farnsworth's son, Jeremy, now coming up for the end of his first month as Rae's assistant. 'Jeremy can't speak highly enough of the help that you're giving him, and how patient you are,' Farnsworth had said.

Rae had replied in kind. 'There's really nothing for him to thank me for. He's a bright kid. He's a fast learner – picks things up real quick. It's a pleasure to watch him.'

Rae and Jeremy Farnsworth had been back to the brownstone on 53rd Street once more since that first time, and the pattern had been much as before. Only this time the shy young man had needed no encouragement, and he had fallen upon Janelle like a tiger as soon as Rae had left the room, pulling her dress down to bare her breasts and up to expose her buttocks, and taking her like that, with headlong passion. Rae had licked his lips wetly as he watched, savouring the sight of the boy's slim buttocks clenching and unclenching as he drove his piston home to a rapid climax.

Tonight, they were going again, the boy simultaneously shamefaced and excited when Rae had suggested 'another little dinner with our girlfriends', at first declining, and then agreeing in spite of himself. 'You won't regret it,' Milton had said. 'I happen to know that the girls are cooking up something very special.'

When they had arrived after another wordless journey across town, before they got out of the car, Jeremy had turned to the older man. 'Er, Milton. I don't think I ought to, really. I've been thinking . . . I guess I ought to just get a cab home.'

'C'mon, Jeremy. Janelle's expecting you. She's very fond of you, you know. Lou-Ann was saying how much she talks about you. You can't let a good-looking girl down at the door!'

'Um – to tell you the truth, er, Milt, I've been having some trouble at home. About getting back so late. I guess . . . '

'Didn't you tell your folks you were going out with me?' Milton's face shone with pale greed in the street lights. 'As long as you don't tell them where we went, they shouldn't worry.'

'Oh, yeah. I told them I was working late, and then we'd grab some dinner. My mom said: "Okay. Then you can get back by midnight." Believe me it's not worth it if I don't get back then.'

Milton reflected that this boy was remarkably under his parents' thumbs for a college graduate. His delicacy and shyness were much of what made him so attractive. But it wouldn't do to have him run away now. It had cost Milton a small fortune so far – girls like Janelle are easy, but not cheap. And then there was the stuff. Lou-Ann had got some special Nepalese hashish for tonight, instead of the usual Mexican weed. That was another couple of hundred bucks. Rae had too much invested to let his plans be thwarted now by the timidity of this nineteen-year-old.

He gave an avuncular chuckle, that was as false as the kindliness and humour in his eyes. 'Hell, boy. Is that all? Well, that still gives us the best part of six hours, and I'll take personal responsibility that you get home before you get turned into a pumpkin.'

He grabbed him firmly by the arm. 'Now let's go. There's certainly no time to waste sitting here arguing.' And he forcibly propelled the faun-like youth out of the car door, grinning good naturedly all the while. He was glad that the boy looked so much like David Kline, but he was even more pleased that Jeremy Farnsworth lacked David's force of character. He was getting too old to waste time with too much persuasion.

Once inside, Rae kissed Lou-Ann, and said to her: 'Best get on with it, baby. Got to get the youngster all tucked up at home by bedtime.' Farnsworth blushed, but honey-skinned Janelle whispered something quickly to him, and his young face relaxed. She was good, that one, thought Milton. Good as well as beautiful. Perhaps it was time to . . . He glanced at Lou-Ann, at the little wrinkles under her arm, where the big breasts had been artificially uplifted by a sturdy brassiere. Then he looked at Janelle. She was braless, and he could see through the low-slung sleeve-holes of her flimsy vest that the breasts swelled firmly without the need for any support, and that the nipples were small and pert.

They drank tequila sours, and ate quickly – a light meal of fine seafood, served with iced Californian Reisling. Dessert was a confection of spun sugar and whipped egg white. Then Lou-Ann stood. 'I have a treat to serve with the liqueurs.' She motioned the other three to sit on the end of the gigantic bed where not long ago Jeremy Farnsworth had lost his virginity, and quickly erected a home-movie screen. She dimmed the lights, pressed a switch to start a projector running, and then settled on to the bed between Milton Rae and Janelle.

Selecting a ready-rolled joint from a mug by the bed, she lit it, and passed it to Janelle who took a puff, and passed it to Jeremy, who refused. His expression was shocked. Janelle just laughed, took a deep lungful of the pungent smoke, then leaned over, tousling the youth's hair. Then she fastened here lips over his, and blew the smoke into his lungs. Flushed with drink and desire, Jeremy went into a paroxysm of laughing and coughing, and leaned his head back when Janelle took another lungful of smoke.

Her hand found the tag of the zip-fastener and made its way inside the trousers, where it released the swollen bulge of the boy's impressive erection.

The air in the room was thick with stale smoke and the musty smell of human secretions, and overheated by the radiator at the curtained window. Clothes lay abandoned as they had been flung aside. A broken liqueur glass had been covered by a mount of flimsy underwear, and a shard of glass had cut a slice through a satin negligee.

Milton Rae, awakened by the throbbing pain in his head, took it in through a blur of sleep induced by excess in drink, drugs and sex. Gradually, he registered the events of the night before. Then the thickness and disorientation suddenly left him, and he sat erect with wide-open eyes.

'Jesus Christ!' he said. 'Jesus H Christ!' And he disentangled himself from the sprawling figures of the two sleeping girls. He switched on the light, its suddenly harsh glare clearly illuminating a scene of recent depravity. Stumbling from the bed, he narrowly missed cutting his foot on the broken glass. Grabbing his trousers from the floor, he nearly stumbled as he thrust a foot too hastily into a tangled leg. Then he put on his shoes without the socks, and turning back to the bed shook Lou-Ann from her stupefied sleep.

'Fucking hell! What's the time? Where the fuck is Jeremy?'

Bursting out of the room, he thundered through the apartment. 'Jeremy! Jeremy! Jeremy!' he shouted. He was about to run upstairs when Lou-Ann appeared, hastily tying the belt of a dressing gown. Its pink flimsiness derided Milton Rae's panic-crazed terror.

'Christ, Lou-Ann,' he shouted. 'What's happened to the boy? For God's sake, where's he gone?'

'Milt, take it easy,' she said, her voice thick with sleep. With her hair crumpled to one side, and the wrinkles of the pillow etched on her sleep-puffy cheek, she looked old and ugly. 'He prob'ly woke up and took a cab home.'

'Stupid bitch. His clothes are still there.'

'Then he's in the other bedroom.'

'He's not there. Jesus. I've just looked. He should have been home by midnight. His folks have probably called the police.'

Lou-Ann looked exasperated. 'Is that *all*? Shit. The kid's old enough to spend the night on the town. We'll spruce him up, think of an excuse he can give his folks. Calm down, will'ya. He's probably in the upstairs closet, puking his guts out. Not surprised, after the treatment you gave him last night.'

Milton raised his hand threateningly, and the hooker cowered. But he had more important things, and turned on his heel, and covered the stairs two at a time. He ripped the closet door open, then stood back. The silence as he held his breath was a chill omen that ran down Lou-Ann's spine. And then he started screaming.

'Oh my God! Oh my God! Oh my God!' He slumped to his knees, and then crumpled entirely, his face buried in his hands. 'Oh my God! Oh my God!'

When Lou-Ann reached him, he was crouched at the door, shirtless, his undone trousers revealing the top of obese buttocks in the pale light of the early morning.

Then she saw Jeremy. His delicate young face was bloated and a blue tongue protruded in a gesture of grotesque disgust. His limp naked body was disfigured by an erection, and the electric flex he had used to hang himself from an overhead pipe, had buried itself into the smooth skin of his neck.

And at his feet, Milton Rae knelt sobbing on the floor tiles.

CHAPTER NINE

Gerald Rule arranged his toothbrush precisely in the cup so that the bristles pointed downwards. He carefully straightened out the toothpaste tube from the bottom, and put it away in a wash-bag. Then he arranged the bag exactly on the shelf, squaring it up carefully, and smoothing a wrinkle from one side, before stepping briskly from the room.

He dressed carefully, selecting clothes from among obsessively neat shelves – a white shirt, a bright blue tie, and a navy pin-stripe suit. 'Goddammit, I'm even looking like a Limey now,' he thought, as he stepped back after knotting the tie just so in the mirror. With his close-cropped hair and horn-rimmed glasses, this was a long way from the truth.

He was about to leave his suite in The Frances when the first spasm of pain crossed his face. 'Jesus.' He clasped his stomach, and turned back into the room. 'Already.' He sat on the bed again, and fished a Maalox tablet from his pocket, and crunched it between his teeth. It was all this tension. Like a load on his back. And it kept piling on.

'Hagridden,' he thought. He had come across the word the other day, in one of those long-winded Limey newspapers, in a court report about a man who had lived all his life with three domineering sisters and his mother, and at the age of 62 had methodically killed them all, by feeding them sleeping pills, then driving a cold chisel into each of their skulls, one after the other. 'I understand just how he felt.'

He could cope with the pressure of business. In fact, he enjoyed it. But that was in New York, where his mind was attuned to the crisp way of thinking, and where he meshed with the pace of the city. London was something different. He hated England, he hated living in The Frances, and he hated all the insincere formality, and the old-boy network, where he moved like a fish out of water.

As if that wasn't enough, there'd been another of those calls from his wife last night. It made no odds to her that 8 pm in New York was 2 am London summer time, no matter how often he told her. 8 pm was the time she started feeling chatty; so 8 pm was the time she rang Gerry. And 9 pm, he reflected ruefully, was the time she rang off.

Last night, as usual, her voice made shrill by the trans-Atlantic line had been a jangle in his head as he fought his way up from deep sleep to listen to her tirade.

'Gerry, when is all this travelling going to stop. I tell you, honey, I really loathe it here when you've gone. This place gets so creepy, and the boiler's making those ghost noises again.'

The couple had married nine years before; the brisk, rather gawky accountant and the timid, third daughter of a US Army colonel. Since then, though he had prospered in business, his home life had been less idyllic. Gerald Rule, they discovered after four fruitless years of trying for a child, was sterile; and this fact had turned his wife's timidity into bitterness. The only trace that remained of the vulnerability that he had found so attractive was this play-acting. It meant she was in a bad mood.

'Take it easy, honey. It's only air bubbles in the radiator. And don't worry – you know Frank keeps a pretty tight watch on the apartment entrance. There's no reason to be scared.'

'But I am scared, Gerry. It's been so cold that I haven't been able to go out all day. I've hardly seen a soul all week. Gerry, why does it always have to be you who goes away?'

'Sweetheart, we've been through all this. It's part of my job right now. And you know I hate it just as much as you do. Anyway, I won't be here much longer now. And I'll be coming back again this weekend. Listen, why don't you call your sister, go and have lunch with her tomorrow.'

'It's because you're under that woman's thumb.' It was as if he hadn't spoken. She was getting warmed up now, thought Gerry. It was a familiar theme.

'It's because you don't stand up for yourself. You're like a lap dog. She clicks her fingers, and you're up at attention, waiting for the next job that nobody else wants to do.'

'Honey,' Gerry interrupted, hopelessly, 'it's not like that. I'm ...'

She continued, oblivious to his words. 'Or is it different? Am I being naive?'

'Is that what it's all about? A chance to get her pet Gerry away from New York. Sometimes a girl can't help wondering, you know, just why some dumb blonde can't wait to get her husband far away from home, in a strange bed in a foreign city. Is that it? Is she there now?'

'Mary, for Chrissakes.' Rule knew his attempt at firmness would result only in a more vigorous tongue-lashing, but he owed it to his pride. 'I don't like what you're trying to suggest, and I wish you'd drop it.'

'You know what's wrong with you?' she cut in.

'No dear. Perhaps you'll tell me.' Gerry spoke quietly. He blamed himself for the change from the bashful creature he had married to this bitter and pitiful woman.

'You're a coward. I should have seen it from the start. You've got the mentality of an accountant. And that's why you'll never make anything of yourself. You're going to spend the rest of your life being sent all over the world for other people, waiting for the promotion that will always pass you by.'

'Honey, you know it's not always going to be like that,' he had replied.

'Easy to say, hard to prove,' she shot back.

And Gerry Rule resigned himself to another humiliating and tedious half hour of abuse from his wife.

Frances arrived at Heathrow on the flight from Geneva at nine that morning. The Boeing had come in low over Surrey. It was March, and the signs of winter were still everywhere; in leafless orchards, and banks of old snow in the lee of the hedgerows. Even from that height, Frances had been aware of a pervasive layer of clammy mud.

The Daimler had been ready for her at Heathrow, and Rule, punctilious in pin-stripes, was waiting for her at The Frances.

'It hasn't been easy, Frances.' He looked tired.

'Spare me the details for half an hour, will you, Gerry,' she said. 'I like to be fresh when I hear bad news.'

When she had settled at the antique desk beside the big picture window, he told her: 'I'm having trouble securing the last five per cent of the Bristol shares.'

'I've been talking to a bunch of different shareholders, and just one of them would give us enough. But the rumours are out that something big's happening, and they're all sitting tight. I'm already over our top limit – I've been offering $6. And they don't look as though they're going to budge.'

'Double it, Gerry. Treble it, if you have to.'

Rule sat back, stunned. 'But that'll cost . . . '

Frances interrupted him. 'Gerry, I've told you to let me handle the money side. Believe me, it's going to be okay. At the end of the day, it's not really going to matter what we pay for the last shares.

'What is important is that we've got to get this deal through fast. I want you to get those shares, and then I need you back in New York. Things are beginning to cook.'

'Don't I know it,' said Rule. 'I just heard that the Japanese are moving fast. They're well into human trials, with volunteer groups in two cities. And from what I hear, their results are good.'

Frances listened in silence. Rule's information was habitually accurate, and this meant the Japanese must be neck and neck with her on PS. She wondered if it had been them who had approached Professor Rocher, if they had run up against the same stability problem.

Then she spoke. 'I have some bad news of my own. I tried my hardest to persuade him, but Professor Rocher is really violently opposed to big business, and he has refused to come to New York. I don't hold out much hope that he will change his mind.'

Frances reflected with some surprise, as she dialled her son's number, that David had been at the back rather than the front of her mind on this trip to London. Instead, she had been thinking of Rocher. Frances could not fully understand their nexus. His face, his correct speech, and his kindly manner had remained with her, never far below the level of consciousness, often breaking to the surface.

She had tried to imagine how it was for him. Could it be that nothing more than a similarity of age could have unlocked the old man's love for his lost daughter? Yes, she decided. It could. But instinctively she felt that there was something deeper.

She couldn't bring herself to intrude on his privacy more than she already had. To invade his life with her obsession. She had gone to persuade this distinguished scientist to leave his home, and to work for the things she believed in. She had failed. And she'd have to find another way.

David was not at his studio. Instead, she was told, he was in Spain, on a shoot.

Of course! Frances remembered he had told her. It was actually Gaby's assignment, modelling for a new range of lingerie. She had shown Frances the test shots – fine white silk stretched across her olive-brown skin. She had wangled a place for David in the production team, and they were away for a full ten days.

Suddenly, she felt she had to talk to him. She set a secretary

111

onto finding out from the client where the shoot was taking place, and forty-five minutes later, she was connected to David at the hotel in Barcelona where some indoor sequences were under way.

His voice was excited. He was dismissive of her questions about Spain, disparaging about the work he was doing, and resentful of the time he was having to spend there.

'I can't wait to get back to London, Fran. Actually, I hope I'll be back there tomorrow.'

'Why?' she asked. 'Is there some problem, David?'

'Problem! Are you kidding? Fran, I just landed me the best contract I've ever had, and I want to get back and get to work.'

'David! Tell me more.'

'It's that cosmetic deal I was pitching for when you were last here. I got the job. A six-figure budget, Fran. Biggest thing I've ever done.' His voice was jubilant.

'Fran – I've made it. I'm set now. I've got to get the works – my own office suite, and I'll need to hire assistants. So I'm leaving here tomorrow to get things all set up.'

'David, that's fantastic. And I've just had a nice deal come off here too, so there'll be some new hotel business to add to the pile.'

There was a sudden reserve in his voice as he answered. It was the same as there had been in London, but this time Frances did feel it.

'Fran, thanks anyway. But I don't need any favours. I'm on my own in London, and it's going great. I can make it on my own.'

'That's fine, sweetheart. I'm glad for you. Just take it slow.'

'Slow! Forget it, Fran. I'm on my way now.' Then he broke off for a minute, and she could hear him put his hand over the mouthpiece, and shout something over his shoulder. Then he came back. 'Ah gee, I'm sorry, Fran. I gotta go. I'm wanted on set.'

And they had rung off without exchanging another word.

* * *

112

Later that afternoon, Frances wrapped up her paperwork and neatly packed her briefcase. She locked the centre drawer of the desk, and put the key in the case.

'Sufficient unto the day is the evil thereof', a dimly remembered quotation from the Bible, that an Episcopalian friend had been fond of repeating. There had been plenty of them today. Not 'evils' exactly, but significant events, and she had enough of them.

It had been just before lunch that Rule had called. 'We got our fifty-one per cent, boss-lady,' he said. He had offered the remaining shareholders $7 a share, and a lot of them had jumped for it. 'We can take our pick,' he said, 'and tell the rest that they've missed the boat.'

'Well done, Gerry. Except nobody has missed the boat. I want you to buy all the shares you've been offered.'

Rule looked frankly baffled. '*All* the shares? But Frances . . . '

'What will our percentage holding be then?'

'Oh – about seventy per cent.'

'Okay, then this is what you do. You make another offer for the rest of the shares, and then another offer after that. You keep going until you hold ninety-one per cent of the shares in the Bristol group.

'Then, Gerry, you make an unconditional offer to the remaining shareholders, at the price of the last deal. They are bound by law to accept.'

Now the scale of Frances' plan became clear to Rule. The strategy was daring and clever . . . typical Kline. It was a classic exercise in asset-stripping. Once she held the balance of the shares, she would put the company into voluntary liquidation, and then sell the assets either one at a time or even in a job lot.

'I see. Then we'll pull all the currants out of the currant bun.' His heart sank as he thought of how much extra work would be involved in separating and selling the assets . . . and how much longer it would keep him in London.

'That's why I told you not to worry about the cost. Don't be concerned about selling the assets, either. I have two US

113

companies who have agreed in principle to take the High Street properties, at a price of $5.8 million, *after* paying off the bonds. Seems to me we come out on the winning side.'

Rule screwed up his eyes for a quick bout of mental arithmetic. 'That's brilliant. At worst, we're going to get all the shares for $12.6 million. Your sales realize $10.8 million. That means we get the Marley Hotel for $1.8 million. That's ten per cent less than Blake offered for it in the first place!'

'Correct, Mr Gerald Rule. That's what you get for staying on your toes.'

Frances planned a quiet dinner in her room. There was nothing more she could do about Rocher's refusal now, except eliminate it from her mind for the present. She had done so by sending him a cable.

'PLEASE RECONSIDER.'

She signed it, simply, 'FRANCES'. She would not accept that his rejection had been final. Not yet, anyway.

She had drawn her bath, and perfumed it with expensive oil, but had not yet got in when the telephone rang. It was Gray Barnard. This time, not yet dripping wet, she was able to laugh at the interruption.

'Not again! You always ring me here when I'm about to get into a bath. Gray, where are you?'

'No more than twenty minutes away.'

She felt her heart jump. 'How did you know I was here?'

'Never mind how. The important thing is this: will you have dinner with me tonight?'

Frances hesitated . . . but as he had before, Gray cut in. 'Don't think too much about it. Just tell me what you'd like to eat. Except for salt beef on rye.'

Frances laughed again. 'Make it roast Highland beef, rare, and you're on.' She needed somebody to talk to, and she could think of no-one better than Gray.

CHAPTER TEN

Less than two hours later, she had taken a cab to the Carlton Towers in Connaught Square. Gray was waiting, pacing up and down the pavement, examining each cab as it stopped. As physically vast as he was, he looked as eager as a child.

He opened the door, reached in, and lifted her clear. The gesture was familiar, then set her down on the pavement without embracing her as she had half-expected.

She was awestruck again by the size of him, the effortless physical power within him – this man – deeply tanned, huge-boned, weathered and strong. She felt her body respond to him; it rang like a crashing orchestral chord right within her. It was like the music of high mountains and wild places, and Frances was powerless but to let it echo through her.

'I hope you're hungry, Franci.' His words cut the tension, and the clipped accent struck the chord again. 'I have already placed our order. It should be waiting for us.'

Then he stepped back and looked at her. Frances was wearing a black dress, the calf-length skirt clinging to her legs under a short sable fur coat, with a flash of sapphire and pearls at her throat. She almost blushed under his gaze. Then he spoke: 'It's an honour to dine with such a beautiful woman. Everyone in the restaurant is going to stare,' and Frances dimpled with an unaccustomed shy pleasure. How long it was since she had really felt like a beautiful woman?

When they were seated at a discreet table in the corner, he turned to her again, and their eyes met with sudden intimacy. A slow smile spread across his face. Neither of them spoke.

They were interrupted by the arrival of the roast beef – an elaborate ceremony with silver platters opened theatrically, and the violent swishing of a long knife being sharpened by the head waiter. The meat was carved almost transparently thin, a hard-baked crust on the outside giving way to a deep red tenderness within. 'Plenty of horseradish sauce,' said Gray to the waiter. And then to Frances, 'we have a lady here who needs to put on some weight.'

'God forbid,' said Frances. 'I spend most of my life trying to get rid of weight.'

'But you're skinny.' Gray leaned across and put the span of his huge hand across her waist. Her body reacted immediately in the very quick of her. But she held herself still as his hand lingered there for a moment, dropped to her lap, and then moved across to his own. Her body was yearning for him to touch her again but Frances wasn't ready to acknowledge its demands openly.

'You really could put on a few pounds, you know,' said Gray. He tasted the Chateau Lafite Rothschild, and motioned the wine-steward to fill Frances' glass as well as his own, against the wishes of her raised hand.

'Fat women aren't taken seriously,' said Frances.

'It's the same with men,' said Gray.

'Not quite,' said Frances. But she was unwilling to be drawn into the politics of womanhood. She'd made her own statements of liberation, by her very lifestyle. It was her own affair, and she wasn't about to make any sermons about it now.

Gray seemed to pick up her thoughts. 'Is all this success as easy as you seem to find it?'

'How do you mean?' Frances transferred a forkful of tender Scottish beef to her mouth, and carved a delicate wedge of Yorkshire pudding to follow, scooping it through the rich brown gravy.

'I mean getting into the big league, as a woman.'

'It wasn't easy getting there, and it isn't easy staying there.'

Gray was forging through his own plate of food. 'Tell me more.'

'Oh, it'll be boring.'

'Come on,' he urged. 'How do you stay on top?'

'By showing results.'

'And how do you do that?'

'By taking risks.' Frances gave a thin-lipped smile. The word was exciting them both. This very dinner was a high risk. So was their whole relationship. A risk that neither of them were able to resist.

She talked about the Cranston Group, and how she'd built her division from a small, unimportant element to a major profit centre. She told him about Maxwell J Bennis. 'He didn't exactly mentor me, but he never blocked me, either.' And she told him about the six-month deadline.

All the while Gray sat opposite her, his face devoid of expression, but his eyes attentive, and his occasional questions intelligent and far-sighted. Quite unruffled, he disposed of the last of his plate of roast beef. She noticed he left the Brussels sprouts until last, but cleaned his plate entirely before he would accept the proffered second helping. As she spoke, their legs touched lightly under the table. Neither of them pulled away, and the pressure became a constant, gentle warmth.

Frances spoke about her strengths and weaknesses – how she'd exploited the former and tried to compensate for the latter. She told him how she complemented her business talents by delegating the details to hand-picked subordinates, and of how she set the tone and mood of her division. 'It is the person at the top who creates the ambience. I have to keep feeling like a winner to keep my people feeling the same way.'

Gray smiled. 'It's hard to imagine you as anything but a winner.'

Frances smiled in return. 'Oh, don't kid yourself. It's the small things that get you in the end. I always smile at the joggers who are scared of the big trucks. I watch out for the bicycles and the potholes.'

She had neglected her dessert as she spoke – hothouse strawberries, exotic in the midwinter chill. Now she ate with a good appetite and vigour. Gray watched her closely, smiling with approval as she washed down a mouthful with a swig of the rich red wine.

Then he looked in her eyes, and asked her: 'Do you do this often?'

'You mean: Do you go out with all sorts of chance-met men?' she said quietly. 'The answer is no. My private time is very private. In any case, I have a son in London.'

Across the tablecloth, Gray's face remained impassive. 'Oh, really?'

'Yes. He's beautiful.' She knew at once that the epithet or the statement itself had jarred Gray. She ran her finger round the rim of her wineglass and said no more.

Gray changed the subject at once.

'Do you enjoy power, Franci?'

'Yes, I guess I do. But I wouldn't put it like that. Power for its own sake is a little like loving love instead of loving the person. It's dull, *passé*, and a little dangerous. It wears you out, and in the end there's nothing.'

'I just wanted to be successful, and I have been. But I think travelling is sometimes more exciting than arriving. Don't you?'

And then, 'Is there anything else you want, Franci?' His expression was deadpan – almost a challenge.

She ignored the ambiguity.

'Lots and lots of coffee.'

Rae had even considered the possibility of hurling himself from the window. He thought of the glass shattering, the sudden emptiness in the room behind him, and his own body, sprawled and crumpled on the paving stones below – one polished shoe off, and his limbs lying all awry. But it was only a diversionary tactic, to take his mind off the real horror of his situation.

'Can't understand why the police didn't contact Meg and me,' said Farnsworth, for the third time since Rae had arrived. He looked older, his face drained of colour, revealing blotches on his forehead and cheeks. He had heard of his son's death in 'premises believed to be the apartment of a call-girl' only four hours before. His wife had collapsed, and he had been unable to comfort her. It was as though everything they had lived for had been destroyed in front of their eyes.

Rae shifted uneasily as the steely-grey-haired lawyer replied. 'Uh, it seems he didn't have identification on him. Probably because of where he was going. He didn't want the hooker to know who he was, in case maybe she'd blackmail him or something. Rae here seems to think that maybe Jeremy had mentioned his name, or the Cranston Group. So the cops got onto him first of all.' His tone of voice showed clearly that he didn't necessarily think along the same lines.

This was Milton's trial of strength. He had somehow summoned the control, that morning, to instruct Lou-Ann and Janelle on how to handle the story. It was essential that they get it right – for his safety and for theirs. For he had already thought, as he flung on his clothes, and hastily eliminated all obvious traces of himself from the flat, of the legal team that Farnsworth Senior would inevitably assemble. Now he was himself face to face with its leader.

Rae had raced home at 4 am, squealing the gigantic limousine through the deserted street. He was just in time to field an apologetic call from the desk sergeant at the 53rd Street local precinct. 'Mr – er – Milton Rae? Sorry to call so early. It's the police.'

'What? Who?' Rae made his voice sound thick with sleep.

'Do you know a Jeremy Farnsworth?' And the bald details of the youngster's death had followed. 'Looks like suicide – but we need positive identification before we can proceed.'

Rae had driven directly back to the brownstone, and had been taken through to the bathroom, where he had little trouble in showing genuine shock at his second sight of the body – blue now, with bruising around the neck and at the ankles. He had made the identification, and then had been allowed to go. He was pleased to see that both girls were well out of the way. All this had gone according to his plan. If he was able to identify the body on the scene, then there would be no need for Farnsworth himself to see where his son had died. Rae felt, somewhat absurdly, that if he could spare Farnsworth the full sordid details

119

of his son's 'suicide', then perhaps his desire for vengeance might be less.

'Blackmail! Yes, indeed. That was why I phoned you from there, Jim.'

Farnsworth looked up gratefully. 'Milt, I can't tell you how grateful I am for what you have done.' Then he dug the heels of his hands into his eye sockets, and massaged them strongly. 'Oh God. It's just so ghastly.'

Fritz Clements cleared his throat. He had been a family friend as well as lawyer to the Farnsworths for the past twenty-five years, and his father had been legal adviser to Jim Farnsworth's own father. 'Jim, I guess there's nothing much anyone can say to make it easier for you. But you must not blame yourself, and you must put Meg's mind at rest too.

'The report the police filed stated they suspected Jeremy had probably been under the influence of the drug they call angel dust – phencyclidine. The stuff's been out on the streets recently. If Jeremy had been taking that, then there's absolutely nothing anything could have done.

'Angel dust is a vicious drug, Jim. A high percentage of users take their own lives or die in bizarre accidents. It drives them out of their minds, and they feel immortal. They believe they can fly, or that they are immune from danger. Jeremy probably didn't deliberately kill himself. So you really cannot blame yourself in any way.'

'I wish I could say that helped, Fritz,' Farnsworth almost snarled . . . Then he stopped. 'Yeah, sure. I'm sorry. But the boy has gone, and it really doesn't make much difference how it happened.'

Fritz Clements showed no reaction to his outburst. His thin face, with incongruously fleshy jowls, remained calm and carefully in control. 'One important matter is that of publicity. Of course, we can't hush it up entirely, but if we can keep it out of the papers for a few days, it will lose its impact as a news story.'

'My office will take care of any statements that are required.

And I've given the desk sergeant five hundred bucks so he'll keep his mouth shut if any reporters come nosing around.'

Milton Rae couldn't prevent himself from asking: 'Have you spoken to the girl at all? I understand there were two women in the house.'

Clements swivelled his blank, attentive eyes across to scrutinize Milton, who wished at that moment that he smoked, so he could camouflage the anxious and incessant movements of his hands. 'They need no . . . ah, encouragement to remain silent. In their profession, not talking to newspapers is a stock in trade.' Across the desk, Farnsworth flinched at the word 'profession'.

'As yet, I have not interviewed the two women, but I will do so later today. I have seen their statement to the police.

'The younger woman said she had met Jeremy in a singles bar, that he had gone home with her for the night. He had been acting strangely all night. When she awoke at 3.30 am, he was not with her. She and the other woman looked for him, and found him in the upstairs closet. He had been dead for about one hour.'

This was the first time Jim Farnsworth had heard the bare facts of his son's death, and he was hungry for detail. He questioned Clements and Rae closely. It was acutely uncomfortable for the Cranston executive, and he was relieved when a convenient pause gave him the chance to excuse himself, pleading an urgent appointment.

Farnsworth collected himself. 'Milt. Thank you for all you've done. We must not delay you any more.'

'Jim.' Rae shook his old friend's hand, and hoped his clammy tremor wasn't noticeable. 'I can't tell you how sorry I am. I feel responsible. I was the last to see him when we left the office together. I'd hoped to take him to the theatre, as he may have mentioned, but he said he had something else to do after all. If only I'd insisted he stay with me . . .'

'Milt, how could you have known?'

'Well, Jim. If there's anything I can do over the next few days, you mustn't hesitate. You know where you can get me.' He

121

turned and nodded to the lawyer, and thankfully left the room.

They walked a full fifteen minutes in the cold, before they hailed a cab to take them to The Frances. In the coffee bar, they found a quiet corner, and sat on the couch talking into the night.

'Tell me about your farms,' Frances asked Gray.

'We have nine. Our family has been cultivating vineyards for the past six generations. Nowadays we do a lot more besides – orchards, sheep, even fertilizer. And we export all over the world.'

Frances tried to picture the smartly-suited giant in front of her as a patriarchal farmer. It was quite easy. 'Do you farm yourself? I mean, get your hands dirty, deal with animals, till the earth?'

He delivered another rumbling laugh. 'Of course, yes. I am a farmer.' And he faced Frances directly and moved across to take her hand.

She responded at once, leaning forward, an intimate smile teasing her lips. Involuntarily, she felt her legs part slightly and realized that she was actually feeling dizzy.

Then she remembered where she was, and pulled back. Startled, she realized it had only been the fear of being seen by The Frances hotel staff that had prevented her from allowing this man to find a way of getting his huge body pressed against her own.

Deliberately, she stepped back from the abyss of irreversible commitment. 'So what brings the earth-stained man of the soil to Europe?' she said lightly.

He held her gaze until her eyes fell, before speaking.

'To see you, of course. To London, anyway.'

'Then on to Paris to visit the cosmetic factory. I told you about my co-operative farming venture.'

'Ah, yes,' she said. 'The kibbutz.'

'Right. It produces a herbal substance that we use as a base for all the cosmetics we manufacture in Paris.'

Frances felt her interest quicken. 'What sort of cosmetics?'

'Mainly body lotions – moisturizing creams. But it is only a small concern. It could be bigger, with some aggressive marketing. The sort of thing you could do in your sleep . . . I'm better at making the land work for me.'

'Although even that's getting more difficult than it used to be. I have to fly home urgently tomorrow to sort out some labour problems. I've had three strikes in the past month. None of them were due to specific grievances, but the unions are inexperienced, and there is a lot of miltancy.'

'It's hardly surprising. These are the first stages of unionization, the first time these people have had a collective voice in living memory. They have been unheard for so long that they are overreacting. Irrespective of whether an employer is good or bad, they feel they have to strike. Can't say I blame them.'

'Is there violence?' asked Frances.

'Sometimes. Not so much on the farms, but in the cities. We have an old man who has lived on my home farm all his life. Last week, his grandson was beaten up and nearly killed because he refused to strike.

'In another case, an old firm went to the wall because two unions were fighting for control of the work force. In the end, nobody won, and hundreds of workers lost their jobs.'

'Are you under the same sort of threat?' asked Frances. She was eager to hear his views, not least because of her own South African concerns.

'I don't think so. But I could be wrong. The situation is very volatile. Even though I have always been close to my staff. Many are classified as 'migrant labourers'. So I have a continuous battle with officialdom to keep them living on the farm where they have been for generations.

'These are just growing pains. Most countries have been through something similar. But I see it's particularly complicated for us because of all the other problems we have. The government only make matters worse. But while they've proceeded with their stupid, schemes for so-called separate development, it is Business – with a capital B – that has been trying to invest in a realistic future for the country against some rough odds, I might add.

'Blacks and whites often work side by side nowadays; rates of pay have improved considerably – in some cases, not without a bit of union prodding. This has made a growing middle class of relatively affluent blacks, who have a definite interest in maintaining the status quo, as well as the hope of an even more affluent future – especially compared with other countries in Africa.'

'That's not what the American public read. Your public relations is really lousy.'

'That I know,' said Gray. 'Business would do a better job of it than the politicians. In time they may have to.'

He mused in silence for a minute, and then Frances asked him: 'Does it upset you to talk about it?'

'Yes, of course. It is a very distressing situation. But I feel also it is my duty to talk about it.'

'Your duty? That sounds very old-fashioned.'

'Franci, I love my country.' He leaned towards her – his expression deadly serious. 'And I'm afraid for it.'

Frances was a little scared by his intensity. Then he quickly broke the mood with a small smile. 'You know, I'd love to show you my farms. Especially the one I told you about.'

'I'd like to see it.'

'God, it's a beautiful place. It's ten thousand four hundred acres of land, in amongst the mountains.' He paused, as he remembered the scent of sunrise over the peaks, and the baking midday summer heat.

'We provide the land, implements, water and training. The farmers then operate the farms in the interests of the co-operative as well as on their own account. We have all sorts of people there – white people who want to be self-sufficient, labourers who have lived on the land for generations, young and ambitious black families from other parts of the country. Actually I have set up a family trust to run it, so I hope it will continue after I have gone.

'It's made history in South Africa. It is completely multi-racial. We even have a multi-racial school for the kids.'

'Do you need special permission for that sort of thing?' asked Frances.

'Of course. But I wasn't able to do it officially, so I went ahead and did it anyway. So far, when presented with a *fait accompli*, the government has turned a blind eye. But there is always the threat of possible trouble. I'll cross that bridge when I come to it.'

There was a short silence as they each comprehended this unpalatable fact. Then Frances asked: 'What do you grow there?'

'All sorts of things. Some of the tenant-farmers are self-sufficient; others grow cash crops for the market. But the co-operative side of the venture is concentrated on a curious little plant that is used as a base for our range of French cosmetics.

'It's a medicinal plant that grows well in that area. The locals have known about it for generations . . . they boil it up, and make a sort of stewed ointment. Then they bind it onto the skin with some of the leaves. They used it on me as a kid, when I had a rash that the doctors couldn't cure. It worked almost immediately. I began to wonder about the ritual significance they attached to this plant. Just what was the magical property it contained?'

'Later I had the plant analyzed by our chemists at the fertilizer factory. They found an active ingredient that we now use as the basic ingredient of the cosmetics that we produce in France.'

They continued talking into the night, engrossed in their own company, colouring in all the details. Frances was surprised when he looked at his watch, and said: 'Two am. Time to take you to your room.'

Again he took her hand. This time, in the darkened room, she didn't pull away.

'Franci, let me come up to your room.'

Frances shivered in spite of the heating, and drew the fur close round her shoulders. She heard her answer stir deep in her body, felt again the music in her loins.

Then he took her hand in his, and drew it to his lips. First he kissed the backs of the fingers, breathing in her fragrance. And then, with an abandon that thrilled her whole being, he slipped her first two fingers into his mouth, and he caressed them with his tongue.

She felt him tease, his legs clasp her knees firmly. Then he took his hand, and ran the fingers down her moulded body, pausing as they ran over her small breasts, the nipples springing erect, and then moving down her legs, and the arrow-mark between them. The movement was quick, but it stayed in Frances' mind for a long time.

Something in her suddenly made her draw away. Despite the primitive stirrings.

'Gray,' she said, her voice thick with wanting him. 'I'm frightened of this. Please don't come up.' And she rose quickly to her feet, and walked from the room without a backward glance.

Gray sat there for another thirty minutes, refusing the waitress's offer of more coffee, and not even noticing a noisy party of late-night revellers. He too was haunted by doubts and fears, though his face hid them with its craggy equanimity.

He knew one thing. He had fallen desperately in love with this petite tycoon from New York. There was no reasoning about it, no logic. Just that the fiercest desire he had ever known was to make this woman part of his life. And he would do it, and count the cost later on.

He, Gray Barnard, was a man who was used to getting his own way.

Upstairs, Frances sat equally alone. A glass of Perrier water fizzed beside her as she sat on her bed, and every few minutes she took a sip.

She lifted her hand to her mouth, and licked the fingers. Then she ran it down the side of her neck, to her breasts, and then to her groin, following the course of Gray's fingers.

Then, with the same briskness that she had left the table down-

126

stairs, she picked up the telephone and dialled home. Web answered, and she found it surprisingly easy to lie when he asked her what had kept her up so late.

After she rang off, though, the fleeting reassurance was replaced by an emptiness. She did love Web, and he loved her. That she knew. But this wasn't enough to stop the ever-increasing erosion of the once-so-solid ground between them.

She was awakened again by the phone. It was Jo-Beth. 'Frances? I'm sorry to phone so late, but I just spoke to Web, and he said you were still awake.'

'I have some bad news, I'm afraid. We've just heard that Ed Potter collapsed at his desk this afternoon. A coronary thrombosis. He's still alive, but they don't know for how much longer. I thought you'd like to know as soon as possible.'

CHAPTER ELEVEN

'Mighty Munch are killin' us. They're sellin' so short that they might as well give 'em away.'

It was the hundredth call of its type that morning. They had begun as soon as the Cranston Group's switchboard had opened; they had come from all over the States, with a special concentration from California and Illinois, the main areas of operation of the rival Mighty Munch chain of fast food outlets. They were from franchise holders of the Cranston's own popular fast food chain, Blockbusters – all of them stunned by Mighty Munch's latest promotional offer . . . three burgers for the price of one.

'Okay, take it easy,' said Carl Hecht, yet again. 'We'll be getting straight onto you when we know which way we're gonna jump. Meantime, just hang on in there.'

'And remember, you've got the Cranston Group right behind you. We'll be fighting back, but we want to do it right.'

'Perfect,' said Frances Kline, after the young man had rung off. 'You handled that just right, Carl. Keep it going like that, and don't worry. And call in at my office tomorrow morning, and we'll work out a strategy.' She had landed feet first in the crisis from London that morning, and was feeling a great deal more flustered than she looked.

Only when she had left the Blockbusters head office, and was en route back to her own suite two floors above, did she allow her shoulders and her features to slump for a moment, unseen. What fate, she wondered, had decreed that Mighty Munch's bid to displace her own Blockbusters chain should strike at precisely the same time as Ed Potter's heart attack.

Ed Potter was her vice-president who had headed Blockbusters ever since she had bought and relaunched the franchizing operation four years before, a trusted aide. Now he was gone, perhaps forever. She would have to handle the situation herself, but she already had too much on her plate. She wondered whether thirty-two-year-old Hecht would be able to cope if she delegated all responsibility to him. He would have to. She'd think of a plan and he would execute it. She'd soon see what the young man was made of.

For the next thirty minutes, she went through her mail with Jo-Beth. All the time, part of her mind imagined the thousands of countrywide Blockbusters franchise holders watching the great hungry public hurrying over to Mighty Munch. Frances had to find a way to make them feel strong again.

She and Potter had expected the Mighty Munch attack. They hadn't known what form it would take, but it was obviously going to be big. Statewide, a food packaging conglomerate had acquired the Mighty Munch chain a few months before, and had also brought up a string of smaller operators across the country, revamping them under the MM banner.

'I'm going to sit tight, Ed,' she had told him three weeks before. 'I'm not going to be panicked into hasty decisions by a

128

competitor who has not yet shown his teeth. We'll be ready for them when they do make a move.'

'I hope you're right,' Potter had said, his face showing the signs of some consternation. 'Statewide has put a lot of financial clout behind Mighty Munch, and our franchise-holders are getting worried.'

'Ed, Statewide have a limited number of possible strategies. When they move, we'll strike back.' Frances' green eyes were glowing as she spoke. This was the side of business she enjoyed the most. She thrived on competition.

Unable yet to swing her trusted team into action, she had visited Ed Potter in hospital, where he lay in the intensive care unit, the anxious silence broken by the thrum and hiss of the machines whose wires and tubes were attached to his ashen-white body.

The medical prognosis had been fair. Potter had suffered a 'moderately severe' heart attack. At first, his condition had been critical, but now he was past the worst. They expected him to survive. But he would be off work for six months, maybe more. Just at the time Frances needed him most.

After checking and signing a sheaf of letters, and dismissing Jo-Beth, Frances ran through her earlier conversation with Potter.

They had decided that the greatest probability was that Mighty Munch would cut prices – as had in fact happened. Potter had suggested Blockbuster should follow suit. Frances had rejected the idea.

'Ed, for a start, it would be a mistake for a market leader like Blockbuster to be seen to follow the lead of an inferior product. We set the pace, we don't let others dictate it.

'More importantly, it would be real bad for our image. Consumers generally assume that a drop in price equals a drop in quality. I'm not cutting prices, or service, nor advertising and marketing budgets. We put a lot of capital into establishing a name for good quality, and fast, friendly service. I'm not prepared to write that investment off.'

This was one of the lessons Frances had learned the hard way,

129

back in California. One of her first new product launches in the USA had been a running shoe. It had been successful enough to prompt an Austrian competitor to launch a copy-cat shoe at a lower price. In response, Frances had cut her prices to match. But the consumers had swung away to a third brand of shoe, leaving herself and the Austrians out in the cold. Frances had commissioned follow-up market research to explain this surprising turn of events, and had discovered – indeed had virtually had her nose rubbed in it – that people have an ingrained conviction that high price means high quality, and that running shoes were among those products for which people *preferred* to pay more.

She spent the rest of the day working through possible Block-busters responses to the Mighty Munch attack, producing contingency figures, and comparing the end results. For the moment, with her gift of total concentration, the problems of PS-21 were eliminated from her mind.

Then, Jo-Beth had brought through a telex message. 'I thought you would like to see this yourself,' she said.

'ARRIVING NEW YORK SWISSAIR FLIGHT SR110 FRIDAY.' It was simply signed: 'ROCHER'.

Frances arrived home that evening both exhausted and exultant. She burst into the sitting room, eager to hug Web, and tell him her news. But inside she discovered Web and Petra Lang together, the latter cosily tucked up on the corner of the sofa, her long slender legs curled beneath her.

The two were deep in discussion, and Web had hardly looked up when Frances walked in, pausing only briefly in his disser-tation on the psychology of rape.

Petra Lang, however, smiled warmly, and presented a cheek to be kissed. She was, Frances had suddenly realized a year or so before, her closest friend, this svelte 37-year-old New York retailer.

They had met quite by chance, at the complaints counter of a

Fifth Avenue shoe store, both having had the strap break in the same place on an identical pair of sandals. The friendship had progressed from coffee in the store's restaurant to a visit to Petra's nearby upmarket florist shop . . . and it hadn't taken long for the pair to become close friends and confidantes. Petra's relationship with Webley had at first been strained. But over the years it had warmed and mellowed, encouraged by the fact that Stacey and Petra had naturally taken to one another with an affection that was quite unfeigned.

Now it was quite natural for her to find Petra surrounded by the day's debris of books, newspapers, and Stacey's kicked off sneakers, awaiting Frances' return.

Frances tripped upstairs, to shed her smartly formal working garb. With the same deliberate care that she had that morning selected the Valentino ensemble she was now removing, she selected a once-worn baggy T-shirt with a faded slogan: 'Run for your Life – Joggers Unanimous', and a slightly crumpled pair of denims. She replaced her Gucci shoes with a pair of red sneakers, then, after her usual glance in the mirror, she ruffled her hair before turning to the door. Before she got there, it opened, and Petra came in on exaggerated tip-toes.

'Don't go yet. You looked so excited when you came in, and excited girl talk is just the kind I need right now.'

The two friends curled up on the bed together – both leaning against a pile of pillows, and talked for an hour as only two close friends can.

'You look tired,' said Petra.

'Thanks for noticing. Nobody else has,' said Frances significantly. 'I love the pressure, but I've never had so much as I have right now. You know, things go smoothly for a while, and then the crises all pile up on top of one another.'

' "Troubles come not single spies, but in battalions" ' said Petra, 'or something like that. It's Shakespeare. So why don't you take a break, Fran? Can't they spare you for a few days, or have you made yourself too indispensable?'

'It's just not like that, Petra. You take a break, you miss the

131

breaks. Besides, I'm on the brink of something so big, I just can't leave it now.'

Petra laughed. 'Fran – you've been saying that ever since we first met. Yet every time you achieve something, it's never enough. You're already burning rubber in pursuit of the next big dream. You've gotta take it easy sometime, you know.'

'Anyway, remember that if you want to leave Stacey with me for a few days, I'll teach her some tricks of the big bad city that she'll thank me for when she gets older. And I'll give her cooked meals, three times a day.'

Petra left after supper – a soufflé that the two women had prepared together. Frances went upstairs, to where Stacey was just finishing her bed-time bath.

Frances handed her a hot towel, and gave the slender, pale body a brisk rub, until Stacey giggled and wriggled free. 'Stop tickling, Mommy.'

'So, how has your day been, sweetheart?' Frances asked.

Dispensing with adult banalities, Stacey replied: 'Mom, can I go and stay with Adele Johnstone on Saturday? She's having a pyjama party for all the girls.'

'Sounds okay to me, honey,' said Frances.

'Mom,' said Stacey, again with nine-year-old directness, 'when are you gonna stop going away all the time? When is this travelling going to stop?'

'Honey, I'm real busy at the moment. It won't last forever, but it's something I have to do in order to do my job properly. I'd prefer to stay home with you, just as you would prefer not to go to school. But sometimes we have to do things we'd rather not do at the time, in order to be happier later on in life.'

'But none of my friends' Moms go out to work, and they're always happy. Why do you have to have a job? Are we poor? Anyway, I love going to school.'

Frances resisted the temptation to take up her daughter's last remark. To a nine-year-old, loving school one minute and hating it the next was perfectly logical. How could she impose adult logic to explain that fulfilment at work made her a better mother, when her daughter was quite simply missing her.

She decided not to try. Instead, she hugged her so the smell of her wet hair was rich in her nostrils, and said: 'Stacey, some day you'll understand. Until then, you've got to remember that I love you, even when I'm far away. And the best time for me is when I come back to you.'

Later, as she lay and soaked in her own hot bath, Web came into the room. As he shook his trousers off, she spoke. 'Honey, I've been lying here wondering what gives with you and the book. It goes on forever and ever. When is there gonna be something to read?'

'C'mon, Frances. It's not like one of your big deals. You don't just make a few phonecalls and it happens, you know.'

'Take it easy, Web. I just want to know how it's going, that's all.'

He started manoeuvring his body into the water behind her. 'Oh, it's okay, I guess. The basic research is done. Now it's just my own case histories.'

'Well, that's good news,' Frances said sincerely.

'Yeah. I've been looking forward to it. But I've got too much material. Don't know what to leave out, and what to put in.'

'If you want, I can help.'

'Do you want to read it?' asked Web.

'Of course,' she replied. Actually, she felt like sleeping, but she didn't have the heart to say so.

'When?' said Web. 'Now?'

'Sure,' said Frances, grimacing to herself.

'Well, actually it's not really ready for me to show anyone yet,' said Web, looking depressed. Then: 'So how was the trip?'

'Okay. I wish you'd come. Please try and do it next time, Web. Petra's offered to take Stacey for a few days.'

'Uh, maybe, honey. We'll see.'

Maxwell J Bennis was wearing his Thursday suit, Frances

133

observed – the charcoal wool with the grey fleck. She had dropped into his office by chance, on her way to her own, and the scheduled meeting with Carl Hecht. She was fairly sure he would be free to see her: Bennis did not overwork himself.

'Morning, Kline,' he beamed affably, as Lilly showed her through. 'Good to see you.'

'Morning, Max. Got a minute?'

'Of course. As long as you like. You know that.'

'I just thought I'd update you on the food division, Max,' she began, arranging her hands neatly on her lap.

'Yes. Awful news about Potter. Such a young man, too.' He ran the palm of his hand over his bald dome. 'Lilly tells me they hope he'll be up and about in a few months, though. Mind you, when the heart starts giving up . . . ' He shook his head.

Frances remembered a snatch of conversation she had over-heard Web delivering at a cocktail party – about how the fear of the approach of death affected successful businessmen. 'It makes them feel what they have achieved is not important,' he had said. 'Instead of enjoying the fruits of their success, they get bored with it instead.' She had thought at once of Maxwell Bennis.

'Bad timing, too,' said Frances. 'Just as Statewide's Mighty Munch mob launch a most aggressive attack on Blockbusters. But it's all in hand. I'm putting Carl Hecht in charge – he was Potter's assistant; and we have a strategy all lined up. We may have to live with marginal profit for a few months, but I know that Blockbusters will be able to ride out the Mighty Munch campaign.'

'Well, Kline. What's your line of action?'

'Mighty Munch have effectively slashed prices, by giving away free burgers. They can't hold out long doing that, but I believe they'll continue to hold prices down in some other way, in the hope of pulling us into a price war.

'I've been expecting something like this ever since Statewide started moving on Mighty Munch. But I'm not being sucked into that kind of public slugging match . . . and I'm definitely not going to cut prices.'

'So what is the Kline way, then?' asked Maxwell, with a smile in his prematurely old eyes.

'I keep my product priced just where it is right now, with extra ingredients, and better service. I pay for that by a budget created from the loss we *would* have incurred if we had reduced prices.'

'Extra ingredients! I don't follow the logic.'

'We've always played on size, Max. So now we add to it and reinforce with good advertising. Blockbusters will come out of this smelling of roses, with an even better image.'

'Well, Kline, I'm sure you can handle it,' said Max. 'Maybe you don't realize it, but the Board has a lot of faith in you, and so do I.'

'C'mon, Max. Why the flattery? You know that sensible girls don't believe a word of it.'

'I do mean it, Kline.'

Frances grinned. 'I know you do, Max. And thank you for engineering six months grace on my Prostaglandin-S project.'

'How is that going, by the way?'

'Great news. That's another thing I came to tell you. Professor Paul Rocher is coming to New York.'

Bennis looked puzzled. 'Professor who?'

'Professor Rocher is the man I went to Lausanne to see. He's the Nobel prize winner. He's coming to New York later this week, and going straight to work on Prostaglandin-S. I am confident he will solve all our problems. He's the man to do it.'

At that moment, the door opened. It was Milton Rae, looking strained and drawn. 'Oh, I'm sorry, Max. I didn't realize you were busy,' he said.

'Like hell,' thought Frances, as she gave him a routine smile.

'Don't worry, Milt,' said Maxwell. 'Frances was just going. She was just telling me about how we've got a Nobel prize winner coming to work for the Cranston Group. What's his name, Kline?'

'Rocher. Professor Paul Rocher,' said Frances reluctantly,

noting with displeasure Milton's startled reaction, before she quietly left the room.

When Frances arrived in her office, it was to find a smartly liveried young messenger. He had a small parcel, and had been directed to deliver it personally to Frances Kline.

Jo-Beth had lingered a while, curious to see what this unusual parcel contained, but Frances thought of a hurried excuse to get rid of her.

Then she had torn off the plain brown wrapping to reveal a black-and-gold jewellery box bearing the legend of Sotheby's auctioneers in London. Carefully opening it, Frances unwrapped the cotton wool nest.

It was an exquisite ivory paperweight, banded and inlaid with a filigree silver pattern, and made in the shape of a heart. It was obviously very old – it had a patina that made it glow with a life of its own. Frances caressed it in her hands, feeling its time-worn smoothness, and wondering who else's hands had made the same caressing motions in the past. There was no need for her to wonder this time who had sent it, even though the Sotheby's card accompanying it was perfectly blank.

Then the desk intercom broke into her thoughts. 'Carl Hecht is here for your meeting,' squawked Jo-Beth.

'Ask him to wait. I'll be ready in a minute,' Frances replied. And then she quickly put the ivory heart into a drawer, and walked to the window to gather her wits. For a top New York huckster, she decided, she was behaving like a silly teenager.

She called in Hecht, and spent the first few minutes reassuring him. 'You have to stop worrying, Carl. Here's how we're going to handle it.'

As she outlined in more detail the strategy she had described to Maxwell Bennis, she could tell from Hecht's expression the awe he felt for her. This was his first time alone in her office, and his reaction reflected the reputation she had among the junior executives. They had read about her in *Time* and *Fortune*, and regarded her as a superhuman example of business acumen and success. Frances didn't fully approve. After all, she saw herself as a perfectly normal forty-two-year-old woman who jogged, had a husband and children, and still did irresponsible things – like walking through the streets of London with a giant South African's arm around her shoulders.

When she reached the end, Hecht asked her: 'What advertising did you have in mind, Mrs Kline?'

'I'd like a Norman Rockwell style illustration for a nationwide poster campaign, and a slogan that hits straight at Mighty Munch, and emphasizes the extra size and quality of our product. "more than just a munch" . . . no: "More burger than just one munch". That's better. Something along those lines.'

Hecht was furiously scribbling notes as she spoke, so she paused to let him catch up. He needed all the reassurance he could get – and if a notepad of her words gave it to him, then that was okay by her.

'Let's get some ideas on promotions for the whole family: "Who can make the biggest burger?" maybe. Run it national then bring the winners to New York. Let the agency figure it out, but *don't* offer any cheap handouts. There is no way I want the public to associate Blockbusters with any cost-cutting. So we hold firm all the way down the line.

'The first thing you must do is to brief the regional managers. You'd better do that at once, before the franchisers get any more panicky than they already are.'

As Hecht left her office, looking just a little bewildered, she called him back. 'And Carl, as of Monday next, you and I are going to monitor Blockbusters sales every two days. Go with it, and good luck!'

Cruising home that evening, flowing with the heavy commuter traffic, Frances suddenly swung off the expressway on a whim. She threaded her way through the suburbs to the beach at Locust Point. It was a beauty spot she and Web had discovered together when they had first arrived in New York. She hadn't been there for years.

She parked the Mercedes on the beach road, deserted at this season and at this time of day. She took a long, quilted coat and lined overboots from the trunk of the car, and pulled a fur-lined beret down over her ears. Then, bracing herself against the biting sea wind, she walked almost to the edge of the surf, and watched its cold, creamy lace curl almost up to her toes. She stood a long while, as the sky darkened as the sun set. Shafts of light reached over her shoulders, across Long Island Sound.

At ease with her solitude, she began to walk along the shoreline, in time with the advance and retreat of the sighing water. Lulled by the rhythmic flow at her feet, she gave free rein to her mind, letting it wash her thoughts at will.

The image of Gray Barnard floated persistently among the swirl of her thoughts. It nudged comfortably against the other blurred images. It wouldn't go away.

She had been struck by his gift, but was a little angry as well as delighted. She felt pressurized, and though she didn't want to escape – she entirely liked the whirlpool in which she was caught – she needed time to think.

Then after a while, the glow of phosphorescent foam at her feet made her notice that it had grown quite dark. Suddenly, she thought of Stacey, waiting at home, and hurried back to the car.

She drew up in the car park at about 8 pm. She had barely switched off the engine when Stacey came rushing out of the house, followed by Lexington, loping clumsily through the shadows.

'Hey, Mommy, Mommy. There's a call for you. Long-distance, the operator said.'

Hugging her daughter along the way, and pushing the excited animal aside, she hurried indoors. Marita, her Mexican housekeeper, was on the phone in the hall. There was no sign of Web.

'Hold on,' Marita shouted, unnecessarily loudly. 'Here she is now.'

It was Gray Barnard.

'I couldn't get you at the office,' she heard him say. 'So I thought I'd chance a call at home. Hope it's okay.'

Frances had no answer.

'I need to see you again, soon,' said Gray.

'I got your parcel,' she blurted out.

She felt, rather than heard, the front door open, then heard Webley's footsteps in the hallway behind her.

'Of course,' she said.

'Franci, is it difficult for you to talk?'

'Of course,' she said again. Web came up behind her, and affectionately grasped her by the neck.

'I'm sorry, Franci. I shouldn't have phoned. Call me tomorrow.' His deep voice with its characteristic accent sounded frighteningly loud in her ear.

'I'll do that,' she said, trying to force a matter-of-fact tone of voice. She was quite sure it hadn't worked. Then she cut the connection, turned to Web, and forced a smile.

'You okay?' He looked through narrowed eyes. 'You look weird.'

'I'm okay,' she said, too abruptly. Then, to conceal it, asked: 'How are you?'

'Fine,' he said, turning away to hang up his coat, then walking through to the family room. 'Who was that?'

'London.' To her own ears, it came out sounding unnaturally high-pitched.

'What do they want you for at this time of day,' he said grouchily. 'It must be four in the morning over there, for Chrissakes.'

'Oh, just some problems at the hotel. A small fire. It's okay, but I asked them to keep me posted.' This time, the lie came out more easily.

Web had settled back in his favourite chair, loosened his tie, and taken a deep draught of whiskey. Then he had switched on the TV, and settled back. 'Great game on tonight,' he said.

Frances was amazed. He had caught her red-handed, in the thick of her guilt. And he hadn't even noticed. Is that how far

139

apart they had grown? How had it happened? How had he allowed so much just to slip away?

Suddenly, the absurdity of the extremes of her life hit home, and she had to force herself not to laugh out loud. On one side was her guilt, her fear of being found out; on the other was her anger at Web for not finding out. Was she really mad at him because he wasn't suspicious?

Yet it was tragic. Once, she and Web had been so close they had become as one. It had seemed like a perfect marriage. Had that very closeness destroyed the relationship?

And, Frances, reflected ruefully, something had happened to the fierce attraction and desire.

If it was like that for her, why should it be different for Web?

Then a new thought: perhaps he just didn't care. It had never occurred to her before.

The idea was so uncomfortable that she took a sleeping pill that night, the only way she could stop the destructive whirlwind in her head.

CHAPTER TWELVE

Among the milling throng coming through customs at John F Kennedy airport, Professor Paul Rocher looked very small, very old, and very bewildered. He was flanked by a pair of burly, expressionless security men, arranged by Frances, who made him look smaller, and more foreign still. How many like him had arrived in this great city, Frances wondered, looking much as he did now, peering about him as if bemused by what he was seeing.

He wore the same grey flannels he had worn when she first met him in Lausanne, their creases still meticulous. A new maroon patterned tie and an old suede jacket completed the picture of an old-fashioned European abroad.

When he spotted Frances, his mournful old face lit up. 'Ah, Frances. It is good to see you again.' His voice was full of pleasure. Snow-white hair stood out around his bald pate in an irregular halo. Frances was shocked to notice that he looked older than when they had last met . . . fragile, and hesitant. She supposed the journey must have been gruelling for the old man.

He embraced her in the formal European manner, brushing first one cheek and then the other against her own, then they stood back, smiling into one another's faces. He enveloped her hand in both of his, the skin dry and papery, but the grip firm and steady.

'It's good to see you, Professor. How do you feel after your long trip?'

'A little tired. Yes, definitely a little tired. But I shall feel fine after a rest. It will take me some time to become accustomed to the fact that what feels like the afternoon to me is still morning here. But I will adjust.'

'Let me take those,' she said, gesturing at the small overnight bag and the oversized box of Swiss chocolates he was carrying.

'No, no, my dear. I can manage perfectly well.'

'What about the rest of your baggage? Is it following on?' She turned to a security man to arrange for it to be collected.

'Baggage? I have no baggage, my dear. This is all I need.' He held up the little suitcase proudly.

They walked close together, a security man on each side, towards the exit and the waiting car. Suddenly, a white flash cut through the artificial light. Rocher stopped mid-stride, looking nonplussed.

Frances first thought the flash was intended for someone else. It was only when two more flashes were repeated in quick succession that she realized they were aimed at her. Then she saw the photographer, crouched on his haunches directly in her path, about to fire off another shot that caught her directly in the eyes, leaving her momentarily blinded.

Then a brash-faced woman was alongside her, lips bright with

141

cheap lipstick, and a contrastingly severe hairstyle. She jabbed a microphone under Frances' chin. 'Mrs Kline. *New York Times.* Would you care to tell us why you've brought Professor Rocher to New York?'

During the following seconds of Frances' speechless surprise, one of the security men stepped firmly forward, shouldering in between Frances and the reporter. 'No comment,' he said brusquely, pushing the young woman aside.

The cameraman flashed again.

'Professor Rocher?' Ever-persistent, the reporter had slipped round the side of the human security barrier. 'Are you in America for . . .'

'Lady,' the security man confronted her. 'I said no comment. Now beat it.'

While he engaged her in argument, Frances, Rocher and the other security man slipped away to the nearest exit, emerging some distance from the waiting car.

Rocher was visibly shaken. Frances in turn felt a mixture of shocked confusion and pure fury. Somebody had blundered, and she was terrified it might scare the Professor off.

They walked quickly to the car – a low-slung Cadillac with blacked-out windows. Frances had shied off using the Cranston helicopter, as being too ostentatious. It would only have drawn attention to an event she had hoped to keep secret – and she also wanted to isolate the Professor from too much direct contact with the corporation he was working for.

Once they had settled in the car, she spoke. 'Professor, I am terribly sorry about what happened back there. Please be assured it was nothing to do with me.'

'Come, my dear. It is alright. It was not your fault, I am sure.'

'Still, I am sorry. It means there has been a leak. I had hoped to keep your visit incognito, at least for the present time.'

As they wheeled out of the airport, he settled back into the cushions of the wide bench seat. Then, suddenly remembering, he thrust the big box of chocolates at Frances. 'Here. These are for you.'

She thanked him, then looked down at his shabby little suitcase: 'Is this really all you have?'

'Everything I own,' he said proudly. 'Possessions only tie one down.'

As the limousine swept through the morning traffic, Rocher gazed at the uninterrupted jumble of concrete and humanity. Then they caught their first glimpse of the sky-scrapers of Manhattan Island. To Rocher, as to every newcomer to New York, it was a breathtaking sight in the morning sun. Man's monument to himself. Rocher gripped Frances lightly by the arm.

'Quite something, huh?' said Frances.

Rocher nodded. 'Quite something,' he agreed, rolling the American inflection around his mouth.

Suddenly, Frances became aware of the enormity of her dragging the old man from his settled existence halfway across the world to fulfil her own ambitions, to further the ends of the Cranston Group. 'Did I bully you into coming?'

'Please! Once I had made up my mind, you wouldn't have stopped me.'

'Professor, what was it that made you change your mind?'

He turned and smiled. 'I have always wanted to see New York. All my life. I decided to take this chance.' But the answer came too quickly, and they both knew it wasn't the real reason. After a short time, he spoke again.

'To tell you the truth, Frances, I came because of you. And because of Michelle. That was my daughter's name. You seem so similar and I couldn't get the likeness out of my mind. And, you know, once I had decided to come . . . well, I haven't felt so alive for years.'

Spontaneously, Frances slipped her arm through the crook of his elbow.

As they crossed over to Manhattan, the water still and silent beneath them, Professor Rocher started to talk.

'I told you I lost everything when they died. But that was not true. I did not lose the will to go on living. Even though there were many times when I was sure that I would rather be dead.

143

That was the worst torture of all, the prolonging of my own life, after everything that was important to that life had been taken away from it.'

'What happened, Professor?'

'It was in 1944. We were living in France. It was the Maquis who shielded us from the Nazis, and in return I worked closely with them, giving whatever help I could. Through the underground network of information, it was obvious that the war could not last much longer. The Nazis would be defeated.

'We really thought then that we had survived the horror, that we had been spared the scourge. The family was intact.

'By then, the three of us – my wife Mathilde, Michelle and myself – were adept at living on the run. Michelle was just two . . . she had never known any other kind of life. We were living on a remote farm in the hills near Clermont-Ferrand, down south. We had joined up with a small group of other Jews, refugees like ourselves. Somebody betrayed us.'

As before, neither his face nor his voice showed any emotion. But again Frances could feel through her touch on his arm that his body was quivering.

'The Gestapo came at 4 am. They woke us up. One man who tried to escape was shot dead on the spot, and left lying in the mud while they made us stand for two hours in our nightclothes. They loaded the women and children into a truck . . . my wife died in Mauthasen. My daughter . . . well, I told you I never found her. I don't know how I could have said so much, on our first meeting.'

'And what happened to you, Professor?' Frances asked, quietly into the silence.

He gave a dry laugh, and continued almost mechanically. 'To me? Well, as you can see, I survived. I already had something of a reputation as a bio-chemist, and the Germans recognized my name. They had a problem that they needed me to solve, so they deported me to Wiesbaden. Their penicillin moulds were suffering from bio-contamination, and it was my job to find out why.'

Frances was uneasily aware of the similarity with the present situation, but if the Professor was also aware of the irony, he gave no sign.

'The war ended before I solved the problem.' He smiled bitterly. 'Before I was of no more use to them.'

Frances felt the weight of generations of sorrow resting on him. They sat very close together, and neither spoke a word.

Then Rocher said into the silence: 'And now, I think I would like a chocolate.' It broke the mood, and together they selected choice delicacies of dark truffles and rich nuts, and sat companionably until the big car turned finally into Fifth Avenue, and drew up outside the imposing portal of The Barrister.

Frances accompanied the old man up to the penthouse suite she had arranged for him in the hotel. It consisted of three rooms – a bedchamber, a sitting room, and a small study – and Rocher was just looking round at his new surroundings when Frances seized him by the arm. 'This is no good. You must come to my home. Please come and live with me and my family.'

'No, no. My dear child. Please, Frances. I have made you feel responsible. This is an adventure for me. It is exciting. This room . . . it is more than I am used to in Lausanne. It is more than enough for me, and it is where I would be the most happy – where I can live in my usual way, without inconveniencing anybody – taking care of myself.'

She relaxed her grip, and his old hand grasped hers. 'Remember, you and I understand one another.'

The old eyes shone as they rested on her face. Then the old man sank slowly into a chair. He closed his eyes for a minute – for long enough for Frances to wonder if he was alright. He looked very small, and very tired, and again she noted his fragility. Then he spoke again.

'You go. I will sleep, and tomorrow we still start. We have a lot to do. Now, I need to be alone. I need to make my peace with God in a new country.'

Before Frances left, she went to open the curtains to the window. The view was onto trees and acres of green.

'Is that a park?' asked the Professor.

'Yes. It's Central Park,' said Frances.

He laughed. 'Why yes, of course. How foolish of me.'

'If you need anything, Professor, you only have to ask. I have left my telephone numbers at the office and at home for you. Please call me. I do hate to leave you alone.'

'I'm not afraid of being alone. I am old enough to be comfortable with myself.' He chuckled. 'And I never take myself by surprise. I am quite predictable.'

Frances stopped off in the foyer of the hotel to make a call. It was to her own office.

'Hi, Jo-Beth. Anything urgent?'

'Nothing that can't wait. Where are you?'

'I'm at The Barrister. I've just dropped Professor Rocher off. And Jo-Beth, I won't be in until after lunch. I'm going on strike for the morning. If you want me urgently I'll be at Jean-Louis' Beauty salon having the full treatment.'

To Frances, a session with Jean-Louis was a resource she turned to when her life was going very smoothly, and conversely when – as now – the pressure was really on. Two hours isolated under a mud-pack or under a hair-dryer were a peaceful retreat, interrupted only by the skilled ministrations of Jean-Louis' expert hands.

When she returned to Cranston Towers that afternoon, she looked beautiful, and felt restored. It was the same sort of sensation brought on by her jogging, a rushing of blood just below the level of the skin.

She sat down, and immediately buzzed Jo-Beth. 'Ask Joe Mitchell to come to my office right away, please.'

Joe Mitchell was Frances' Vice-President in charge of Communications and Public Affairs, a position he had held for the past four years. He arrived at her office within five minutes, his young face as clean-shaven at three in the afternoon as an after-shave ad. It was Frances' normal practice to select young

146

men for junior executive posts, choosing for ambition and flair, as well as for an ability to follow her instructions to the letter. Men much older than herself, she had discovered, if they didn't dislike taking orders from a woman, often placed their own rather liberal interpretation on those orders when it came to carrying them out.

She motioned Mitchell to a chair, and came straight to the point. 'Alright, Joe. Who put the story out?'

'What do you mean, Frances?' He looked genuinely bewildered. 'What are you talking about?'

'I'm talking about a reporter and a photographer from the *New York Times*, who just happened to be waiting to meet Professor Rocher when he arrived at Kennedy this morning and will alert the entire American public, if not the world, to the fact that he's here working with us.'

'Holy Cow!' said Mitchell.

'They tried to get a story from me, and they took pictures of the two of us together.'

'Frances, I can tell you for sure that the leak didn't come from PR. It couldn't have. I am the only person who knows, and I have kept it right under my hat. After you briefed me, I put nothing down on paper for any of my staff to find. There is no way they could have found out. The leak must have come from somewhere else.'

As he spoke, Frances' searching eyes were holding his young gaze with steady scrutiny. She was satisfied the young man was not lying.

'Well, if it wasn't you, Joe, then who was it?'

'It shouldn't be too difficult to find out. I'll call the *Times* newsdesk, and if that doesn't work I'll try my contacts among the reporters. I should have an answer for you within half an hour.'

Frances shook her head at his departing back. She didn't think he would find the answer so easily. If the tip-off came from a chance casual remark, then maybe it would work. But if it had been a deliberate leak, then the source would have protected himself, secured anonymity. And if that was the case, Mitchell would have as much chance of finding out as he would of stopping publication. And that was no chance at all.

Still, at least she had been able to knock one suspect off the list. Apart from the respective secretaries – and it was unlikely to have been them, except by carelessness – this left Gerald Rule and Maxwell J Bennis whom she had told willingly, and Milton Rae, whom she had told most unwillingly. Bennis might easily have mentioned the fact to other executives, while Milton Rae might have passed on the information to his own Prostaglandin research team. Frances sighed, and wondered if she would ever know the truth.

Next, she called for Gerry Rule. He'd wrapped up the Marley deal within a week, and had been back in New York for a few days. Already he was looking better, the grey fading from his complexion.

Rule was emphatically happiest in his own empire, surrounded by his own staff, his beloved computers, and immersed in budget runs and great sheaves of print-outs and data.

Frances was almost as pleased to see him back as he was to be back. They made a good team, and she did not seriously suspect that he was the source of the leak. Rule was a real corporate man, and if he had to make a choice between her and the company, Frances was sure he would choose the latter.

When they had first worked together, during her early days with Cranston, she had often said to Rule – as she said to all her senior executives – that she wanted him to strive for her position. 'I may only be running a small division at Cranston, but it's not going to stay small for much longer.'

Like so many other people, Rule had at first been sceptical and amused by this little woman with big ideas. But as her empire grew, his attitude changed to one of respect that was untainted by more than normal envy. 'Frances, you *are* this division,' he had once said to her. 'It relies completely on your energy.'

'Yes, Gerry,' she had replied. 'But only for now.'

He stepped jauntily into her office, immaculately dressed as always, in a brown worsted two-piece suit with a silk burgundy

148

tie. 'Afternoon, boss-lady,' he said. 'Your little prof get in okay?'

'A bit too okay,' replied Frances. 'We had a press leak.'

'What!' Rule seemed quite genuinely astounded. 'How the hell . . .'

'That's exactly what I'd like to know,' said Frances. 'You got any ideas?'

'Well, it's gotta be out of you, me, PR department, security staff, or our own laboratory.'

'And Maxwell Bennis,' she reminded him. 'I told him yesterday.' She had been going to add Milton Rae's name, but something made her pull back. If it had been him, then the only reason could be to pursue a personal vendetta against Frances and her Prostaglandin-S. If so, she would deal with it personally.

'Well, gee, there's your answer,' said Rule sourly. 'He's well known for shooting his mouth off over a few drinks with the boys.'

'Whoever it is, I aim to find out,' said Frances.

Frances bent forward to study the yellow legal pad in front of her. 'I want you to give everything you've got to Prostaglandin now, Gerry,' she said. 'We've got one tight schedule ahead of us, and we can't afford any slips.'

'Don't I just know it,' said Rule. 'That's nothing new. You're always putting your neck on the line. And you always get away with it.'

Frances gave him a downturned smile. 'You may not think so when you've heard the bad news.'

'Well, let's hear it. I'm feeling strong today.' Rule beamed cheerfully.

He could afford to, thought Frances. The risks are all mine.

'I want all the projections for the next quarter, and all the budgets. By tomorrow morning.'

'That's easy. So what's the bad news?'

'I need a minimum of $10 million dollars.'

'What!'

'I've got to have ten million dollars. If this thing works out, we're going to need to set up our own factory. Though I haven't decided where to put it. Worldwide distribution would be better from Europe, and I think the image would be better too.

'PS is going to be quite a shock to the world market. It's such a new concept. Europeanizing it gives it a link with the past. Makes people more comfortable.

'On the other hand,' she went on, 'a US base would make control easier. We have the production right on our doorstep, and we can use existing means of distribution – and Epipharm have agreed in principle to make their distribution network available. Of course export regulations are a great deal easier in the Common Market than the States.'

In her own mind, she had always seen PS-21 as a French product. This would emphasize its cosmetic connotations, where its origin in the US would only highlight its pharmaceutical side. Even though the product would be in the form of a tablet, she wanted consumers to see it as a beauty and healthcare aid rather than as any sort of medicine.

'Maybe,' Gerry was saying, 'we should look at Spain. They'll be in the Common Market soon, and costs are low. But terms of image, it would have to be a country with a reputation for quality. Germany, Belgium, France . . . even Britain.'

'Gerry,' said Frances. 'Give me a while to think about it. Of course I'll need you to handle the details once I've made a decision.

'And Gerry,' added Frances, as he was leaving the office, 'for God's sake don't talk to anyone about it.'

'Yessir, boss-lady.'

'Hello.' It was Gray's voice, deep and slightly clipped. Frances was unable to speak for several seconds.

It was 4 pm in New York. Frances was in the middle of dictating a letter to Athabasca's head office in Johannesburg. While she spoke, her mind had been on two levels – the letter to South Africa, and on the man in South Africa, whose image lodged like an ache in her throat. Since that last evening in

London, her attraction to Gray had been with her constantly. As she caressed the ivory heart, she could imagine Gray's own hands as they too must have caressed its roundness, and then she could feel them move to her own body, where her breasts and her buttocks echoed the plumpness of the ornament.

'One moment,' Frances replied, waiting what seemed to her like an interminable age after she had dismissed Jo-Beth from the room.

'Are you there?' Gray's voice had been doubtful, as she returned to the receiver.

'Gray.' She breathed his name slowly.

'I've been missing you,' he said.

'And I you.' She had no other answer.

'I love you.' The words were as rousing to Frances as if it had been his lips instead of an electronic loudspeaker which had relayed them to her ear.

'Please don't,' she had replied.

'I want you, Franci.' He spoke more boldly now. 'And you want me.'

Frances remained silent.

'Are you there?' he asked again.

'Yes,' she replied weakly.

'Franci, stop fighting it. It's going to happen.' The statement made its impact low down in her body.

'Please, Gray. It's gone too far.'

'Not far enough, Franci. Not for me or you.'

After he had rung off, she stared at the telephone for several long minutes, and then leaned forward to the intercom. 'We'll finish that Athabasca letter in the morning, Jo-Beth,' she said. 'You can go home now. I'm staying on a while. See you tomorrow.'

Frances wanted to be alone, to enjoy the sensation of abandonment. It was as though she was floating. Gray had created a new feeling in her; an experience so personal that it would allow no intrusion from the world outside.

After sitting still for a while, she began to leaf desultorily

151

through the mail that Jo-Beth had left on her desk. She needed to try and understand what was happening to her; why her life seemed suddenly so hollow, and why that void should be filled by the huge South African.

Later, driving the Mercedes home through a world coloured orange by the sunset, the first signs of spring in the air, Frances Kline turned her Clarion cassette player up to full volume. Powerful loudspeakers turned the inside of the car into a vibrating concert hall, with the perfect fidelity that is the hallmark of expensive equipment. The voice of Barbra Streisand filled the air around her and Frances allowed herself to be carried away on the swelling billows of sound.

She drove home slowly, barely aware of the traffic around her, following her route by instinct, until she abruptly swung off the expressway to follow quiet local roads the rest of the way home. Savouring the music, and the unmoving sky, Frances burst into song. Then her voice knotted up, and she began to cry.

CHAPTER THIRTEEN

The face stared from across two columns of the *New York Times* with startled eyes, all the kindly contours and furrows bleached out under the harsh glare of the flash. The headline over the top was cryptic: NOBEL GLAND MAN IN JFK PUZZLE; and the story beneath was several inches deep. It was pure speculation – necessarily so, in view of the lack of hard facts the reporter had to base it on.

It named both Professor Paul Rocher and Frances Kline in the first paragraph, and described how the reporter had been elbowed aside with a brusque 'no comment' at JFK. The second paragraph homed in on Frances. 'What's new from Cranston's wiz-woman?' the reporter asked.

She went on to speculate briefly about possible Cranston Group developments in the field of pituitary gland hormones - for which Rocher had won his Nobel Prize.

Then followed a brief rehash on Rocher's career; and an even briefer one on Frances Kline, describing her as 'one of New York's top three business women', getting her age wrong by two years on the credit side . . . an error that had been started by a misprint in the *NYT* business section six years before, announcing her Cranston appointment, and perpetuated ever since.

Far more disturbing to Frances was the astute way the report implied some sort of mystery surrounding the Professor's arrival. The words 'secret mission' were designed to titillate the reader's imagination, to lend a conspiratorial tone. And they were used three times.

Frances read through the report for the sixth time since she had first seen it before breakfast that morning. Then she cast it down, and frowned across the desk at Joe Mitchell.

'So this is the only paper to carry it?' she said. 'Well, I guess that's something, except that the damage is done. Talk about open-house for the competition.'

The young man opposite her looked undeniably flustered. 'Frances, I'm real sorry,' he said, his fresh face clouded. 'I tried to get the newsdesk all day yesterday, but it seems they'd been warned off speaking to me.' He slid a typed memo across the desk to Frances. 'I got through this morning.'

'So?' Frances resisted the obvious remark that this was a little after the event. 'It took a mighty lot of pushing,' he said. 'The reporter wouldn't give me her source – gave me the whole bit about the *Times* being independent, and that as far as she was concerned, a Nobel winner's arrival in New York was news, and the public had a right to know.'

'Damn,' said Frances under her breath. 'Sorry, Joe. It's not your fault. The story was too vague to do us too much harm, not so far, anyway. There's been no link with PS, or Prostaglandins of any sort. If we can keep it at this, it'll be okay.'

'What worries me is that the leak came from *somewhere*, and if we don't plug it now, you can bet we're going to have a lot more problems.'

Joe Mitchell looked puzzled. 'I don't know, Frances. This could have been a pure chance thing. A keen young reporter, checking through the airline passenger lists. Nobel Prize winners don't come out the nickel-and-dime store, you know. She goes out to JFK just to see what she can pick up. It's a slow day for news, so she gets lucky.'

'Could be,' said Frances. 'I'd like to believe that too. But there's too much coincidence in it for my liking. I'm not prepared to take any chances.'

'Joe, from now on I'm going to hold my cards so close to my chest that I'm not going to be able to tell you everything that happens on PS.'

Mitchell looked crestfallen. It had always been part of his role to keep confidences. He needed the whole picture to be able to issue statements to the press.

'It's not that I don't trust you, Joe,' she added quickly. 'If I didn't, I wouldn't be telling you this. I just need to narrow down the field. Sorry, but that's the way it has to be.'

'Meantime, we have the problem of defusing any interest that the *Times* story may have started up. We'll have to admit everything, and give away nothing. Any reporters who call, I'll handle. Now I must go to the Chairman.'

Bennis was sitting at his desk amid the usual haze of fresh smoke rapidly going stale in the drapes and furniture. 'You've seen the papers,' he said gruffly, as Frances entered his office.

'Of course I have, Max,' she replied. 'The paper, to be precise. Only the *New York Times* had any story.'

'Yeah,' he replied in a sarcastic tone. 'And it was only on the front page.'

'Kline, do you realize what this means? You're going to get Wall Street all hyped up. They're going to go crazy speculating. God knows where it could end.'

'Max, I think you're overreacting.'

'No!' He thumped the desk, sending his burning cigarette toppling from the ashtray, depositing another little errant pile of ash on his desk. 'I am not overreacting. Once this kind of thing starts, there's no knowing where it might end. You've got yourself into a Mickey Mouse woman's-magazine product, and you're going to have the whole of the country laughing at us.'

'Max, what's eating you. There's an innocuous story that tells nothing beyond the fact that Professor Rocher is in town, and connected to the Cranston Group. The interest will all have died down in a day or two.'

'What are you going to do when all the other papers get on the line?'

'Tell them the truth: that Rocher is here to do research work, and that we are not ready to make a statement.'

'I should have been consulted,' Bennis said petulantly.

'About what, exactly?' Frances' eyes were beginning to look dangerously piercing, if Bennis had but noticed.

'Goddammit, Frances, about this whole business of bringing Rocher to New York.'

'Max,' she replied, 'I did tell you.'

'You told me you were going to Lausanne in the goddamn elevator,' blustered Bennis.

'I've made bigger decisions every day of my life at Cranston, Max,' said Frances, 'without having to clear them all with you. And as long as I stay here, I'll continue to make the decisions that I think are right for the Cranston Group.' Her voice was patient, but it was an effort to keep it so.

'Milton was right,' said Maxwell J Bennis. 'We should never have allowed Cranston to get involved in this sensationalist sort of thing.'

'So,' said Frances. 'Milton's been talking to you.' Now she understood.

'Sure he has. He's as worried about this as I am.'

'Max,' Frances was angry now. 'You've got to make up your mind whether or not you are behind me on this. I know that PS-21 is a winner. You promised me six months to prove it. Now, on the face of a story that contains nothing more than idle speculation, you let Milton Rae panic you into an about face.'

'Milton has been with Cranston for twenty years, Kline. You have been here precisely six. He is a highly experienced executive, who has the good of the Group at heart.'

'I wish I could agree, Max.' Frances spoke quietly, but something about her tone made Bennis pay attention.

'What do you mean?'

'Just this; it smells to me like this story was deliberately leaked to the *Times*. And it didn't come from my department, I'm quite sure of that.'

Bennis remained silent for several seconds. Then he said quietly: 'Kline. You'd better be very careful with statements like that. You'd better make very sure of your facts before you make any accusations.'

'I will, Max. I will.'

Frances spent the rest of the morning in her office, going through the routine of managing her division. But her mind was with Rocher, and as soon as she had cleared her paperwork, she checked out with Jo-Beth, and caught a cab to the laboratory she had arranged for the Professor.

It was just three blocks from The Barrister, and contained all the equipment and manpower he had asked for. He had been typically undemanding, asking only for the bare minimum, and making it clear that he preferred to be left alone to get on with the job. Frances had added a confidential secretary, and a small kitchen where this discreet, middle-aged Cranston employee could prepare meals for him and his assistants.

Now she took the stairs up to the laboratory two at a time, excited at the prospect of seeing him at work.

Three minutes later, she was on her way to his hotel in another cab. She clutched her handbag, knuckles white with anxiety. The old man was ill, and she felt responsible.

At The Barrister, she telephoned Rocher's room from the lobby. 'Frances,' he replied, 'you are exactly who I would most like to see. Come please to my room – I am lying down for a little while.' His voice was steady but sounded weak, full of fatigue.

Frances took the elevator to his suite, and the bell-hop opened the door for her with a pass-key. She went straight through to the bedroom. Rocher was lying with his eyes closed, and his cheeks sunken. His skin was the colour of parchment. She was aghast at the change in him since the day before.

Softly she sat on the bed, and spoke to him. 'Professor, it's me.'

He opened his eyes, and summoned a slow smile. 'Frances. I am sorry this has happened to me so soon. But I will be better. By tomorrow you'll see . . . '

'What is it?' Spontaneously, she clutched at his hands. Their dry coolness gave her a start. She wanted him to stop talking. She didn't want to hear what he was going to say. He was ill, desperately ill. She could see that much. And she, in her folly, had brought him headlong into the middle of this project, a high pressure project to say the least. 'Tell me the truth. What is the matter?'

'I have not been well for several months,' he spoke so softly that she had to bend to hear the words. 'The day before you came to Lausanne, I had been to the hospital for a series of tests. It's what I feared, what I knew in my heart. I should have gone to hospital earlier of course, but the old have to die and make room for the new.' His mouth creased as he mustered a slight grin. 'It's too late now to operate. It's cancer of course.'

Frances felt a sudden tide of nausea rise within her. A sob shook her whole body. Die, die . . . His words hit her as surely as if it had been a well-aimed fist.

They sat in silence as the horror sank in. Frances began to whimper softly. But the old man shook his head feebly. 'No, no don't. No, my dear. You must not cry. I am ready to die. As much as a man can be ready to die. But first I must assist with this obession of yours.' Then, after a short silence, he looked at her. 'How green your eyes are. Just the same shade as my Michelle's.'

Frances squeezed his hand. 'How can you talk of dying?' she choked.

He smiled again. 'I have to get used to the idea. It is no great hardship. The doctors told me that the end would come soon. I will have attacks, like this one. But I have some time left. About a month, I would guess.'

'A *month*!' Frances could not prevent the horrified expostulation.

'My dear. When it is the rest of your life, it seems like quite a long time.'

Frances had left the Professor to rest, and had wandered in a dazed condition down the hotel corridors and to the elevators. In the lobby, she had had to sit down. Her relationship with the old man had taken on a new dimension. Now her responsibility for bringing him so far from home, to die in a foreign land, seemed too heavy to bear.

She felt quite desperate . . . and it had nothing to do with PS-21.

Frances arrived home weary. She needed to talk. But Web's station-wagon was missing from the carport, and she found a note on the hall table. He had taken Stacey for her first lesson at the school junior cheerleaders' class. Damn – she had promised to take her. She'd forgotten.

She had to talk to someone. The strong image of Gray Barnard appeared before her. Yes. She would talk to him.

Quickly, she looked up the Stellenbosch number in her diary, and jabbed the buttons hastily, as if to start the action before she changed her mind. Only when the clicks and buzzes of the international line ended, and were replaced by a rhythmical ringing, did she wonder at the madness of what she was doing. What if Web came home. What if Barnard's wife answered?

Then she heard that familiar accent, and her body relaxed. His voice was slowed and thickened for having been awakened from deep sleep. 'Hello. What is it?'

'Gray. It's me. Frances.'

'It's you.' He suddenly sounded fully awake, gleeful, excited. 'I knew you would phone. I was waiting for your call when I fell asleep.'

'I must be careful,' she said. 'I'm calling from home. I wanted to to know . . . '

'Franci, what is it, is something wrong?' he cut across her.

Frances released the avalanche.

'He's dying,' she said in a high-pitched sob, pent up inside of her.

'Who?'

'Rocher. Professor Paul Rocher. I brought him to New York to work in PS-21. He's going to die here, soon. I feel so guilty.'

'Don't be.'

The hiss of the big station-wagon as Web pulled up in the driveway, jerked her back to consciousness. She heard the clatter of Stacey's feet on the porch . . . Heard her call excitedly: 'Mommy's home.'

'Gray, I've got to go,' she said. 'Web's arrived.'

'Hold on a minute, Franci, please. I'll do the talking.'

'Gray, I . . . '

Webley Kline came into the hallway, saw Frances, and grinned.

'I'll get back to you,' said Frances. 'Bye.'

'I'll call you tomorrow,' he said and the line went dead.

Web returned from hanging up his coat, and gave her a mechanical kiss on the cheek. 'I tried to get you at the office this afternoon.'

'I wasn't in much. We had a crisis.' Suddenly, she was reluctant to talk to Web about Rocher.

'Yeah, I saw the *Times*. What's it all about?'

'Some hack reporter tried to get smart – hooked onto Rocher's arrival at JFK, and tried to get a story out of us at the airport.' She spoke dismissively, congratulating herself on the way she calmed her voice, in spite of the trembling within.

'Had a lousy day myself. Writing's a bitch. Sometimes you go backwards instead of forwards. Wanna drink?'

'Yeah.' This was spoken with unfeigned sincerity. 'I guess I deserve something stronger than Perrier after today. Campari and soda, please.'

Web raised an ironic eyebrow. 'Don't drink it all at once, huh.' Then he started shuffling through the bottles on the shelves. 'Where the hell is the goddamn Campari.'

'Web, why don't you and I and Stace take Rocher away for the weekend? Drive up to Cape Cod or something. We could leave early Friday, and stop off somewhere on the way.'

His response was as undignified as it was unexpected. Rising suddenly, he cracked his head on the top rail of the bar. Ignoring the impact, he spoke loudly. 'Oh shit, Fran, I'm sick to death of you and your business friends.'

Frances bit her lip. 'Web, he's not a business friend. He's just an old man – a very dear old man. An old man who has risked his life to help me.' She saw from the grim set of Web's jaw that he was intent on an argument, and felt the futility of it all.

'Tell you what to do, Fran. You go. You take him. Show him the sights, have a good time. Stacey and I will just carry on with normal family life here. Any time you feel like a slice of it, then you just stay home for a while. Or would that be too dull for Mrs Kline?'

'Leave it, Web. It's not important. We'll forget Rocher, okay?'

Web splashed soda viciously into her Campari and his Scotch. 'Oh yes, it is important. Everything you do is important. So important that little things don't rate too highly. Like promising your daughter you'd take her to her first goddamn rah-rah class. I guess you thought she'd forget, huh?'

Frances was battling to control herself. Web was spoiling for a fight. Then, unseen by either of them, Stacey came to the doorway, paused for a moment sensing the atmosphere, and slipped away again disconsolately.

'Web, please,' Frances implored. 'I know I've been away a lot. I know it's rough on Stacey. But I've been doing it for us. And I've explained that to her.'

'For us!' Web was almost shouting now. 'You've just got to be kidding. It's for you and your outsize ego!'

'I don't know how else you imagine you'd have the chance to write the book that never gets written.'

Web turned on her fiercely. 'Aha. So it's money again, is it? Your money, that makes it possible for me to do what I want.'

'My money, your money – what the hell is the difference? That's the point, Web. It's *our* money.'

Web didn't reply. He just picked up his drink, and walked firmly out of the room towards his study. When he got there, he slammed the door, and Frances heard the brief electronic tone which meant he had switched his word-processor on.

She sighed, as she felt the anger die within her. She couldn't understand the arguments she and Web had about money. In the beginning, when they had none, they had never discussed the topic. Now they had more than enough, they seemed forever to be wrangling about it.

Then Frances walked briskly through to the bedroom wing, and found her daughter lying down clutching her tattered black scottie dog, her constant sleeping companion from the age of four. She was crying without noise, tears rolling down the smooth-skinned cheeks. Frances grabbed her shoulders, pulled her up and hugged her, wiping her tears and crooning softly. 'Freckles, freckles. Where did you get all these freckles.'

Later, she made a tray of open sandwiches and a mug of hot, strong coffee, and sat with Stacey watching *The A-Team*.

'Don't you love 'em, Mom?'

'Not like you do, Stace. Not like I love you.'

Later, she took Stacey to bed. 'I'll sit with you a while, honey,' she said. And in the child's bedroom, her face soft and young in the night-light, she tried to figure out how to balance all the forces in her life, all pulling her in opposite directions.

First she thought of Gray. Then of Rocher, lying desperately ill and all alone. And then Webley, simmering a few rooms away.

Finally she relaxed, and let her fatigue take over, wrapping around her. Gray loved her. Rocher was dying. Her marriage was falling apart. Her mind couldn't cope with anything more than those three gigantic truths.

Rocher had recovered as quickly as he had been struck down. He was back in the laboratory the next day, and working all hours. She called in to see him there every day . . . he regularly stayed until 7 pm, and was usually too busy to do more than exchange a friendly greeting, before turning back to his test tubes and calculations.

Although he did not suffer any more attacks, to Frances, knowing his condition, he seemed a little weaker every day. She was distraught with the guilt at having shackled a dying man to this intensive labour. Even though he seemed to be enjoying it.

Finally, after three weeks, he called her office for the first time. His voice sounded as spry as she had ever heard it.

'Frances, my dear.' Rocher spoke as if their last conversation had been but minutes before. 'I think we may have a solution. We should talk. Would you be free, perhaps this evening?'

Her heart leapt, as much from the evidence of his apparent good cheer as the news his words conveyed. 'Of course. As soon as you like. I can come at once.'

Thirty minutes later, they shared a fresh brew of herbal tea in the small room off the laboratory. Anxiously, Frances scanned his face for signs of pain, for the ravages of the disease that was eating him from within. He looked better now than he had since he had arrived in New York. His disease was a sly, deceptive one.

The Professor could hardly contain his excitement. 'I cannot actually *show* you anything. But I think I have found a vital link in getting your wonder product made.' He paused, to twinkle at her from his bright eyes, his floss of white hair a crown on his old

162

head. Frances waited expectantly while he sipped his fragrant black tea.

'I'm quite pleased,' he continued. 'Quite pleased. As you know, apart from our shelf-life problem which I am working on to make Prostaglandin-S commercially, we have the problem of synthesizing the stabilizing agent. For manufacture, you are going to need supplies in bulk.'

'Why should it be a problem?' Frances was thinking quickly now, planning ahead, running through dates and schedules in her mind.

'Because no large quanities are at present available. I have been able to procure sufficient quantities for my experiments from Merck in Germany so far. They synthesize it for use in their diagnostic enzymes. But already I have nearly exhausted that possible source.

'It is very difficult to synthesize, and very costly, even for small quantities. The thought of synthesizing it on an industrial scale is completely out of the question. We've got to find the substance in natural form.'

'Well, can we get hold of it?' Frances refused even to consider that the solution would be taken away from her before she could even grasp it.

'Perhaps. This is why I wanted to see you. I now know that the substance does occur in nature, in small concentrations in succulent plants. I have just got the feedback I've been waiting for. The only known significant high concentrations are found in a plant called *Dorothaneum*.'

'It is a common plant?'

'It is not rare. It grows abundantly in the wild, when conditions are right. But it is very fussy. It flourishes only in dry, sandy soil, on hot coasts where a cold current flows. Currents like the Humboldt and the Benguella.'

'I know the Humboldt. Flows past South Africa, doesn't it?'

'Very good.' His old eyes twinkled. 'Past Chile, to be precise. And the Benguella current runs up the west coast of South Africa. This colleague of mine in Lausanne, a botanist, he tells

163

me that *Dorothaneum* grows most prolifically along the western Cape coast of South Africa.'

Suddenly, the old man looked tired. He sat silently as he concealed a spasm of agonizing inner pain. Then he smiled at Frances. 'Leave me now, my dear. I need to rest again, and then I have more work to do to finish my research.'

Frances leaned forward, and kissed him on the forehead. 'Thank you, Professor. Thank you very much. I will see you tomorrow.'

She left the room, and caught a cab to her office. She knew what she had to do.

Striding into her office with a passing greeting to the puzzled-looking Jo-Beth, she picked up the phone. This time, she gave no heed to who might answer, as she dialled Gray Barnard's number.

CHAPTER FOURTEEN

The walls of the over-decorated room pressed in, searing into him the brand of his own perversion. The furniture loomed stark and implacable. The ornaments – brass and wood – had been silent spectators to his mortification. They had witnessed the last hideous hours of Jeremy Farnsworth. Now they taunted him.

Another swig of neat bourbon – his third since arriving ten minutes before – scalded the back of his throat. Milton Rae sat within the confines of his fear, and regarded the woman refilling her own glass at the cocktail cabinet.

'I want to know,' she said over her shoulder, 'what the hell's going on. You said you'd fixed it up. That there'd be nothing more. A straight suicide, you said. Since then, I've had three different cops nosing around here, and the last one threatened me with Vice.'

'But it was a straight suicide,' said Rae. 'Just tell it like it was . . . except that I wasn't here.'

'Yeah, sure. Meantime Janelle and I carry the can.'

'Listen.' He raised his voice. 'It's okay. There's nothing for you to worry about, and I can take care of Vice. Just keep doing as I tell you to the cops – he was just another mixed up kid who got in over his head, and took the easy way out. They'll lose interest soon.'

Now she spun around, her face old and ugly in its anger. Milton wondered how he could ever have desired her.

'No, Milt,' she spat. 'You listen to me for a change. Seems like you don't know the police you "fixed up" did an autopsy. And you know what they found?'

She drew herself up into a ludicrous imitation of a New York cop. 'Evidence of abnormal sexual assault.'

Milton sank back in the chair. His face was contorted. 'Jesus! What did you say?'

'What could I say? I said nothing. And that's when they started threatening me with Vice.'

'So?'

'So it's been handed over to the DA's office.'

'Oh Christ! Have they spoken to Janelle?'

'How the hell should I know. I haven't seen her since, and when I called the model agency, they said she'd asked to be taken off the books for a month or two.'

The claustrophobia now reached unbearable intensity. Milton Rae had a sudden and almost uncontrollable urge to attack the woman, to relieve himself of the reality of her and the events she represented. He rose to his feet, and clutched blindly about him for an instrument. Then the matching terror in her own eyes jerked him back to his senses.

Christ, he thought. It would be so easy.

Biting hard on his fury with his back teeth, he stormed out of the house without another word.

Gunning the Lincoln down the expressway, he weaved through the evening traffic, the big car swaying clumsily as he

wrenched the steering this way and that. The tortured tyres expressed perfectly his own frenzy as he broadsided round the final
corner, and then skidded into his driveway three doors down. He
switched off the car and leapt out before it had stopped rolling.

Margaret Richardson met him halfway down the hallway,
wringing her hands on her apron. 'Yes! What do you want?'
Without realizing it, he was shouting.

She lifted a finger to her lips. 'Quiet, Mr Rae. Julian is asleep.'

'You can go, Mrs Richardson.' He controlled himself with
teeth clenched, fighting again the urge to attack, as her bovine
figure shuffled away down the corridor of polished wood, and
she retired to the bedroom suite she occupied next to Julian's
room. Every two hours she emerged from it to turn his son, to
relieve his agony of lying forever in one position, without the
ability even to flex his muscles against the mattress.

Alone at last, Rae poured himself another bourbon, and carried
it through to Julian's room. Standing over the bed, he looked
down at the sleeping figure. He should have been a fine, vigorous
youth. Instead he was something disgusting. His heart filled with
mindless hatred as he contemplated the living death, the foul
object that was his own flesh and blood.

When he was first growing used to the blow of the misshapen
replica of himself, the doctors and the useless comforters of the
church had tried to convince him that his first-born was merely
an unfortunate error. Hiding respectively behind science and an
assumed proximity to a traitorous God, they had reassured him
that Julian was just a genetic accident. The fault lay in the stars,
and not in his seed.

As if it mattered. Julian had killed the only woman he had ever
loved. And since then, with the passage of the years, Milton's
mind had become a distorted parody, like his son's body. Milton
almost revelled in it. It made him feel a kinship with the pitiable
object that lay grunting and snuffling in the bed in front of him.

'Look, Sergeant Mannering. This is crazy. Surely there's no

166

need for you to come to my office? I made a full statement on the morning of the tragedy!'

'Sorry, Mr Rae, sir. But the police surgeon's report has thrown up some new factors that I've gotta follow through.'

'Like what?'

'Can't say over the phone.' The reply was dour, and gave nothing away. 'It's just a matter of routine. Maybe it'd be easier for you to call into the precinct. It shouldn't take too long.'

The thought of the precinct filled Milton with dread, and he felt the quick clutch of claustrophobia again. He calmed his voice with difficulty, thinking fast.

'The precinct's a bit out of the way for me. Maybe it would be better here. Can you make it after hours?'

'Uh . . . no problem,' Sergeant Mannering replied, with weary resignation.

'I have a board meeting until five thirty, maybe later,' Milton lied. 'Can we make it around six?'

'See you then, Mr Rae, sir.'

It was 3 pm on the afternoon after Milton's encounter with Lou-Ann. Milton took a moment to clear his mind, and then started to act. First he buzzed his secretary. 'You've a meeting with Johnstone in ten minutes,' she reminded him.

'Cancel it. Cancel everything for the rest of the day, and hold all calls.

'And give me a private line, will you.'

He dialled Lou-Ann's number as soon as the line was put through. She let it ring for several seconds before she answered it, and her voice was coy and giggly. 'She's drunk,' thought Milton. And then a half-second later. 'Or she's with another man. Probably both.'

'Hi, honey,' she said. 'How's you?'

Rae cut across her false flirtatiousness. 'Where's Janelle?'

'Why, Milt. I don't know. What do you want her for?'

'Cut the crap,' he said harshly. 'Just give me her number.'

He scribbled it down and cut the connection without saying goodbye.

'She's not taking calls,' the woman at the model agency drawled. 'Nor messages.' Rae could hear the cud-chewing of her wad of gum. 'Perhaps another girl might suit you, Mister?'

Rae cut her short. 'Lady, this is police business. If you want to keep operating, you just tell me how to contact Janelle. And fast.'

The gum-chewing had stopped now. There was a moment's pause. Then the Brooklyn-accented voice queried: 'You sure? I don't wanna take the rap from Janelle if you're lying.'

'Just give me the number,' he snarled.

Two minutes later, as he listened to Janelle's home telephone ringing, he nervously doodled elongated patterns on the scrap pad in front of him.

'Hello.' The voice was cool and cautious, and thick with innate sexuality. Milton felt a sudden stirring in his loins.

'Janelle, where the fuck have you been?'

'Cool it, Milton. I don't have to account to you.'

He changed his tone immediately. He recognized at once that antagonizing this self-assured young model and hooker would get him nowhere. 'Okay, baby. I've been worried, that's all. I just wanted to know what was going on.'

'What do you mean?'

'Have the police spoken to you about that business the other night?'

'Sure.' Her voice was lazy, teasing him. 'The cops have been round a couple of times.'

'What did they say?'

'Nothin' much. Just checking it out, I guess.'

'Well, for chrissakes, what the fuck did they want?'

'Milton,' her voice was jeering at him now, 'keep your balls on. What's the panic?'

'Please, Janelle.' His voice dropped a semi-tone. The pleading in it was quite clear. 'Please tell me what they said.'

'Okay. But it wasn't said exactly. More kind of implied. You know what cops are like.'

'They kinda suggested that Jeremy had an asshole job before he took his life. They wondered if I knew anything about that.'

'So what did you say?'

He could almost see her languid shrug. 'What do you think I said. I asked them where they thought I'd found the equipment to do the job.'

'And?'

'And nothing, Milton.'

'Did they ask about me?'

'Sure. They wanted to know what your relationship was with Jeremy.'

Janelle deliberately refused to elaborate, threading his anxiety through the needle of her guile.

'And?' Milton was forced to ask again.

'Well, you surely didn't expect me to lie to police, did you?'

Ice gripped at his chest; he felt the muscles in his legs go liquid. If he hadn't been sitting, he would have collapsed. 'Christ, you bitch. What did you tell them.' He was shouting now.

'I told them that they had better ask you.'

'Do you swear that?' The wash of relief was expressed as a long sigh.

'Milt,' her self-assurance developing an overtone of smugness. 'I am the sort of girl who knows which side of the bread has the peanut butter on it.'

'That's just great. You're terrific, Janelle.'

'Sure I am.' Her words were languid and luxurious. 'And I'll be around, of course. For some peanut butter. Remember?'

'Of course, Janelle. I'll see to that. Anything you like. Within reason, of course. I'm sure you'll be realistic.'

'You can be sure of that, honey. Before you go, why don't you and I have dinner some time. Just the two of us. Without Lou-Ann. We can talk business.'

Again, Milton felt the stirring. 'Any time, Janelle. Any time you like.'

Sergeant Mannering arrived on the dot of 6 pm. His face was heavily fleshed under the eyes; beefy along the jawline. His skin was the colour of rubbed brick, and his eyes were alert under a glaze of tiredness.

He sat down beneath the Matisse, without waiting to be invited. The heavy proportions of his body pushed upwards and outwards, threatening the seams of the grey serge suit he wore; his lower shirt buttons in danger of being torn out by the roots.

'So,' said Milton Rae. He closed a slender folder in front of him, and leaned back in his chair. He was assured, secure in his own environment. He'd had time to think things through, and the call to Janelle had boosted his confidence. His role was clear – he was a top executive at one of America's largest corporations, donating some valuable time to help the police with their enquiries. 'What's all this about? How can I be of assistance, Sergeant?'

'Just a coupla questions. Routine stuff.' Mannering waved a podgy hand dismissively, as his eyes scanned the office brazenly, pausing briefly to register the distorted faces of the modern-art portraits behind Milton's head.

Milton looked at his watch. 'Fire away. I'm afraid I'm on a pretty tight schedule. The sooner we finish, the better.'

'Oh, sure. Darn right! The sooner the better.' Now he stopped his scrutiny of the office, and switched his attention to Rae. 'I'll come straight to the point. The autopsy guys said there was evidence of anal intercourse prior to Jeremy Farnsworth's death.'

Rae felt himself muster a facial expression combining distaste with astonishment. He considered that he had done it rather well. 'Oh dear. What does this mean? Had the boy been assaulted?'

'Well, there were no signs of what you might call forced entry. We don't know what it means, really. Just another one of those goddamned loose ends. Gotta be tied up.' The sergeant looked very weary indeed.

'Well, how do you think I can help you.' Rae was quite calm.

'Basically, we'd like to know whether you might have been aware of the victim's sexual preferences. As his employer, I mean. I know you guys go into a lot of background before you take anyone on.'

170

'Yes, we certainly do.' Rae laced his fingers across his belly. 'Especially when the work is of any sort of a confidential nature. But you must realize, sergeant, that Jeremy Farnsworth was not your run-of-the-mill employee. I took him on as my assistant as a personal favour to his parents, who are old friends of mine. You must know all this from the files, surely?'

'Yeah. I know. But did you know that Jeremy Farnsworth was a fruitcake? Gay?'

Milton Rae gave a slightly exaggerated pause for thought. Then he spoke. 'I suspected it. He was rather effeminate. But there was never any direct evidence.

'Anyway, Sergeant. It's so common nowadays that one just has to accept it, no matter what one thinks. Here at Cranston, we have a policy not to discriminate against employees on the basis of their sexual preferences, in the same way that there's no prejudice about colour or sex.' It was the sort of bland statement that was easy to make, and hard to contradict.

'I'm sure. I'm sure.' The square face lapsed into silence. It was as if he had suddenly run out of small talk with a fellow dinner guest. He sat without a word, his attention apparently captured by the mournful Modigliani on the wall behind Rae's head.

Then Rae could keep his silence no longer. 'Is there anything else, Sergeant?'

The policeman suddenly came to attention, as if startled. His eyes refocussed on the man in front of him.

'Uh? Oh. No. Thanks a lot. That's all.'

And that was it. Mannering simply rose from the sofa, and departed without so much as saying goodbye.

His silence and then his abrupt departure rekindled all Rae's anxieties. He could not help feeling the interview had gone badly. He was the victim of all that his own wild imagination could muster, and by the time he arrived home he had already gone through the worst of the consequences several times over.

It was not Jim Farnsworth that he feared. The possibility of a vengeful father was a human matter. It could be dealt with, by lies and by manipulation.

Far more terrifying was the prospect of his exposure to the Board. That he could not face. To be pilloried by his equals, to be rejected and cast aside, to be labelled pervert, and to drag the name of Cranston with him through the mud. That would be the ruin of everything he had strived for.

Shortly after he arrived home, as he was preparing to face the solitude of his second bourbon, the telephone rang. It was Fritz Clements – legal adviser to Jim Farnsworth.

His voice was unthreateningly soft. 'Hullo, Milt. Sorry to ring you at home.'

'No problem.' Behind the veneer, Rae's heart was sinking. He knows, he thought to himself. He knows. He must have guessed.

'I'll be brief. The DA has sent me a copy of the autopsy report on Jeremy Farnsworth. It doesn't make very nice reading.'

'Oh?' Alarm bells were jangling inside Rae's head.

'The report raises the question of an abnormal sexual assault prior to death. The DA's question is this: Could the boy have been coerced into a homosexual act which might have induced him to take his own life?'

'That explains why the police came back to see me again.' Rae took refuge in rational talk, as if it really was a light-hearted conversation.

'Can I be straight with you, Milton?' the lawyer asked.

'Sure. Go ahead, Fritz.'

'Did you screw the boy at any time on the night that he died?'

The bland question took Milton completely by surprise. Panic-stricken again for the fourth time in twenty-four hours, he blustered out a reply. 'Jesus Christ, Clements! What the hell are you trying to suggest?'

The response was delivered in the same perfectly equable tone of all the lawyer's conversation. 'Milton, you were seen going in there that night. Your car was seen outside. You were seen leaving in the early hours of the morning.

'The police don't know this, because they're not that interested. But I do.'

Milton sat in stunned silence. Now the blow had fallen, he had no words, and no reaction. He could only sit, slumped in his chair.

'Milton. You're a businessman. I'm a lawyer. We're both adults. I'm not moralizing on the issue. But I do know the facts.

'At the moment, this is between you and me. And you've committed no crime. Not in New York. Not unless anyone can prove you actually raped the boy.

'What I'm saying is that we can keep it between ourselves. But there's a price, Milton, just like there always is.'

'What do you want? How much?'

'Get off Frances Kline's back. Just leave her alone. Stop blocking her moves.'

Rae exploded. 'I don't believe this! You're blackmailing me to protect that bitch. What's she got on you?'

'If you don't, I have a fully prepared written statement that confirms your guilt absolutely. And a copy of it will reach the Cranston Board on the same day that you let me down.'

Clements had rung off then, leaving Milton Rae staring down at the receiver. His first reaction had been a wave of relief. At least nobody else knew the truth. Not yet.

So it was that fucking Kline woman behind all this. Well, he wasn't about to take orders from her.

He made a note on the pad beside the telephone. See Cutler, tomorrow soonest. Then he added, to himself: 'Let the bastard do some work for a change.'

CHAPTER FIFTEEN

She spotted Gray instantly, leaning over a counter at the far end of the airport arrivals lounge. He was dressed in navy slacks and a navy blue blazer, his white shirt open at the neck, showing a patch of deeply tanned and weathered skin. The sun-bleached thatch on his head reminded Frances of baled hay that has stood under the sun for a long time.

Frances suddenly felt very small and very shy, as she walked across the polished expanse towards him. He had seen her, but remained motionless, only his mouth moving, spreading into a slow smile. She felt as though she was being examined minutely, and she lifted her head high and walked proudly, living up to the casual free-spiritedness of the winter white cape and matching trousers-suit she had purchased a year before, but never worn – she had been keeping it, she realized, for this moment – off-set by an electric red beret set at a jaunty angle.

'You look gorgeous,' he said. His expression of pride showed that he meant it literally.

Frances had taken a connecting flight from Johannesburg to Cape Town, high over the vast plains of the Karroo, featureless from the air, the gentle undulations flattened, and the *kopjes* – flat-crowned, free-standing hills – disappearing into the soft khaki shading. Like so many first-time air travellers before her, Frances Kline was struck by the power of the sudden change as the massive folds of the Cape mountains came into view far below . . . the earth's crust like rolling waves of rock surging towards the Atlantic.

As the 737 canted to the right, losing height now, the slate-blue of distance was revealed as walls of hard rock brooding over soft green valleys. Dark forests clung to steep mountainside, above white-walled and black-thatched farm dwellings, scattered among the quilt-work of wheatfields and vineyards. Then came the dense population overspill of Cape Town, a sprawl of close-packed, shadeless slums, in sharp contrast to the red-tiled luxury of the white dwellings on the hillsides, with their blue swimming pools strung like jewels among the trees.

Nearing DF Malan airport, Frances saw for the first time the distinctive outline of Table Mountain, standing guard over the Mother City. She could understand the emotion with which Gray spoke of his beloved Cape.

Their meeting was rather formal, a swift kiss on each cheek. It was, Frances realized, the first time they had kissed, but it was as natural as if it was the thousandth. After that, words seemed superfluous, and silence was more comfortable and actually relaxed.

Frances remembered the shyness he had spoken about that first evening in London . . . a reserve peculiar to very big men.

He led her out to the car park, bright in the southern winter sun. Carrying her big Samsonite suitcase as if it weighed nothing, he strode towards a black Porsche 928, squatting frog-like, and he hoisted the suitcase into the trunk.

He held the V8 engine at a burbling fast idle as he reversed out of the parking place, and manoeuvred the low car out from among the mundane machinery that surrounded it. It was a car that suited him perfectly, thought Frances: under-stated power and a construction so solid you could feel it simply by touching the dashboard.

'First, to Cape Town, to your hotel,' he said. 'We'll check you in, and then you come home to *Goedgeluk*.'

'And what is *Goed* . . . ' Her tongue struggled with the unfamiliar Dutch word.

'It is my farm.'

Frances gave herself over to the luxury of having decisions made for her. It was a feeling she had forgotten.

Barnard drove the Porsche decisively through the Cape Town traffic, using its acceleration with delicate precision to slice smoothly through the stream without disturbing its flow. He swept the car down the curve of De Waal Drive, past pastel-painted semi-detached houses squeezed between modern highrise apartment blocks.

As they descended towards the foreshore of Cape Town, the bulwark of Table Mountain crags above them, Frances looked back to see the cable station, a nipple against the skyline, about to be covered modestly by a sheet of cloud that seemed about to pour over the edge and engulf the city. They drove past open market stalls huddled under colourful awnings, cheek by jowl with the glass flanks of modern skyscrapers. Chic high-heeled

175

women mixed with ragged, noisy half-breeds, the mixed-race descendants of early white settlers. They were called 'Coloureds' here, Frances had learned with some surprise – one of those strange quirks of a society where everybody has an official label of race.

Passing beneath a concrete tangle of fly-overs and inter-changes, they flanked the harbour, and turned past the grey-black factory buildings and warehouses of Paarden Island. Somewhere later, they encircled an expanse of lawn with a fountain at its centre, and a statue of a man in breeches on a pedestal.

Then they drove up to a small hotel with a little courtyard, and discreetly shuttered windows beneath a grapevine that ran along the eaves. 'I reserved a suite for you here,' said Gray. 'They will keep messages for you. Now you go and check in and sign the register, and we'll go home.' There was no point protesting. He had made up both of their minds for them.

It made the deception easy for her, and she signed the register without a second thought before running down the steps again to the car, feeling again like a naughty teenager on an illicit adventure. 'It's all part of growing up,' she thought wryly to herself.

'I'll have to come back tomorrow,' she said, as she slipped into the leather cockpit.

'Of course,' said Gray.

'Or perhaps after the weekend.'

'Of course.'

'I'll need to check my calls.'

'Of course.'

'Gray. You're not listening to me.'

'Of course.'

They broke into laughter at once, in unison, both glad of the relief.

Soon they shed the outskirts of the city, travelling north along the road to Stellenbosch. Frances was suddenly overwhelmed by fatigue, and she stifled an involuntary yawn, as the car drew up at some traffic lights.

'Sleep, Franci,' said Gray. 'We have more than half an hour. Sleep now.'

And he leaned across the divide between the seats, and took her face in both of his enormous hands. Turning it towards him, he looked over her, and kissed her on the lips.

It was gentle at first. He pulled away briefly, and she heard him draw breath sharply. Then he kissed her again, so hard that she felt as though her lips were being bruised. Only when a car behind them hooted did he look up, see that the lights were green, and accelerate away sharply with a quick laugh.

Frances lay back in the seat, the belt holding her tight into the bucket. She put her hand across to touch Gray lightly on the leg, and fell asleep like that, with nothing in her mind but the delicious numbness of her lips, and the animal strength and sexuality of the big man beside her.

She awoke with a change of the rhythm of the wheels, as they turned off the asphalt and onto a sand road. They were driving through a tunnel of ancient oaks, the setting sun filtered by the leaves to a darkness so profound that it took a while for her eyes to adjust. A carpet of acorns and leaves crackled under the tyres. The moist warmth of forest-floor smells filtered into the car. Barnard drove slowly, steering carefully over the ruts, giving Frances time to absorb the stillness of the huge trunks and warped branches.

They rounded a long curve in the lane, which revealed a pillared gateway at the end of the avenue. An old man with grey, peppercorn hair smiled a toothless greeting as they clattered across a cattle grid between the tall white pillars.

'*Goedgeluk*,' said Gray. 'This is where I was born. And my father, and my grandfather.'

They didn't see the house until they had rounded two curves of the crunching gravel driveway, between the thick greenery of oleanders. Then it was upon them, a great white-washed gable over a solid wooden door. High up on the façade, the figures '1802' were raised in relief.

The rest of the house stretched away from the façade. Grey-black thatch sloped over wooden sash windows, set symmetrically into wings that flanked the central gable. A wide terrace, now catching the afternoon sun, ran the full width of the house. An ancient bench waited alongside the front door, its sloping armrests infinitely patient, the wood burnished into a yellow glow by countless weary limbs.

Stepping from the car, Frances stood awed by the silence. Massively placid, the house rested in the dying heat of the afternoon. Somewhere in the distance, she heard the raised voices of men at work, calling in a strange and musical language, rolling in across the lawns and flowerbeds that surrounded the house. She saw a green lizard scuttle along a wall, its scales iridescent in the sun. The breathless air was broken momentarily by a sharp noise from somewhere in the house. A pot being put on a stove in the kitchen, she thought. And the brooding silence returned. The place was thick with family history, and Frances felt very inadequate. What did she have to offer, with all her New York chutzpah, to compare with these generations.

Barnard came round, and without a word put an arm round her shoulder. Now, from the side of the house, a thick-set Coloured man, as brown and wrinkled as the man who had greeted them at the gate, came towards them. Barnard acknowledged his deferential greeting in Afrikaans, and spoke a few more sentences. Smiling at Frances, the old man took her case from the back of the car, and carried it inside. 'That is Klein Piet. He was also born here. He and his wife look after me here. They are the oldest friends that I have.'

Frances wanted to ask where his family lived, but the silence of the house kept her tongue still. Gray cupped her elbow, and led her through to the front door. Broad yellowwood floorboards, hand-hewn and worn smooth with almost two centuries of polishing, stretched the full length of the vast central hallway.

Now she did speak, and was a little shamed by the inadequacy of her words. 'It's magnificent,' she said.

'It's one of the oldest buildings in the region,' said Gray. 'I've had to restore parts of it, but it is completely authentic.'

The room was divided by an intricately carved lattice-work screen, reaching almost to the black roof-beams. Frances could glimpse through it a door opposite her, opening to a sun-drenched courtyard. On either side, the walls were hung with huge oil paintings in heavy mahogany frames: portraits of Gray's forebears, craggy men and sombre women, staring down eternally on the room they had occupied in life.

'Is this a traditional homestead?'

'Yes,' replied Gray. 'Cape-Dutch. It has become a kind of museum, where I keep most of my family's heirlooms. Nobody lives here, but I use it as a sanctuary. Sometimes, I come home for two or three days at a time.'

He paused, then continued, looking shy again. 'It sounds strange, but it helps me to get in touch with the spirits of my ancestors.'

Frances felt her heart jump within her. They were alone. She was not intruding on another woman's home. This was Gray's house.

'Where do you live then?' she asked.

'On the neighbouring farm,' he said. 'About five miles away. It's called *Nooitgedacht*.

'It belonged to my wife's grandfather, and he left it to her. There's a modern house . . . electric light, a swimming pool . . . It's an easier house to live in, and better for the boys . . . at least when they were growing up. There's no electricity here, you see. And I didn't want to electrify *Goedgeluk* because it would have spoiled the whole meaning of the place for me.'

'I love this house,' said Frances spontaneously. She did feel like an intruder upon history, but a welcome alien. Now the expressions on the portraits on the wall did not look so accusing; and she discerned a twinkle in the man's eyes that she was sure had not been there before.

'So do I,' said Barnard. 'When I come here, I feel safe. I suppose it is the memory of my childhood. Here, I feel very close to myself. I don't usually bring anyone here. Especially not strangers.'

179

'And your wife?' The words fell out. Frances had been holding them in for too long now.

Gray shook his head. 'She has no interest in the old place. And she dislikes the way I become introspective when I am here. Rita has her own interests.'

She was relieved by his answer. 'Gray, I need to bath and change. I feel as though I've been wearing these clothes for days.'

Gray led her into the biggest bedroom she had ever seen. It was dominated by a vast four-poster bed, uprights made from stinkwood and yellowwood; the canopy of pale, undyed silk. Again there were portraits, and against one wall a heavy wooden washstand, with a giant porcelain wash-basin and a matching water-jug.

On a small table under a window, a vase of wildflowers caught the light on spiny petals. Many-paned French doors were at the opposite side of the room, leading onto the same courtyard. Now Frances could see it was paved with stone, and had a tranquil pond as its centrepiece. Water-lilly pads floated on the surface, and fat golden fish caught flashes of sunlight as they glided among the stems.

Gray left her alone, and Frances sank back for a moment into the softness of the imposing bed. She felt an expectant tremor between her legs, and allowed her hand to wander down over her body. She knew that she and Barnard had crossed the threshold now. There was no turning back. She wrenched herself from the comfort of the bed and her thoughts, and bathed quickly in the huge claw-footed cast-iron bathtub.

Then she slipped into her tracksuit and running shoes, and went in search of Gray Barnard.

He was nowhere in the house, which she walked through timidly, peeking into room after room. As she passed through the huge old farm kitchen, with its huge coal stove and racks of copper pots, a Coloured woman with downcast eyes nodded shyly.

She found Gray in the neatly-terraced herb garden beyond the kitchen among the scent of lavender, rosemary and wild thyme. He was on his haunches, tossing crushed grain to a flock of birds that surrounded him – squat birds, with the bare skin of their heads a bright, turquoise blue, and the plumage on their fat bodies a salt-and-pepper grey. Her sudden approach sent the flock scattering in a whistling frenzy and a clumsy clutter of wings.

'Oh, I'm sorry,' she said, as Gray turned. 'I scared them.'

Gray laughed. 'They're guineafowl. My special pets when I am here. And every so often, I eat one of them.' He stood up, and their eyes met for a minute, before both of them looked away shyly. The feeling of desire between them was electric, almost tangible. Then it was as if Gray completed the circuit, taking her hand firmly.

'Come,' he said. 'I want to show you something.'

He led her down a path past the rose-garden, and on through the apple orchard, leafless now.

Gray was walking fast, and Frances had to break into a run from time to time to keep up with him. The pressure of his hand was constant and firm. Finally, they passed through a gap in the hedge and they were in a vast and silent forest of pines. At their feet, down a small stone path, stood a tiny building, with creeping flowers overhanging its narrow windows, and a cross on a small gable above the front door. It was a chapel, and in a plot beyond it was the family graveyard, ancient stones standing guard over well-kept tombs.

'Can we go in?' Frances spoke in hushed and reverent tones.

'Of course. Come this way.' Gray drew a giant key from the pocket of his slacks, and opened the door.

The inside was tiny. Frances noted there were only ten seats, and a plain altar at the far end. They stood silently for a long time. Their bodies were touching, and she felt the pressure of him overwhelmingly. A pulse beat in her temple.

Gray turned quickly, and almost bore her out into the fading light. She seemed to float a little way into the pine forest, into a small clearing, with a dry soft floor of deep pine needles. Then he drew her towards him, and she surrendered to the urgency of his touch.

They kissed with a passion that surprised them both, his tongue exploring her mouth, hers flickering back teasingly. His hand had found the zip of her tracksuit and pulled it down firmly, before capturing a nipple between his fingers. Frances could feel how it sprang to attention at his touch.

Together, face to face, they sank to their knees, and he bent lower to kiss her face with almost animal intensity.

Then he broke free, and taking off his jacket, he laid it down on the carpet of needles.

Now he took control again. Frances had no power to resist; nor did she wish to. She abandoned herself to his strong hands, and meekly let herself be laid down on the soft fabric, making no protest at his roughness, as he stripped the clothes from her: first the top, leaving her breasts to fall free to his eyes, nipples pert and erect. She felt rather than heard him catch his breath, and then his head was down, and he was kissing her breasts, catching them in his teeth, and biting just into the threshold of pain.

Harshly he ripped off her tracksuit bottom. She heard the small tear of a seam giving way, and felt his hand between her legs, probing urgently, and she lay back and opened herself out to him.

He too was naked, and she caught a glimpse of his manhood, thick and slightly curved in the growing dusk, before he moved over her, suspending his magnificent size above her body, and entered her with one powerful thrust.

How, Frances wondered briefly, can a man so big fit so perfectly into my tiny body. Then he began to move, and her instinct took over again. She raced with him, rocked with him, emitting mews of pleasure and biting uncontrollably at his shoulders. Their eyes met as he drove again and again into her, and his rhythm began to accelerate, to grow frantic.

Simultaneously, Frances felt her own orgasm swell. She lay back without moving with it, letting waves of pleasure wash through her and over her, carrying her to a level of fulfilment that culminated in a long, shuddering cry.

It was the signal for Gray's own release, his own deep-throated cry of passion assuaged.

And then he crumpled half on top and half alongside her with a sigh that seemed to take forever. 'Franci,' he said. 'I love you. You are mine now.'

She held his head close to her shoulder, and buried her face in his hair. Yes, it was done. She had given herself to this man and there was no going back.

An hour later, flushed and slightly giggly, they sat eating fresh lobsters in the courtyard, under the deep African sky, studded with stars.

They had dressed hurriedly in the pine forest, Frances suddenly afraid that somebody might arrive, in spite of Gray's assurances. By the time they arrived back at the house, heavy shadows from the mountains around them had swept over the house and the garden. Darkness had fallen with surprising suddenness.

In the house, kerosene-fired Miller lamps – antique curiosities – shed a soft yellow glow that pushed the gathering gloom into the corners of the room and up under the thatch. The fragrance of jasmine and moonflowers filled the house through open doors and windows; and the early evening insects were striking up a deafening chorus.

Gray had fetched a bottle of wine from the cellar and they sat on the front terrace and drank the cool straw-yellow liquid. Frances could feel gentle warmth rising from the flagstones of the floor.

Gray spoke first, and Frances was content to let his conversation engulf her as she had been content to let him control everything about their lovemaking.

He told her about the flint-dry white wine they were drinking, about how his father had lovingly developed the vine-stock, with an instinctive knowledge of exactly how or when to graft or prune, when to reap, and exactly when to bottle the wine. By degrees, and by inspiration, he had arrived at the vine that best suited the soil of *Goedgeluk*, and had perfected the wine until it was one of the finest in the land.

'Is it the same for you?' asked Frances.

Gray chuckled. 'I'll never have the same feeling for the grape as my father. But we manage well enough. *Goedgeluk* estate wine is quite highly regarded; I sell all I can produce.'

As he spoke, Frances could feel the natural, unhurried pace of the man, and the tranquillity of his thoughts. It was a contrast, she realized, to the man she had known in London, who now seemed edgy and nervous by comparison. Here, he was restful, close to his country and the traditions with which he had surrounded himself. Or was it because of their lovemaking – so recent that the memory of him was still imprinted in her loins.

Reaching across, she took his hand. Stopping in mid-sentence, he answered with a quizzical smile, and a pressure in response.

Then he spoke again, suddenly deadly serious. 'Franci, what about your husband . . . ' He didn't finish the sentence.

'What about him?' she parried. It was too soon for this discussion.

'Do you love him?' Gray's eyes looked at her with piercing intensity.

She met his eyes. This was not the time for playing games, and he demanded an answer to a question she had avoided asking herself.

'Web and I are connected in so many ways that I can't explain,' she said. 'Things of the present and things of the past. They're all intertwined, and we take them for granted. But they cannot be denied.'

'I understand that,' said Gray. 'But it's not the same as loving him.' He paused, as if wrestling with himself. 'Does that mean you wouldn't leave him?'

'I've never had to think about that before.'

'Well,' he said. 'Think about it.' He stood quickly, and moved towards the dark shape of the door. 'I'll see about food.'

Frances could feel his jealousy and indignation bristling from his departing back. She understood, but the power of his posses-siveness frightened her too.

'Gray,' she said. 'You want more than I have to offer.'

At this, he turned, and looked solemn. 'Franci,' he said. 'I will take anything I can get.'

He disappeared into the dimness of the house, and returned a few minutes later, carrying a steaming, covered copper bucket, burnished and dented with decades of use. At his heels was the same old woman Frances had seen in the kitchen, bearing a gigantic tray of plates, sauce dishes, napkins and cutlery – fine old silver and crisp linen – which she set out on the table.

'This is Japita. She is Klein Piet's wife.' Again, the flash of a shy smile. Then he said: 'I hope you like lobster.'

'Are you kidding? It's my *best*,' said Frances. Suddenly, she was ravenously hungry.

'I picked it up in Cape Town this morning,' he said. 'It's quite a luxury now. Not like the old days. You could buy a bucketful for a shilling. But we would rather go and catch them for our-selves.'

Taking a white napkin, he plucked an enormous lobster from the pot. Wrapping it, Barnard cracked the carapace expertly, and opened it out. Succulent steam rose from the plump white flesh that he laid in a silver tray between them. 'Garlic?' he asked.

'What else?' said Frances, and watched as he took a silver sauce-boat, drenched the flesh with molten butter and crushed garlic, and then added a dash of hot peri-peri sauce.

They ate with their fingers. Gray kept up a steady supply of the shellfish, extracting pink morsels from the claws, and crescents of sweet meat from the bodies.

Before long, each of them was oily with melted butter, dripping down their fingers and smearing their mouths. Then Frances plucked a choice morsel from the dish, and fed it to Barnard. He clutched at her wrist, and engulfed her whole hand with his lips, his tongue licking between her fingers, before he took the food. It sent a fresh thrill of desire coursing through Frances, and when Gray in turn passed her a piece of the flesh,

185

she teased it delicately with her tongue before playfully nipping his fingers.

'Dangerous,' he murmured. 'Just like the Moray eels when we were fishing for these things. Stick your hand in a likely hole in the rocks, and if an eel fastens on, the only way to get your hand back is by ripping the flesh off. They have reversed teeth, and you often used to see Black women along the shoreline, with their right hands maimed.'

As Frances gasped her horror, he took her hand to his mouth again, and bit on the mount of Venus at the base of the thumb. Then he was leaning across the table, and kissing her again, licking the oil from her lips, and offering his to her.

'Gray,' she pulled back. 'What about Japita?'

'She's gone. So has Klein Piet. Come now. Come to bed.'

Their second lovemaking was as placid and varied as the first had been wild and brutish. First Gray lay back as Frances moved over him – a nymph on a massive statue – with her lips and flickering tongue, tasting every inch of him. Then she lay back as he mapped out her body's centres of pleasure. When they joined eventually, it was with slow luxury.

Then, too early to sleep, Gray brought the rest of the wine, chilled in a bucket of ice chips, and then the coffee pot from the old stove. Together, they lay in the great four-poster, and talked, Frances getting a little drunk as they laughed at shadows, sharing secrets and intimacies. 'Do new lovers always act this way?' Frances giggled. 'I feel innocent and childish. Please don't remind me of who I really am.'

'Would you ever give up working if you had me?' asked Gray.

Frances considered the question carefully. 'I think I need both, you and work.'

'I've never considered my life here as work,' said Gray. 'Making wine is a calling. Or a passion. Not a job.'

Suddenly, Frances envied him. She would have said the same thing about her work for the Cranston Group. But she doubted if she could have said it with the same conviction as he did. 'My job at Cranston is fun; it's just that I spend too much energy fighting battles that are politics. Nothing else. Often I'm not sure if it's that they're afraid I'll fail, or that I'll be too successful,' he said.

'I suppose it is important to you to succeed?'

'Of course,' said Frances.

Gray laughed dryly. 'Most people are afraid of success. In themselves, or in others. That's how the weak destroy the strong. Mediocrity is the real enemy of the achievers.'

Frances found comfort in his easy wisdom, and in the size of the man, at home in the vastness of his land. She saw herself as a small person – frenetic, working too hard, too often and too fast. Gray absorbed all that, with a silent acceptance that refreshed her.

An hour later, talked out, exhausted, she fell asleep, nestled in his massive arms like an oversized doll.

He lay still beside her long after his arm had gone numb, wide awake, eyes fixed on the play of shadows cast on the wall by the flickering paraffin lamp.

CHAPTER SIXTEEN

Frances awoke knowing exactly where she was, and who she was with. There was no clawing herself back to consciousness, no sudden realization. Just a warm and luscious feeling of security and comfort.

She was even a little dismayed at her lack of guilt, at her total freedom from any pangs of conscience. That in itself was exciting, and it struck a chord with the throb that still filled her body. She felt young and beautiful, vital and energetic. Every fibre of her body echoed her happiness.

She was lying on her side, as she always did when she slept soundly, snug in the curve of Barnard's own body. She didn't wake him, just lay and enjoyed the rhythmical push of his stomach against her back in time with his breathing. When she did stir, quietly, so as not to disturb him, she was surprised to hear him speak.

'I've been awake for hours. I didn't want to disturb you.'

'And I've been lying still to avoid waking you.' They started the day by laughing together, and then, suddenly he kissed her hard, the stubble of his chin harsh against her face.

When Frances came back from the bathroom, Gray had gone. She climbed back into the huge welcoming bed, not ready herself to break the spell of the night. Outside, the morning chorus of forest birds flooded in through the windows. It was already light, not yet 7 am. Plenty of time for the day – and she would have to get down to work.

Then Gray came back into the room, walking awkwardly backwards, to manage the tray he was carrying. 'Breakfast in bed,' he said. 'Service with a smile.' At that moment, the towel round his waist became unfastened. Unable to catch it, he let it fall to the ground. 'And not much else,' he added with a laugh.

The tray bore coffee, cream, a huge bowl of strawberries, and another of what looked like lumps of dried bread. Gray put it on the bed, and they sat cross-legged on either side of it. He poured them each a big mug of coffee, and then picked up one of the hard-baked hunks from the bowl and dipped it into his coffee, pulling it out just before it disintegrated, and transferring it quickly to his mouth. 'This is the way we eat our rusks down on the farm,' he said.

'Rusks?' said Frances. 'They look more like *chalah* that's been broken up and left out to dry.'

'That's exactly the way the farmers' wives make rusks,' Gray replied. 'They bake soft white bread. When it's done, it looks like a lot of round balls stuck together. In Afrikaans, we call it *mossbolletjies.*'

'Well, whatever you might call it, that's *chalah*. I'm a good Jewish girl, so I should know.' She smiled, and dunked a rusk into her coffee.

188

After that, with barely a passing thought for her diet, she took a big bowl of strawberries, sprinkled them with sugar, then drenched them in cream. When she had finished them, she sat back with a contented sigh. 'Now I understand what they mean by "the cat that got the cream",' she said. 'That was delicious.'

'Franci,' Gray replied, looking serious. 'I am not quite sure what you have done to me.'

'What do you mean?'

His eyes belied his solemn expression. 'I want you.'

'Again?' She laughed. 'Again!'

He took her hand, and drew it across into his lap. He was hard again, and her hand lingered in wonderment, slipping inside the towel to feel the silky skin and hot flesh. Gray bent forward, and whispered intimately into her ear.

The words shocked and thrilled her. A new feeling was burning within her – a wildness she had never known with Webley. Her husband had never spoken to her with such blatant sexuality.

She heard herself moan as Gray scooped her buttocks off the bed and sank his teeth into the soft flesh of her belly. He moved down between her legs, and she moaned again as his tongue found the growing bud of her desire.

Then he was off the bed, pulling her legs roughly towards him. The sight of her drew an involuntary cry from his throat. 'Oh God, Franci, I must have you.' He drove into her again and again until she came to a shuddering climax that seemed as if it would never end.

Afterwards, she bathed again, but her mood changed now. She was done with luxuriating, with enjoying letting Gray set the pace and make all the decisions. Now it was time to work.

She emerged to find Gray drinking fresh coffee on the verandah. 'The life of a country gentleman suits you,' she smiled. 'But not me. I have work to do. You said you could help me find the *Dorothaneum* plant. Where do I start looking?'

'First things first,' he said. 'I also promised to show you my "kibbutz" as you persist in calling it. Then we can look for this

189

plant. Though I don't know what sort of quantities we'll find.'

'Gray,' she said, a little exasperated. 'I'm really on a tight schedule. Couldn't we leave the farm until another time?'

'Well, maybe the full tour can wait. But I want you to see it first. I'm afraid I must insist.'

He was teasing her, playing games. Somehow she trusted him, and didn't protest as he poured her another cup of coffee.

Before she had time to finish it, Barnard was on his feet. 'Come on, Franci. We've got a lot of ground to cover today.' He led her to the Porsche, parked in a lean to, and fired up the engine, warming it for a minute before he reversed out and burbled carefully along the dirt road.

He drove down the avenue of old oaks from *Goedgeluk*, and onto the main highway. Frances, accustomed to Webley's erratic and frenzied progress in a car, enjoyed the way he handled the Porsche like a precision instrument. His driving seemed to epitomize the self-assured direction in his own life.

With the windows up and the heater taking the chill out of the morning, the speeding car was quiet.

'Tell me about your wife,' said Frances, keeping her tone deliberately light.

'Rita and I were married when I was twenty and she was eighteen. Both our families looked on it as a perfect match. It meant that *Nooitgedacht* and *Goedgeluk* could be combined to make a larger and more profitable farm, and also that the land stayed in the family. For us, it wasn't so perfect.' He laughed grimly, and shook his head.

'You didn't elope with her, did you?' Frances was free from jealousy now, but filled with curiosity.

'Absolutely not. You see, Rita and I had to get married. Not that she was pregnant. Heaven forbid.'

'Why then?'

They were swinging round a long bend, Barnard choosing a smooth line that took the car from the outside to the inside of the curve, where he put the power on again and drifted back to the left. Then he took his eyes from the road, and looked at Frances.

'For you to understand that, you would have to know something about Afrikaners,' he said. 'Otherwise it is not easy to explain.'

'Tell me anyway,' she said.

'Well, in the eyes of the traditional Afrikaner – and both our families were very traditional Afrikaners – sex is only for the begetting of children. It is part of an old Calvinistic heritage, and the Calvinists can be very hard on you if you let them. They preach a fear of God so profound that it is a sin to be happy in the way of human happiness.'

'They sound like the Lubavitch Jews,' said Frances. 'All pigtails and piety, and a joyless life in return for a better hereafter.'

'Well, one long Sunday afternoon, her father caught us in the shed at *Nooitgedacht*, behind some wine vats. We were only kids, and we were doing as kids do; discovering the difference between men and woman. 'It was quite innocent, really. A few shared kisses, a hand on the breast – outside the skirt – for a few minutes. When he found us, I was playfully pulling up her skirt. It would have gone no further – she wouldn't have let it. But it was enough.

'Her father was enraged. Especially since it was Sunday, the Lord's day. He ranted and raved about the work of the devil, that I was the son of the devil, and a whole lot more. Within another day, it was a scandal throughout the valley. The incident was exaggerated out of all proportion. Rita and I were shunned, and I remember people whispering behind my back after I had passed them in the street.'

'I can't believe it,' said Frances.

'It's true. Eventually, the *dominee* – the priest – was called in, and he gave the two of us a long lecture about carnal sin. He quoted from the Bible, mostly in High Dutch. He thundered and he raged for two full hours, then he told us that the only way God could forgive us was if we got married.'

'For Chrissakes!' said Frances. 'So you did?'

Gray sighed deeply. 'Young, and living in that sort of society, it isn't difficult to be pushed into such a decision.'

'That's terrible. It's worse than a Henry Miller play.'

'It certainly isn't a formula for a happy marriage,' said Gray. 'And it was the end of any pleasure in our sex life. Rita became devoutly religious, and from then on, sex was only for the begetting of children. We had two boys who are now grown up, and she devotes most of her life to working for the church.'

'Wow,' said Frances, somewhat at a loss for words. 'It makes Web and me seem so normal. We just fell in love, went to bed when we wanted to, and then got married.'

At the mention of Web, she again sensed Gray drawing back into himself. Then came an interruption from outside. They had driven into a deep cutting in the road, where it sliced through the shoulder of the land mass tumbling down to the sea, when Gray had to stop suddenly to avoid a troop of impertinent baboons who refused to give way. They were squabbling over a broken pumpkin in the roadway, and Frances was delighted when one jumped onto the car's hood, and began peering through the windscreen, ducking its head from side to side as it tried to fathom out its own reflection.

'Look,' she trilled. 'She has a baby clinging to her belly.'

'Keep your window shut,' said Gray. 'They bite.'

As they accelerated away again, Gray did make an effort to acknowledge her home life. 'Tell me about your son,' he said.

'David is very special to me,' she said. 'He looks like a male version of me, with a bit of Web around the mouth. Now is a difficult time for us. He needs his independence and I have to give it to him. That's why he's in London, instead of New York. I think he ran away from me. It's Catch 22. I want to do so much for him. I could set him up in business, help him to be successful. But I dare not. The fact is,' she went on musingly, 'that I am his role model. He strives to be like me – and it makes him hate me. That's true whether he succeeds or fails. He has to make it on his own.'

Then she smiled, and squeezed Gray's knee. 'So you see the sort of person I am now . . . I'm just another Jewish Mama in disguise. When I bring you your first bowl of chicken soup, then you'll know and see the real me.'

They were silent a while, the noise of the tyres and the murmur of the engine filling the car. Then Gray spoke.

'You're different from me, Franci,' he said. 'Perhaps it is because I'm an Afrikaner, or perhaps it's because I'm a Protestant. But I believe a man should earn for himself what he wants out of life.'

'You didn't,' she countered. 'You had your farms handed to you on a plate!'

'It's not the same,' he said. 'When my father handed *Goedgeluk* to me, he burdened me with a tremendous responsibility. He gave me a living thing, that needed to be fed and cared for like a child, every hour of the day, every day of the week. It was not a gift. It was my heritage.'

'So what's the difference. What I want to give David is his heritage too.'

'It's not the same. Your success belongs to you and the corporation. You can't hand it down.'

Then his mood changed again. 'Now, tell me about your business in South Africa. You need *Dorothaneum*, and plenty of it. Is this for the rejuvenation drug that you told me about?'

'The very same,' said Frances. 'I'm up against a deadline on it. The Board gave me six months to finish development, or else the project will be aborted.'

'That's crazy,' said Barnard.

'It's corporate politics,' said Frances. 'So you can see the reason for the rush. It's all so complex . . . I'm beginning to think I'd rather have let the competition do the development, and go into the market as a follower.'

'That doesn't sound like Frances Kline,' laughed Gray.

'No, I suppose I don't really mean it. But we've had so many problems, especially in stopping the active ingredient from deteriorating. At first, it didn't seem possible that we could get it to last longer than a couple of minutes. Anyway Rocher is working on that one . . . Then there's the problem of making it in large quantities. He says *Dorothaneum* holds the answer. So it's crucial to the success of the project, absolutely essential that I find a source of supply.

'So here I am.'

'Okay,' he said. 'I get the point.'

They passed through a little village of clustered cottages, neat gardens and an old church and vicarage, near a working water-mill. 'Mamre,' said Barnard. 'It means "among the oaks". It used to be a Moravian mission, now it's a haven for artistic types with beards.'

Half an hour later, they reached the sea, and swept past an azure lagoon, surrounded by distant mountains. In the shallows, what seemed like thousands of flamingoes made a floss of pure white and delicate pink. Below the level of the road, the beach stretched white and endless, disappearing into a salt-haze from the breakers. On the open ground, wild flowers grew from among the arid stones. 'Saldanha Bay,' said Barnard. The name was vaguely familiar to Frances, but the strange beauty of its setting was something new. Her eyes were trained on the scrubby hills of California, and the closeness of New York and Europe. Here, the emptiness seemed to have a wild and lonely song of its own.

'How far to the farm?' she asked, rather curtly. She was fighting against her own impatience to be doing things, trying to stay calm and in tune with the sensuous pleasure of the Porsche on the roadway, and Gray's placid farm.

'Another half an hour,' said Gray. And he drove on fast along the wild and deserted sea shore.

After that time had passed, when the road had veered away from the coastline, he slowed outside a rustic gate, and manoeuvred over a ricket cattle grid.

Then he parked just inside the gate, and got out of the car. '*Eerstevallei*,' he said. 'Its means "First Valley". From here on we walk.' Frances heaved a sigh of relief that she was wearing her running shoes . . . the road that led inside the farm was stony and rough, and deeply rutted where the mud of wheeltracks had dried in the sun. From where they stood, a wide patch of wild and rocky ground stretched towards the sea, dropping away out of sight. It was dotted with wild flowers and scrub-like plants, the grey-green of their succulent leaves a subtle contrast with the deep blue-green of the Atlantic Ocean far below. The roadway ran parallel to the shore, and then out of sight round a bulge of steep hillside. 'The valley is beyond there,' said Gray. 'Not too far.' And he set off with his long stride modulated to match Frances' quick bouncing step.

Around the corner, the prospect opened out into a softly-curving valley, rimmed with high mountains which seemed to trap the clear blue sky. In the centre was a large barn with windows set in; and spaced out across the flat floor of the valley were little homesteads, each the hub of its own web of little fields, hen-hutches and animal pens, butting up against one another on the flat valley floor. The hillsides did not appear to be cultivated, although there were vehicle tracks at regular intervals, and scorched land at the upper boundaries where fire-breaks had been burned.

As they entered the valley, Frances was struck by the combination of moisture and heat, even on a cool winter's day. She mopped at the sweat that suddenly started at her brow, and opened the zip of her tracksuit top.

'This is the co-op,' said Gray. 'The land stretches right across, up the valley out of sight and right down to the shore. You can feel the humidity. It's caused by temperature inversions: the ring of mountains traps hot moist air in the plains. That's what makes it so fertile here. That, and the fact that the floor is made from centuries worth of alluvial top-soil.'

He reached down beside the road and plucked a handful of rich loam. 'Smell that,' he said. 'That is the smell of life. Each of the tenant farmers runs his own little plot. He is allowed to develop it in any way he chooses, as long as a majority of other tenants agree. We find with the ethnic mix of people that there's an equally wide choice of crops, so there haven't been any fights. Yet.' He grinned, clearly proud of what he was showing her.

'What do they grow?' she asked.

'All sorts of things. The Africans grow Sorghum, a Chinese family has terraced and flooded their plot to grow rice. It's been very successful too – selling to health-shops and vegetarians. Almost everything seems to grow well here, given irrigation in the dry months. That's why we have so many dams.' He gestured around, to where small reservoirs were strung along the stream bed in the lowland floor. 'We built them all ourselves.'

They had reached the barn by now, and Frances lingered outside in the thin sunshine as Gray went inside. Then he emerged, and strode over to a battered Land Rover parked outside. He vaulted aboard, and gestured Frances into the passenger seat. 'Come,' he said. 'I want to show you the view from the top.'

The diesel engine grumbled reluctantly to life after some coaxing, followed by some rather rougher work with the accelerator pedal. Then they bumped away along the rutted road, Frances getting thrown out of her seat as they crossed a patch of big half-sunken boulders. 'Can't afford to slow down,' said Gray. 'Might never start her up again if she stalls.' And he laughed out loud as he hurled the rickety old workhorse over the rudely carved track across the valley floor, splashing through the river and sending sheets of spray into the air. Then he jolted on straight up the ever-steepening side of the mountain until the old vehicle groaned to a stop.

He leapt down, and lifted Frances down as he had from the taxi in London. This time he did follow through with a long, hard kiss on the lips.

'And here,' he said, 'you can see the communal crop.'

'Where?' asked Frances, scanning the valley now laid out beneath her.

'No, not there. Right here, where we are standing.'

Frances looked closer at hand, and saw that the ground around her was now thickly carpeted with the low grey-green spines of the plant that had been growing wild at the entrance. She looked up beyond the firebreak and the boundary fence, now close by, and noticed that although the same colour was in evidence everywhere she looked, it was only in isolated clumps, not the continuous sea that surrounded her.

She picked up a leaf and examined it, feeling how the flesh and hard, dusty skin stored moisture away against the beating sun.

'This is our export crop,' said Gray. 'The one we use for the cosmetics that we produce in Paris.'

'The one that cured your rash when you were a boy?'

'That's right.' He smiled down at her.

'What is it?'

'It's a member of the *mesembreanthemum* family. It's called *Bokbaaivygie*. Translated literally, it means "Goat Bay Fig".'

'Strange name,' said Frances, breaking the spiny leaf and looking at the jelly-like flesh and the triangular cross-section.

'Scientifically,' continued Gray, his face immobile again, 'it's known as *Dorothaneum*.'

CHAPTER SEVENTEEN

Frances placed her knife and fork neatly crossed on her plate. 'There's only one thing for it, Gray. You're going to have to join the project.'

Gray leaned back, and raised one eyebrow. He said nothing, but the expression on his face said it for him. Then he threw back his great head, and gave a shout of laughter.

'No, Gray. I'm serious. I don't mean you should come to New York, or become an employee, or anything like that. But since you control supply of the essential plant, and if – as you say – it has to be processed on the spot, then I can't see PS-21 working without you. And also, you have ready-made production facilities in France. The whole thing ties up, you see. Gray, what an opportunity, especially for the co-op. It's not as though either of us is doing it for personal gain. C'mon, Gray. Say you'll do it.'

They were eating lunch on the vine-shaded verandah of an old country inn, about twenty miles from the farm. Frances had barely stopped talking for an instant on the drive except when Gray was answering her machine-gun fire questions. Suggesting that he should be involved in PS-21 in some way was the culmination of her conversation, but the idea was so personally thrilling to her, as well as being the most obvious business solution, that she had approached it with the utmost caution. Little did she know that Gray had seen it coming all along.

First, she had cross-examined him on the cultivation and reaping of the plant.

Bokbaaivygie, she learned, grew wild all over the western Cape, but local peasant farmers invariably had at least one plant growing at home for its curative properties. The *Eerstevallei* experiment was, as far as Gray knew, the only place where the plant was grown in large quantities.

Bokbaaivygie bloomed only in the spring, turning the countryside briefly shell-pink with its sudden effloresence of paper-thin petals. That was the time when concentration of the active ingredient in the sap – the amino-butylic acid, the discovery of which had led Rocher to the plant in the first place – was fifteen to twenty times higher than during the rest of the year.

'We have only about three weeks to harvest the crop,' Gray told her. 'And then it must be processed within the next few days before the potency starts to drop.' Gray was able to make a section of his fertilizer plant available for the highly seasonal processing, and then he transferred the extract to Paris, in liquid form, where it was used as the basis for his small range of cosmetics.

'The cosmetic side isn't big enough to use our full possible growing capacity of *Bokbaaivygie*, but it gives a nice predictable return, and the whole operation remains a manageable size,' he said.

Then Frances had explored the possibilities of starting Cranston's own *Dorothaneum* farm. Gray told her that the right conditions would be easy enough to find in the area, but it would take more than two years before she could start to reap significant quantities of leaves. 'You will be able to plant soon,' he had said. 'The middle of August is the best time. But then you will have to wait until the third spring, twenty-seven months later, before the plants will be strong enough to survive the cropping, and big enough to give you any leaves.'

'Hmmmm. Doesn't fit too well with a six-month deadline,' said Frances ruefully. The bottom line was obvious to them both. Gray Barnard's co-operative controlled the world supply of *Dorothaneum* as well as the processed extract . . . at least for the next three years.

They had eaten hurriedly – first *paté* and coarse brown bread, then a fragrant stew, with a pulpy, fibrous vegetable sharing the rich gravy with tangy chunks of mutton.

'What do you think of the food?' said Gray.

Frances took a reflective chew on the subtly-flavoured and altogether unfamiliar delicacy, and said: 'Interesting. It's a bit like young asparagus, or, ummmm, a kind of potato. But different.'

'It's *waterblommetjie bredie*,' he said, and enjoyed her perplexed look at the strange collection of syllables. 'It means "water-lily stew". Those are the buds of the flowers. See what we Afrikaners can do with plants!'

They finished with strong coffee that tasted as if it had been boiled for a long time. 'Railway coffee,' Gray called it smilingly. Then he asked her what she wanted to do for the rest of the day. 'A swim in the Indian Ocean? Or the view from the top of Table Mountain?' It was, Frances realized, the first choice he had given her since she had arrived.

'I want to work,' she said. 'Can we get back to the farm. I need to call New York.'

Gray had remained non-committal on the question of his co-operation with the Cranston Group, but she could see that his

199

mind was working. He hadn't rejected the idea. In the car on the way back, she had covered everything possible about Prostaglandin-S, even information she hadn't revealed to anybody else beyond her own researchers. She was sure that if she communicated her excitement about PS in this way, then Gray too would be infected.

'I plan to launch in two phases,' she had told him. 'First, PS-21 – to get the market accustomed to the concept of a "youth drug", hence the 21. It is a mild form, with minimal potency. Our research has shown that it has a marked effect in slowing the ageing process of skin, and that the results are visible within the second thirty days of use, because the initial softening action on the skin is quite dramatic. Quick results, and easy to see. To help people get used to the idea, especially women, the drug will be in pill form, to be taken one a day. Like a contraceptive pill, and packaged and taken in just the same way. Though of course missing a day's dosage of PS-21 will not be quite so potentially disastrous! The important thing is to get the trend-setters in every country to use it. Should be easy enough. I can't see any Hollywood star rejecting the chance of hanging on to their youthful allure for a few more years. And if the international jet-set take on the idea, the bulk of the market will follow on.

'This is really all to prepare the ground for the real Prostaglandin-S development. The one that retards the whole cosmetic ageing process, and not just that of the skin.'

Gray let out a low whistle. 'Rejuvenation! You really mean it.'

'Well, not exactly,' said Frances. 'PS can't actually reverse the process, but it sure can slow it up. The case histories are really remarkable, though the results depend on the age of the person taking the drug. It is most effective between the ages of thirty-five and forty-two,' she said. 'Something to do with the stability of the hormonal balance. Before and after that time, the results are not nearly so significant.'

'Good God,' said Gray. 'That means we'll end up with a world full of thirty-five-year-olds who will never die.'

Frances laughed. 'It strikes a lot of people that way. But I'm afraid I can't offer immortality. The effect is mainly upon the skin, hair, nails, and muscles. It only improves appearance.'

Gray gave another whistle. 'If you're right, everybody in the world will want it.'

'Eventually, yes,' said Frances. 'But that will take quite some time. It's a huge innovation – and the market won't be able to accept it all at once. There are different cultures to consider, different religions. It's not going to be easy. But it can be done.'

Gray was fascinated now. 'But waiting before releasing the major product . . . won't that let the competition in ahead of you?'

'Yes and no,' said Frances. 'PS-21 will always be the first, and PS-35 will follow eighteen months later. Within another year, I plan two more brands. So we won't leave any obvious gaps in the market. Besides, competition is good. It gives credibility. After that, it's just a question of improving the product, and keeping the market standards high. And of course, looking for ways to get production costs down.

'Gray, now you can understand why I've been so excited. Prostaglandin-S products are the biggest thing . . . since I don't know what. Bigger than the aspirin. It's a quantum leap . . . in science, cosmetics, marketing – in every possible way. It's going to change the world, Gray. Imagine growing up, knowing that you will never look old. No grey hairs. No wrinkles. No sagging flesh. Gray, I don't want to put pressure on you. But I need you in. Even the France thing just adds up perfectly. I'd more or less decided already to manufacture in France, because it's still perceived as the centre of the beauty culture.'

She was looking very businesslike now, in the passenger seat of the Porsche, where yesterday she had been languorous. But she still looked very feminine, thought Gray, as she sat with her knees together, and her serious eyes.

'I'd like to buy up your complete operation. What do you say? Would you be prepared to sell?'

'The thought had crossed my mind already,' admitted Gray. He was driving slowly now, as he swung off the asphalt and onto the dirt road of *Goedgeluk*. 'It struck me as a very expensive way for you to get the drug that you need.'

'Not really. Not in the long run. It means that Cranston secures control of the existing supplies of the extract, and that gives us a three-year head-start.'

'Certainly, I would consider it. If it is important to you, then I would sell the business to you . . .'

Frances cut in. 'No, Gray. I don't want that sort of decision. That's a personal judgement, and we're going to have to keep business matters and personal feelings apart. You sell only if it makes sense to you and to the co-op.'

'Okay,' he said. 'Then it becomes a matter of how much you are prepared to pay. But Franci, you must understand one thing. I would never consider selling the co-operative. It's not a business exercise, not an agricultural enterprise, that could be bought and sold. It is an important social experiment, and as long as I am alive it must stay directly under my control.'

He drew up outside the great front gable with a crunch of gravel, and led her inside the old house, now so welcoming where before it had seemed withdrawn and slightly disapproving. Frances felt at home here, at ease with herself and her surroundings.

Five minutes later, waiting for tea on the shady side of the terrace, she spoke again.

'Then we could form a joint company, here in South Africa between Cranston and the co-op. Of course you would be in control. That company will deal with crop procurement, processing and export. The co-op will remain independent, and share in the joint company . . . in return, the joint company will own all the co-op's *Dorothaneum* crop.'

'Franci, it's sounding better and better.'

At that moment, the tea arrived – fine old silver, and delicate old china cups. It was an exotic Indian tea, which Gray served her weak and without milk.

Licking her lips, she continued. 'In France, the Cranston Group must retain control. We will take over the factory lock,

202

stock and barrel. You will have to drop your line of cosmetics, because PS is so much bigger. As part of the purchase price, the co-op can have a minority percentage of the equity. With the sort of profits we're expecting, that will more than compensate for the loss of foreign income. I'll have to do some homework, but something around ten per cent.

'Don't say anything now, Gray. I must leave tomorrow morning. Tell me then. I want us to enjoy the rest of the time we have together.'

'Franci, must you go tomorrow? Stay a little longer.' His voice was peremptory; the switch from business matters to their personal relationship was instant.

'Gray, I can't stay in your life. You know that.'

'Then you must come in and out of it when you can.'

'I am not free, Gray. I am not able just to help myself to freedom. I told you I can't give you what you ask.'

'Why not?' said Gray, his voice very quiet, his face a little pale. 'If you love me, why not? What are you waiting for . . . your husband's approval?'

His words were harsh, and they hit Frances like a slap. Gray had homed in with perfect accuracy.

She always sought Web's approval for her actions, and the recent apparent withdrawal of that approval had left her doubtful and insecure.

'Gray, don't be angry. I can't think only of us. We both have families. I am not ready to run away from mine. That doesn't mean that I don't love you. God knows, I am more certain of that than I have ever been of anything. Let the future take care of itself. Tonight is for us.'

He stood, his sudden anger still narrowing his eyes, and walked to the low wall at the edge of the terrace. Lifting one foot onto the rail, he looked outwards. In the foreground, a Hoopoe speared beetles on the lawn with its curved beak, its crest a Roman mane of feathers. In the distance, blue-hazed mountains raised their buttresses to the sky. 'Franci, we must look ahead,' he said.

Frances was suddenly struck by the thought that he looked just like an advertisement for life insurance and told him so. Fighting to control her incongruous mirth, she said: 'Yes, Gray, but not only for ourselves.' One second later, she was laughing; and a minute after that, Gray was laughing too, and hugging her.

'Okay, Franci,' he said. 'For now, I'll play it your way. But it won't be forever.'

After bathing again in the gigantic claw-footed tub, Frances telephoned home. She wanted to speak to Stacey. But had to wait until 6.30 pm when it would be 12.30 in New York, and the little girl would be home from school for lunch.

Stacey answered, then Web had taken over. 'When will you be back,' he had asked tersely.

'Day after tomorrow,' she had replied. 'I'll be home about lunchtime.'

Then: 'Where've you been?'

'Web, I'm on a research trip. I've been in the field.'

Running away with her lie, amazed at how easy it was, she continued: 'Spent last night in a little country inn . . . I've seen some amazing countryside. Web, you should come here.' She immediately regretted having said that. What if he should accept! But he cut across her.

'Jo-Beth's been trying to reach you for two days. Some crisis with your precious Professor.'

Suddenly, Frances felt her gut wrench with a pang of anxious guilt. 'What? What did she tell you?'

'Nothing, Fran. Really, I wasn't that interested. Call her, why don't you.'

After he had rung off, Frances held the instrument against her breast for a few minutes, trying to analyze how she felt after the first words she had spoken to her husband since sleeping with another man. She felt no guilt, only exhilaration. She decided she was feeling too damn good about herself. She dialled through to her office in New York.

When she returned to the terrace, Gray was in the garden. She walked quietly up behind him, flung her arms round his waist, and put her head against his broad back in the golden evening light. 'Rocher is ill. Very ill. I've just spoken to his assistant, Rademeijer. Evidently they've had a breakthrough. The old man has found the catalyst he needed to combine *Dorothaneum* extract with Prostaglandin-S to give it sufficient shelf life. If only he could live to see it on the market.'

Gray turned, and took her head in his hands. 'Franci, come here. I'm sorry.' He enveloped her in his arms. And then: 'Your idea of a joint company is a good one.'

'So, does that mean yes?' she said.

'Why not? Yes,' he said firmly. 'Why not.'

He took her in his arms and kissed her with increasing passion.

Gray made love to her roughly that night, thrusting down hard into her body as she lay spreadeagled on the bed. It was, she thought, like losing her virginity again. She had never known lovemaking as powerful as this, in all her marriage to Web. It wasn't so much lovemaking as possession, and she allowed her body to be rocked in rhythm with its almost vicious desire.

'Make it last, Gray. Make it last,' she said.

Only one thing marred her ecstasy and that one thing kept hammering in her head. Rocher had collapsed.

The sky had filled with heavy black clouds as Gray drove her to the airport early the next morning. A slash of sudden lightning, and an almost simultaneous thunderclap that sounded as if it came from inside the automobile made Frances flinch. Barnard reached across and touched her, his massive hand over hers. 'Divine retribution,' he had said. 'That's what the priests would say.' Then he smiled dryly.

Almost immediately, huge drops of rain had begun to spatter on the windscreen in a violent crescendo, and within a minute they were engulfed in what seemed to be a solid wall of water. The rain drummed deafeningly on the car, a torrent that overwhelmed the screen wipers. And then the hail fell – first small crystals of ice, then larger stones, threatening to crack the windscreen. Gray pulled off down a side road.

'It'll be over in a few minutes,' he shouted over the din. 'I'm going to wait until it passes.' By the time he had pulled under a roadside tree, they could barely see ten feet ahead.

Sitting, isolated by the sheets of rain and hail, they held onto one another across the space of the seats. They pressed close together, feeling the comfort of their body warmth through their clothes.

'Franci, I love you.' Gray's hoarse whisper rose above the roaring around them. 'And I'm going to fight to have you.'

Frances knew what she should have said. But she said nothing, and held him close, her fingers twirling through his thick blonde hair.

The storm passed as quickly as it had come. The sun shafted back in from the remaining empty-bellied clouds, and the air smelt clean and freshly washed. The mountain peaks glistened where fresh springs caught the light, and the Porsche's tyres swished on the roadway, an audible reminder to them both of the perpetual passing of time and distance.

Neither of them spoke again. Then, at the airport, Gray said suddenly: 'Franci, I'm coming with you to Johannesburg. I'll fly back here tomorrow.'

'No,' she said, her tone low, and without emotion. She had got used to the idea of saying goodbye to Gray. She couldn't go through it again. 'Gray, please put me off outside the airport. I don't want you to come in.'

'I don't want to say goodbye.'

CHAPTER EIGHTEEN

'Sorry, Max,' said Frances. 'I was dreaming. I must be jet lagged.'

Maxwell Bennis gave what he imagined was a benign chuckle. 'Just got back, have you, Kline? Where from this time?'

'South Africa,' she said. 'This morning. And I've brought some pretty terrific news with me.'

'Good. That's great, Kline. Let's hear it.'

He was blustering. That much was clear to her. As usual, he was at sea, and would need reminding of all the details. Frances glanced at one of the wartime photographs on the wall behind him. It was strange to think that this man who had once commanded a PT boat had grown so ineffectual with age.

Briefly, she brought Bennis up to date on Rocher's breakthrough, the joint venture with Barnard and the co-op. 'And that's about it, Max,' she concluded.

'I've got to hand it to you, Frances. When you move, you move fast.'

'I'm preparing a full memorandum for tomorrow's executive meeting,' she said. 'I'll see that you get a copy this afternoon, so you have some time to go through it.'

'Sounds good, Kline.'

There was something about his tone that made Frances wary. She looked up, and there was doubt in his eyes.

'Max,' she said. 'There's something on your mind. Let's have it.'

'Quite frankly,' he said through a cloud of smoke, 'there's something that worries me.' He chopped his hand vaguely through the air. 'Don't misunderstand me. I think you've done a great job, and I want to . . .'

'But?' said Frances firmly, forcing him to come to the point.

'It's just that you're so strong-headed. The Board's already finding it difficult to swallow the whole PS thing. It was damn difficult for me to persuade them to give you this extra six months. Damn difficult.' He rubbed his face, looking exasperated. 'Now you go and get the thing involved in South Africa, of all the places in the world to choose . . . there's rumours of a disinvestment scare. Was there really nowhere else where you could look for a supply of this wonder-plant?'

'No.' Her reply was emphatic.

'It's not only that, Kline. The business in the newspapers about the Professor has made a lot of people very jumpy. The feeling is that you've been on thin ice for a long time, and that if I don't hold you back, you're going to have a big fall.'

'Who says that?' Frances' eyes were blazing. 'Milton Rae?' Frances was sure now that it had been Rae who tipped off the press, and who was behind the problems at Board level.

Bennis shrugged uncomfortably. 'He's one of them, but he's . . . '

'He's behind all of it!' she spat out. 'Face it, Max, the man is scared shitless. He knows that my Prostaglandin product is going to beat his, and be the biggest thing we've ever done. And we all three of us know that he should never have given it to me in the first place. Max – he's running scared. Surely you can handle him?'

The old man looked dubious.

Frances could not prevent her sudden flare-up. 'For Chrissakes, Max. Do you want me to confront him?'

'Absolutely not. I forbid it!' He glared at her from under bushy eyebrows. 'I want to go through your report on what you've got us into in South Africa.

'But I can tell you this. I don't like it, Kline. The sooner you can buy this South African and his growers out of the project, and out of anything to do with the Cranston Group, the better.'

Frances said nothing.

Then Bennis changed tack. 'Kline, I assume that this is all within your monetary discretion?'

She held his gaze. 'Max, I need to ask you this again. Do I have your support?'

208

He heaved himself up from the slouch he had sunk into while she spoke. 'Kline,' he said. 'It looks as though I don't have much option.' He sighed. 'You've done it already. Alright, I'll do my best.'

'Good,' she replied. 'Because later today, I am announcing PS-21 to the world press.'

'What!' This time he really did sit erect. 'But that'll be before the meeting tomorrow has had time to discuss it. You can't do that.'

'Of course I can, Max. And what is more, it's already too late for me to stop myself.'

'Kline, your impetuous actions are going to ruin you. I just hope they don't ruin me too, or Cranston. You'd better be damn sure that you've got a fallback position.'

Frances smiled sweetly. 'Haven't I always, Max?'

'All went through perfectly, boss-lady,' he said. 'The end price for the Marley was just a fraction over 1.6 million dollars. We've had all the papers through, the last came yesterday.'

He giggled, his eyes small behind the thick glasses, a red polka dot bow-tie keeping time with the shrill laugh. 'When I told Jonathan Blake we'd got the hotel for seventy-five per cent of his offer that they originally refused, he hummed and hawed in that pompous way of his.' He shook his head, delighted with his own image of the Englishman's discomfort.

'Good. Then we can leave him to it. Because I need you for the PS project now. Gerry, we have a runner.'

Rademeijer was documenting the last of Rocher's research – now she filled in the final gaps of the past five days, the news of the final breakthrough, with details of the press launch she had scheduled. 'The world will know about Prostaglandin-S tomorrow,' she said with a smile. 'I'm going public immediately to secure our position.'

'Position with who? The competition? . . . the Board?'

'Both.' She faced him squarely.

'That's fantastic!' Even now, she thought, she was still able to astonish Rule by her fast and fancy footwork. The thought both pleased and amused her.

She filled him in on the planned joint venture with Barnard. 'The deal must be signed by the end of the week – and we've got to be one hundred per cent certain that we have exclusive access to their entire crop, for as long as we need it. Check it all out, will you Gerry? And after that, I'm afraid you're going to be back on your travels for a while.'

Rule's podgy face fell. 'Not London again,' he said. The prospect clearly filled him with genuine horror.

'No. Paris. But only for a week or so. I've decided to set up the manufacturing base in France, and I've arranged to purchase Barnard's existing cosmetics plant as part of the deal. The premises are big enough, a modern building in an industrial estate on the southern outskirts of the city. But the production facilities will need to be updated and expanded a whole lot. I need you to be there on my behalf; then Randy Wise can take over production.

'I figure the best way to give PS-21 a European image is to use a genuine Paris advertising agency for all the campaigns. There's no way we can hand over control, though, so we will have to buy into a small Paris agency. I want you to look into what's available, and make sure it's in the correct *arrondisement*. Even the ad agency has to have a classy image. Can you leave tomorrow or the next day?'

He was looking a little dazed, as if waiting for another spasm from his ulcer. Paris, he thought. Could be worse. But Mary. Now she was another problem.

He nodded grimly. 'Okay, boss-lady. But I want to get back real soon, please.'

'And I need you back, Gerry. PS has got an enemy inside this corporation, and I might want you here to help me fight him.'

The resigned look on Rule's face was instantly replaced with one of startled concern. 'Who? How do you mean?'

'It's pretty obvious who it is,' she said. 'It's Milton Rae. What

I don't know is if he is operating out of simple jealousy of our potential success with a product he cast aside – or whether he has some deeper motive. I also don't know just how far he's prepared to go.'

Rule looked stunned. 'But that's crazy.'

'Yes,' said Frances. 'That's the problem. What are the limits to a crazy man's actions?'

'Could he kill off PS-21?'

Frances looked serious. 'Yes.'

'Jesus. Can't you stop him? What are you going to do?'

'Nothing yet,' said Frances. 'I want to give him the chance to show his hand.'

'But by then it could be too late,' said Rule. 'Why don't you take it to the board? They have the power to stop him.'

'I can't do that. I'm not in a position of strength. Rae has influence with the Board members, and he has already used it to prejudice them against PS-21. If I raise it with the Board, I create an issue, and I don't have any real evidence. Gerry, we just have to wait. But when Milton makes his next move, you can bet that we'll be ready for him.'

After Rule had left, Frances had an appointment with Joe Mitchell. Before he came, she quickly scanned through the pack he had prepared for presentation to the press that afternoon, with the information embargoed until midnight that night. The first media to carry the information would be the early-morning radio and TV news shows, leaving the field clear for a big splash in the morning newspapers.

It was a comprehensive document, explaining PS-21 in full, both in layman's terms and in some of the scientific detail. It contained selected case histories, supported by 'Before and After' photographs. It stressed the importance of the product, and contained a formal photograph of Frances at her desk. There was a photograph of Rocher as well, and brief biographies of both of them.

It had been drawn up several months before, and modified in detail as the project developed. She needed now to be absolutely sure that it was correct in every respect, that there was no information in it that could not be substantiated. One flaw would be enough to destroy PS-21.

Joe Mitchell was clearly excited when he came in. His young face, framed with close-cropped brown hair, was glowing with importance. The forthcoming launch was the biggest thing he had ever been involved with. He had been anticipating a break like this for years. Frances ordered all calls held, and for the next two hours she briefed Mitchell until he was word-perfect, and knew exactly how much information to make public, and how much to keep back. 'We want something in reserve for the time that the product gets to the shelves,' she told him.

Frances had been incubating the format of her launch for even longer than Joe Mitchell. Today's news release would be the 'generic' launch, introducing the public to the concept of a rejuvenation drug, and telling them to expect the product within the next six months.

The dossier would be sent to local and international press and TV. From New York, it would then be beamed out all over the world.

Joe had also produced short films suitable for display on TV news shows – clips of laboratory tests; animated cartoons showing how the PS-21 effect worked; close-up skin shots of the 'Before and After' subjects collected; and more material on Frances, showing her at her desk, relaxing on the beach, and jogging through the early morning mist.

There was also historical footage of Professor Rocher, receiving his Nobel Prize. The TV and newspaper editors would find everything they needed, in just the form Frances wanted to present it to them.

Finally, she was satisfied. 'It's over to you now, Joe. And we'll see tomorrow how the world's press reacts. Good luck!' And she smiled briskly as she dismissed him from her office.

After Joe Mitchell had left, Frances allowed herself to slump in her chair for a moment. She was exhausted, and almost emotionally spent. And she was dying to get home.

First, she buzzed Jo-Beth. 'Any word about Rocher yet?'

'Nothing doing. I've been phoning every half-hour since you got in. Same answer every time . . . he's asleep, and they have strict instructions not to disturb him.'

Frances felt the alarm rise within her. Something was seriously wrong.

'Get me a cab, please Jo-Beth. I'm going over to The Barrister. But first, I want you to connect me to the South African, Gray Barnard. I gave you all the details this morning.'

'Gray? Gray,' she heard herself say over the telephone. Simply saying his name brought back the twenty-four-hour-old memories of his face, his body, his huge nakedness.

'Franci, my love,' his voice so clear he might have been in the next room. 'Where are you? Did you get back safely?'

'I'm in my office. I'm missing you. How is *Goedgeluk*?' She could smell the wood-odour of the yellowwood floors in her nostrils, the woodsmoke from the giant stove.

'It's empty,' he said, his voice genuinely forlorn and wistful.

'Gray,' she said, businesslike now. 'I have spoken with Max, and the legal side is being done.'

'What did he say?'

'Nothing much. The South African connection is very sensitive here. There's the start of a real hype on disinvestment, and he's worried about that.'

'Tell you what, Franci. Why don't I come to New York. I have to go to Kuwait next week. I could make a trip of it.'

The thought shocked Frances. Gray in New York. Out of the question. She just wasn't ready yet for that. In any case, like most South Africans, Barnard was expecting to receive a sympathetic hearing, and a chance to make his case. It just wasn't going to be like that – the crusaders weren't interested in the details, only the moral issue. They wouldn't want to deal with

213

anyone involved with the system, no matter what side they were on.

'There's be no point, Gray.'

There was a silence from the other end.

'Please don't withdraw from me, Gray. I need time.'

'When will I see you again?'

'In Paris. Soon. I promise.'

The bedroom in Rocher's suite at The Barrister was darkened by drawn curtains, the pale afternoon sunshine showing faintly round the edges. Rocher was in bed, lying on his back, and asleep. His spectacles were balanced on his chest, and a book lay open where it had fallen beside the bed. His hair, tousled by the pillows, was a cloud of white around his relaxed features.

Frances was astounded by his appearance. His cheekbones were standing out, his lips were pale. She stood irresolutely at the door, not wanting to wake him, then tiptoed over to the bed. She had folded the book and was picking up his glasses when his eyes opened.

She tried to help him to sit himself up in the pillows, but he was too weak and fell back, his head to one side.

Frances examined the old man carefully for signs of the devastation of his disease. They were plainer for her to see now. He was visibly shaky, and the pain had left its mark.

How ironic, she thought, that in unlocking the secret of eternal youth he had himself grown so old.

She had wanted to call her doctor, had begged him on several occasions. 'He can help you, perhaps.' But Rocher had persistently refused the offer just as he had declined her invitations to come home with her to Westchester, even for a weekend.

'Frances,' he had said the last time they'd talked, 'I am dying. We both know that. My only request is that I be left to die in peace. I do not want to go to hospital; I simply want to stay in the hotel where I can be by myself as I have been my whole life. The last thing I want is a strange doctor around for my death.'

Her eyes filled with tears. Sitting beside him on the bed, she bent over him and put her arms round his thin shoulders.

Then she stood and bustled around the room, straightening the pile of books on the bedside table, re-arranging the old wrist-watch and cuff-links, pouring him a fresh glass of water from the chilled carafe, knowing he probably wouldn't drink it. She was busying herself to control her almost overpowering emotion, but feeling her uselessness all the more keenly as she did so.

Later, when he didn't waken, she bent forward and kissed him on the forehead, pressing her lips to the dry furrows of his brow. She had never kissed a man as old as he, she realized. 'I will come again tomorrow,' she whispered into the deathly silence.

She switched the music off. It intruded on the pleasure of returning home. Like a horse to its stable, she thought. She felt she had been away very far, and for a very long time.

She had hardly stepped from the car when Stacey came flying down the porch, jumping up at her and almost knocking her over. With squeals of delight, she buried her face in Frances' hair and hugged her painfully around the neck.

Frances looked up to see Web appear on the porch, a broad grin of welcome on his face. Then he strode across the asphalt to hug her too, before hoisting her cases out of the trunk.

By the time they reached the front door, they were a regular parade – Stacey hauling Frances' overnight bag clumsily, Web bringing up the rear with her big suitcase. And then Lexington came romping down the hall, and hurtling full-tilt into Frances, sending her cannoning back into Web with the force of the charge.

It was a perfect homecoming, thought Frances. What was it inside her that made her want anything more than this?

Webley had a real fire burning in the family room, and a lump of coal fizzled and spat a greeting to her. Sitting on the sofa, Frances unzipped the bag and hauled out presents for everybody, including a rubber bone for Lexington. By the time Webley

215

returned from stowing the suitcase, the little girl was already playing with the black plastic doll dressed in African beads, and the soft felt elephant with ridiculously large ears.

'This is for you,' she smiled at Webley, handing him a bottle of *Goedgeluk* estate wine, wondering if she'd ever have cause to regret the choice. It's from an estate that I visited while I was looking for my plant. I found it, by the way. Rejuvenation is on!'

'Great, Fran. Glad to hear it. Send me some on Skid Row, won't you.' He went into his wino-parody routine, slewing around the room and pretending to drink from the bottle, much to Stacey's vocal delight. Then he went to the bar, to fix them both a drink.

'What have you been doing?' she asked him.

'Hard at work,' he replied. 'In fact, I was hoping just to grab a salad now and then get back to it. I've got to keep running now I have the speed up.'

'Why not wait and have some sandwiches a little later with me and Stacey,' she said. 'I haven't eaten since yesterday, and I sure could do some damage to a piece of lettuce.'

'Okay,' he said. 'Then I want to get another hour in before I call it a day.'

A few minutes later, with Stacey taking her new toys away to introduce them to her old ones, and Web withdrawn into his study, Frances was left alone with a sense of loss that was a sharp contrast to the joy of her return home. She was a different woman now, she thought. She was a faithless wife. Nothing would ever be the same again . . . and yet Web was just the same as he had always been. He never would change, she thought. And that was the trouble, because she was changing all the time.

Suddenly, she felt the need to call Gray. Then she realized that there was a good chance that Web might pick up his extension phone and make a call of his own, and he would overhear her. She felt trapped, and wished she had stayed at work. But that was absurd. She wasn't trapped – Web allowed her as much freedom as she wanted. Was that the trouble?

On an impulse, she made up a tray of coffee and biscuits and took it through to the study. Web was at his desk, fingers poised above the keyboard, studying the screen of his word processor.

'Coffee, honey?' she said.

'No thanks.' He had replied without looking up.

'Why don't you come for a walk. The fresh air will do you good, if you've been cooped up in here all day.'

'No thanks, kiddo. You go.'

Left with no other alternative, she took the tray out of the room without another word.

She went to the family room, and picked up the latest copy of *Fortune* that she had brought home from the office. Then she threw it down. She couldn't concentrate.

Then she began to pace around the room restlessly, examining her old ornaments as if she had just discovered them for the first time. She put some Dvorak on the turntable, and turned the volume up loud. Still unable to settle down, she began to straighten out the room.

Glancing out of the window, she saw Webley strolling across the lawn into the dusk. Without a second thought, she went through to the hall telephone and dialled Gray Barnard's number. Before it had started to ring, she hung up.

When she slipped between the sheets that night, waiting for Web to finish his bath and join her in bed, she wondered whether or nor he would want to make love. He had been so occupied since her return that she had been unable to assess his mood. Even in their shared bath a few minutes before, he had been withdrawn, soaping absently, and not saying very much. He was cheerful, though, and she had discarded any fear that he might have guessed.

If he approached her, she couldn't refuse him. She would have to let Web make love to her – she had no option. But for the moment, true intimacy was something that she shared only with Gray Barnard.

She awoke at 6 am, and immediately pulled on her tracksuit and went for a long run, revelling in the early sunshine and the prospect of the day ahead.

Today was the day of the worldwide press launch of Prostaglandin-S, and she was pumped up with the prospect of public reaction to four years of unremitting hard work.

At 10 am was the executive management meeting. She was going to announce that PS-21 was ready for production. There was only one thing to do. Present them with a *fait accompli*. And if she was going to have a fight on her hands to keep the project going, she was looking forward to it.

Over towards Long Island, another early riser peered out at the dawn. Battered and bewildered by the events of the past few days, Milton Rae looked rather small and rather rumpled. He smoothed out the creases in front of the bathroom mirror, then dressed hurriedly, and drove to Cranston Towers. He too had a big day planned.

His suite of offices was deserted when he walked in at 7 am. He had just sat down at his desk when he was amazed to hear his private telephone ringing.

It was Fritz Clements. 'Hi, Milton. Tried to get you at home, but you'd gone already. I'm glad I caught you.'

'Yes, what is it?' Rae's voice would have sounded as harsh as he meant it to, had not a small tremor given the game away.

'Just checking, Milt. You've got a big meeting on today, haven't you? Well, I am quite sure you won't forget our little arrangement, will you?

'You stay off Frances Kline's back, and your little secret is safe with me. If not . . . ' He let the thought hang in the air.

'You're her messenger boy now, are you?' Rae's voice was full of scorn. 'You're Kline's whipping boy. Well, I know exactly how I stand, then. And you'll know what to do. Let me tell you, Kline doesn't scare me. So you get off my fucking back.'

The last words were shouted. Milton hurled the receiver back on the rest to cut the connection.

CHAPTER NINETEEN

Frances breakfasted to the sound of her own voice and the sight of her own face on TV, paying tribute to Professor Rocher, his work on the drug the news media had dubbed the 'Fountain of Youth'. In the car, she heard her voice on the radio. And when she arrived at her office, an array of newspapers was laid out on her desk – from the *New York Times* to the *San Francisco Chronicle*, and everything in between. All of them had given yesterday's announcement front page coverage. Joe Mitchell had done his job well.

In the main, the reports were positive and encouraging. The drug was variously described as 'another triumph for American know-how', 'the product that mankind had sought from the dawn of time', and – by one doubting Thomas on a Deep-South daily – as 'the seed of complete moral ruin'.

He had found a religious leader to describe the new drug as 'the work of the Devil . . . an evil to rank with the heresy of Darwin's theory of evolution'. Some other religious comments were guarded but not as hostile, weighing the benefits of good mental and physical health against the sin of vanity, expressing concern at the effect of rejuvenation on the standards of the American people.

But this was not a question that concerned many of the newspapers. They had seized on the announcement as a child with a new toy – and were occupied in shaking it around and holding it up to the light.

Most of all, Frances appreciated the editorial comment in the Chicago *Tribune*, whose thinking was much in line with her own. They anticipated problems from the older generation, who had missed out on the opportunity; and the 'back to nature' alternative youth culture, among others. They also saw the announcement as significant as that of the motor car.

'When the refrigerator was invented, it was rejected in Britain as 'unsaleable'.

When the motor car arrived, the law decreed that a man had to walk in front waving a red flag.

When the aircraft was invented, they said:

"If God had meant us to fly, he would have given us wings."

Now we have the prospect of cell rejuvenation. There will be those who will identify this with the ultimate potential of eternal life. They will try to ban the drug not on the grounds of its actual effect, but on some imagined potential.

To these, we offer an update on the old quotation.

"If God had not meant us to fly, he would not have given us the brains to invent the aeroplane." '

It so perfectly expressed Frances' own views that she made a mental note to send the editor the first available free sample of PS-21.

Then she had turned to the continually growing pile of telex messages on her desk. Some expressed congratulations, one or two suggested joint ventures, a huge pile were from foreign newspapers, seeking more information.

She was fascinated to find one from the Pentagon, marked HIGHLY CONFIDENTIAL. It requested an early meeting to discuss the military implications of the drug. It could mean trouble, she thought, or it could mean an enormous contract.

Then she came across one from the White House, from a presidential aide requesting more facts for the President.

These she put to one side. She wanted to deal with them personally.

There were also countless demands for television news interviews, and invitations to appear on discussion and chat shows. Those from the NBC and CBS in the States, and from the BBC and ITV in London, as well as one each from Japan, Germany, France and Italy, she would accept – the rest she would pass on to Joe Mitchell.

Frances did not enjoy television appearances – the medium was too much open to interpretation by the producer, who could select unflattering camera angles and edit out favourable parts of interviews. But she recognized the need, and that her youthful good looks were a powerful point in her favour.

Now she worked through her diary, fitting in what she could over the next week. It would be a time of high stress, but it was essential in order to have the public licking their lips and eager to buy by the time PS-21 reached the shelves.

Frances Kline was the last to arrive in the boardroom of Cranston Towers for the executive management meeting. Her fellow divisional presidents were already seated round the big table. Maxwell J Bennis sat at the head, smoking a cigarette, and inclining his head to his right to listen to what Milton Rae was saying. They were talking in low tones, while the rest of the executives were apparently engrossed in Yale Duke's views on the prospects of the New York Mets and the Yankees in the forthcoming baseball season.

'Good day, gentlemen,' she said as she strode to her vacant chair. They broke off their discussions, and variously nodded or mumbled their greetings.

Bennis opened the meeting immediately, sticking to the formal progress of events as if there were nothing more important on the agenda than the increase requested in the staff canteen budget. But the way he kept discussion brief, and the eagerness of everybody to move on, showed that they were all keen to get to the matter of her Prostaglandin project as quickly as possible. She was sure they had been discussing it before she came in, and wondered if they had reached any consensus in her absence. Most of them would have learned more from the papers that morning than they already knew from within the Cranston Group, and she anticipated some hostility for that reason alone.

When her turn came, Frances ran through the memorandum she had drawn up. She gave a detailed report on the proposed

221

manufacture of the drug, and reminded them of the distribution deal with Epipharm. Milton Rae's mask was stony and expressionless. She outlined her budgets and her proposed expenditure; and explained the broad outline of her marketing strategies. Every face in the room was staring at her.

Finally, she dealt with the negotiations she had been through with Gray Barnard, and the acquisition from him of a ready-made cosmetics manufacturing plant in France. She was getting rather good, she reflected, at talking about Gray like any other business colleague.

There was a long silence after her report, that was eventually broken by Maxwell Bennis.

'Well, I think Kline ought to be congratulated. Apart from the unfortunate press leak concerning the Professor's arrival in New York – and that fizzled out before it became serious – the whole thing seems to have gone pretty well.' He took another draw on his cigarette, balancing the ash, this time successfully. 'In fact, it has all gone very well indeed.'

The table nodded their agreement. Frances found the reaction uncanny. It was all going too smoothly. When was Milton Rae going to attack?

'Thank you, Max,' she said. 'And, of course, the rest of you. It hasn't been easy, but it looks like we've made it. And I'd like to put it on the record that without the assistance of Professor Paul Rocher of Lausanne, we would not have been able to get the product off the ground.'

Yale Duke was the next to speak. 'The only thing that concerns me,' he drawled, 'is the connection with South Africa. The Board's views on dealing with South Africa are quite clear.'

This was more like what Frances was expecting. Her answer was couched mildly, but was barbed. 'The Board's views have always been flexible enough to accommodate the current political climate in the States. And the Board is quite amenable to my division's continuing involvement with the Athabasca mines – mainly, I imagine because Athabasca pays big dividends.'

'True, true,' replied Duke. 'But I'm sure I speak for all of us here when I say we'd still rather not involve ourselves in South Africa if it can be helped.'

'For my money,' said John C Cunningham, head of Shipping, 'I'd like to see us cut all ties with South Africa. I can see anti-feeling build up quickly now . . . with Tutu winning the Nobel for Peace. I know we're stuck for now with Athabasca. But let's not add to our problems with another link to the country.'

AJ Moretti of Heavy Industries was next to chime in. 'We stopped supplying to South Africa five years ago. I feel pretty strongly on the subject, and Frances knows it.'

Other voices joined in, cut across by that of Merill Lamb. 'Forget the morals of the thing,' he said. 'We could argue those all day. The real problem is press reaction and public opinion. There's simply no way to make South Africa sound acceptable.'

Frances Kline held her tongue, allowing them to voice their objections. She had expected all this.

'Surely there are other options,' asked Duke. 'If there isn't any alternative natural source, couldn't we cultivate the crop in the US?'

'There's Chile,' Frances answered. 'But quantities are small, and there are no established cultivated crops. In any case, many of the same objections apply to Chile . . . as a fascist dictatorship the government there doesn't exactly endear itself to the campaigners for human rights.'

'Gentlemen, I have considered the alternatives carefully. Even if we could find a country with the right politics to go with the right geography and the right weather, it would still take a minimum of three years to establish a crop if ever.'

'You might remember setting me a six-month deadline at our last meeting. That set the seal on it . . . even if it had been possible to wait three years, while all the competition climbed in on the act. I'm afraid I had no option.

'And now you have no option. Cranston is committed.' She wondered how many of them realized she had made the press announcement specifically to block any counter-moves from within the executive.

Milton Rae could have been reading her mind. For the first time in the meeting, he spoke: 'That's because you made the press announcement too soon.'

'Too soon for what, Milton?' She felt the tension and pressure in the room now that her main adversary had broken his silence. 'My job is to secure our leadership. Any delay would have jeopardized that.'

'Being first is your obsession, and it's high risk,' replied Rae.

'My obsession, and my carefully planned route to making my division a market leader.' She shuddered inwardly. Web had often called her obsessive, bound to her work like some drug-crazed addict. Rocher had used the same word. But she had asked herself a million times . . . did she know any high achiever who wasn't obsessed?

'I think it is goddamn irresponsible. You've committed Cranston to a major project that most of us consider fraught with serious political and business problems,' continued Rae.

'Milton.' Frances spoke with conviction. 'I have kept this executive fully informed of every move I have made. I have acted within my mandate. And I am also quite sure the rest of the executive can speak for themselves.'

'I am referring to the press announcement,' Rae persisted. 'I am quite sure you purposely released the information to the media before this meeting, knowing that you would then commit the Group before we had a chance to object.'

The silence in the boardroom was palatable. Each of the men looked straight ahead, with the exception of Rae. He flicked his eyes from one to the next, seeking affirmation from at least one of them.

Cunningham broke the silence. 'It's just too damned politically sensitive. I accept all the reasons for being involved in South Africa but I feel we should take immediate steps to establish our own source of supply, so that in two years we can get shot of this Barnard character. In the meantime, we use him as much as we can without any future involvement.'

Frances' immediate reaction was to defend her association with

224

Barnard, but she was more conscious than ever of the need to remain objective.

'The South African connection is the source of only one ingredient in this project,' she said. 'The action is in France. The South African connection is a technicality. I don't intend to go public on that fact.' She looked directly at Rae and added, 'And I hope no-one else intends to. Far more important at the moment is the question of security, and the danger of industrial espionage.'

'That's a red herring . . . ' began Milton, but Frances sailed on regardless.

'And if there is any political criticism, the Cranston Group can be proud of its association with the kind of progress Barnard has going there. The report I gave you all today describes how the *Eerstevallei* Co-operative is a multi-racial organization representing a much more significant blow against the apartheid policies of the South African government than anything we would achieve.'

She began to assemble her documents, and replaced them in her briefcase.

'What is required here, gentlemen, is a vote of confidence. And I shall leave the meeting to allow you to decide.'

As she stood up, she caught Maxwell J Bennis's eye. He looked shocked, struck dumb. She felt the stunned surprise of the rest of the men round the table as she calmly stood up and walked to the door.

Only when she had closed it behind her did she allow her emotions to show. Never before had she taken such a drastic step She had always been prepared to argue her point of view, and then go with the majority. That was one of the things she'd learned working for a large organization. But this time, she felt too strongly. She had to show strength.

Walking out of meetings was, she reflected soberly by the time she returned to her office, one of those things you could do only once. That might yet turn out to be once too often.

* * *

She was surprised to find Gerald Rule in her office when she returned . . . and he was equally surprised to see her. He was dropping off a memo on her desk, and instead passed it to her. 'Here's the final on the Marley,' he said. 'But what are you doing here? Aren't you supposed to be at the meeting?'

'Milton has got to all of them,' she said tersely. 'Either they give me their confidence, or else I'm out.'

'Come on,' said Gerry. But sensing that Frances had said all she was going to say, he walked heavily from the room.

Half an hour later, Maxwell J Bennis tapped on her door, peered round it almost timidly, as if expecting attack, before he walked in. 'Is that you, Kline? You shouldn't have done that,' he said, looking solemn. 'In any case,' he went on, 'you have our vote of confidence. Don't do it again, Kline.' He was looking stern, bushy eyebrows knitted over her faded eyes.

Then he grinned. 'Still, I must say I admire your guts.'

His smile was infectious, and Frances couldn't help herself grinning in return. Feeling conspiratorial, they laughed together. 'I wonder,' said Bennis, 'if this corporation will ever have a woman as the Chairman of the Board.'

'You look good,' said Petra Lang, smiling across the table at her. 'In fact, you're shining like a beacon. You must tell me how you do it, Fran.'

'I starve myself, and I work myself into the ground,' smiled Frances.

She and Petra met for lunch religiously once every couple of months at pre-arranged dates set months in advance. Her first instinct had been to postpone today's meeting because of the pressure. But she needed a break. She needed a confidential chat that had nothing to do with either Prostaglandin-S or the Cranston Group. Besides, neither of them had ever cancelled before. At a corner table of a quiet seafood restaurant just off Fifth Avenue, they sat face to face.

'I don't mean your figure,' said Petra, who was looking

stunning in a slinky woollen one-piece that was half a skirt and half a trouser-suit, and that left one shoulder quite bare. 'I mean your face. It has that special kind of radiance. Fran, it can mean only one thing. You, my girl, are in love.'

Frances kept her attention firmly on the menu she was examining. 'Goodness me,' she tinkled out of character, her laugh sounding so false to her that she wished she hadn't tried it. 'You do have the weirdest notions, Petra.'

'Maybe so,' her friend replied. 'But I can tell you this. The look on your face is the same as all women have either when they are pregnant, or when they are in love.

'And I assume you're not pregnant.'

Frances felt absurdly awkward. She looked intently at the menu, keeping her head down and desperately searching for some way of changing the subject without giving herself away. The attentions of the waiter gave her time to think, and time to realize that if Petra had guessed the truth so quickly, there would be little point in her hiding it.

'Does it show that clearly?' said Frances, her shyness quite genuine, her eyes still downcast.

'My God,' said Petra. 'So I was right!' Their eyes met – Frances' embarrassed, Petra's shining.

'It shows to me,' Petra continued. 'But then I'm different. My femi... :uition doesn't often let me down.' Her words were over-bright, a bit embarrassed. 'I'm your friend, Frances.' She reached out, and touched her hand.

Frances felt an immediate sense of relief, an unburdening of the enormous secret she was carrying around with her. Inwardly, she had wanted to talk to Petra about it. She needed to involve someone else in her confusion, without having to grapple with complicated explanations and a web of lies.

Until that moment, she hadn't realized how important it was to her to share the load. It was the sort of thing, Frances realized, that mothers did instinctively for their children, but seldom adults for other adults. Petra was the only person she could share it with.

At that moment, the clam chowder they had ordered arrived. Frances picked at hers, watching Petra launch into the hot, creamy brew with gusto.

'I've been waiting for someone to find out,' said Frances. 'I thought it would be Web.'

'He'd be the last to know, Fran. It wouldn't occur to Web unless you spelt it out for him.'

'I can't understand why,' said Frances. 'I feel so different that I can't believe it isn't written all over me. Surely Web would notice such a big change?'

Petra shook her head. 'Believe me, Fran. Web won't notice. And if he did, he'd push it out of his mind . . . because he doesn't want to notice.'

Frances, watching her friend eat, suddenly felt great warmth for her. Petra's life had been tough, and Frances was privy to most of the details: an early marriage to a man who was mentally sick, and turned violent on the first night of their honeymoon; one much-loved daughter, followed by a miscarriage after her husband had assaulted her, which had left her sterile. Soon after that, he had been killed in a drunken brawl, and she was left penniless. In spite of all this, Petra accepted the world without bitterness, living for her daughter for whom, she always said, she had created her successful small chain of florist shops.

Frances refocussed on her own concern. 'Maybe he is waiting for me to say something.'

'Like what, Fran?' Petra asked, not trying to conceal her mirth. 'Are you going to drop to your knees, confess everything, then beg his forgiveness?'

Frances didn't smile in return, her brow remaining furrowed. 'But, Petra, what is it that wives who have taken lovers are supposed to say or do? Lie?' She paused. 'Petra, I've never lied to Web before.'

'Frances, for pity's sake, don't tell Web the truth. Not unless there's no choice and you have decided to leave him. You have to lie to avoid hurting him. It's part of what affairs are all about.'

Frances said nothing, so Petra went on, no longer attempting to make a joke of it. 'Fran, think of it another way. Try and be objective and dispassionate for a moment, if you'll pardon the pun. You need to get this affair in proportion.'

'Men do it all the time – they have nice uncomplicated little affairs, then go back to their wives, and probably the marriage is a little better as a result. One thing they never do is tell. And everybody's a little happier afterwards. You have to try and keep it at that level, no matter what you feel.'

They were interrupted again by the waiter, dyed sideburns and too-black moustache intruding between them as he removed the soup plates and brought their main course – sliced abalone for Petra, and a grilled sole for Frances, each with a side-dish of fresh green salad. Frances wondered if he slipped away to have affairs, or if he had a mistress tucked away somewhere.

'Unless, of course, this is serious.' Petra was leaning forward now, her generous lips pursed in her concern.

'I do love him, Petra.'

'That's a bitch, Fran. That's a real bitch. But maybe you just feel that for now. If you didn't feel that, you wouldn't have got involved, would you?'

'Petra, you know me well enough for that.'

Petra said nothing for a while, chewing thoughtfully on her abalone. Frances continued into the rapt silence: 'But I'm not ready to leave Web, and I have to think of Stacey. I just have to figure out a way to go on with the relationship without having it break up my family.' She bent to her food.

'Fran, please. Brighten up. You're not doing too badly, you know. At the moment, you've got the best of both worlds. Anyway, how about the idea that falling for another man right now could be the best thing for your marriage. Think of that for a while.'

'Yes, but what about Gray?' Frances blurted out in her anguish.

'Gray? That's his name?'

'Yes. He's a businessman I met, a South African . . . '

229

'And you love him? A South African?' The tone in Petra's voice was accusatory now.

'Yes,' Frances replied.

Petra shook her head. 'You don't make it easy on yourself, do you? That's the backside of the civilized world.'

Frances made no reply, picking instead at the grilled fish in front of her, flaky white flesh coming away easily from miraculously symmetrical little bones.

Petra continued. 'What makes him so special. I mean, you could choose your man, Frannie.'

'I don't know. I never set out looking for anyone in particular, or anyone at all, for that matter. He was . . . well, I suppose just there. When I needed something . . . or someone. God knows. It works. What more can I tell you?'

'Well for one thing what's he like?'

'Massive, assertive, uncomplicated – expansive, yes that's it I guess, expansive. Like his country. Can a man be expansive, Petra?'

'I guess so, Frannie.'

Petra clicked her fingers at the waiter, hovering close enough to eavesdrop without being too obtrusive. 'A bottle of . . . Mmm . . . *Cordon Rouge* champagne, please.' Then she turned to Frances. 'Then this calls for a celebration.'

'Hold on, Petra,' Frances began to laugh. 'This isn't . . . '

'Frannie, darling,' she held up a hand. 'Listen to me. Think of this as the best thing that has ever happened to you. You have to ease back and enjoy it for what it is. Roll with the punches, go with the flow. A love affair could turn out to be just what you've needed in your life for all these years.'

'And what about Web?'

'There you go again, burdening yourself. Fran, you're going to have to abandon either Web or Gray, if you don't learn to live with it and yourself. Web need never know.'

'But if Web found out, it would kill him, Petra. He does love me.'

'Yes,' her friend replied. 'And resents you. Everyone can see that.'

230

'How do you mean?' Frances knew exactly what she meant, and knew that Web confided in Petra.

Petra piled another forkful of abalone into her mouth and started chewing. Frances waited expectantly.

'Fran, you're still competing with men, you know. For power, money, position. And you've forced Web into competing with you. You're a maverick, Frances. And for any man to love you, he has to hate you a bit as well.'

At that moment, a hand fell on Frances' shoulder. She jumped guiltily, and turned to see the smiling face of Denny Cotton, a friend of Webley's. 'Hi, Fran. Saw you in the newspapers. This rejuvenation thing's a real bombshell! Wow!'

Frances answered him as politely as she could, then turned back to Petra as he left, grinning cheerfully.

'Then why doesn't Web get off his ass and do something about it?'

'Because he's Webley. He's not the competitive sort. He's a dear, clever, witty, companionable man. But when it comes to having to challenge his own wife, he'd rather back off. That's because you out-distanced him in the beginning, and now you are so far ahead that you're not even in the same race. Fran, he knows you've left him behind. So he has internalized, withdrawn. He's leaving the field for you.'

Petra lifted her glass, and raised it to her friend. 'So here's to you, Frances.' And she took a deep draught of the palate-tickling champagne.

Frances didn't return the toast. The issue was too important to abandon so easily. 'You're close to Web, aren't you?' she said softly.

'I understand him,' Petra replied.

'Web's just not giving me what I need right now. Obviously I'm not giving him much either.'

Petra turned away from the shellfish, and was stabbing the air with her fork. 'So what's new? And what about this guy from South Africa? How long will he be happy with this mad life you lead, Frances?'

231

They were both silent for a while.

'How do you feel, Frannie, really? I mean, deep down where only you know.'

'How are you supposed to feel when you pull the most sturdy tree in your life from the earth, and you discover that the roots you were relying on were riddled with rot? How should you feel when you take your first really analytical look at something you thought was okay, and it turns out to be lousy? How, in God's name, are you supposed to handle it?'

'You're asking me?' smiled the most abused and least scarred woman Frances knew.

'It's like being on a fairground ride that has gone out of control.'

'Hang on then, Fran, and enjoy the ride.'

Confiding in Petra had lightened the load.

She loved Web. It had withered, but it would never die completely. Gray was new and exciting, and filled gaps she never knew she had. Strangely, she thought, both bonds were strong. Each was so different from the other.

It was, she thought, like blood and wine. She needed both.

'Take it *all* away? Already? Blimey, it's only been two or three weeks. The kid's hardly got started. Taking the stuff away now will finish him.'

'You've got it. That's exactly what I intend. Take the whole thing away from him. Do it at once. Give any reason you like. Just do it fast.'

The click and buzz on the line indicated that the trans-Atlantic connection had been broken abruptly, and in London, Tony Geek looked resignedly at the instrument in his hand and shook his head, before he wearily pushed the telephone cradle down once to get a dialling tone, and connected with another London number.

* * *

'He's been peaceful, but he is very tired. He's beyond pain now, and sleeping most of the time. Go in quietly.'

The nurse Frances had installed in Rocher's suite had met her outside the door. In fact, though she had not told the Professor, the 'nurse' was a fully qualified doctor, and her prognosis was bleak.

'It happens often like this,' she had told Frances. 'The end comes quite suddenly. If we moved him into an intensive care unit, perhaps we could keep him alive for several months. But without hospitalization, he could just slip away at any time.'

'He doesn't want to go to hospital,' said Frances. 'How . . . how long has he got? I mean, will he . . . '

The nurse took her hand gently. 'Yes, he will . . . '

Rocher was lying quite still. His cheeks were even more sunken than she had seen them before, and the infacing cancer cells made his skull fleshless and cadaverous.

As Frances sat on the chair beside his bed, his eyes opened. He moved his head slightly towards her.

'Waiting for you . . . '

She strained to hear him.

'We have done a good thing together, you and I . . . ' the voice was quavery.

'Yes, yes, I know.' She thought of the executive meeting and how the pleasure had been sucked out of her. His eyes were on her and she smiled through her tears.

'I am so proud to have known you,' she said, choking on the words. 'So proud of what you have done.' He didn't move. Could he hear her?

Her nose was running. She took a tissue from her bag to wipe her face; it came away stained with mascara.

'Say Kaddish for me, Frances . . . please . . . Kaddish, Frances, Kaddish please . . . '

She nodded her head vigorously and clasped his hands, feeling the fragility.

233

Then, he gave a rattling sigh. 'No,' she whispered. 'Please, no.' But she knew he had stopped breathing. She could feel his old hands slowly relax as the tissues were emptied of life, and the pulse in his veins finally ceased. This was the closest to death she'd ever been.

For a few long minutes, she sat and watched him, holding his dead hands in her own. She leaned forward to close the old eyes.

Wondering only briefly, whether women were allowed to say the ancient prayer for the dead, the words that send a shiver down the spine of every Jew, she began to chant the Hebrew syllables.

Yisgaddal v'yiskaddash sh'meh rabbo . . . '

The strength drained out of her. She stopped, and whispered: 'I'm sorry, Professor. I only know the first line.'

Then she turned and walked out of the room.

CHAPTER TWENTY

That morning, Rademeijer had phoned at 6 am. He'd insisted they meet immediately. It was now 7 am. Any second now, he should arrive, Frances thought glancing down at her watch.

'Impossible to wait,' he had said, breathing urgently into the telephone. 'I must see you immediately, Mrs Kline. Immediately.'

She'd hardly said a dozen or more words to the man in private, she realized. He'd worked closely with Rocher. Except once; yes, she recalled now, once quite recently when he had told her about the breakthrough, he'd ventured that Rocher had taken to long bouts of working totally alone.

She sighed deeply at the thought of Rocher. Would she ever strike out his memory?

Cranston Towers was more or less deserted. The inside, that is. Even at this early time, however, Frances could have sworn she'd seen a small knot of reporters awaiting her arrival.

It had been like that all week, ever since the announcement of PS-21. The running dogs of the great newspapers of the world had besieged her, all begging, cajoling and even threatening, in order to get some extra snippet of information. Frances had altered her routine to cope. She had taken to arriving in Manhattan at different times each morning, and leaving equally erratically after dark. She would park her Mercedes Benz two blocks away, in an expensive garage off Lexington Avenue, and take a cab to Cranston Towers. Once there, she instructed the cabby to drive at speed straight into the underground parking garage, where she could jump directly into the elevator to the executive floors. She had found one woman journalist waiting in her office one morning, and had been sufficiently impressed by her enterprise to grant her an exclusive instant five-minute interview, before calling security to have her escorted out.

She collected her thoughts at her desk, preparing herself mentally for Rademeijer's visit. What could the man want this urgently? He was already late.

The feverish level of interest in her new product was of course gratifying. For her and for her staff. There had been an excited hype at the eleventh floor since the first headlines. But it did place heavy demands on her and everyone else who had spent most of their time fielding telephone calls from all corners of the globe.

Seven ten. The man was really late now. She began to get irritated.

Well, she was beginning to feel the strain of the past few days. She'd appeared on national network television twice, taken part in a debate via satellite with church leaders, politicians, and a medical delegation, and, believe-it-or-not, a rival company who had pooh-poohed the whole concept. The doctors had extracted a promise from her, in front of the entire American nation, to publish the research in a medical journal when a sensible period of time had passed. A promise she'd have to keep.

It would settle down, she thought, at least until their next carefully selected piece of information was released, and then the next . . . all designed to keep interest in Prostaglandin-S running high.

At least the extra load had taken her mind off Rocher's death. Or partly, anyway. It would, she knew instinctively, take a long time for her to get over the tragedy. If she ever did.

'Mrs Kline.' The knock was faint. 'May I?'

'Of course, come in Dr Rademeijer. Sit down, please.'

The old scientist walked towards her. Diffidently, she noted. For the first time she noticed he had a limp. How could she have missed anything so obvious before?

'I'm sorry to bring you out so early, Mrs Kline . . . this is urgent, of course.'

'Of course, Dr Rademeijer.' She looked down at her watch. Seven fifteen.

He took a deep breath and looked at her over a furrowed brow. 'Mrs Kline, I'm sorry to have to tell you that the compound has decomposed.'

She sat up rigid. 'You mean Prostaglandin-S?'

'Exactly, Mrs Kline. I . . . '

'But I was assured, Rocher, you yourself told me that . . . '

'Exactly, Mrs Kline. The Professor, he was positive. He told me, his exact words, I remember them; I can see him in front of me. "Willem," he said, "it's done. Conclusively." '

She hardly heard the outpouring which followed, her mind racing ahead, trying to think through the ramifications of what the man was saying.

Now she was on her feet, her body swaying slightly. Rademeijer got up and followed her to the window.

'On paper, Mrs Kline, it's impossible to tell . . . ' he said quietly.

Which means Prostaglandin-S could be delayed. She wished the man would keep quiet so she could think.

236

'Of course there's still hope. We won't give up trying . . .'

Which means with the deadline she had, the whole project could be in jeopardy.

'Without Rocher, well, Mrs Kline, you can understand there's no way of telling how long it . . .'

Just what Milton Rae wanted. She wondered vaguely whether he had something to do with it.

'Mrs Kline . . .'

'Dr Rademeijer, could you please be quiet for a few minutes. Let me get a few things straight.'

'Yes, Mrs Kline.'

'You're saying the formula Professor Rocher left you with is inaccurate.'

'Well, technically . . .'

'Or rather, has led to destabilization?'

'That is correct.'

A picture of Rocher came at her forcibly.

'Despite his reassurances.'

'He was a sick man, Mrs Kline. At the end, maybe he was too far gone. Hallucinating, you know what I mean?'

'Dr Rademeijer, if you don't mind.' She felt explosive. Goddammit. What was the point. She needed this old scientist on her side.

'Perhaps,' he interrupted her thoughts, 'perhaps we should have insisted he include us in the experiments. He was very secretive especially . . .'

'But he documented everything, didn't he?'

'Meticulously to the last detail.'

'So?' She looked at him for reassurance.

'As I've explained, Mrs Kline, on paper it's perfect. Impossible to tell.'

'Can you fix it? How long do you need?' She wouldn't let the man consider a 'no'.

'It's not a question of fixing it, Mrs Kline,' he said, patiently. 'It's finding it. There's no way of knowing. Physiologically, what we've got is sound. It just doesn't last chemically.'

'Rademeijer, I want you to make it last.' Her eyes flashed at him. 'I want you to make it last at any cost.'

'I'll do my best, Mrs Kline.' He turned to leave.

'Dr Rademeijer, one more thing before you go.'

'Yes, Mrs Kline?'

'No one – absolutely no one is to know about this. Understood?'

'Understood, Mrs Kline.'

Damn, damn, damn! She felt the panic move through her body. Cold and heavy. Why the hell hadn't she checked? But how could she? How could she make any sense out of the scientific scrawl anyway? Who else could she have involved without blowing the security?

Some voices from the outer offices reached her faintly. She leaned over to her buzzer.

'Jo-Beth, are you there?'

'Morning, Frances. You're here early.'

'Some coffee please.'

'Sure thing. Anything else? Are you there . . . ?'

She'd been wrong. Wrong, wrong, wrong. If only he hadn't died before he could speak to her. Could Milton be behind this? There was no end to how low he would go. Important she remain positive. She would have to wait . . . what was she waiting for? A miracle . . . A goddamn miracle. That's what. Only a miracle could save her and Prostaglandin-S from this nightmare.

Jo-Beth had just brought in the coffee when her private telephone rang; mechanically she picked up the receiver, and brought it to her lips. 'Yes?'

Voice high-pitched and frantic, it was David.

'Fran, I'm devastated. I just can't believe what's going on.'

'What?'

'One month, just one fucking month, and they've taken the

238

whole account away from me.' Frances felt absurdly relieved. She listened to his voice go on. 'It's unheard of. I just can't understand it. Our work was superb. I can't even begin to piece together the reasons why. Fran, you know what this means? I am finished. Kaput!'

'David, David. Calm down.' Already she was feeling more in control of the situation. Automatically, she reached out for the ivory heart on her desk, and stroked its comforting form.

'Now tell me slowly, what has happened?'

'That new cosmetics account I told you about. Well, I gave it my best shot and produced brilliant work. The best I've ever done. It's cost me thousands; models, studios, printing . . .

'Now they've just pulled out. No "thank you", no explanation. No nothing. Just out!'

'David, surely you can do something to save it. Don't just give up.'

'Save what? They loved my ideas, they loved the testshots we did. Three days with five models in a London studio – Christ, it was good enough to publish . . . just for the goddamn *test* material. It was class, Fran, real goddamn class. Then all of a sudden, their marketing director rings me up. He's cancelling. Goodbye and goodnight. There's nothing to argue against.'

'Don't you have some sort of a contract, David? Surely you got an agreement in writing before you started spending your own money?'

'It's not like that with creative work here, Fran. It's all verbal agreements, you know . . . In a way, it almost looks as though I were set up for it. I'm the punchline in some totally obscure, goddamn private joke!'

'David, now listen carefully. If it's over, it's over, so just leave it behind. I've got something else for you. Something far bigger.' Please God, she thought wanly to herself. 'Can you come to New York directly? Can you do that?'

'Drop everything? That's rich. Everything has just dropped me.'

'So you can do it, then?'

'Yeah, I guess.' He sounded calmer now, happy to let Frances take over, and rescue the situation.

'Good. Leave tomorrow morning. I'll arrange a ticket – you just phone Pan Am to fix where to pick it up.'

The last thing she needed now was an orientation luncheon with her staff. With her plans for Prostaglandin-S the main issue on the agenda. There was no option. She had to go through with it. As though everything was on schedule.

At the lunch table, Frances smiled sunnily. Just beneath the surface, her heart was pounding. Still reeling from the Rademeijer bombshell, she had tried to consider all the implications. She needed to talk to someone, but dared not risk telling a soul. Except Gray. If only the man was with her. She needed him as a sounding board.

The lunch was an informal affair she had arranged especially for her Vice-Presidents. Jo-Beth had booked the banquet room at The Barrister, and ordered a smorgasbord combining variety with plenty.

It was a conciliatory gesture, really. She had built up her management team by instilling a stronge sense of commitment in them, and that had been achieved by keeping them fully informed of all the future developments of the division. It gave them a share in the future, and a sense of belonging.

But Prostaglandin-S she had kept to herself. It was so important and sensational a product that she had been forced to break her rule, and she knew that some of the executives were inevitably resentful.

She had greeted her V-Ps warmly, then left them to enjoy the food and wine. After they had eaten, she rapped on the table for silence, and began to speak.

It was amazing to her that she could so readily summon a flow of words, when her mind was in turmoil.

'You will all understand, when I have finished talking to you, of the need for complete secrecy on the action plan for Prostaglandin-S. I haven't been able to take even you into my confidence until now. Everything I am going to tell you now is secret. At the moment, Cranston has the lead in rejuvenation, but the competition is fierce, because this is going to be the biggest thing in pharmaceutical cosmetics since God was a boy.'

The incongrous profanity raised a small ripple of laughter, and Frances was sure she was getting them all on her side again.

Now she turned to one of the executives – Randy Wise, a staff man whom she'd plucked from management of a chemical manufacturing works that had closed down two years before, impressed by his quick grasp of the complicated business of production. Since then, she had been holding him in reserve for the right job.

Speaking mainly to him, she announced her intentions of and reasons for manufacturing in Paris. 'Gerry Rule is already there, overseeing redevelopment of the factory I have bought, and looking out for a French ad agency to promote the product. Randy, I'm going to ask you to go to Paris to take control of the manufacturing side.' The young man's earnest face beneath an old-fashioned crew-cut, back in mode again, was split by a wide grin. 'Meantime, the rest of us here are going to have our work cut out.'

'The significance of this new product is gigantic. It has the potential to generate more turnover and to make more money than anything the Cranston Group has ever tackled. And we are all part of that.'

She sat down to a round of spontaneous applause. Confidently, she held her smile in place. How could she tell them that there was a possibility Prostaglandin-S would be stillborn? That the odds were stacked high. And not in their favour.

CHAPTER TWENTY-ONE

Her telephone shrilled. Who could that be at this hour?

'Frances? Already here?' The false geniality in Milton Rae's voice sent a small shiver down her spine. 'I hoped I'd find you. It's the perfect opportunity for a confidential chat. Any chance you could pop up to my office for half an hour?'

She'd left home at the first crack of a chilly dawn. Webley had roared after her: 'It's not normal, Frances. Do you know what time it is?' as she'd swung her Mercedes out into the slippery roadway.

'I'm rather tied up, Milton.' She was dressed in black. To match her mood, she reflected wryly.

'No problem. Then I'll come down to you. See you in five minutes.'

And he had rung off before she could reply.

He stepped into her office glowing with urbanity, but Frances noted the sheen of cold sweat across his brow. She looked up without closing the file she was studying, eyebrows raised.

'Hi,' he said, before helping himself to a chair. 'Another early bird. I've been coming in this time for years, once or twice a week. An hour now is better than five after lunch.' He looked pointedly at the cup of coffee on her desk, but Frances decided to ignore the courtesies.

'Was it anything in particular, Milton?'

'A little plan . . . a little plan. One that could be of great benefit to us both.'

'Let's get on with it, Milton.' She rattled the papers angrily.

'It's about PS-21.' He hesitated.

'So . . . ?'

'Let's face facts, you're dabbling, Frances – it's a big project and you're out of your league.'

'Will you get to the point, Milton.'

242

'The point is that my division has the experience and knowledge of the market, and you don't. We need to put our heads together and get a bit of synergy going.'

'We already have a signed agreement to use your sales force,' she said. 'Seven per cent on sales. You signed it four years ago, remember?'

He ignored her. 'Cranston doesn't need a cock-up, Frances. So what I propose is that we take over the whole headache from you, Paris included. We'll make PS-21 and sell it for you.'

'At a price, of course,' said Frances, vaguely amused now.

'Of course. But you'll cream off the top, with no hassles. We'd leave you to handle advertising and promotion. You're good at that. We'll pay you a fee – naturally.'

Frances Kline began to laugh. She had not laughed so loudly for a long time. 'Milton, you've just got to be kidding!'

She was tempted to tell the fool that there might never be a Prostaglandin-S; that his efforts were wasted. But instead she said, 'I've seen the whole PS project through from beginning to end – against, I might add, sustained opposition from you. Now that I've won through, you expect me to give you a slice of the action!' She snorted derisively. 'Forget it, Rae. Just put it right out of your mind.'

Now he too stopped playing games. His nostrils were slightly flared with anger, and his eyes had a burning intensity that made it uncomfortable for Frances to meet them. She could see now that he had been drinking.

'Frances, you seem to forget. Your deal with me . . . I'm the deal.' The threat was implicit, but he spelt it out anyway. 'I could make it awful slow going for you. So clean up your act, Kline.'

'Get out.' She dropped her head again to the papers in front of her.

The effect on Rae was electrifying. He leapt to his feet, snatched the papers from in front of her, and flung them across the room. He was insane with anger.

'You fucking bitch! Just you listen to me. I've had as much as I

243

can take. I . . . ' He broke off, looking wildly round the room.

Frances was genuinely scared now. Suddenly it was painfully clear to her. Milton Rae was totally mad.

'I could finish you,' Rae said. 'I could finish you right now. You think Clements has me on the run? Hah!'

'What do you mean?' Frances said. 'Who is Clements?'

He moved quickly round the desk, and was at Frances' side. She braced herself, feeling around in her desk drawer for the spare Gazapper she kept there.

He did not try and strike. Instead he leered at her, then leaned his face over hers. The stench of bourbon was stale. Clammy skin, slavering lips, moist and hungry against her mouth. She wanted to scream. Frantically, she pushed him away, pummelling at his chest.

Abruptly, he stood back. Dusting himself down, he gave a smile that was almost prim. Frances felt a cringe run through her, as if a slug was inside her dress. In mute shock, she stared at him.

'I should have known you were a waste of time,' he said. 'You and that faggot son of yours.'

It was then Frances lost control. And she struck out. The first time in her life she could remember hitting anyone. The sting of his cheek against her hand was immensely satisfying.

He continued, unperturbed. 'You're exactly like him, aren't you.' He took a buff-coloured envelope out of his suit pocket, slapped it down on Frances' desk, and then walked steadily to the door. There he turned. 'A little something to think about, Frances.' Then he was gone.

The mention of David had filled her with dread. A chill cut through her, razor sharp. She picked up the envelope and slit it open. Inside was a photograph. She drew her breath in sharply. Madness! Milton was insane.

Two naked figures. It was a pornographic picture with two men lying intertwined on a bed. She only glanced at it before slipping it back in the envelope.

Then she drew it out again. It wasn't just two men. The older man was Milton Rae, a leer on his face just like the one she had seen a moment before when he had leaned over her.

The younger man, and there was no mistaking him, was David.

She had gazed at the photograph horror-struck. She could see from his haircut that it had been taken in New York when David was seventeen. Now, from her desk, it was staring up at her, the intense expression frozen on her son's face, an ironic echo of her own stricken stare.

Agony. Sheer agony at the image of this boy in the arms of her most bitter enemy.

Quickly she slammed the picture face down. She was shaking from head to foot. And she was cold. She was always cold when she was this distressed. Had she ever been this distressed? she wondered.

Absently she began to flick through papers on her desk. She would have to confront him, and soon.

She sat hunched, her head in her hands. To know so little of your own child. Was it possible?

'She doesn't look good to me . . . ' A stranger's voice.

'She's fine. Frances, are you alright . . . ?' Jo-Beth with a stranger.

What does he want? She felt herself shiver. 'What does he want?' She repeated it aloud. She looked past them.

'I'm sorry, Frances, this man insisted. I couldn't stop . . . '

'Who is he, Jo-Beth?' The man coughed and sneezed. He looked vaguely familiar.

'The Barrister, ma'am. I'm the doorman . . . ' Frances closed her eyes, wishing them gone.

'I'm sorry, Frances. I'll get rid . . . '

'The Professor, Mrs Kline. Rocher. He sent me . . . ' He kept on coughing.

Frances shot upright.

'You can go, Jo-Beth.' She kept her eyes on the man.

'The Professor told me to give you this.' he held an envelope in his stubby fingers. 'Gave me the exact time and day to come, too. I was two minutes early . . . ' He beamed at her.

'Please give it to me.'

The old man shrugged, handed the envelope over and rambled on, 'Sure, we used to chat often . . . '

My dear Frances,

'He knew he could trust me – he said so . . . '

By the time you receive this

'I'm real sorry ma'am to have to burst in on you like this . . . '

I will be dead.

'Yes, thank you, er, Mr . . . er.'

'Ford, ma'am. Herbert Ford.'

'Mr Ford, I'm very grateful. Would you mind . . . ' She gestured towards the door.

I've given this letter

'Mr Ford, I really would like to read.'

To Herbert

'Oh yes, ma'am. Of course.' She felt the man shuffle towards the door.

Ford, the doorman at The Barrister.

'Thank you, Mr Ford.' She must remember to tip him.

I am afraid I might die before you return from Johannesburg. I completed the last part of the research last night, but as fate would have it, my strength has gone with it.

By now you will know that the formula I left behind is unstable. Science is so exact. So predictable. Not like human beings at all. Here is my little secret.

Her eyes skipped the spidery scientific hieroglyphics. *Give it to Rademeijer. He will know what to do. You can trust him. But the corporation. That's another thing. It is crawling with unseen enemies. So you see, Frances dear, I could not take a chance.*

What Willem has now is the second last formula. This one will have the same clinical effects, but it also has life. Technically, all

246

I've done is reposition one of the side chains of the molecule. (Did you know that if the sugar molecule is inverted, it is no longer fattening?)

But enough of all this. You must get on with it without me. And so you will.

I will send another copy of this to my Swiss banker friend in Lausanne with instructions to forward it to you. Just in case.

Goodbye, dear Frances. There will always be a special bond between us. I deliberately did not get too close. But for a birthmark Michèle had behind her left ear you could have been my own.

Now I must leave you with the last bit of my jigsaw. And with the responsibility.

Paul Rocher.

David Kline looked far too beautiful to be a man. The feeling struck Frances every time she saw him after a prolonged absence – this time the thought had a cutting edge.

His features, hewn by a sculptor with a sharp chisel, were almost too symmetrical and perfectly formed; his blond hair was softer than her own. His collar bones met precisely at the base of his lean-muscled neck, his Adam's apple a medieval codpiece that punctuated his words. But it was his eyes that held the attention, and for the first time – now that she was looking for it – she saw a loneliness in their depths.

He had, she thought with an inward shudder as the image of Milton Rae passed through her mind, a very touchable beauty. Stacey was boisterously clambering all over him. It seemed so long since he had been in Westchester County and the house overlooking Rhode Island Sound.

'Hey, Stace. I've only just got home,' his mouth grinning broadly at his sister's affectionate display. 'Give me a chance. I've hardly said hello to Fran and Dad.'

'They can see you while I'm sleeping.' She clambered onto his shoulders, catching fistfuls of hair. 'I can only see you now.' And he finally had to give in to her devastating logic, to be led away to her room, smiling and shrugging at Frances as he left.

An hour later, with Stacey pacified and playing happily in her room, and Web working in his study, Frances took David through to the small room she used as a workplace. They sat on a tiny sofa, the only furniture in the room, and he raised his eyebrows expectantly.

Frances felt so calm and self-controlled that it was almost as though the whole thing was happening to someone else, and she was a dispassionate observer. She had no way of knowing how David would react to what she had to say. But it had to be done and it was best done at once.

Without a word, she withdrew the buff envelope from her pocket, and slid it unopened across to her son. Then, when he had picked it up, she said: 'David, can you explain this to me . . . '

He drew his breath in fiercely and slid the picture back into the envelope. His face pale, he stood up and looked away from Frances and out of the darkening window. 'Look at me, David.' When he did meet her eyes, the expression in them tore at her. She felt the years fall away.

'Fran,' he gave a sigh that was halfway to being a sob. 'I never wanted you to know.'

'Well, now I know.'

'Did he tell you?'

'Of course.'

'The bastard.' David's head fell forward in shame, but Frances resisted the temptation to reach for him, to cradle his head against her body.

'Now it's just a question of what he wants,' she said.

David pulled back. 'You mean . . . okay, I get it. You mean he's blackmailing you. Oh Jesus.'

'David, you must tell me the truth.' Frances was sitting straight, quelling her emotions with the need to cope with the situation.

'Fran . . . it's all over now. All in the past. It's something that happened, that I've forgotten. Please don't make me go through it all again.'

Suddenly her anger surfaced. 'I'd like to kill the sonofabitch.'

'No, Fran. No. He isn't all bad. He taught me a lot – about art, about nature, about life . . . '

'I bet,' said Frances. The remark created a pause, and they fell silent for a while.

'When you left,' Frances cut across the quiet, 'I thought you were running away from your father and me – me in particular.' For an instant, her voice let her down, choking on the words. 'But it was him you were escaping, wasn't it?'

'Yes, yes, yes,' said David. 'But it's over, Fran. For God's sake let it be. I'm okay now. Straight. You know . . . Gabs and me.'

He looked completely distraught. Then he moved across the room, and sat on the sofa beside her. 'Please, you do believe that, don't you?' He was sobbing now, and he sank his head on his mother's shoulder.

Frances felt so remote, almost trance-like. She hugged her son to her, and ran her fingers through his hair. There was nothing to be said except, soothingly, 'It's okay. It's okay.'

That was Frances, the mother; Kline, the businesswoman, was busy inside, thinking through the consequences . . . deciding firstly not to tell Web, for that would be to betray David . . . realizing her own vulnerability, and the danger that Milton Rae represented to her. He couldn't blackmail her without destroying himself in the process. But he was mad enough to try anything.

Then she sat and embraced the young man who Milton Rae had loved. Filled with loathing.

After they had eaten, and Stacey had finally been put to bed, they sat together in the family room.

David stretched lean legs towards the fire. 'So, Fran, what have you got planned for your very prodigal son?'

'Plenty,' she said. 'I'm sorry you lost your big cosmetic account, but I don't think you'll miss it much when you see what I have got to take its place.'

'This PS thing certainly has taken the world by storm,' replied

David. Frances marvelled at the way he was able to target in to work, after their recent conversation. She smiled: it was a gift he had inherited from her.

'Yes,' she replied. 'And tricky. We've got to sell it very carefully, or else the whole thing is going to go right out of control.'

She drew her chair closer to his, leaning forward, getting into her stride. 'What we have to do is achieve a delicate balance between medical credibility and aesthetic appeal. PS must be neither a pure drug, nor a pure cosmetic. In the minds of the public, it must contain elements of both. And that's where you come in – with a co-ordinated advertising, packaging and marketing campaign.

'It's not going to be easy. But I know you can do it. But it sure is the most complex product I've ever handled.'

'That's for sure,' said David. He turned to Webley, who was looking benignly on. 'What do you think, Dad?'

'Your mother has a minefield there,' said Web. 'I've warned her already.'

'A minefield is right,' said Frances. 'That's why the creative side of the campaign is so important. And security. That's another reason why I want David.'

She told David all the unpublished details of the work so far on PS-21, finishing up with the story of how the Professor had discovered that the *Dorothaneum* plant contained the vital ingredient for commercializing PS-21, and of her search to find it.

'I was lucky,' she said. 'I managed to find and tie up the world's only plentiful source of the plant within a couple of days when I was in South Africa recently. Now we have a factory in France, and supplies of the raw material. We are ready to run.'

'Why South Africa?' said David, his eyes narrowing.

'Because that's where the plant grows, David.'

David was silent, looking stern, while Webly ostentatiously played no part in the conversation.

'So,' she went on and described the *Eerstevallei* setup, 'I have

250

gone into a joint partnership with the co-op and Gray Barnard who also owned the cosmetics plant in France – the one we bought.' She felt a flood of emotion as she spoke Barnard's name, and hoped that it didn't show.

'I'm not interested in doing business with any South Africans,' retorted David.

'David. Just listen, will you. Stop allowing your own prejudices to colour your feelings. Barnard set up this whole multi-racial community, against stiff opposition, simply for the welfare of the people. He makes no profit from the co-op deal.'

'More wine?' It was Webley, a determinedly non-committal spectator. Frances put her hand over her glass, and continued talking.

'I'd like you in on this, David. I really need someone I can trust. I am in the process of purchasing a Paris ad agency. I would want to put you in charge of it, particularly for the creative side. I can supply all the administrative talent you need . . . that's easy to find. It's your creative ability that we need. You'll have to wind down the agency's existing accounts, and devote the entire resource to PS-21 . . . at least for the next year.'

'You want me to move to Paris?' She could see he was weakening.

'For a while. Not that many people would complain about that!' She reached out, touching him on the knee. 'It's a big, big chance.'

'And South Africa?'

'David, I explained it. There's no way around it.'

'What about this South African guy?'

'What about him?' She suppressed a frisson of excitement.

'It would hurt Gaby if I had dealings with a South African.'

'David, it's an American product. An international American product. Some of the raw material comes from South Africa . . . and without that raw material, there's no product. It's all put together in France. And it will be sold all over the world. That's the way global business goes.

'You won't hurt Gaby if you take the job. But you will hurt

251

yourself if you don't. This is a gigantic breakthrough. The work and the money that have gone into it are enormous – but nothing compared with the eventual potential. More important, it's the beginning of a new era. An historic event. Don't you want to have a part in that?'

'Frances,' Webley spoke for the first time in ages. 'I think you are pressurizing the boy.'

David hated being called 'the boy' by his father, a fact that Frances knew, but hadn't had the heart to tell Web.

'Okay.' Frances looked at David. 'I won't put any more pressure on you. But I want you in on this, and I will think you are crazy if you don't accept. You discuss it with Gaby. I am leaving for Paris in two weeks. If you agree, I'll need you to meet me there. Now I'm going to leave you men alone for a while, and make us all some wonderfully strong Irish coffee.'

Webley and Fran again, in the bathroom, she resting the nape of her neck on the smooth enamel, watching as he shed his clothes, dropping them where he stood. He seemed miles away, and she wished she could plumb his thoughts. He hadn't questioned her about her trip to South Africa at all, not even in a superficially polite way; and she hadn't volunteered any information. That fact engendered an uneasiness she preferred not to explore further.

Then Webley, brushing his teeth, spoke through a froth of toothpaste. 'I think you're leaning a little hard on the boy, you know.'

'So you said. And you really must stop calling him that. He hates it. But he must make up his mind. As far as I'm concerned, it's a straight business offer. And a good one, at that. If he doesn't want it, he can turn it down. I certainly wouldn't take offence.'

'Fran,' he said indistinctly. 'You know how he feels about you. About how he wants to emulate you. This is a hell of a decision for the boy. If he screws it up, he'll crack, you know. Really crack.' He pointed the head of his toothbrush at her to emphasize the point. 'You'd better believe that, Frances.'

'I believe it. But I also believe he won't screw it up.'

'Well, I sure hope you're right. I want to see him succeed as much as you do.'

How much Web seemed to know instinctively, Frances thought. He understands about David without knowing anything about him.

Her thoughts were broken by a sudden shock of cold on her scalp, and then a squirt of hot water from the hand-shower. 'Jesus, Web!' But he was on her, dowsing her hair – and the rest of the bathroom – with the shower of water, then leaving it to plume up the tiled wall, as he held her down and started to shampoo her hair. She was laughing and trying to squirm away from him, his hands slippery with the creamy soap grappling at her shoulders, laughing also, and splashing water until it welled over onto the floor.

Exhausted, she eventually collapsed, and laughingly submitted as he showered the soap off her. 'Kline, stop it,' she said. The horseplay had taken her back to the earliest, happiest days of their life together.

She hated the feeling of wet hair against her pillow, she thought, just before she drifted off to sleep. And she smiled at her husband's unexpected display of high spirits.

Then she frowned. How could this be happening to her? She was deeply in love with one man, and sharing her life with another.

It couldn't go on for much longer.

CHAPTER TWENTY-TWO

The drive from Nice took them through Venice, along the mountainous contours of the old road, cuttings edged with stone bulwarks to hold back the aggressive greenery. Gnarled old olive trees, and tall-stretched cypresses.

The road dipped and swung between a clutch of villas facing out to sea, staring sightlessly at the Mediterranean horizon from windows shuttered against the sunshine. They passed tiny farms, interspersed with huge holiday apartments, then the road swung inland, towards Grasse, drawing nearer to the white-boned skeletons of the ancient hills rising into the heat-haze.

They had flown into Nice airport that morning from Paris. The runway terminates abruptly at the sea and Frances had recalled the lurching panic she had felt one morning flying into Hong Kong, its runway absurdly small. This time, Gray Barnard was sitting next to her, and the palm of his hand confidently enveloped her fingers.

In the weeks of separation she had felt consistently close to him. They had spoken on the telephone once, often twice a day. If anything, the separation had given her the space to analyze her feelings for him with more objectivity. An objectivity that convinced her that the relationship offered her a vitality and sanity she needed.

Randy Wise had been hard at work setting up the factory. She knew from his reports that it simply wouldn't have been possible without Gray's help. Gray had made two trips to Paris that month, and his experience and local knowledge were invaluable at speeding things through.

A fortnight ago, his voice plaintive, he had asked her: 'Do you know how long it is since we've been together?'

'Three weeks and four days,' she had answerd without hesitation, and they had both laughed.

Then Gray continued. 'Can't you come over to Paris, Franci. Come at least and see the factory.'

'I can't, my love. I can't. There's been so much trauma here with PS-21 that I've been neglecting other things. I have a whole lot of catching up to do. Please understand.'

'Then come for the weekend. We could go down to my villa.'

'You have a villa? Where?'

'In the south. Near a town called Grasse. It is the centre of the perfume industry.'

'You do surprise me,' she had said. 'Gray, I'll be coming to Paris at the end of the month. I know that I've taken advantage of you, Gray. But I'll make it up to you. I promise.'

He ignored the remark.

'Well, then I definitely will come to New York.'

'No,' she had said quickly. 'Not now. I'm not ready yet.'

'Will you ever be ready?' he had replied, and had rung off. It was their first argument, and left a lingering pressure-point between them.

Now all that was forgotten, as Frances lay back and enjoyed the heat pouring in through the sun-roof of their rented Peugeot. She and Gray had passed through the stage of talking furiously when they had met in the airport in Paris, and on the flight to Nice. Able, at last, to relax she felt comfortable without having to talk.

She wondered how Gray and David would get along together. It was impossible to conceive that two people she loved so much would not find common bonds. But they would have to make their own relationship work. She could not be in the middle.

David and Milton Rae. Eventually she would have to handle that. But right now she could do nothing. Any confrontation would result in so much hostility and cause a ripple effect throughout the organization. And the nett result . . .

She would compromise her position and be forced to resign.

Exactly what Milton wanted.

*　*　*

Rule was lying on his hotel bed, telephone to his ear, listening to the babyish tones of his wife's voice. This time he had managed to forestall one of her painful telephone calls, the ones that gathered momentum and ended in floods of costly, trans-Atlantic tears. He had telephoned her, and found her in an expansive mood.

'Gerry, what are you going to buy me in Paris. I want some silk lingerie, oh, and some Chanel perfume. And maybe one of those funny stripy tee-shirts they wear.' Her version of Paris was via Hollywood.

'Sure, honey,' said Rule, laughing affectionately. 'And some onions, and a bicycle, and some Gauloise cigarettes.' He was determined to keep the mood light.

'You're alone in Gay Paris for the weekend, are you? I thought you said your Frances Precious Kline was going to be there.'

'She's checked in and checked straight out again,' he said. 'Be back first thing Monday morning.'

'So what will you be getting up to?' Her voice was becoming more plaintive, as she saw images of French tarts in fishnet tights, skirts slit up to the waist, berets seductively rakish over heavy make-up.

Rule calmed her with a chortle. 'Just the usual, sweetheart. I'll be painting the town red, giving the girls something to remember me by, drinking champagne at dawn under the Eiffel Tower.'

The joke backfired.

'Sweetheart, you can ring me right here any time of the day or night, any time you want to check up on me.

'Don't worry. After this is over, we're going to take that nice, long holiday I've been promising you.'

As the road climbed a stony ridge, Gray suddenly swung off onto the verge. The view was nothing short of sensational, back to the deep blue of the sea, where the great mountains marched into the Mediterranean, and up to the Alps beyond, jutting skyward, as if the land was trying to link the heavens and the depths.

Frances was drinking it in when she felt Gray seize her firmly, and turn her small shoulders towards him. 'Franci, Franci,' he said, and then kissed her again in that way she remembered so well, starting tenderly, but then growing rougher as their passion rose.

Then he broke free, just when Frances thought he was going to take her, right there in the car, just when she realized that she wouldn't be able to resist if he did. 'Oh, Gray, it's been such a long time. I've missed you.'

They resumed their journey with the car suffused with the warm secretions of their desire. It was something that infected both of them, a musky feeling that was patient but would not wait much longer.

Frances spoke again, the curiosity burning about Barnard's marriage. 'Does she ever come with you on your trips? Your wife, I mean. Has she been to the villa?'

'Not for years. She doesn't enjoy leaving her home. She last came when my elder son, Deon, was here, seconded to the Royal Navy for Special Anti-Submarine training. Deon was always her child, and he was the only thing that would have enticed her to leave home, even then. Actually, she spoiled the boy. Always lived for him, and still does even now.'

Frances was struck by the echo of her feelings for David. 'And your other child?' she asked, thinking of Stacey.

Barnard gave the deep-throated chuckle that she knew meant a tenderness had been touched inside him. 'Lukas? He's different. He seems closer to the ground.'

'Like you?'

'Yes. My child, I reckon. He and I grew up together. He reminded me of the values that my father taught me, and which I had forgotten. I relived my whole childhood through his eyes. I tell you, even the smell of his model aeroplane glue brought a whole segment of my own past back to life. One day, I'd like you to meet Lukas.'

'I'd love to,' she replied mechanically. His talk had been unexpectedly painful, conjuring up an image of a Gray she had never seen, happy with his family. Then she added: 'You're going to meet David soon.'

'That's very important to you, isn't it?' he said. The observation was acute. 'Actually, I am a little nervous to meet him.'

'Don't be,' she said. 'You'll only make it harder for him. He's only a kid, with a head full of bright ideas.' Not wanting to drive a wedge between her son and the man she loved, she avoided mentioning David's violent, anti-South African stance. Since both of them ultimately agreed on the basics, they would no doubt work out their own solution.

Now the road began to climb steeply, the engine humming in the lower gears as the road twisted up from the plain. 'We're nearly there,' said Gray.

'Nearly where?'

'Grasse. My villa is in a tiny village, hidden away from the town. There are only eight houses there.'

'What a place,' she said. 'Breathtaking! It looks impossible to get there.' She stared up at the impregnable walls that rose above them.

Then Gray turned into a narrow gateway set in the weather-beaten, old stone and drew up in a courtyard, with a grove of cypress trees, all standing to attention. 'Nous sommes arrivées,' he said, switching off the engine with a Gallic flourish.

As Frances climbed from the car, her nostrils were assailed by a scent both strange and achingly familiar, the scent of grandmothers and covered coathangers, of old farm gardens. Leaning her head back so her hair fell sensuous from her head, she sniffed deeply.

'Lavender,' said Gray. 'It grows wild here.'

He waited as Frances took in her surroundings – acorn-brown stone, the rust of old clay tiles . . . each house within the walled village like a bas-relief carved from the living rock. Three young children – brother and two sisters, by the similarity of their tightly curled black hair, small hands and olive skins – came and looked silently up at her with enormous eyes, then ran away again shyly as she smiled and extended her hand in greeting.

Then she saw a curtain flutter across the courtyard, and all but caught a glimpse of a ghostly old face behind the lace.

'Which one is your villa?' she asked, her voice metallic in the thick heat of the air.

'At the end,' he said, taking their baggage from the car, and setting off across the square into the intimate gold of the twilight. In the centre, a fountain gurgled. It was fashioned in the shape of an urn, with the water spewing from the mouths of four time-worn gargoyles. A woman crossed the square, clad in black. Without looking at the strangers, she filled a jug from the fountain.

'The village water supply,' said Gray. 'Until recently, it was the only water supply. Now we have pipes laid to all the houses. But the villagers prefer to drink this water. It comes straight from the mountainside. Taste it.'

It was like crystal, sparkling and light, a sharp tang of granite, and full of life. Frances drank deeply, then stood back and wiped her mouth.

Before they reached the final alleyway leading to the farthest row of houses, an old man and woman rushed out to meet them – he shrunken and nut-brown inside baggy clothes, she with the complexion of an apple dried at full ripeness.

They walked in through cool stone walls, in to tall rooms, with creaking dark-stained floorboards. The kitchen was hung about with old copper pots, strings of onion and garlic, and bunches of fresh lavender, hung from the ceiling to dry. In one corner, wine bottles had been stacked to the ceiling.

The old woman spoke to Frances, but her dialogue was so rapid and so heavily accented that her own schoolgirl French could not cope. Looking puzzled, she turned to Gray. 'She wants to know if you would like fish for dinner,' he grinned at both of them.

Frances turned and smiled at the old woman. '*Oui, s'il vous plaît*,' she said, doing her best. '*Poisson c'est bon, merci beaucoup*.' Now it was the turn of the old Frenchwoman to look puzzled, until Gray translated.

They walked through narrow French doors leading onto a paved terrace, almost overflowing with pots of herbs and a multitude of shrubs. The ground sloped steeply to the valley below.

From the upstairs window, when Gray took her to their bedroom, they could see clear to the Mediterranean, a thin silver of blue-black contrasting with the red-gold of the sky. She was gazing out of the tall window when suddenly Gray was behind her, his arms round her waist, pushing up under her breasts. She turned to face him, within the circle of his arms, then he produced from behind her back a small box that had been concealed in his fist.

'Please open it,' he said, 'then I'll explain.'

Frances had never seen anything like it before. It was a gold locket on a short chain, obviously very old, with a large diamond set into the boss in the centre, and a delicate tracery of engraving on the back, the initials lost by years of wear.

'It belonged to my great-grandmother,' said Gray. 'That was the first diamond the family has ever owned. And those were her initials . . . the same as mine.' His fingertip sketched out the elaborate GSB for her to see.

'What does the S stand for in your name?' Frances asked, and thought simultaneously, 'How little I know of the man.'

'Sebastian.'

'Gray Sebastian Barnard. I like it.'

She turned the locket over and over in the palm of her hand. Then she thrust it back at him. 'Gray, I can't take this. It is part of your heritage.'

He held up his hand. 'So are you,' he said.

'Gray, it's exquisite.'

Now he unclasped the chain, and gently put it around her neck. Then he turned her, so they were both reflected in the floor-length mirror against the wall . . .

The image brought tears to Frances' eyes. Gray, so big and steadfast behind her, framing her fine-boned delicacy, and the ancient jewel sparkling against her skin.

'There's something inside it,' Barnard said. 'No, you can't open it. I had it sealed. That makes the power ever-lasting.'

'The power?'

'About thirty years ago, I found a very old man wandering about the veldt near *Goedgeluk*. He was a *sangoma* – what the white men called a "witch doctor" – and we became friends. I used to spend a lot of time with him. He told me about the ancient witchcraft of Africa, the combined use of medicinal herbs and superstition . . . a force of remarkable power. Quite often, we used to sit in silence beside a rough fire. He was a man of great inner peace and strength.

'One day, he brought me a small pouch made of the skin of a jackal. He told me I must always keep it . . . it contained something that would protect me all the days of my life. Two days later, he disappeared. Many years later a skeleton was found under a rock on the mountainside. He had curled up in the hollow, and waited to die. He must have known death was coming.

'Inside the bag he gave me was a small patch of fur – baboon fur, I think. It was steeped in herbs, and it had a bitter, acrid smell. Some I had set into the back of my watch. Here you see; the rest I sealed up in this locket for you.

'It is one of the most precious things I own, and I want to share it with you.'

They clung to each other until the sun sank into the bosom of the brown hills, until they heard the old woman with the food.

In the vast upstairs bedroom, they ate on the floor – grilled bream on a large platter, a bowl of garlic mayonnaise, a long thin loaf of white bread, and a wedge of ripened Brie. They drank *Côtes de Provence*, a full-bodied rosé and devoured the delicious fish to the last pure-white flake. Cool night air, scented with strong Mediterranean herbs and jasmine wafted through the open doors.

The wine, and the richness of the air, lent Frances a feeling of floating. She moved the plates aside, and lay back on the cushions. Then she began to laugh, uncontrollably.

Gray joined her on the cushions, and – laughing as wildly as she – removed all her clothes as they rolled around in glee, until they were both naked among the debris of their meal, only the gold locket winking between her breasts in the soft light.

Frances pulled Gray down onto her, roughly thrusting up toward him. 'Gray. Now. I want you now.'

She climaxed as soon as he entered her.

The next day passed like a Provençal idyll. They were awoken by the sombre majesty of church bells, and Frances looked out of the window to see the peasants and bourgeoisie treading the old cobbled streets, in answer to the summons. Old women wrapped in black and work-hardened farm labourers contrasted with the family of a smart-suited young executive as they shuffled beneath the tall stone portals of the ancient church.

They breakfasted on coffee and *brioches*, then Gray took her riding, the horses picking their way down a steep path, and then cantering across the fields below. Frances had ridden as a child, but had to concentrate to stay on. When she did get a chance to look at Gray, she was struck by the fluid unity of the big man and the large animal. They moved as one, and when they paused by an outlook to gather their breath, she complimented him on his skill. 'I was born on a horse,' he chuckled.

They raced home, the smell of crushed lavender and the rich damp sweat of the horses mingling unforgettably in Frances' nostrils.

Then they drove down to Grasse, where Gray bought her an enormous bottle of perfume, and – suddenly starving – they bought huge chunks of pizza and ate them on a bench in a street lined with trees, licking their fingers, laughing and hugging, speaking hilarious French at the tops of their voices.

As the light began to fade, Gray drove her to St Paul de Vence, a town direct from a rather menacing folk tale, clustered with its knees drawn up on the summit of a precipitous hill.

At sunset, golden rays picked out the snow-capped peaks of the Maritime Alps.

As darkness fell, they walked to the Café de la Place, a small café-bar, with coloured lights strung in the twisted olive trees outside. It had belonged, Gray told her, to Simone Signoret and Yves Montand, and Frances wished she could understand the conversation round the bar, invested somehow with so much extra wit and wisdom because it was in colloquial French.

The click-click from the floodlit courtyard at the back summoned them, and they were cajoled into playing *boules* with the locals – Frances emerging victorious in a sensational bout of beginner's luck.

Then, exhausted, they drove back to the villa, and fell asleep in one another's arms.

Frances knew she could never be that happy again.

At Orly early the next morning Frances was aware how far behind her were the smells and sounds of the south of France. Just a couple of hours, but also a life-time away.

Gray was a different man now, as he stood beside her, smartly suited; and she was a different woman, in the Versace gear every inch a crisp businesswoman, as she scanned the faces of the incoming flight from New York.

When she had awoken in Grasse that morning, she had been overcome with a deep and deadly melancholy, and had answered Gray monosyllabically, until he had pressed her to discuss it.

'It's the price, Gray. For pleasure, now it's back to work.'

He shook his head mutely, one eyebrow raised.

'Okay. It's you, it's Rocher, it's David . . . it's . . . '

'David?'

She told him about Milton's clumsy attempt at seducing her, and then the photograph she had had thrust in her face. Everything. Including David's tearful reaction.

When she finished speaking, he took her hand. 'Don't judge him too hard, Franci,' he said.

'I'm not judging him,' she said. 'I'm judging myself. Web once told me that women who have homosexual sons are usually relieved when they discover the truth. They know then they will never lose their sons to another woman. I don't feel like that. I suppose I am to blame. I was too possessive, too protective. And Web and David . . . well, they never connected in the way he does with Stacey.'

'Frances, it's obviously long over. Put it behind you.'

'That's the problem. I can't. Because Milton Rae is able to brandish it over my head whenever he likes. At least now I understand his vendetta against me. It's not just the PS-21 project. It's David too.'

'That bastard. Would he expose himself?'

'I think he's just capable of it.'

'Then what will you do? Can't you tell Bennis?'

'Tell him what? I dare not precipitate things.'

Now they were waiting, each in their own pocket of thought, for the moment she had been hoping for and dreading, the moment her son would meet her lover.

She saw Gabrielle first, clinging firmly to David's arm, and steering him round people. She waved, and they hurried towards her, smiling eagerly. She hugged them both and kissed them, before standing back and introducing them to Gray. The two men looked serious, but smiled politely. 'How do you do,' was all David managed, before escaping with his eyes. And then, as Barnard reached for Gaby's hand, David grabbed the two women by the shoulders and swept them away, leaving Barnard's hand in mid-air, with no option but to trail along behind the tight-knit trio.

'First the hotel,' said Frances. 'I've booked you in for a month – until you can find an apartment. And then the agency, straight away. When you work for me you have to get moving.'

Then she noticed how David pointedly excluded Gray, and self-consciously disentangled herself from his arms. She felt the

264

discomfort in Barnard's clear eyes. David had rejected him. Instantly.

'And then we can go and see the factory,' she said brightly. 'Gray can show us around.'

'Let's skip the factory.' David's tone was unfriendly. 'I'm only really interested in the agency.'

Gray, she could see, was building up to a simmer of irritation. She shuddered at the explosive potential of the situation.

'David, I think it's important to you to get as broad a picture of PS-21 as possible. I want you to know the product from the ground up. You're going to spend quite a lot of time at the factory, one way or another; so you might as well get to know it. Preferably before I leave tomorrow.'

'You're leaving tomorrow?' David's surprise showed in his voice – Barnard's only in his watchful eyes.

'I have other things to worry about as well as PS, you know. So has Gray – though I hope he will be able to stay a bit longer to help you settle in.' Both men were silent.

They dropped their baggage at a small hotel close to the Seine, and went directly to the agency nearby. Gerald Rule was waiting for them there.

He had in fact found the agency on only his second day in Paris. It was a relatively new firm, Agence de Lasaere. Guy de Lasaere had furnished his small premises in lavish style, with a modern sharp-cut touch that spoke of efficiency at work. He had established an excellent infrastructure, and a good reputation, with few but select clients.

Frances had approved of the price Rule had paid, and the speed with which the deal was done. Now he was waiting to introduce them to the departing de Lasaere, as well as to the staff who were staying on . . . accounts director Christian Olivier and copy chief Françoise Delibes, a chic, 40-year-old divorcee to whom Frances had warmed at once.

They were drinking champagne to celebrate the signing of the contract when Rule spoke again. 'Boss-lady – there's someone else I guess you should all meet. The creative director resigned when he heard of the take-over. But I managed to find an excellent replacement at very short notice. He is a talented creative man, with a strong sympathy for the product. I hope you will like him.'

Xavier Chatelaine appeared a second after Rule had telephoned to summon him. He had obviously been waiting for the call. He was the epitome of languid youth, looking no more than twenty, with a clear complexion and a hint of olive to his skin. His fine black hair was cropped fashionably close, with a thick hunk falling over his eyes. He wore a tight, red, V-neck sweater over baggily cut trousers and sneakers.

Frances had felt rather than seen David's reaction when Xavier entered the room. It had been like a spark of static electricity. Frances heard herself say: 'Glad to meet you,' as she shook the young man's hand. His grasp was cool and lifeless.

'*Enchanté, Madame.* I am most happy to make your acquaintance.' His English was charmingly hesitant, and strongly accented.

Then he was shaking hands with David. Frances noted the way their eyes met.

As if to reassure her, she saw David draw closer to Gaby, and hold her firmly round the shoulders.

Then, as they left the room a few minutes later, David was holding Gaby very close to him. Almost, Frances thought, like a shield.

CHAPTER TWENTY-THREE

It was like being struck in the solar plexus. Web never met her at airports . . . not since they had moved to New York. He said they had an unhealthy atmosphere, of partings and sadness, so Frances had made her own way to and from her frequent flights.

She had spotted him quite by chance, as she idly scanned the throng outside the glass doors of the arrivals lounge. Her mind had been filled with Gray Barnard, and memories of his power and tenderness. Suddenly Web's fall figure, standing out above a sea of faces, anxiously scanning the arrivals.

Her first thought was one of blind panic. Something has happened to Stacey! And fear clutched at her throat as she pushed her way through the plate glass doors and through the press of people beyond.

Webley spotted her only when she was a few feet away. His face broke into a wide welcome.

'What's the matter?' she almost shouted, over the shoulder of a fat woman who seemed determined to block her way. 'Where is Stacey?'

'Nothing's the matter,' said Web, still smiling rather foolishly. 'I just came to meet you, that's all.'

'C'mon, Web. It's the first time for years. What's the story?'

'Really, Frances, there's nothing.'

Guiding her through the crowds with a courtesy that would have been comical if it had not been so unexpected, his mood seemed buoyant, and his step jaunty. Affectionately, he helped her into the passenger seat, and carried her bags round to the back. It all simply made her more sure that something was wrong.

In the automobile, she grasped his arm as he reached towards the shift lever.

'Web, for Chrissakes. Will you tell me what the hell is going on!'

'Fran, don't be ridiculous. I had some time going free, so I thought it would make a nice change if I met you. Stacey is with Petra, and we'll pick her up later. Hey, don't knock it.'

He was playing some sort of game. That was obvious. Now Frances looked him over carefully. Dressed in brand-new clothes. They were well cut, and carefully chosen . . . totally foreign to Webley's pattern. What was he trying to hide? She remembered vaguely reading in a womens' magazine that when men got involved with other women, they often smartened up. What irony that would be!

Either that, or somebody had told Webley about her and Gray Barnard. Even so, why was he behaving so strangely?

She scanned her husband's face, almost as if for the first time in twenty-three years of marriage. Smooth skin, so unlike the rugged brown sandpaper texture of Gray Barnard's; uncommonly small hands, well-manicured, uncalloused, sleek from never having wielded an object heavier than a pen.

She did love Webley, and she loved him for reasons that nobody could change. Although she could see the vacuum her marriage had become, she felt herself being siphoned back into it.

Now Web spoke. A casual but completely uncharacteristic enquiry about how her trip had gone. 'And how was David? Has he settled into Paris okay?'

It occurred to her suddenly that David might have exposed her affair to his father. Impossible. David had not confided in Web-y for years. 'Have you talked to him?'

'No. I phoned your hotel twice. But you were both out.'

'Why didn't you leave a message?' An icy feeling moved down her neck, making her hackles rise.

'I didn't want to interfere,' he replied.

'Interfere? Goddamnit, Web – stop treating me like one of your neurotic patients. Tell me what's going on.'

They had pulled up at home and Lexington came galloping out to meet them. She felt a sudden rush, almost like an ache, at the familiarity of her surroundings.

She watched Web as he went to pick up the baggage. Inside his dapper new clothes, he looked a little smaller than usual, not quite so sharp around the edges. He was either going to confront her, or make a confession, thought Frances, and she wished he would get it over with.

'Stace?' she called down the bedroom corridor, as if to reassure herself the child wasn't lying there ill. She returned to the phone, but Web had already got there and was dialling Petra's number. Frances noticed the practiced ease with which he punched out the code on the push-buttons.

She uneasily wondered just how often Web dialled that number. Then she was talking to Stacey.

'My baby! Are you okay?'

'Sure, Mom. When did you get back?'

'Just arrived. I'll see you later.'

That was all Frances could manage. Then she passed the receiver wordlessly to Web, not wanting the child to hear the sobs that were racking her body, quite beyond her control.

Webley's arm encircled her. 'I'll fetch you later, kiddo,' she heard him say. 'Bye, honey.'

Then he turned to Frances and led her gently to the sofa. 'I'll fix us some strong coffee,' he said. 'Then we'll talk.'

Left alone, Frances' mind cleared rapidly. This whole homecoming thing had been so deliberately unsettling. Almost as if it had been stage-managed. As, of course, it had. Damn Webley, and damn his bloody manipulative mind. He knew about her affair, she was sure of that now.

When Web returned with a tray of coffee, Frances turned on him. 'You did that on purpose,' she said, her voice strangled by a mixture of anger and grief.

'What do you mean?'

'This whole scene; meeting me, having Stacey away. You did it to punish me, to make me afraid and insecure. It's what you've always done, isn't it? And I was too dumb to see it. I was too goddamn grateful you were around to stand in for me.'

She was close to hysteria, looking for any release from the tension that Webley's false cheerfulness had engendered. Standing abruptly, she walked to the window.

'Too fucking naive to realize that you've spent the whole of this so-called marriage of ours just tolerating me. You dangle my emotions on a string. You've allowed me the privilege of working, only to use it against me whenever it suited you.'

'I don't know what you're talking about, Fran,' he said. His

269

manner was clinical, and Frances wheeled round to face him, her face stained with tears.

'You hate me, don't you,' she said.

'Hate you?' Webley's voice was unfuriatingly mild and controlled. 'You are my wife. I love you. But I hate what your career has done to you, to me, and to Stacey. But hate never.'

Frances was screaming now. 'You resent me. You resent my success. You're trying to drag me down to your level.'

'Frances, I resent what you've become. But I love the real you.' Again, he was earnest and understanding, and Frances could stand no more of it. 'The real me? Web, for God's sake, this is the real me!' She jabbed her chest with her thumb, then she flung out of the room, slamming the door behind her, and locked herself into the bathroom.

Lying in the hot bath, she composed herself, gathering the shards and fitting them together. She washed her hair. And as she massaged her scalp, she remembered the feel of Gray's fingers, holding her head firmly while he skilfully pleasured her. She needed him with her right then.

Wrapped in a black and gold Terry towelling robe, she returned to the family room in search of her husband. He was sitting by the fire, engrossed in the blue and orange flickerings. A fresh pot of coffee was on the tray beside him.

Frances took a chair, and joined him in his scrutiny of the embers. He poured two cups and passed one to her.

'We must talk,' she said. 'How did you find out?'

Suddenly, she felt close to Web. Remarkably. She felt totally guiltless. Her major concern was not Web's reaction to her infidelity, but the fear that it might have been David who told him. How ironic, she thought, that by loving Gray I should lose David to Webley.

'I called the hotel,' said Web, in measured, level tones. 'Both you and David were out, so I thought I would leave a message. It was the *concièrge* . . . not anything she said, but just her tone, and the way she bracketed you and Barnard in the same way as she did David and Gaby. It made me suspicious.'

270

He was sitting forward, with his elbows on his knees, his eyes fixed on his tightly-clasped hands.

'I called again, half-an-hour later. By the time we'd finished speaking, I knew.' Now he looked up, and gave Frances a crooked smile. 'My training didn't do me much good when it came to my own wife, did it?'

He rose. 'Fran, we don't need to talk about it now. I love you. We'll sort it out. I'll go and fetch Stacey, and then I'll rustle us up some omelettes. When you're ready, you can tell me.'

Frances exploded at the condescension in his tone. 'Web! You're treating me like one of your goddamn patients again. I want to talk now. I want to tell you. It's necessary.'

She told Webley the story as honestly as she dared. He did not interrupt, staring into the fire, and making no attempt to delve further. Frances suddenly remembered a conversation they had once had, back in the mists of the years. 'I probe the sludge-baskets of people's minds all day. At home, I need peace.' Right now, Frances needed to talk. Long and hard.

When she had finished, she heard Webley speak, as if from far away. 'What's done is done,' he said. Frances was astonished by the complete lack of jealousy in him – as if part of him was missing.

'The point,' he continued, 'is what we're going to do about it now. We've got years ahead of us. You and me and Stacey.' Frances managed to avoid flinching. This was Web's deadliest stab.

'Now that it's behind us, we can try and make things work better. Put them together more strongly. Let's learn from this, and grow as human beings.'

The absurdity of his words struck Frances hard. Webley had always said that if she were to be unfaithful, he would leave her. Now it had happened, and he was talking about learning from it.

'We can't change what's happened,' he continued. 'I'm not about to throw up our lives because you've slept with another man. It happens. Though, I must say, I never thought it would happen to you. What I'm actually trying to say, Fran, is that I

271

can forgive you if you stop seeing him. Then we can heal it all up. We both know that.'

'For Chrissakes, Web. Stop being so fucking condescending. You haven't been listening to me. This isn't an affair. I *love* the man. And I went through hell trying to avoid . . . '

'Fucking him?' enquired Web mildly.

'Yes. Sleeping with him. Anyway, that side of it was incidental. He makes me feel like I haven't in years. I don't want to lose that.'

'You will in the end,' said Web. 'They all end the same way. How much are you prepared to destroy before you see that for yourself? It's an affair, that's all. A fling. Now it's over.'

'That's my decision, not yours,' she retorted. 'Whether I end it with Gray is not even at issue here. The issue is you and me. Our marriage, Webley, has been empty for years. I've always blamed myself and my work. Chrissakes! I was even grateful to you for enduring it, for allowing me to do my thing.' She snorted at the memory. 'And I lost sight of the real problem . . . you and me.'

'Frances, how many marriages work even half as well as ours?' Web raised his voice a tone, and Frances congratulated herself for having unleashed some real emotions in place of his psychiatrist's veneer.

'Goddamnit, we're married, you and I. We can't change that. You can't just wipe away the years just because you're cock-struck by another man. I presume it's a man, and not men.'

'Web, that's unfair. That's beneath you.'

'Fair!' he shouted. 'Fair! What do you know about fair?' He stormed out of the room, his coffee undrunk.

Cradling the receiver close to his face, he breathed the name to the switchboard operator. This was one thing he wanted to get over and done with, and although he was alone in the room, his speech was hardly audible.

When he was put through, he spoke more boldly.

'It's me . . . Hello. Can you hear me?'

'Well?'

'They've connected. It went like a dream.'

'You think it'll work?'

'I'm damn sure it will. You should have seen their eyes when they met. Like raisins in a fruit cake!' He laughed.

The other man let out a cynical snort. 'Well, I'm sure you're right. It can't fail.'

Stacey arrived in her usual carefree mood, hyped up as always after a day out. If she detected anything in the atmosphere, she didn't show it. Frances hugged her for an extra long time. As she clung to the little girl's boyish body, she felt an emotional pull so strong that it all but blotted out the void inside her.

She had disappeared for a while, into her bathroom to cry it out of herself.

Then she bathed Stacey, washed her hair, toasted her a ham-and-cheese sandwich, poured her a glass of milk, and tucked her up in bed.

'When are you going to stay home with us, Mommy?'

'We'll see, baby. We'll see.'

'Daddy's lonely without you. He said so.'

'Okay, baby. Go to sleep now.'

'Did you see Davey?'

'Yes. He says he loves you.'

'Did he write me a letter?'

'He will.'

By the time she went to bed, she thought Webley was asleep. And then, late in the night, he spoke, his voice husky with emotion.

'Just don't leave me, Fran.'

Maxwell J Bennis was in one of his more alert moods that morning. His suit was as creased as ever, but his prematurely aged body inside it seemed less flaccid. He was definitely pleased with himself.

The reason was plain to see. It front of him on the desk, a copy of the *Wall Street Journal* was open. It showed a picture of him – an old picture, Frances noticed – and an interview that quoted him at length on PS-21, and the impact on the world. CRANSTON CHIEF: LIFE EVERLASTING? ran the headline.

'Quite a stir, yóu seem to have caused here, Kline,' he said.

'Uh-huh,' said Frances. Perhaps now he'd been told about it by the *Wall Street Journal*, he would appreciate the significance of her Prostaglandin project.

It was six weeks since her return to New York, and her confession to Webley. Six weeks in which she had kept going on the daily trivia of life, and twice-daily telephone calls to Gray. Now, he was continually demanding that he come to New York, or she to Paris. And she countered the same way every time. 'Gray, darling. Give me time.' She knew it could not last much longer.

'Nice write-up in the paper here,' Maxwell continued, friendly and interested. 'They called me, you know, for my comments.'

'I saw.'

'I'm getting very good feedback on this one, Kline. When do you start manufacturing?'

'In about a month to six weeks,' Frances replied. 'Then we'll need another six weeks to build up stocks and get the product distributed. We're using Hamburg, Zurich, London, New York and Los Angeles as centres, with of course Paris at the hub.'

'Tell me how it works. I'm a little hazy on the technicalities. And what's the next step? They seemed very interested in that.'

'Well, PS-21 is low dosage – less than ten milligrams a day. We can sell it over the counter,' she said patiently. 'Next comes PS-35. With a dosage three times bigger. It's a whole different ballpark. We're still testing it; it won't be out for two years or so. We have positive evidence on file that PS-35 will rejuvenate a whole lot more than the skin. It retards arthritic changes, it can restart the growth of lost hair, and it even halts the ageing process within the lens of the eye. It's quite revolutionary.'

'Frances, that's remarkable. Why didn't you tell me this before?'

'Read the confidential reports, Max. It's all there.'

He ignored the remark. 'Anyway, the whole thing sounds very exciting. How are the production plans shaping up?'

'Well. Everything is on target, and all our supply lines are open. And we're about to finalize the marketing strategy and packaging.'

'What do you have in mind?'

'It's quite complex. On the one hand, we have a lot of technical information that we need to put across to the market; on the other, we don't want to confuse the buyers with medical jargon. But the agency we bought has a good record. Last year, they managed to capture seventy-five per cent of the market in France with a diet food . . . and selling diet-food in France is some achievement, Max. Their research was brilliant, taking in medical opinions and including the profession in the product right from the start. The result is that it's even being prescribed in some hospitals. It's just the sort of impact we need for PS-21. And with David in charge, I'm sure that we can make the most of it.'

'Are you sure David is the right man for the job?'

'Absolutely sure. And there's a big advantage for security. The agency is small, and he can control it all tightly.'

'Well,' said Bennis. 'Your track record shows that you know which horse to back, so I guess you can ride it through.'

'How is Ed Potter, by the way?' asked Bennis.

'It's slow, Max. Very slow. It'll be another six months before he's fit to get back to full-time work. I'm having Jo-Beth take the computer sales-runs to him twice a week, but that's more therapeutic than anything.'

'Why don't you go and see him, Max? He's only on 42nd Street – it's ten minutes by cab.'

'I'll try, Kline. I really will. But I've got a real load of work on at the moment.' They both knew he wouldn't go.

275

As Frances rose to leave, Maxwell Bennis appeared to remember something. 'By the way,' he called her back. 'Milton tells me he's having some trouble accommodating you on distribution.'

'What?' Frances spun round. 'What do you mean "difficulty", Max?'

'Well, you know, with his profits down, he feels the need to put more effort into their existing lines.'

'For Chrissakes, Max. Can't you see through his goddamn game plans?'

'I'm in the middle here, Kline.'

'Right, Max. And that's where you'd better stay. But you better keep your head down, out of the cross-fire. Because I'm going to take matters into my own hands now.'

'Jeez, boss-lady. That's *serious*. What can we do? Can we go it alone?' Gerald Rule shifted his glasses on the bridge of his nose.

Calling Gerry had been the first thing Frances had done after she'd stormed back to her office. She was livid – with Milton, for carrying out his earlier threat; and with herself, for not having anticipated his move. Well, now she would act. And if Milton thought he could assassinate PS-21 at this late stage, then he was wrong.

'There's no way, Gerry. We could set up a worldwide distribution network in a couple of months, but it would be damn difficult, and unbelievably expensive. No – there's only one way to handle this.'

'And what's that?'

'To do exactly what Milton least expects. We'll take it to the opposition. I will contact Merill and Fitch today and set up a meeting.'

'Merill and Fitch.' His frown redoubled in its intensity. 'That's dynamite, Frances.'

'Gerry, they are as hungry as anybody. They won't refuse a profitable deal. We'll make them an offer they can't refuse.'

'Can't you talk to Rae? We have a watertight contract with him.'

'No. He's dangerous, Gerry. Milton will stop at nothing to destroy Prostaglandin-S, and me with it.' She could have gone further, but she couldn't tell Gerry just how vulnerable she was to Rae. 'We're better off without him.'

'This will make waves in the corporation, Frances. I mean, involving the opposition is no joke.'

She sighed wearily. 'So what else is new? I have no choice. My back is against the wall.'

Frances spoke to Gray twice, sometimes three times a day, as he travelled between *Eerstevallei* and Paris. Having him involved gave Frances a wonderful feeling of sharing and security. For the first time, she was able to delegate to someone else with total confidence. She knew she'd needed him on the project, irrespective of her personal feelings for him. As a colleague, he had been exceptional, handling the operation with precision and speed, ahead of schedule, matching her energy and skill, and adding a synergy to the whole experience.

Moving together towards the climax of the launch, in touch with each other's pent-up emotions and energies, had made their separation easier to bear.

Frances knew that soon she would have to take drastic decisions. Right now, she needed breathing space, at least until PS-21 was off the ground. This was a cop-out of sorts. Frances was much too honest and aware of her emotions not to know that. Both Gray and Web were important to her. Both were a part of her life.

Working with Gray as well as loving him was a new sort of exhilaration. The one fed the other. But she could never allow her love to colour her business judgement. She was far too disciplined for that.

Gray had no illusions about the fact that he was intruding on her relationship with Web. In fact, he told Frances he had

277

reached the stage where he intended to. It was one of a pattern of growing demands. Twice in the past month, he had called her house and spoken first to Web before asking for her. Frances had toyed with the idea of the interaction between the two men, with her as a silent observer.

'Lover-boy okay?' Web asked the second time, as she replaced the receiver.

'Oh Web, for Chrissakes. If you want to talk about it, let's talk. But I can do without the sarcasm.'

She could feel his pain through the silence that followed. Then he spoke. 'I'm riding this one out, Fran. There's nothing to discuss. I told you – do what you must, until it's over.'

'You mean you're really hoping this will disappear. That we'll wake up one morning, and it will all be gone. Dammit, Web. Why can't you confront the issue?'

'I am confronting it, Fran. I know human beings well enough to know that this will wear off. We have too much together, our bonds are too strong. Stacey is too important. There is no way this marriage is about to be ruined just because of one affair. Do it, and get it over with.'

He turned to face her. 'You take your time. What is important is that you come back to me of your own free will.'

During the six weeks, Web hadn't attempted to make love to her, as though afraid that the physical act would bring about new uncertainties. But at night, he would hold her and stroke her gently to sleep, as if to create closeness without invading her sexual privacy.

As she fell asleep, Frances wondered how much of his concern was that of a loving husband, and how much the watchful experience of a predictive analyst.

The heat around his neck and chest was stifling. He tugged at the tie, and loosened his top button. 'Yes?' he said into the receiver.

'Milt.' The voice was light and casual. 'Still giving trouble!' Clements was turning the screw, but anyone listening to him would have thought the conversation was of no more importance than the giving of directions to a cab driver.

'You listen here,' said Rae. 'Just you get off my back. And tell your fancy-pants lady to get fucked.'

'Really, Milton. I don't think you're taking this seriously enough. Have you forgotten about poor little Jeremy?'

Rae sat fuming in silence. He was searching for words, but the image of the boy dead on the washroom floor was suddenly vivid in front of him again.

'Play ball, Rae. Just play ball. Or you are out!'

'Go to hell, Clements,' Rae yelled. But the lawyer had already rung off.

Then Rae replaced the receiver slowly on its cradle, his face preoccupied, his eyes filled with a growing fear. Whatever it was that Kline was into, it was starting to look more massive than he had bargained for.

CHAPTER TWENTY-FOUR

After six weeks in Paris, David Kline felt as if he had walked every inch of the banks of the Seine near his apartment in the Quai des Celestines. He had spent hours on end studying the old motor barges that plied the river, and moored beneath his windows, watching the way the bargee families went about their waterborne lives, and envying them the companionable atmosphere.

He loved Paris for her cultural riches. He communed with the Post-Impressionists in the *Jeu de Paume* gallery, and tramped the corridors of the Louvre. Paris fed his sense of ancient history, and he followed the few remaining traces of the Roman occupation, visiting archaeological sites and museums, enthralled by what he saw.

He enjoyed discovering the other side of the City of Light – the human side, tucked away from tourists, and kept for the locals.

There was no doubt about it, though – since Gaby had left to take up modelling commissions that were just too good to miss, David had been desperately lonely. At first, he had enjoyed the solitude. Now that Rae had let his secret out, he was relieved, and felt closer to his mother than he had for years. His only concern was that he had made her vulnerable to blackmail. That was something he tried to avoid thinking about.

At the agency, he had been guarded about making friends. He felt it was easier to maintain his authority without the complication of personal relationships. The responsibility was a new-found pleasure; he was good at making decisions, and at making them stick; and having to do so taught him a new respect for Frances. Until now, he had taken her business skills and her rapid rise to the top for granted. Now he appreciated her calibre, and admired her the more.

The plans for the PS-21 launch were progressing well. David had designed a simple graphic logo in two shades of green, an allusion to springtime and fresh growth that was carried through in the packaging. He had found a glamorous French model, whose looks belied her age of thirty-eight, and devized a strategy that clearly placed the first-generation PS product in a niche of its own, between patent medicines, and cosmetics. The work was of course top secret, and Frances was the only person outside the agency who had seen the proposals. She had changed the concept only slightly, to include the model's three children in some of the visuals, to add a sense of family, wellbeing.

Aside from the solitude, only one thing had marred David's six weeks in Paris – the necessity of dealing regularly with Gray Barnard. Though the giant South African was unfailingly polite, and clearly had a brilliant flair for business, it was his relationship with David's mother that counted more than David's antipathy for the politics of his homeland.

It had not taken long for David to realize that Barnard and Frances were lovers. In fact, he had suspected it from the first. It was the way Frances looked at Gray – David had never seen her eyes look so green. It showed in the way they walked together, the natural way their hands brushed against one another, and in the unspoken bond that made David feel like an outsider when he was in their company.

It was not the cuckolding of his father that upset David. He had already grown to abhor Webley's weakness, and his own relationship with his father had been empty for many years. But he loved his mother, and Gray Barnard was an intruder.

Sometimes, the very thought of the sun-browned Afrikaner mounting and penetrating his mother rose so strongly in front of David's mind's eye that he had to try and walk it out of his system. Now, leaning over the parapet of the Pont Boulevarde Sully, staring at the tourists like goldfish beneath the plastic dome of a sight-seeing river boat, he resolved to try and cope . . . for the moment, at least.

There had been one exception to his standoffish approach to the agency staff – Xavier Chatelaine. His creative director had been friendly to him from the moment they first met, and David found he was spending more and more time with the languid young man, with his gentle manners and quick rather cruel sense of humour.

The occasional lunch together and the odd movie had now turned into several evenings a week, sitting at a pavement café talking late into the night, over glasses of the cloudy Anis liqueur that Xavier eventually taught him to enjoy.

Xavier had turned out to be a real professional asset. He had produced excellent copy, sharp and to the point, which conveyed precisely the kind of image David and Frances had envisaged.

It was professional respect as much as personal admiration that had drawn David to him at first, though the initiative had come from the young Frenchman, and now David had come to rely on Xavier to relieve the worst of his depressions before they began. The two men – the blonde and lean-muscled American and the dark, languid Frenchman with long eyelashes over eyes like deep pools, shared their thoughts with a growing intimacy.

And yet no warning bells rang in David's head. His relationship with Milton Rae had been so different.

It had all been so long ago. It started at a dinner party at the new Kline home in Westchester County. David had left the company early, and was bathing, slithering his soapy hands over his young erection, his mind wandering over formless erotic images, when suddenly the door opened. It was Milton Rae, who met his eyes wordlessly, then stepped inside to finish off his pleasuring for him with a deft hand. The relationship had lasted for two years, until David had finally fled from New York to escape it.

In fact, he had already spent a night with Xavier, after an evening's drinking had taken David too far. He dimly remembered a short taxi-ride, but it was not until he awoke the next morning, his head thick and his tongue dry and swollen, that he realized he was in Xavier's apartment, in Xavier's bed, with his young friend offering him a cup of strong coffee.

'Jesus,' said David. 'What happened?'

Xavier laughed. 'Nothing. You just had too much to drink. I didn't know how to get you into your apartment, so I brought you here instead.'

'I'm sorry,' said David. 'But if I slept in your bed, where did you sleep?'

'Next to you. No problem.' Xavier's smile was direct, his eyes unveiled. Vaguely, David remembered the silkiness of his skin, and the warmth of his body. Yet there was no embarrassment in it for either of them, and the innocence of the experience instead made David feel reassured.

Ten days before Frances was due to return to Paris, Xavier and David were finishing a meal at an intimate restaurant close to his apartment. 'David,' said Xavier, the lilt in his voice as charming as ever, 'I have an uncle, Comte Duvernet. He is, how you say, a widower . . . a very *rich* widower, living in the most beautiful chateau you have ever seen. He has no family but myself, and I always make a point of sharing at least one weekend a month with him. I would love it if you could join me there this weekend.'

'Xavier!' David laughed. 'I never knew you had aristocratic connections.'

The Frenchman also laughed. 'It is a cross that I have to bear.'

'I'd really like to,' said David. 'When are you going down?'

'We can leave straight from the agency on Friday evening. It's a lovely ride down, and the countryside is wonderful. But the old man is a bit bleak – don't expect a lot of laughs at dinner. Still, we can have a good time.'

To an American, the very thought of ancient European nobility exercised a powerful fascination – a fact that David recognized in himself with wry amusement. 'Gee, the closest I've been to real nobility was a one-night stand with a forty-year-old who claimed to be a Polish countess. This'll be a real cultural experience for me.'

'A countess I can't offer you. One of the Comte's pretty country housemaids, perhaps. But bring a smoking.'

'A smoking? What the hell's that?'

'What the English call a dinner jacket. The Comte is very formal. Not to say formidable.'

Once they had escaped from the traffic that choked Paris, it was a drive of an hour-and-a-half along winding country roads, through dark and brooding forests, and tiny villages clustered around café-bars that seemed deserted. Once, as they paused at a junction, an owl swooped low in front of the car, gliding soundlessly on wide-spread wings.

Xavier drove an open Alfa-Romeo in pillarbox red, that had seen better days, but could still muster an impressive turn of speed. He drove with more exuberance than skill, relying on the car's agility to get them round bends, tyres screeching on the hard surface to be answered by a whoop of delight from the Frenchman.

David was nervous at first, and in the dim light of the dashboard, he could see the whites of Xavier's eyes. He seemed to be in a state of euphoria. Then David abandoned himself to the same state, and the two men grinned at one another as they soared down a straight section at death-defying speed.

It was as if they were drunk on the speed, their minds turned by the chilling wind that whipped at their hair, and struck at the back of their throats.

Then Xavier swung the car off the forest road and into the deeper blackness of a single track which ended at the foot of a pair of huge wrought-iron gates, their pillars almost disappearing into the dark night sky. Floating in the glow of the headlights, a pair of arthritic legs in flapping blue dungarees hobbled to the latch and swung the gates open. They were clearly expected.

Arrogantly, Xavier revved the engine and shot through the gate, wheels spinning and kicking up the gravel, ignoring the faceless serg who had let them in. Even after they had climbed from the car, they both had difficulty in containing their exuberance.

A servant, skin creased by the folds of age and his voice softened by aeons of servitude, led them stoop-shouldered through to a black-beamed room, walls heavy with laden bookshelves and huge tapestries, the aged yellow glow of rural electricity fighting a losing battle against centuries of darkness trapped within the old stone walls. Only now, amid this powerful atmosphere, did the elation evaporate, and David felt suddenly rather humble.

They had been shown to twin bedrooms, one alongside the other in a wing lined with doors that seemed as though they had been sealed for centuries. In these surroundings, the enormous antique furniture looked normal-sized, and David felt overawed by the history. Subdued now, he dressed in his rented dinner jacket, and waited until Xavier called him for the evening meal. Dressed up, each flicked an appraising glance over the other's finery.

If possible, Comte Duvernet was even more decrepit than his

manservant, and it seemed to take whole minutes for him to lower himself into the heavy, high-backed chair at the distant end of a long rosewood banqueting table. It was only after he had tucked his napkin into his collar and sat back that he haughtily acknowledged Xavier's introduction of David Kline. Though his manner was dry, his civility was most courtly, and his English perfect.

'It is thoughtful of you, Xavier-Pierre, to bring a guest with you. I am too often alone. However, I must remind you that here you do not have licence to behave as you do in the sewers of Paris. I am sure that Monsieur Kline is of the finest breeding, but I advise you strongly not to have him splash about in the muddy waters of your usual choosing.'

There was no answer to that, and an oppressive stillness descended over the table, broken only by the shuffling of the servant as he set a dish of simple salad in front of the three dinner companions, and then the sound of heavy silver cutlery against old bone china. David ate slowly, more than slightly in awe of the old man's presence, commanding in spite of his senility.

The oily salad was followed by a course of meat that David was unable to identify, it was so drenched in sauce, and then the meal was apparently over – the end signified only by the fact that the servant shuffling over the flagstones stopped bringing wine, and instead brought a decanter of port.

The old man spoke again. 'An English custom, I believe,' his yellow teeth bared in a humourless smile. 'One of the few that is worth following. Ah – but of course you are American. A land that has given us no worthwhile customs at all.'

The tension made David want to giggle, and as he met Xavier's eyes, he did so, behind his table napkin, a brief explosion.

The old man gave no sign of having noticed. He drank only half of his small glass of port, then signalled to the manservant with a shrunken hand. The ancient retainer came and helped him from the chair, and then – stooping alongside him – led him shuffling from the room.

After the servant had swung the heavy door closed painfully,

Xavier spoke for the first time. 'David, there is no doubt about it. I think that he likes you.' Then he flung his head back, and shrieked with laughter. Hesitantly at first, and then with a return of their former exuberance, David joined in, as Xavier seized the decanter of fine vintage port, and splashed both of their glasses to the brim.

'Ah, these rich old men,' Xavier shook his head, and quaffed deep on the musty-sweet liquor. 'He may be my uncle, but he would be better off dead. It is to me very sad that men like the Comte cannot enjoy their wealth.'

'At least it is his own, so I suppose he's entitled to do with it what he will,' said David.

'What nonsense. But don't let us bother about it. Let us take advantage of the old man's money, and enjoy it in a way that is fitting.' With that he rose, and led David through a different door.

They went into a small reception room, the ceiling ornate with gilded beams, and the furniture of rich wood and red velvet, reflecting the elegant grace of the Louis XIV period. The tiled floor was scattered with exotic rugs, and ornate ceramic figurines cluttered the mantelpiece – delicate china on exquisite polished cherry-wood. A large silver tray with crystal decanters and glasses picked the subdued lighting into points and stars, while an ice-bucket was dewed with condensation.

'Come, *mon ami*,' said Xavier 'Let us drink and be merry. We know how to enjoy life.' And he poured each of them a large measure of whiskey. Xavier's exuberance was new to David. He had known him happy, and always enthusiastic. But never this euphoria, as brittle as the crystal glasses they drank from. It was when Xavier took a small lacquered box from his pocket, and took out cigarette papers and a block of something that looked like henna, that David realized why – especially when he glimpsed a small square of paper folded like a miniature envelope remaining in the tin.

Xavier was stoned.

David had smoked grass before, though never as hashish. He watched as Xavier rolled a joint, and drew deeply when he passed it to him. But he knew marijuana alone could not account for the young Frenchman's mood.

Then Xavier took one of the pictures down from the wall, polished the glass front, and laid it on the table. Taking out the folder, he scattered a small amount of white powder on the glass. Then he took a straight-bladed knife from his pocket, chopped the chunks into a fine powder, and assembled it into two lines on the glass.

As he did this, he didn't look at David. Only when he had finished did he look up, and meet his friend's astonished gaze. Slightly embarrassed, he smiled. 'Don't worry, David. It's just a little cocaine. Nothing heavy. Why don't you have some.'

'For Christ's sake, Xavier, what are you into?'

'David, please. It's just coke. Just the occasional buzz. Over weekends. It helps me to get my head together – it regenerates my creativity. It's not dangerous, like heroin. Have a little.'

David knew that cocaine was common in fashionable circles. It was the champagne drug, what the jet-set used to make their parties go with a swing.

Quickly, he nodded, and then watched as Xavier rolled up a crisp ten franc note into a cylinder, and inhaled the larger of the two lines before passing the picture, with the note still balanced on it, across to him. Quickly, he sniffed, feeling a slight sting at the back of his nose, and then a sudden rush of well-being that made him sit back in his chair with a slow smile.

What he hadn't noticed was that the powder he had inhaled had come from a different compartment within the white envelope, and that when he was overcome with drowsiness half an hour later, Xavier's eyes were still bright, and rather greedy, as he slipped his arm under David's and helped him up the stairs.

The boy, for that is what Xavier had become, had about him a hairless silkiness that slid luminescently against David's skin. He was smoother than anyone he had felt – smoother even than Gabrielle's dusky pelt. Limbs entangled with limbs in an

287

infinitely calm slowness, a melding of flesh with flesh.

It was the most natural thing in the world, to be in bed with this boy, to be kissing him, to answer his caresses with his own gentleness, to enjoy every inch of him, stretched alongside him in the big old four-poster bed.

All the time, David had clarity of mind such as he had never known before. It was as if the inside of his skull was lined with polished glass; as if he were floating weightless inside a transparent balloon. All he saw and did had about it a heightened brightness, a sharpness of edge that he had never experienced before.

He was aware of the silvery moonlight striking against the heavily buffed furniture, the washstand and its bowl, the brass dome and ceramic toggle of the light switch beside the door – even the tongue-and-groove ceiling boards, and the cleanliness of Xavier's perfectly manicured fingernails, as he lifted his partner's hand to his own lips.

This was different from the crass and guilt-ridden hotel-room fumblings with Milton Rae, different even from the alternately powerful and lazy lovemaking with Gaby, who never seemed satisfied, who always wanted it to last a little longer, to start a little sooner, and to happen a little more often.

This was quite different from anything he had ever known before.

With Xavier, the sensation was total. He felt he was attaining the ultimate in physical contact; making love to himself. But more than that, even – it was as though he were holding his own image, separate from himself, in his own hands, moulding the separate tissues into his own body; kneading the softness and hardness, the smoothness and the hairiness, of a body he had known since birth.

Awash with a chemical ecstasy, he allowed himself to explore and be explored. He exposed every sense and every organ. And then, as their release came together, David marvelled: like waves crashing on the floor, like stars in the sky . . . like every cliché I've ever read about – only far, far better.

CHAPTER TWENTY-FIVE

Possessed, David ran across lawns wet with dew. He was dressed in shirtsleeves, sockless, but he didn't notice the dawn chill in the air. Only one thing in his mind . . . escape.

He ran towards the wrought-iron gates without a glance back at the chateau, stone brooding upon stone, impassive and unyielding. Fumbling for the catch, he let himself out, and ran on, down the sandy track through the forest, towards public roads. Only then did it occur to him that he didn't know where he was. Oh God, he thought. Anywhere, but not here, and not now.

Six hours later, he was in his apartment on the Quai de Celestines, steaming in a hot bath. The journey had been a humiliating nightmare, but still a welcome release from the remorse that threatened to drive him mad. Now as he lay in the soothing balm of the hot water, he leafed through an encyclopaedia of drug abuse, until he found the section on cocaine. The drug, he read, has a mild effect, especially on first-time users. It stimulates the mind to a state of self-confidence, makes the user talkative and exuberant. Nowhere did he read that it causes drowsiness, nor an abandonment of usual behaviour patterns. Nor, he read, does it necessarily stimulate sexuality.

It was then that he suspected he had been doped.

It was late on Sunday night that he finally summoned up the courage to call Xavier. A day spent moping along had helped him come to terms with his loss of self-control: now he wanted to find out the facts. In any case, he would have to face Chatelaine at the agency the next morning. Best to get it over with.

Xavier's voice was quiet, almost shy. 'David, I'm coming to your apartment now,' he cut him short. 'We can talk about it then.'

As he waited for his lover to arrive, David paced the small

apartment, prowling from sitting room to bedroom and kitchenette, making himself a mug of instant coffee, then discarding it for a stiff Scotch. Thinking the matter through, he was surprised at his violent remorse. It was not the morality that concerned him – on the contrary, he had enjoyed the encounter, and could quite easily contemplate repeating it. It was his failure to keep his word to his mother that upset him . . . his own weakness.

His feelings towards Xavier were similarly mixed – resentment at the suspicion he had been doped against his will, combined with a strong desire to be with him again. Then he heard his characteristic knock.

'David.' Xavier's anxious little smile and the uncertainty in his voice pulled at a string of sympathy in David's confusion. 'What happened? How did you get home? I have been infinitely worried.'

David did not give Xavier a detailed description of his appalling journey home – how, clad only in a shirt, trousers and shoes, his appearance had caused passing motorists to accelerate by as though he was some sort of troublesome vagrant. Stumbling he had walked for two hours, with painful feet, quite exhausted, into the village of Le Chatellet-ren-Brie. He had made for the *gendarmerie*, where he had been treated with suspicion. Without money or identity documents, not even knowing where the chateau was, and unwilling to tell them the truth, they had simply not known what to make of him. When they assumed he had been bankrolled by a hooker, he was happy to agree. They had insisted on delivering him to his apartment to establish his credentials.

'Never mind that. I hitched a ride. I got home okay. Listen, Xavier. I want the truth. What did you give me last night? I'm damn sure it wasn't cocaine.'

At first, Xavier said nothing. He sprawled on the couch, misery in his eyes, his jaw muscles rippling beneath his soft skin as he clenched and unclenched them. Then he spoke quickly, with a false snicker. 'Nothing much, David. Just a little smack mixed in. Just a bit of fun, that's all.'

Suddenly, David became angry. He rose to his feet, fists balled. 'Fun! You gave me heroin for fun? Jesus Christ, Xavier – you'd better tell me everything. Or else you're finished, you Goddamn junkie faggot!'

Then Xavier sat up straight, met David's eyes, and launched into a tortured confession.

'David, it is all my fault, my fault entirely. What you say is true. I am a junkie. It's not just coke and marijuana. I'm on heroin. David, I'm hooked!'

It was a cry from the depths of human despair, manifesting a pain that David could only begin to imagine. For the moment, he forgot himself, overcome with sympathy for the lost soul who sat shivering and pathetic in front of him.

'David, I am a total failure. Not long ago, I was an example to anyone. The perfect well-bred Frenchman. Then, at seventeen, I started to look for ways to give me freedom that religion and respectability could never give me. It started slowly – the odd smoke with my friends, cough mixtures and amphetamines . . . things that I thought were safe. And then,' - tears of self-pity rimmed his beautiful eyes – 'I found better things. More instant.'

Xavier stood up, his lean frame impeccably clothed in the fashions of the day. Wringing his hands wretchedly, he sank to the floor, curled up like an overgrown foetus. 'Why me? As though God has selected me for punishment. At first, it was all so good. I was able to work for twenty-four hours every day, without sleep . . . to produce the most magnificent creations. Then it started to go sour. I couldn't produce anything without drugs. I needed something stronger all the time. First heroin, just now and then. Before I knew it, I was hooked.

'I stopped caring about anything, or anyone. As long as I could get my supplies. Nothing else mattered. But now it has changed, David. I do care about someone. Believe me you must – I care about you.'

Xavier had stood as he spoke, and then sat down alongside David. He reached for David's hand. David felt a sudden surge of compassion for the man who earlier he felt had betrayed him. Spontaneously, their fingers intertwined.

And then David's arm was around Xavier, hugging the young Frenchman to him as sobs racked his slender frame, patting him and soothing him and smoothing his hair. 'It's okay, Xavier. I understand. I forgive you. We'll work it out together, okay? Just for a start, I need to know where you get your stuff from.'

Calmer now, Xavier spoke without emotion. 'From the street markets, and in clubs . . . the usual way. Until two months ago. Then a dealer I have never met before approached me. He was breaking into the market, he said. He could supply me all that I wanted, at half the usual price. Good quality stuff, and always reliable. So for two months I have had no problems, and no danger. Fresh supplies just a phonecall away.'

'But that's not normal, surely?' said David. 'Why has it been made easy for you? There has to be a reason.'

'I don't know,' said Xavier. 'I suppose they are after my uncle's money. When he dies, I will be a very rich man, you know.'

'Well, then they will call in the tab, Xavier. And you'd better be ready to pay it.' He felt the Frenchman stiffen involuntarily, overcome with a sudden fear that showed in his limpid eyes.

'Don't leave me, David, please. Just stay with me. I really care for you. Please don't go away.'

For long minutes, David said nothing. He stared grimly at the wall, his eyes blank windows to thoughts that he did not wish to acknowledge, let alone speak. Then he drew Xavier close again. 'I won't leave you,' he said. 'Got nowhere to go, have I.'

A cold rattle of windswept leaves, scudding across an autumnal Central Park, greeted Frances Kline as she strode purposefully from the chauffeured Cadillac across the sidewalk and through the automatic glass doors of the Cranston Tower lobby. The doorman saluted her as she passed, and an elevator arrived and swished its doors open almost as if it had been exclusively

292

awaiting her arrival. Good, she thought. That's the kind of thing I need plenty of today.

In her office, she asked Jo-Beth to summon Joe Mitchell and her other vice-presidents for a final meeting before she departed for Paris to supervise the launch of PS-21. It was Thursday. She was due to fly the next morning. A full-scale publicity exercise was planned for the following Monday, at the same time as the production protocols were due to be sent to the laboratories for the final tests and go-ahead.

Submerged in this crucial phase, Frances had had little time to devote to the personal problems of her life and loves. She couldn't understand Web's attitude, but she thanked God for it. There was no re-appraisal of their relationship, no fresh definition to cope with this new problem. She knew he was hurting, but he wouldn't discuss it. Frances saw it as yet more evidence of weakness on Web's part . . . but given the circumstances, she was more relieved than angry.

Even her frequent calls to Gray had concentrated on business rather than the love that was quite undiminished by separation. Barnard had been commuting back and forth between Paris and *Eerstevallei*, and the importation of the processed extract of *Dorothaneum* had proved easier and less fraught by red tape than either of them had imagined possible. The members of the *Eerstevallei* co-op had responded with a will to the increased demand for the product, and had cleared another thirty acres of ground to build up the harvest the following season. The manufacturing works had processed two-and-a-half tons of raw material, which had yielded fifty kilograms of pure extract . . . enough to supply the first six months' projected sales, with more to come.

She had also spoken to David almost daily. He had been jubilant about the work that the Agency Lasaere had produced, although she had sensed a withdrawal in him recently. The campaign comprised not only visual and television advertising, but also one of the best press kits she had ever seen, which was now being sent out to newspapers all around the world.

She had briefed Merrill and Fitch – deadly rivals to the Cranston Group – on distribution and sales plans for PS-21, and they were geared up to airfreight the first production to their depots world-wide. As she had predicted, they had leapt at the opportunity to share in the profits forthcoming from the biggest innovation in pharmaceutical cosmetics for centuries.

M&F's quick agreement had allowed her to outflank Milton Rae. He was swiftly cut out of a deal that would have yielded him millions. For reasons of personal revenge, he had cost his division a fortune. If he was prepared to do that, thought Frances, there was no telling where he would stop.

Joe Mitchell had come into her office looking exhausted but elated. He had returned late the previous night from a country-wide motivation programme for the M&F representatives and the key wholesale outlets. With a video team and an elaborate presentation, he had given them comprehensive information on the product and the marketing plans, and the incentive programme designed to get the product into the shops, bought, tried and repurchased. He had been overwhelmed by the enthusiasm his presentation had generated.

'They loved it, Frances,' he said as he came in. 'The comments were just fantastic. In LA, they gave us a standing ovation!'

'That's great, Joe. I'm proud of you. Now what about Europe and the UK?'

'All planned for next week. It's one hell of a rush, but we'll make it. Sure hope it goes as well as it has here. I expected sceptics, you know – doubters. But I've never seen a bunch of guys so excited.'

And now, thought Frances, the world was waiting – with news reporters, TV stations and gossip columnists daily pestering Cranston for more information, cosmetic houses clamouring for details, even the trainer of an Olympic athletics team trying to get an inside track.

'Joe,' said Frances. 'Is there anything else, anything we've forgotten. Any loose strings? Have you double-checked the Hotel Roosevelt for the press launch in Paris?'

'Yes, ma'am,' the young man flashed a confident smile, his excitement representative of the growing sense of achievement that had pervaded Frances' floor of Cranston Towers.

'Everything is just great. We've been through everything a million times. Nothing, absolutely nothing has been left to chance.'

Milton Rae focussed on Frances Kline from across the room. To anyone who knew him well, he had aged visibly. Stress had made his cheeks sag, and the bags under his eyes – portmanteaux of unresolved problems and lack of sleep – were puffy and stained a deep purple.

Frances was standing, the only woman among a group of men – Maxwell J Bennis, Yale Duke and Stig Petersen, one of the non-executive members of the Cranston Board. She was dressed typically, Rae thought with scorn. Bright colours, that made her stand out – yes, tarty colours. But he was forced to admit that Frances was able to carry them off without looking cheap.

Rae had arrived late at the cocktail party, and already it had divided into distinct groups . . . males, females, and what he called the transit group. These were couples who had just arrived – husbands and wives exchanging pleasantries, before splitting up to join members of their own sex.

In all his years attending the quarterly Board cocktail parties, it had always been the same. Only Kline didn't conform to type. With or without her husband, and Rae noted that this time she was without him, she invariably ended up with the men.

As he watched her, his eyes narrow, she broke away from the group she was with, and moved across to talk to Gerry Rule. Rae wasn't listening to Cutler, who was discussing a client problem, and with his assistant in mid-sentence, he rudely turned his back and moved over towards Kline.

'Gee, boss-lady, I never thought you'd have the nerve. I hear the M&F guys loved it,' Rule was saying.

Frances laughed. 'Yeah. I didn't think I'd have the nerve either. But really I was left with no choice . . . ' She broke off, as she saw Rae bearing down on them.

Rae appeared neither to have heard nor to care what they were talking about. He spoke right across Rule, as if he were not there, his lip curling in a smile that ended up more like a snarl. 'I see you've brought the opposition into your little scheme.'

It took a supreme effort of will for Frances not to reply. She met his eyes for long enough for him to be sure she had heard and understood him, and then turned on her heel. Taking Rule by the arm, she led him away to a vacant spot on the other side of the room.

Rae was left fuming, his eyes bulging. Quickly, he glanced around the room, to see if anyone had noticed the snub. In fact, only Cutler had seen it, and he had turned away to hide a satisfied smile. Rae composed himself, put on a casual smile, and walked over to join his fellow board members.

Frances, meantime, was feeling pleased with herself. She had managed to insult Rae without saying a word. Had she answered back, that would only have been to invite a reply. And who knows what it would have been . . .

Gerry, on the other hand, was not troubling to conceal his anger. He threw a poisonous glance at Rae, and then turned to Frances. 'I don't know how you manage to keep so calm,' he said. 'Can't you get rid of him once and for all?'

Frances only smiled. 'Not yet,' she said. 'Not quite yet.'

Then she started to laugh, quietly at first, then uproariously, until Gerald Rule was infected and he too was overcome with laughter.

CHAPTER TWENTY-SIX

Alone at Orly airport. Frances stood scanning the faces that filed out into the arrivals hall – looking for sun-tans and luggage labels that would tell her the passengers from the Johannesburg flight were coming through.

She had arrived in Paris the day before, for a furious afternoon and evening at work with David and Randy, so as to leave the weekend clear to spend with Gray. The manufacturing process was under way now, with sample protocols ready for delivery to official laboratories on Monday. All tests were expected to be completed within a week – and Frances was so confident that they would be nothing more than a formality that she had given the go-ahead for the machines to start rolling.

She had left David and his agency team hard at work, putting the finishing touches to the print campaign, re-editing the sound-track of the television ads, and finalizing the presentation to the press scheduled for Monday morning. Extra capacity for the hundreds of journalists who had requested invitations to the launch, in addition to those already invited had had to be arranged. They would overflow the hotel ballroom.

Not only did they now have closed-circuit television coverage to two more conference rooms in the hotel, but also simultaneous translation to twelve different languages – including Chinese and Swahili.

She put it to the back of her mind, in the anticipation of seeing Gray again for the first time in almost two months. It had been so long: and she was anxious that time and distance might have created a barrier between them.

She had dressed with extra care, after a cold shower. Freshly shampooed hair a mane of blonde silk, set off her expectant features. Her while silk shirt collar was pulled up to emphasize

297

her profile, and in white slacks and a navy Gucci jacket, she felt gloriously vital.

How familiar he looks. Her first thought as she saw Gray looming large over the crowds now pouring from the exits. It feels as though I've known him for a million years. She could feel the chasm of separation close in an instant as she moved towards him through the crowds.

His face was lined with fatigue, but he was smiling uncontrollably, his eyes like two blue searchlights. As he swept her up into his arms, she had a fleeting thought – that airport lounges were such sterile, impersonal places, and yet people shared their more intimate emotions there.

He was the first to speak. 'Franci. I don't want to be away from you again. Never.' The words and his love wrapped her like a blanket, and then they were talking furiously, the sentences spilling out. Peeling away the weeks of tension and loneliness, she noticed that already he looked younger than when he had first arrived. She suspected that she did too.

They were five kilometres along the road to Orleans, heading south-west away from Paris, before Gray noticed they were heading the wrong way. 'Hey, where are we going?'

'A little surprise. I'm kidnapping you for the weekend. There's nothing we can do before Monday except eat, sleep . . . and make love. I want you all to myself for one-and-a-half days. Any objections?'

Gray gave the grin she loved so much. 'None, my darling. None at all.'

'We start early on Monday. Breakfast with David.' She waited for a reaction. There was none. 'We'll run through the whole campaign. Which, by the way, is sensational. The launch starts at ten – should last less than three hours. After that, straight to the factory, to check out any last-minute decisions with Randy. Then I've planned a celebration dinner for all of us at the Tour d'Argent. After that, we just have to wait a week or so for the test results, and then everything is full steam ahead. Gray, we're almost there.' She gave an exultant whoop.

'And then the problems start,' he said, looking earnest.

'What do you mean?' she said, with a quick, worried frown.

'I mean, what are you going to do for an encore?'

She giggled again. 'No encore, except . . . ' She responded to his earnest look. 'I think I'll buy another hotel. In Paris, this time. Just to keep from getting bored.'

As she spoke, she could feel Gray's eyes on her. She kept her own on the road ahead. His hand had been resting on her shoulder. Now it moved down, tracing the contours of her torso through the thin silk of her shirt, moving across her stomach, then down to her legs, to her knee, and then back up the inside of her thigh. 'Where are we going?' he said. 'I need you very soon.'

She could feel the chemistry of her body give a quick flip, feel the moistness rise within her, her eyelids go heavy with sudden desire. Slamming on the brakes, she pulled off the side of the road and turned to face him. 'If you carry on doing that I'll . . . '

She didn't get a chance to finish the sentence. Gray's arms were around her, holding her roughly. He kissed her hard. She could feel him bruising her lips, his teeth grating against hers, his tongue probing her mouth. She pulled away, gasping for air. 'Let's get to the hotel.' Then, after she had recovered her breath more: 'We're going to a place on the Loire. Near Amboise. The Chateau de Pray – one of the few genuine old chateaux that take guests.'

Soon afterwards, they were in Orleans, passing gay Saturday street markets. They crossed the Loire over a long bridge, with differently designed arches on each side. They passed the Chateau de Me'nars' formal gardens running down to the water's edge. Then they were at an old manor house with a rectangular central block framed by fairy-castle towers at each end, with battlements and conical towers. At the end of a large garden, the Loire slipped past quietly.

A porter in shirtsleeves and an apron came and took their luggage, and a young receptionist showed them to a room with a large, leaded window overlooking the rustic splendour. She opened the curtains, revealing a view of tranquil, autumn countryside in the afternoon sunshine. Then Gray opened the door and ushered her out.

He began undressing immediately, his back still touching the door, looking at Frances without speaking. She felt rooted to the floor, feeling her head going light, and the blood rushing to her cheeks.

Then she started undressing slowly, teasingly, hearing the pitch of her breathing grow harsher, letting her clothes lie around her where they fell. Between her legs, she could feel a hard pulse, moving up under her buttocks and into her back.

Gray watched, naked, without stirring. Then he moved to the bed, watching her follow.

They made love violently, needing each other's flesh, seizing and biting, pumping furiously without a word. His mouth on her hair, entangled with the golden strands.

'I think this is okay now. We've done everything we can to touch up the image. What do you say?'

David Kline pushed back a lock of blonde hair that kept falling over his eyes, and carefully scrutinized the picture in front of him. He had required that the subject be brought out more from the background, which had been achieved by air-brushing on an imperceptible halo around the model's head.

Swivelling his powerful light onto it, he examined the retouched print with a magnifying glass. Then he shook his head. 'It's good, but it's not good enough, Pierre. I can see the spotting. You'll have to try again tomorrow.'

'But you will never see that on newspaper reproduction, David,' said the French artist, looking harassed.

David sat back. He spoke quietly, but his eyes were burning. 'I said it's not good enough, Pierre. Go and do it again.'

When he was alone, he leaned back in his chair and sighed. It was 8 pm on Saturday night, and all key personnel had stayed on at the agency. They would work again tomorrow . . . the trouble with creative work, David reflected, is that it is never finished.

Only a deadline can bring it to an end – apart from that, one can go on and on improving something for ever.

He could hear rock music from the big creative office just outside, and he stood and went to the door. The same tape had been repeating itself since the afternoon, and he walked over to switch it off. Men and women sat at big drawing boards; the floor was littered with proof sheets and discarded paper.

'Okay, guys,' he said. 'I think that's enough for a Saturday night. We start again at nine tomorrow. Try not to be late,' and he cast a mock-angry glance around the room.

Half an hour later, he and Xavier were walking through the wet, lonely streets towards Xavier's apartment. The fatigue that had been oppressive in the agency had lifted from David almost as soon as they had walked out of the door. Xavier was in a carefree state, almost as if he thrived on hard work. David knew it was because the Frenchman had been taking drugs, but even so it was impossible not to be infected by his blithe mood.

Xavier's studio was rather small and very Parisian, in an attic five floors up. It was really just two rooms, each one in the bay of a big window.

He had stopped at the small *alimentation* shop downstairs, exchanged flirtatious greetings with the pert young daughter of the proprietor, and bought long French loaves, a wedge of oozing-ripe Brie, some small roundels of goats-milk cheese and some paté, and three bottles of rough red country wine. Now they sat on cushions on the floor, eating it with gusto, and drinking deep draughts of the coarse wine.

When Xavier rolled a long, slender joint of crumbly Moroccan hashish, David accepted a couple of puffs, and felt the relaxation steal over him. They made gentle love, each one satisfying the other with a skill they might have been practising for years.

Afterwards, they lay together in Xavier's narrow bed. David was exhausted, but Xavier seemed wide awake. The American struggled to keep his eyes open, to talk for a while, but his lids were weighed down. Waves of fatigue overpowered him.

Just before he surrendered to sleep, he had a sudden thought. This was the same feeling he had had at the chateau. The night Xavier had doped him.

He had no time to explore it. He fell fast asleep.

Frances had ordered for them both . . . *boudins aux raisins* – little blood sausages with white raisins, spiced honey bread, and *cremets* – small circular cheeses served with sugar and cream. They drank sparkling Vouvray, very cold, while they talked under the duvet, Gray making her jump by dipping his fingers in the cold wine and then touching her nipple so it stood sharply erect with the sudden cold. 'Careful. You'll make me spill.' It was cosily sensual and very intimate. Suddenly, in the quiet, Gray asked: 'How did you meet your husband?'

'At UCLA. I was a student, and he was a man of the world. I was just eighteen. He seemed to have done everything, seen everything, and understand everything. He was interested in art, travel, music, politics . . . and me. Especially me.'

'And then?'

'Do you really want to know?' She had felt him wince slightly at the tone of her voice. Although he replied: 'Yes,' she knew he didn't mean it.

'At first, it was good. Really good. The happiest time of my life, I guess.'

'Sometimes we'd stay up all night, just talking – afraid to sleep.'

'We bought a yacht, with every last cent we could muster. Just a dinghy really, but it was enough. We used to sail summer and winter.' She looked sad. 'It's gone now, of course. Gone long ago.

'I remember the exact moment I decided to start working. Web had been out for a whole day, a Sunday, with one of his therapy groups. He was good with his patients. I mean, really involved. He came home excited, and spent the whole evening telling me about it. Not that I minded. It was interesting. But not once

302

did he ask me what I'd done that day. That's what really got to me . . . as though his work was important, and I was just nothing, a non-entity, an accessory to his life.

'The next morning, I went looking for a job. And six months after that, I enrolled for a part-time MBA at USC. By then, I wanted a better job.'

'How did he react?' Gray still could not bring himself to speak Webley's name.

'Oh, Web is the perfect example of an enlightened husband. We got a Mexican housekeeper, and he was home more often than not. He gave me complete freedom . . . but you know, in the end the freedom became a sort of bondage in itself.'

She paused, and looked far away, beyond the moulding on the ceiling, the boundary of her vision. 'It's the same now, with you. Web's giving me the freedom again. But in return, I am in his debt, and under his control.'

Gray was lounging on one elbow, gently caressing her arm. She was lying back, her head resting on her hands, hiding in her shock of blonde hair.

'Relationships do change, Franci.'

'Oh, invariably.' She lifted one hand, and put her fingers to his mouth. 'I suppose ours will too.' Then she squirmed with the sensation as he took two of her fingers into his mouth, and sucked at them gently.

He looked serious. 'Can you explain why you still love him?' She knew the question had been difficult for him.

'Maybe it's a habit. The years create bonds, intangible as well as tangible. Children, joys shared, and sorrows too. And not a few neuroses.'

She laughed, then looked solemn again. 'Of course I love him. But it's not in the same way that I love you. It's not a driving force in my life, the way you have become. Not something that enhances my life the way you do. But I feel his pain and it becomes part of my own pain. I carry it with me. I can't explain. Except to give you up would hurt even more. Do you want to hear all of this?'

303

Gray was silent for a long time. Frances moved a little closer to him, and was tempted to tickle his ear with her tongue.

'I need to get into your head.'

'Why?'

'So I can tell if I have a chance to make you happy.'

'Gray, you can make me happy.'

'Will you marry me, Franci? Ever, I mean.'

She looked very solemn. 'I can't think through to there yet, Gray. I never stop thinking about it, being with you – but I always push it away again, to the back of my mind. It's just too big a question to confront right now.'

'Franci, I can't go on forever on just a part of you. I want the lot, and I'd be lying if I said otherwise. I need commitment. And until you leave your husband, I don't have that.'

He was sitting up in the bed now, the tray between them on the cover. His face was solemn, in the fading sunlight coming through the chinks in the shutters.

'I'm sorry, Franci, but there it is. I want everything.'

Frances sat up too, drawing the cover up over her breasts, and shook her head. 'Life just isn't that simple, Gray. Everything or nothing. Black or white. What can I give more than you have at the moment? What extra do you expect, if we get married? I don't feel I have anything more to give . . . '

'Time, for one thing. Having you there whenever I need you, whenever I want to talk to you. To start each day with you, and to end it. Christ, that's not difficult, is it?' His reaction hung heavy in the silence.

'No, I guess not. But disbanding my family, perhaps abandoning my career, leaving New York . . . that is like you leaving South Africa. What would you think of that?'

'For you, Franci, I would do it. Tomorrow, if it was what was needed.'

Frances could feel the ambiguity of his words; a rift growing between them with every passing second of the moments that followed. And she turned over and kissed him gently on the mouth to try and stop it ripping them apart.

'You haven't left him yet, have you, Franci?'

'In a way, I left him a long time ago.' Then she sat up abruptly, and looked away from him. 'I'm sorry. I just wanted this time together to be perfect.' Then she leaned towards him again, determined to bridge the chasm, rubbing his back and leaning her body against his.

He didn't answer. He knew what he wanted. And he was used to getting his own way.

She could see that. It frightened her a little – it was a part of him that she hadn't troubled to acknowledge before. Now he eased away from her, and the space between them felt alarmingly cold and large.

The light breaking through the gap in the curtain was too bright to be dawn. David sat up, and forced his mind to register. He felt sluggish, and raw at the edges, and any sudden thought was jagged and painful. His eyes ached, and there was a sharp acidic taste on the roof of his mouth. It was the same taste he recognized from his panic-stricken morning at the chateau. He knew at once that he had been drugged. Again.

This time, though, he wouldn't panic. He decided to take it step by step.

It was Sunday. He was in a strange bed. Ah – Xavier's bed. The Frenchman was still sleeping, curled into a private bundle. He looked so young.

As David's eyes moved to the gentle green glow of the digital clock, he remembered. Shit – the agency. We should have been there at nine. Now it's – *what* – 10.53!

Roughly, he shook Xavier awake. He was shouting into the groggy young face, shaking his shoulders to try to get some reaction.

'Xavier, you bastard. Wake up! Why did you do it? You didn't have to fucking drug me, you know. Look at the time, Goddammit!'

'Get ready. We were due at the agency at nine!' He shouted:

'Wake up, junkie!' He pushed Xavier so he fell out of the bed onto his hands and knees. Then as if scrabbling to escape he disappeared into the bathroom and locked the door.

In the cab on the way to the agency, David felt Xavier's eyes on him all the time. Whenever he turned towards him, the Frenchman dropped his gaze. Once, David saw tears in his eyes. Xavier turned away. And when David tried to speak to him, he simply shook his head.

Five hours later, across the Atlantic, Webley Kline puffed out his cheeks in the sudden cold as he got from the car. He walked like a man of resolve, a man with a purpose. But he didn't feel decisive. In fact, he had been feeling less and less certain all the way to Manhattan, on the drive from Westchester County.

When he'd left home, Webley had been sure he was doing the right thing. Now he was not so sure. All the same, he had to go through with it. He had come this far . . .

Maxwell J Bennis had greeted him personally when he rang on the doorbell. He wore his weekend outfit: blazer, flannels, and a rather gaudy cravat. He looked disgruntled, and Webley was sure he had dressed up especially, after Web had called him earlier that morning.

'Well, Webley, this is a surprise. Day of rest, you know. Still, it must be important, this – er – matter you have to discuss. Must confess, I'm all curiosity. Come through to my study.'

Five minutes later, Web was ensconced in an easy chair, with a badly-mixed cocktail on his knee, and Bennis leaning back in the chair behind his desk. He wished he felt less like a traitorous schoolboy, and more like a man with a justifiable grievance. After all, Bennis was just another of those big-business pricks, with their country clubs, and store-bought self-importance. Frances would listen to him – if not him then who would she listen to?

He heard himself say how worried he was about Frances, how he felt the workload was too much for her, how it had started affecting their marriage. 'She's over-stretched, Max. That sort of stress kills. You don't want to lose her. Neither do I.'

'Kills? Lose her? Bit strong, isn't it, Webley? It's just what she wants, you know. She's in the driving seat. I can't tell her to slow down. Anyway, she's got ambition, and plenty of stamina. She's perfectly healthy, isn't she?' Suddenly his face clouded.

'I think it's psychotic. The balance has gone. The South African man is a typical example. A symptom of a larger problem.' He tried to sound as nonchalant as he could.

'The South African man? What do you mean?'

'I thought you'd know,' lied Web. 'This man, Barnard, that she's tied up with in South Africa.'

Bennis shifted uncomfortably in his seat. 'Can you get to the point, Webley. Are you telling me your wife is having an affair with Gray Barnard. Because if that's so . . . ' he paused in mid-sentence, visibly off-balance, as the implications sank in.

Again, Web was deceptively casual. 'It's only because she's away from home too much. It makes her vulnerable. And that's why I came to you . . . because I hope you can help.'

Web spoke on, but it was obvious that Bennis wasn't listening. He was deep in thought, his face troubled, biting his lower lip, and puffing furiously on his stub of a cigarette. Web knew he had achieved what he had set out to do. 'I won't tell Frances that I came here, Maxwell. And I know I can rely on you to do whatever you can. Thanks for hearing me out.' And he walked almost jauntily from the room.

Maxwell Bennis sat for a long time at his desk. What to do next? God, if the word got out! A Cranston President, in a liaison with a South African business partner. The whole thing would resound through the press. He didn't know how to handle this. He only knew that Webley Kline had put the ball firmly in his court. Sonofabitch!

Webley still looked confident as he let himself out of the front door, and crossed the sidewalk to his station wagon. It was only after he climbed in that he broke down and wept.

He'd betrayed Frances. Could he ever forgive himself? What

307

was his option? He had done it for Stacey, more than for himself. His motives were clean.

But even though he almost convinced himself that his treachery had been justified in every way, it was a long time before he started the engine and turned the big wagon back towards Westchester County.

Rae's office stank of fear and cigarettes. It was 10 pm, three days later, and Milton looked like a cornered animal as he sat behind his desk, a bottle of bourbon in front of him a quarter full, and the glass beside him half-empty. His hand shook as he drained it at a single gulp, and then half-filled it again, the ice cubes rattling with the quiver of his arm.

What a day it had been. It was all closing in on him now. Clements had called again, but this time he hadn't threatened him. He had spoken with a laugh in his voice. 'Sorry, Milton. You didn't listen. You didn't do as I said, did you.'

'Who told you that?' said Milton. 'Kline. Well, tell her . . . '

But Clements had cut across his bluster with an ice-cool laugh. And then he had hung up.

Then Janelle had called. 'Remember me, Milt?' her voice was sing-song with artificial sensuality. 'You promised me some peanut butter. Am I gonna have to come and get it?'

'Bitch. Fuck off!' And he had slammed the phone down.

And when it had rung again, immediately, he had picked it up and started shouting, 'I told you . . . ' when he heard a man's voice, speaking quietly – a voice that filled him with dread, making a polite request he could not deny. 'In my office,' said Rae. 'Of course 9 pm's not too late. I generally stay late on weekdays. Life's tough at the top.' His attempt at a casual laugh did not come off. 'I'll be here.'

Now he'd been waiting one hour, and he was getting nervous. He was no longer sure that he could brazen this one out. Perhaps he should go home . . . but that would be just putting the whole thing off.

He tried to calm himself looking at his beloved paintings. He had a fine collection – some prints, a couple of originals. They took him away from his problems, and he looked at the misshapen face of his Modigliani portrait. Only this time the gentle eyes were hard and accusing; the Picasso alongside also failed to soothe him – jumbled images jarring rather than slotting themselves into place in his mind. Only the big Matisse on the wall behind the sofa reflected his mood – geometric squares of screaming colours, overlaid with a spatter of scarlet paint. Flung on in an arrangement of spontaneous perfection.

Then came the soft knock on the door. 'Are you there, Milton?' The voice almost diffident.

Quickly, Milton dimmed the room lights and switched on the standard lamp by the sofa. He put the bourbon on the table with the ice bucket. The light cast a warm glow – the office now had a homely corner, with the leather sofa and the two matching armchairs. It created an informal atmosphere. It would make the discussion more relaxed, he thought. Then he walked to the door, fixed a smile on his face, and opened it. 'Hi. Come in. I was wondering what had happened.'

He stepped inside, and Milton closed the door. Then he ushered his guest towards the armchairs and offered him a drink.

'Bourbon? Yes please, Milt. I'd like a stiff one. I'm going to need it.'

He didn't accept Rae's offer of an armchair. Instead he went and leaned back on the edge of the desk. Silhouetted against the night lights of New York, his face was out of the pool of light, his expression impossible to make out.

Milton felt absurdly like a performer sitting in the full glow of the lamp, trying to look affable, but concerned. His smile felt painted on, like that of a clown. He took a swig from his freshly refilled glass, and tried the smile again. 'Now, you said that I could do something for you. What is it?'

'It's really just some information, Milt.'

Milton gave a genuinely relieved smile. Maybe it was going to

309

be okay. 'Fire away. If I know it, and it isn't a trade secret, I'll be glad to tell you.'

'When did you first start with little boys, Milt?' The voice was very quiet and even.

Milton missed a breath. God, what does he know? But years of calculating deviousness and a twisted paranoia had not left him without some skills in a tight spot. His voice was more composed than his mind as he gave a convincing display of outrage. 'What? Do you know what you're suggesting? Remember who I am!'

'When did it begin? I suppose it's been going on for years, hasn't it? How many young lives have you bent and wrecked? Oh – you've had a good front, haven't you. Milton Rae, patron of young artists, business mentor to kid trainee managers. How many, Milton?'

The voice was full of menace now. The speaker had risen from the desk, and was walking towards Rae seated on the sofa.

'You're crazy,' he said. 'Stay where you are.' And he tried to rise to his feet, but the other man was towering above him.

'Well, it won't happen any more, Milton, because I'm going to to have your balls.'

As Rae tried to push his assailant away, he felt the sharp sting of raw spirit in his eyes, and chunks of ice slashing at his cheeks. He fell back onto the sofa, furiously trying to wipe the bourbon from where it was blinding him. He stood again, and when he could open his eyes, he was looking at the barrel of a gun.

'You cradle-snatcher. You cock-sucker. You filthy pervert! You'll never destroy another life.'

'Who told you? Did she tell you? Kline? She's lying, I tell you. For God's sake, don't shoot!'

'Clements told me. Clements told me everything, you stinking bastard.'

And then he saw his adversary's knuckles whiten on the trigger, saw the barrel levelled at his eyes. Time switched speed, and it seemed as if the rest of his life moved in slow motion.

'Damn you, Kline,' he shouted, as the gun barked once, and then once again. Then he crumpled onto the sofa, sitting there long enough for the gunman to ready himself for another shot, before his corpse finally fell to the floor.

On the Matisse behind his head, a fresh splatter of scarlet cut across the original painting at a new angle, shading at the bottom to a fine mist of red droplets.

In a curious way, the visitor mused, it suddenly made the painting look more finished.

CHAPTER TWENTY-SEVEN

Thursday morning in Paris. The reality of wet paving and tarmac, a grey sky reflecting from the polished quaysides. The subdued noise of the traffic and the freshness of the moist air afforded refreshment to David and Xavier as they strode along, casually touching from time to time.

The presentation was over, most of the PS-21 ads were already placed, the pressure of work was off the agency now, at least for a few days, and the two men were taking advantage of the lull for a morning walk along the banks of the river by David's apartment. Xavier had invited himself over the night before, but had been strangely silent and withdrawn, until they had made love with a passion that David had never experienced before. It had been Xavier's idea to walk as well, and now they moved in rhythm together.

Because it added to his sense of peace, David had guided their steps beside the Seine, past the houseboats and barges whose lives he peered into from his apartment. They had been walking for five minutes, in complete silence, before Xavier spoke.

'David,' he said. 'I love you.' It was uttered without a grain of sexuality – a simple statement of truth. 'But,' Xavier went on, 'I have done a terrible thing. It is because I love you that now I must tell you.'

Suddenly he turned to David, wild-eyed, sobbing. 'I wish I'd had the courage to fling myself off this bridge before I had done it. To relieve myself, and you. But I loved life too much. Even my pitiful life . . . the life of an addict.' He summoned up the pride to speak the word with scorn.

'And because I needed the drugs to continue in the life I loved so much, I have brought us to this.' The overplayed melodrama might have amused them both under different circumstances.

'Brought us to what, Xavier?' said David. He was so much more patient with Xavier than anyone he could remember. He wondered why. Was it because he loved him too?

'Because, David, people like you do not realize that there are others who will take advantage of us.'

'Xavier, what are you trying to say? Tell me now.' He knew he had to handle the overwrought young man beside him with care, but now he could feel the alarm rise in himself. Had Xavier exposed their affair? Would his mother find out?

Now Xavier stopped, turned and leaned over the ballustrade, staring down at the water, the cool ivory of his face made the paler by the reflected light. 'David, I cannot keep this to myself another minute longer. But first you must say you will forgive me.'

'For Christ's sake, Xavier, just tell me. Forgiveness doesn't come into it. It's important that you tell me what has happened. Start at the beginning.'

'Okay then. But remember, I couldn't help it. I was caught in a trap a long time ago, and my actions have been manipulated since then.

'It was this new dealer . . . the one I told you about. When I started with him, I was just taking coke occasionally, and I'd just tried smack – heroin – for the fun of it. But soon, with the regular supplies, I was hooked. I had to have the smack. And pretty soon, I found I couldn't pay for it. Of course, it was all part of their plan. I see that clearly enough now. Oh, God – if I could

312

have just said no – no more drugs.' He stared out across the river as if seeking solace in its utter indifference.

'That happened when I lost my job. As I told you, I was with a big American agency in Paris. I didn't tell you I was fired, did I? They caught me and another copy-writer taking cocaine. I thought it was my big chance to break free. I told the dealer that I had run out of money, that I didn't want any more drugs. That's when they told me I could earn enough money just by doing what they told me. And he forced me to take a gram of smack on credit, just to be sure I owed him something. I meant to throw the packet away. But I didn't. When I got home, I took some – and I decided that I would do as they said. At first, it was fine. They told me that I must apply for a job at *Agence Lasaere*. Well, that was only a pleasure. It was a promotion, for a better salary than before. Why should that be a hardship? The interview seemed only a formality, and I was given the job. It was only a few days later that the agency was sold. And then you came along – and they started to make more demands. The other night, you spoke about them calling up the tab. Well, they did. The tab was you.'

David was both spellbound and horror struck. Even as he listened his mind was formulating excuses, or avenues for escape. He didn't want any more trouble. He didn't want to hear what Xavier was going to say. But fascinated, he listened avidly.

'They told me that I must befriend you. Yes, I am sorry, but it is true. Now – you must believe me – now I wish to be your friend only out of love. But it started because they forced me to do it.'

David spoke with an icy calm that he did not feel. 'Carry on. Tell me everything. I want to know everything.'

'David, the chateau, my uncle. They were a fiction. I have no rich uncle. I am not noble.'

He laughed savagely. 'Oh no, certainly not. I am most assuredly not noble. No. All that was a charade, designed to get you into a compromising position with me. They set it all up, they gave me the drugs. And it all went according to their plan

. . . except for one thing. I really did fall in love with you.'

Almost brusquely, David put his arm round Xavier for a moment. The gesture was mechanical. 'I don't understand what it was all in aid of, though. Do they want to blackmail me? Are they trying to get at my mother?'

'I don't know exactly why. But I know what. They wanted me to blackmail you into getting your security pass for the factory. But I couldn't do it – because I love you.' Xavier was almost shouting now, and a flicker of a curtain in a houseboat window showed that they were being watched.

'Let me get this, Xavier. They want you to blackmail me to gain access to the factory?'

'No, David.' Xavier's face crumpled. 'They've already had access. Last weekend. I couldn't blackmail you. I just couldn't so I took the card while you were sleeping. That was why I had to drug you.'

Instinctively, David felt for his wallet, opened it. The card was back in its place.

Now Xavier was clinging to his arm, weeping openly. 'I'm sorry, David. But they would have killed me. I lay awake watching you all night, willing you to wake up, so you could stop whatever was happening. You were so gone that nothing would make you stir. Then they came back, and returned the card to me. I put it back in your wallet. It was all so easy. But you don't know how I've felt since then. I have been in hell – truly in hell!'

David said nothing. He turned, and began walking fast. After a few paces, he realized he was walking away from home, and he turned angrily and strode back in the opposite direction.

Xavier was almost running to keep up with him. 'David, say something. Do something. For the love of God, hit me even. They will kill me if they know I've told you. Please!' The last word was a sob, that David left behind him as he broke into a run. He knew only one thing. He had to go. He had to escape.

The second she saw Randy's face, Frances knew that there was something badly wrong. He had gone a greyish white, and his freckles stood out against an unhealthy looking background. The guest with him staring fixedly at her without seeing. He sat down opposite her at her desk, and then spoke almost inaudibly.

'Oh my God, it's terrible. I've just heard.'

Frances waited a second, and then spoke sharply. 'Come on Randy. What is it?' She rose to her feet, pushing the chair back impatiently.

'The first results. I just heard. Three of the labs have had the same thing. I just can't understand it.'

Gerry Rule was in the room with them, and Gray Barnard. The three of them had been discussing budgets for the forthcoming months when the factory manager, Randy Wise, had come bursting into the room with his ashen-faced laboratory director.

'What do you mean, Randy?' It was Gray, his face drawn in sudden concern.

'I'm not sure how . . .'

'Just say it, Randy. We can handle it.' Frances was standing next to him, looking intently at his face.

'I heard from Zurich first. It's the final protocol samples. They have been destabilizing. Then I called London, and Hamburg. They were having the same problems. I've put my assistant onto contacting the other labs, and so far every answer he's come up with is in accord. The samples have destabilized. In simple terms, the active ingredient has decomposed into several new ingredients. As yet, they're not sure of the effects of those new chemicals – but it appears that it may be having a bad effect on some of the test volunteers.'

'But it's impossible after all this time!' Frances felt a knife turning in her stomach. Heard the blood pounding in her head.

'You've had problems with it breaking down before, Frances,' Randy ventured.

'Yes, but that was shelf life.'

'That's just another symptom of decomposition. But I agree it's peculiar that it should happen so suddenly.'

315

'Is the fact that it was sudden significant?' Gray had been pacing back and forth rapidly, but now faced the scientist who had said nothing up to then.

'Yes, sir. Decomposition usually takes place gradually. We've been manufacturing for months.'

'What can we do?' Frances asked Randy quickly.

'Well, I've already got the lab teams at work analysing the test samples that we held back as a control. I am expecting their results later tomorrow morning, though by tonight we'll have an idea of what they're looking at. But I can't figure it out. I *know* our samples were perfect.'

'Well, if you can't figure it out, who can?' said Gray. He was in a most uncharacteristic state, shouting angrily, a fearsome spectacle. 'If you've cocked up those samples . . . '

It was Frances who appeased the situation, though she felt far from calm herself. 'Okay, Gray, take it easy. We need information. We can do nothing more until we have it.'

'Gray's right,' said Randy, looking very tired and much older than his twenty-eight years. 'I feel personally responsible.'

'No, goddammit! I won't have recriminations now. There's no question of individual responsibility. I carry the can around here. Now let's keep our heads.' She hesitated for a moment to compose herself. 'Randy, you concentrate on getting reports from the sample labs worldwide, and come right back when you have some sort of a comprehensive picture.'

It took two hours to compile results from the various European laboratories. In the interim, Gray had been pacing the office vigorously, distracting Frances irritatingly as she tried to formulate some plan to handle this new disaster. Gerry Rule, fussing over a set of data print-outs, had nothing to contribute – she was alone.

Without warning, Randy and the head of the laboratory team burst into the office again. He spoke rapidly. 'It's worse than we thought. We've traced nine test volunteers admitted to hospitals, with some sort of skin complaint. The results are similar all over Europe. It's a disaster.'

He sat down, looking pale and wasted. 'Oh, God.' The sigh was deeply troubled. Then he handed a sheaf of papers to Frances. 'The reports.'

She put them down without looking. 'Well? What's in the reports?'

'It seems, Frances, that destabilization has taken place at all the laboratories. The results are more or less identical.'

Frances cut across him. 'What has happened to the test volunteers? What are the precise problems there?'

'We're waiting for details. There appears to be a darkening of the skin, severe depression, and high blood pressure. All patients have recorded two or more of those symptoms, and some others as well. In the worse case, trouble with breathing has put the woman in intensive care. That is in Turin.' His hand was moving down the report.

'And what could possibly have caused it?'

'A catalyst of some sort seems the most likely explanation.'

'But how?' said Gray.

'Well, it's a substance that causes a chemical reaction. Like mercury on aluminium. Pour some mercury on the wing of an aircraft, and though the mercury takes no part in the chemical reaction itself and doesn't change, the aluminium is weakened so much that the plane's wing could fall off.'

'I know how a bloody catalyst works. I mean how did the catalyst get into the samples?'

Frances cut in quickly. 'First, I want the names of the victims who have shown adverse response to the samples. Get Joe Mitchell here. He can deal with them and their families personally. They will be cared for and compensated. And above all, kept quiet. And the same thing applies to all of us.' She looked round the room, catching the eyes of each one in turn. 'If this leaks out to the press, we're finished.'

'Right now, our top priority is not why it's happened. We have to save our credibility. And it's best at the moment that there should be absolutely no publicity at all, until we are in possession of the facts.'

317

The chemist nodded dumbly, so did Joe Mitchell. The others just looked stunned. Then she dismissed them all. 'Now I need time to think.'

When they had all gone, she said to Gray, 'I need air and exercise to help me think this thing through.'

Out in the fresh streets, it was a normal calm Parisian Thursday. The atmosphere helped to clear Frances' mind. She looked across at Gray, and spoke firmly. 'It's finished, isn't it.'

'If we can keep it quiet perhaps we can save it,' said Gray.

'No, it's not possible. Our credibility with the laboratories is lost. We can't keep it out of the papers indefinitely. We have to face it, Gray. PS-21 is finished – even before it got started.'

Later that afternoon, Randy returned to Frances' office for the third time. 'We're getting our own lab results starting to come in now, and they confirm the outside reports.'

'Randy, what we need to know now is whether we have a fundamental flaw in the drug, or whether it's confined to the test material.'

'The test material is my guess,' he replied.

'Good God, man! Surely you know?' Gray flared up again.

'Can anyone have got to the test batch, Randy?' asked Frances, again exerting a calming influence. A crisis always strained personal relationships. She couldn't afford to let them get out of control.

'At the various labs and hospitals? I suppose so, in theory. But it's unlikely, it would take a lot of co-ordinating. In any case, that doesn't hold up, because our own control samples show the same problem.'

'Which means,' Gray jumped in quickly. 'That whatever did happen took place right here.'

'You mean a faulty batch?' asked Randy.

'I don't know what I mean,' said Gray. 'But I intend to find out.'

Frances had ordered all her calls to be held – making an

exception only if David should call. She had been trying to raise him all day – but he wasn't at the agency, nor was he at his apartment. His absence formed the focus of a small and separate strand of surging fear within her – which, like her anxiety about the failure of PS-21, she did her best to suppress. She didn't have time to panic.

Now it was 3 pm and she was with Gerry. Gray was following his own line of investigation. She turned her attention to the messages her secretary had held for her.

Top was one from Maxwell Bennis – he had called five times in the past hour. Frances couldn't help smiling at the frustration the old man must have felt to have come up against a wall of Gallic indifference.

She called his office directly, dialling the number herself, and within seconds was through to the Chairman of the Cranston Group.

'That you, Kline? For Chrissakes. Where have you *been*? Never mind that now. Have you heard the news?'

'Yes, Max,' replied Frances wearily. 'We've been working on finding out more all day. I'm surprised you heard it so soon, though.'

'What do you mean? It happened in this damn building. Why shouldn't I have heard?'

For a moment, Frances wondered what he was talking about. Then he went on. 'My God, it was terrible. I had to go and see him, you know. With the police. His face was almost blown away. God knows who or why – though from what the police are saying, our Milton was a bit of a dark horse.'

'Milton? What do you mean, Max?'

'I thought you said you knew? Milton Rae is dead. Murdered. He was shot in his office. Late last night, they tell me.'

Frances felt as though she'd been hit. Speechless, she sank back into the cushions of her chair, holding the handset away from her face, oblivious to its squawkings. Milton murdered! What could it all mean?

Then the disembodied voice brought her back to the present.

319

'Kline? Are you there? Goddammit, answer me, woman. Will you be able to be back here tomorrow?'

'Tomorrow? Oh, no. That's quite out of the question, Max.' She replied with an icy calm, hardly knowing what she was saying.

'Kline, it's not a request – it's an order. I need you back here right now. With Milton gone, we need all our executives in New York.'

'Maxwell, I'm sorry, but I can't do that. I'm dealing with a crisis of my own here at the moment. I simply won't be free to come back for at least a week.'

'Listen, Kline. Let me put this absolutely straight. Crisis, or no crisis, I want you back in New York. Don't you understand that this is the closest you have ever been to an appointment on the Board?'

'I understand that, Max. But I'm needed here. In fact I have to go right now. I'll call you again.'

Abandoned, all the fight went out of Maxwell Bennis. He sounded quite deflated as he spoke weakly, 'Kline, get back here. I need you.'

On Friday, the next morning, Frances was awake early. The night images danced around her head continuously; PS—21 turned into a laughing stock, Milton murdered in his office, David disappeared . . . how could it be coincidence that these things had happened all at once. By 9 pm, emotionally drained, she had taken a Lexotan, and had fallen into a deep sleep almost immediately.

She felt refreshed, almost jaunty, in a paradoxical way. After a quick shower, ending with a thorough sluicing in jets of ice-cold water, she bound her hair up in a towel, put on a hotel robe, and called Gray in his room. 'I've ordered breakfast in my room for both of us. Please come down, darling.'

Her appetite was unaffected by the unheaval – rather she felt a need to eat, to build up all her reserves. As well as *croissants* and *brioches* she had ordered omelettes, ham and waffles – a true international breakfast, and was tucking into it with gusto when Gray arrived, already dressed.

Quickly, and without frills, she told him about Milton's murder, as well as her suspicions as to it being connected in some way to the failure of the PS-21 samples. 'Gray, there is something going on that is impossible to understand. But it's a definite chain of events that is all linked up, and that somebody is controlling. We've got to find out what it is.'

He thought the idea was far-fetched. 'What can a murder in New York have to do with a chemical accident in Europe? From what you've told me, Milton's the kind of guy who made a few enemies. We have to ask who they were – who had a motive for killing him?'

Frances gave an incongruous laugh. 'Put like that, Gray, the finger points clearly one way. Milton's biggest enemy is sitting right here in the room with you. Me.'

The day passed painfully slowly. Frances sat in her office awaiting the results of the assay test, running the various possible answers through her mind, and her possible response to each of them. If the drug had destabilized of its own accord, that meant all her efforts had been in vain. The PS-21 project was doomed. How pleased Milton would have been, she thought.

But Milton had been murdered – and the remembrance made her think again of the likelihood of outside interference to the test samples. Perhaps it had been arranged by Milton – yes, that was the most likely. But the plan had somehow backfired on him, and now he was dead.

There was a word for outside intervention. Sabotage. If that was so, then they might be able to apply for a re-test, and simply delay the launch by a fortnight or so. Bad, but at least a road to recovery.

Then images of the victims of the skin infection flashed through her mind, growing hourly more disfigured – a nightmarish daydream. No, she realized. It had gone too far already. Their credibility had been destroyed. If news ever leaked out about the fact that PS-21 samples had caused disfiguring disease, the product would be finished . . . no matter what the reason, and for all time.

It was late in the afternoon before the final assay results were assembled. Randy had knocked on her door, and come in even more white-faced than the day before. Every fresh event seemed to make more physical impact on the young man – and it showed.

'We've found the culprit, Frances,' he said. 'It's a reactive foreign substance – a sort of enzyme – that is completely new to us. It's never shown up before. It breaks down Prosta-glandin-S within a matter of hours, and leaves a cocktail of chemicals that seem to have an end result almost like scarlet fever. It is definitely something that has been introduced.'

'How did that happen?' asked Frances. 'Was there some negligence in the laboratory?'

'No,' replied Randy, looking pale. 'We've found tiny hypo-dermic holes in the sealing film on our control samples. They have been tampered with. Something was deliberately injected.'

'Tampered with?' Frances felt outrage at the reality of her worst fears. How clever of them, whoever they were. To make it look as though it was just another destabilization problem, a replay of the setback they'd experienced during laboratory testing in New York before she received Rocher's letter.

She saw Gray coming in, and turned to face him. 'The drug was tampered with – made to look like a recurrence of the same old problem,' was all she could manage by way of explanation. 'My God, it doesn't say much for Europe's most sophisticated security system, does it? Damn thing cost us enough. The best security money could buy, and . . .'

Gray was looking grim. 'Frances,' he interrupted, 'there's something I have to tell you.'

Something in his tone stopped Frances mid-sentence. 'What is it, Gray?'

He laid a small bundle of newspapers on the desk. On the front page of each of them, she could see the letters PS-21 in banner headlines. Two or three carried the same picture of a young woman with a disfiguring strawberry scar that had spread from her ear. Frances saw the words 'Scandal', 'Fraud', and 'Hoax', as she sank back into her chair. Her worst terrors had come true.

'Somebody has tipped off the press. I've been holding off all calls until the assay results came through. But they didn't need much from us, anyway. Facts, figures, they've got the lot. Dammit, they even have pictures.'

'Frances, we've been sabotaged.'

At that moment, two telephones on the desk started to ring at the same time. The avalanche had begun.

In David's apartment, Xavier was clinging hopelessly to the young American's arm, while David stormed around the room, flinging objects of value into a suitcase. He took only a selection of his clothes, rather more of his books. The thing that he handled with the most care was his small collection of stone axes, each one carefully tissue-wrapped before he bound them tightly in a special box.

As he packed, Xavier danced around him like an anxious sprite, touching his arm, imploring David to answer him, to tell him where he was going. The young Frenchman was dishevelled and had the distracted look of a heroin addict undergoing with-drawal symptoms. But he was being driven now by a force stronger even than his craving for drugs. He had been waiting outside David's apartment since he had lost touch with him the morning before. He had slept in his clothes on the doorstep – and it looked like it. The sight touched David, but he refused to say a word.

As he scooped up a pile of papers from the desk, a brochure fluttered down to the floor. Feverishly, Xavier snatched it up. It was for the Greek island of Samothraki – a typical tourist folder, with pictures of smiling peasants leading donkeys through incredibly whitewashed villages, of dramatic sea cliffs, and of sunbathers baking on broad beaches.

Xavier remembered the name of the island from a conversation a week before . . . David had been talking of a new archaeological dig that had discovered intriguing new evidence there. The two things clicked in Xavier's tortured mind.

'This is it, isn't it. This is where you're going. Samothraki.'

'David, I am going to come with you.'

But David took no notice, snapping the case shut, taking a final glance around the room, and then stepping out firmly from the apartment. The night before he had slept in a small hotel. Now he had decided what to do – and he could think only of leaving.

Xavier watched him go with a desolate sense of finality. The pamphlet fell from his fingers, and fluttered to the floor, as with a cry, the young Frenchman ran to the door. 'David, wait for me. I am coming with you . . . '

Now the mechanism was becoming clear to Frances. The leak to the press had confirmed it. PS-21 was being manipulated, and until she could identity who was doing it, she was powerless to prevent disgrace to the drug and to herself.

She had to find out how the pieces all fitted together. And at the moment, her data banks weren't only empty, they were scrambled by the force of the confusion.

The press leak was something beyond her control. But what could she say when she was still looking for facts herself. She had issued a blanket statement, that the matter was being investigated, and she could make no comment until she had all the details. Then she had left Joe Mitchell to handle the individual calls, instructing him to soothe the situation as much as he could, without giving away any information.

Now she turned again to face Randy. 'Are you saying that it was only the batch of protocol samples that were contaminated?' Frances was on her feet again, mind racing.

'Yes, as far as we can make out. We've got every technician testing all the other batches, and so far it's all been negative.'

'So we need to know who had access to those samples. Where were they kept?'

'Frances, it was in the maximum security area all the time. Only key personnel have access, and then only under the supervision of one of the eight card-holders . . . that's you, me, Barnard, the key laboratory staff. And of course your son David.' The name struck Frances like a jolt.

Gray seemed to sense her reaction, and broke in. 'So anyone planning a sabotage attempt had access to top-security information as to where the samples were, and how to get to them?'

'Possibly,' said Randy. 'I hadn't thought about that. But maybe security will have some ideas on it.'

'Right,' said France. 'Get the head of security here. I want every centimetre of this building checked for signs of a break-in. And I don't want the police in . . . not yet, anyway. I want some questions answered first.'

Randy glanced furtively at his watch. It was 8 pm – they would have to call security staff in from their homes. 'What, now Frances?'

'Yes – now.'

The head of security was there in fifteen minutes. 'We'll have to wait until morning to do a really thorough check, Madame,' he said.

'What about records – do we have any way of finding out who went into the sample-room?'

'That's easy. Access is gained only by insertion of one of eight security cards . . . and each time one is used, the system records whose it was.'

'Why wasn't I told this?' said Frances.

'We told no-one. In my job, you trust nobody. It wouldn't be a security system if everyone knew how it worked.'

The security report came back in ten minutes, a neat print-out showing the times the main security door had been opened, next to a code to show whose card had been used. The key to the code was printed on a separate sheet of paper.

One of the entries was underlined. The time was O3h21 on Sunday morning. 'It looks like here that they broke in, Madame,' said the security chief. 'The building was quiet – there was nobody working at the time. It would have triggered off all the alarms, if the top-security card hadn't been used correctly.'

Frances hardly dared to ask the next question. 'Whose card was used?'

'See the code there, Madame. It's G34.' He pointed his finger to the list of eight names, and found the code G34. Frances followed his finger across the dotted line.

There she read the name.

David Kline.

CHAPTER TWENTY-EIGHT

Frances and Gray walked past the lights of a small fairground, onto a brightly-lit square of grass, and then out into the darkness, where they could look over the railings into the graveyard. It seemed appropriate.

He had followed her after she had left the room, abruptly dismissing everybody until the next morning. He had loped after her as she hurried down the corridors towards the exit. 'No, Franci. Wait. Don't go out of the front door – the place is besieged by reporters.'

It was a full fifteen minutes later, waiting beside the silent and darkened door, that she heard the noise of a car outside. It was Gray, in a small and rather battered Renault. He had rented the most anonymous car they could drive in Paris.

'I need to walk.' Frances had motioned Gray to pull over. 'I can't face being cooped up – especially in a hotel room.' So they had headed north, to the hill of Montmartre. There they had parked the car, and walked briskly through the cool air towards the *Sacre Coeur*, and then through narrow streets that opened up here and there to give a spectacular panorama of Paris.

After a while, they stopped at a small coffee bar, and drank tiny mugs of strong coffee, washed down with draughts of Perrier water. It made her feel stronger.

'Gray, this is too big for David.

'Whoever is gunning for me has got a lot of pull, and they've used my son. My flesh and blood!

'God, I feel sick. He can't be involved, Gray. He can't!'

'Franci, keep calm.'

'Calm? After this, I doubt if I can ever be calm again. If I could figure out where it begins or where it ends. It's as though my life is a tapestry and someone out there has pulled the crucial thread. And it's all coming to pieces. I feel so utterly helpless – so responsible. I can't do a thing to stop it!'

'Franci . . .'

'Gray, there's so much damage. Where's it coming from? Tell me, Gray. Where?' Her voice was rising in pitch as she tore at a paper napkin.

Gray reached out and put his hand over hers. 'God knows,' he said. 'The Russians? Competitors? Some powerful crank group. I'm too tired to think, Franci, too damn tired.'

'I've got to find David, Gray,' she said. And quietly to herself; 'Why am I sitting here?' Suddenly she felt denuded.

'Not now, Franci. I'm taking you back to the hotel now. We'll get you past the press, and then you stay tight for the night. I'll find David for you.'

And they had driven fast back to her hotel, and Gray had simply powered his way through the clutch of reporters, holding her encircled in his arms, until they had finally made it to her room, and he closed the door behind her.

★ ★ ★

327

At that precise moment in New York, Captain Mannering was contemplating a soggy sandwich that he had just drawn out of his lunchbox. He was about to order a burger instead, when suddenly the door to his office opened.

Sandwich in one hand, the policeman stood staring at the new arrival. It was a distinguished-looking elderly man, crisply dressed in formal evening clothes, quite overcome with fatigue.

'Officer, I understand you are in charge of the investigation into the murder of Milton Rae.

'I have come to save you some trouble.

'I killed him, and I did it because he killed my son. Perverted bastard – he as good as murdered him.

'I have taken my revenge, now you must do your duty.'

Mannering stood motionless.

'My name is Jim Farnsworth. I am Jeremy Farnsworth's father.'

Frances was awoken in the middle of the night by the shrill jangle of the telephone. It was Maxwell J Bennis, and it was plain from his tone that he had heard the news.

'That you, Kline? What the hell's going on out there? The papers have gone wild. Looks like this little scheme of yours has blown sky-high.'

'I'm trying to put the pieces together, Max. But I'm afraid it doesn't look good.'

'You can say that again. The *Wall Street Journal* have predicted that Cranston Group shares are going to plummet! Already they've started to take a real tumble. Tell me what is going on!'

'It's hard to say right now, Max. We're working on the assumption that the test samples were tampered with.'

The voice on the other end began talking furiously, roaring in Frances' ear. When it stopped for a moment, she spoke again.

'Yeah, that's right – that's exactly what I mean. It looks like we've been deliberately sabotaged. Somebody broke into the factory, and poisoned the samples.'

'*What*? Well, what are you doing about it?'

'Everything I can. Security's working on investigating it and so is everybody else.'

'Have you reported it to the police?'

'Not yet. It would only cause an even bigger scandal.'

'Jesus.' The thought of a scandal bigger than that already all over the front pages of the world knocked the breath out of him. 'We don't want that.'

'Exactly. Therefore, no cops. Not yet.'

'Frances, you'd better get your ass here at once. What am I supposed to tell the Board? I want you right here in New York.'

'Max, I'll get back as soon as I can. But I have to finish up here first.'

'Okay, Frances. I know exactly what's keeping you. Your husband came and told me all the details. Now, I'd suggest you leave your South African to clear up the mess. It was he who got you into it in the first place.'

'What do you mean?'

'I mean I know about your affair. The whole messy story. Never mind that now. We'll come back to it later. Right now, I want you back here. There's a Board meeting on Friday, a week today. See that you are back here before that.'

'Max, I don't . . .'

'You've got seven days, Kline.' And he hung up, leaving Frances gazing mutely at the phone.

Why had Webley done that to her? Coward. Traitor! It was hardly important, but it crystallized everything she already knew.

The next morning Frances awoke early, feeling numb and shocked. Her first reaction was to call Gray, but there was no reply from his room. In a lonely sort of daze, she went through the motions of bathing, of washing herself, making up her face, and choosing clothes. It was something she did almost automatically, but she was aware as she took a final glance in the mirror that even without trying, she looked stunning.

She arrived at the factory unprotected from the press of journalists who clustered round her at the entrance. On a Saturday morning, they were mainly from the Sunday papers, with a deadline approaching, and a desperate need to get a good wrap-up story. Frances spoke firmly. 'Gentlemen, I am sorry you have been kept waiting. I will make an official statement in an hour.'

Gerry Rule and Joe Mitchell were waiting inside.

'I want you to call a conference for the pressmen,' she said to Mitchell. 'I want to make as full a statement as possible. I intend to tell them everything that we know so far . . . that our laboratory was broken into on Saturday night, that the test samples were deliberately poisoned. I'll introduce the word "sabotage" as soon as I can – give them something to chew on. Perhaps they'll make a meal of it, and take the heat off us for a while.

'I want them to know that we are looking after everyone who is showing problems after taking test samples, and that we will be caring for all of them. But I must take this chance to make it clear that the real blame lies on the saboteurs, and that Cranston is going to come out fighting when we know who they are.'

'Meantime, we will have to shut up shop here for a while. Randy will take over. Gerry, I want you to stay to see that the operation is wound down, and then you must go back to New York. Barnard has promised to stay on for a week. I'll be back in New York as soon as I can.'

At that moment, Gray Barbard arrived. He looked troubled, and made a private gesture to Frances that he needed to talk to her alone. She dismissed her vice-presidents, and when the door had closed, walked over to Gray to hug him. She needed to be received into his great comforting arms. But he gave her only a perfunctory squeeze, then held her at arm's length.

330

'Franci, I've been looking for David. I'm afraid he has gone.'

'Gone? What do you mean? Gone where?'

'Gone to Greece. I followed his trail, and it led to the airport. He left on an Olympic flight to Athens last night.'

'Are you sure?'

'First, I went to his apartment. The door was unlocked. It looked as though a bomb had struck it. He obviously packed in a hurry. Some clothes have gone, and I suppose his personal things. He's left quite a lot of junk behind.

'On the floor, I found this.' It was the tourist brochure for Samothraki. 'Then I noticed a newspaper cutting pinned up over the desk. It was also about 'Samothraki. There's a big new archaeological dig in progress there – and knowing his interest in ancient history, I put two and two together.

'I went out to the airport next, and looked up which flights had left for Greece in the last twenty-four hours. David was on the Athens flight last night. Then when I was checking to see if he had been on the plane when it had taken off, that little lap-dog of his from the agency came up and told me the rest of the story in between whispers. He'd been left behind, apparently. Just like us. Been sitting at the airport ever since. I gave him the taxi-fare home.'

As a rule, Gray didn't let his feelings for David show. But now he clearly felt contempt, and he didn't hide it.

'Gray,' said Frances. 'I'm going to follow him. I must find out what has happened. I must find out directly from David, so I know the truth.'

'Right, Franci. Then I am coming with you.'

'No, Gray.' She saw the veil come down over his eyes, and she crossed over to him quickly, to slip into his arms.

'Gray, please. You must understand. This is something I have to do myself. Don't be angry. I need you to be here, to help wind down the factory – until I know what the Board will decide. I'm afraid it's out of my hands now. Anyway, Gray, this is something between me and my son. Please, just bear with me. I promise I will come back to Paris as soon as I can. But first I must find

David. And now, we must speak to Randy and Gerry Rule together before I leave.'

Frances was unconsciously mimicking her son's own actions of the night before – throwing important items into a light suitcase, discarding things she wouldn't need. And Gray was unconsciously playing the role of Xavier, following her round the room, entreating that he could accompany her.

'Franci, I don't understand why at least you won't let me come to Athens with you. It would give you a firm base. We don't know that David has gone to Samothraki. I could help you look. Franci, I want to be with you – it's important that we share this together.'

'Gray, to be honest, you would be out of place. If David has fled, seeing you would only make him run away again. I daren't risk that.'

Gray's jaw was fixed like granite. She saw a cloud come down over his eyes. She stopped packing for a moment and looked at him in exasperation.

'Please don't make me feel insecure, Gray. Your love is the one thing I need to be able to lean on right now.' And again she drew close to him, and he almost by reflex circled her in his arms.

'Once again, Franci, it seems I must do as you say. Now, don't talk about it any more. We have until the early morning. I want you to get some sleep before you go.'

All that night, Frances lay cradled in his arms. Then he woke her very early, before dawn. Wordlessly they made love with gentle compassion, and a tenderness that lasted right up until the urgency of the final moments.

Frances again went through the motions of preparing herself. She knew her ordeal was just beginning. The end of PS-21 – that was something maybe she could come to terms with eventually;

but the disappearance of David, and the riddle of his involvement in the disaster – that had to be solved.

Gray had taken charge of the journey, organizing a quick getaway in an anonymous taxi. Without Gray, she knew she wouldn't have made it. He had fended off the small but forceful crowd of reporters and photographers at the airport. Quickly, Frances had wondered how they had known she was leaving. Then the thought was submerged in the shoving throng, and her anxiety simply to get through to the next moment.

One man brandishing a small spy camera in her face, had accused her of abandoning the test volunteers. She wondered what the headlines would be on the next day. Hidden behind her dark glasses, her face pale, she had spoken as little as possible. Then she and Gray were together in a VIP lounge, and he was talking urgently, conscious of the minutes ticking away.

'How will I know where to contact you, Franci?'

'Oh, I'll wire you at the hotel, Gray. Or call. I'll call you from Athens anyway.'

The moment before their parting took place in an emotionally deadened state to Frances. Some defence mechanism within her had come into play to cushion her feelings. And when Gray spoke, she heard and registered the words as though they applied to somebody else.

'I'll stay here for a week. If by then I haven't heard from you, I'll assume you've decided to go back to New York without me.'

They clung together for a moment, then she turned awkwardly away. She wanted to cut this moment short, to rid herself of all the emotional clutter. And she walked away quickly, almost like a stranger.

On the aircraft, her numbed senses gradually cleared. She couldn't face breakfast, but she drank strong coffee, and that calmed her by helping her to concentrate on the essential and to discard the irrelevant.

She re-read the cutting on the archaeological dig on Samothraki. An American team were piecing together an ancient sanctuary. It had been a great mystic centre in 350 BC. Alexander the Great's parents had met there while attending some arcane ceremonial. But the island was best known in archaeological circles as the place where the headless, winged statue of Nike was found, kidnapped by a French diplomat in 1863, and taken to the Louvre.

Frances smiled. She remembered David talking about having seen the statue. She was sure that was where he had gone.

She read on, about how the American team had been digging for thirty years, and had still only uncovered little more than half of the vast site. And how Samothraki was an inhospitable island, even now inaccessible in stormy weather.

Then she turned to the tourist brochure, where the weather was hardly mentioned, and the island was described in glowing terms as a holiday paradise. But the photographs and the map showed it to be a mountainous hunk of rock, thrusting sharply out of the northern-most part of the Aegean sea, and rising to a single dramatic peak.

So this was to be her destination – a lonely citadel of stone, far from home, where she would confront her son and find out the truth of his role in the destruction of PS-21.

Then she slept.

It may have been blind fate, thought Frances, that had put her in the hands of Dimitri on her arrival at Samothraki. But surely it was the work of a kindly God. Here, in this island whose sacred significance stretched back over ancient civilizations, at last something, or someone, was on her side.

Dimitri had been waiting on the quayside, and had come over and taken her baggage without waiting to be asked. He drove the town's only taxi, and it was only once he had seated Frances securely in the back that he asked her where she wanted to go.

Dimitri turned out to be a sort of clearing house for every other sort of function as well. It was Dimitri who told Frances not only that he had seen David arrive three days before, but also where David had gone . . . to the village of Paleopolis, a short distance up the coast, and the site of the archaeological dig. In fact, Dimitri had taken him there himself. But before he would do the same for Frances, he insisted on taking her to his own house where his mother could give her a room. All the hotels were closed now; the tourists had gone. There was nowhere else she could stay; and he drove her up the winding streets to a two-storey house, with grape vines growing up to the first-floor open balcony that her neat little room opened onto.

After leaving Paris hot on David's trail, Frances had spent two frustrating nights in Athens. Gray's hunch had been correct. David had flown to Alexandropoulis, in the far corner of mainland Greece, the closest ferry port to the island of Samothraki. But to Frances' dismay, a strike since then had grounded all Olympic Airways internal flights. Her only way of reaching the island was by ferry-boat . . . a twenty-four hour voyage, with the next boat leaving on Monday morning. Frances had booked her hotel room for another night, and reminded herself that in Greece, life has its own pace, and that she would have to adjust hers to match.

Twenty-four hours aboard the car-ferry *Poseidon* had been a nightmare of claustrophobia and seasickness, as the weather gradually worsened. Homer's 'wine-dark dea' was black as slate, punctuated by white caps driven by the steadily rising wind.

Frances didn't know it, but it was only a window in the storm that allowed them to dock at Samothraki at all.

As soon as Frances had dumped her luggage, she and Dimitri were splashing and bumping along the road to Paleopolis. Driving rain had made puddles out of potholes, and through the smeared screen, Frances could glimpse an angry sea casting spray high in its tireless assault on the land.

On the way, Dimitri filled in the details. 'Of course, the season is over for archaeologists too. They have gone, the Americans, to try and fit together all those little bits of clay that they dig up.' He laughed at the absurdity of it.

'Perhaps they will be back – one or two of them sometimes stay for part of the winter. I told your son. But he seemed – forgive me – a little crazy. He must go there anyway. So I took him.' Then, with an ingratiating glance, he reassured Frances. 'But he is in good hands. You need not worry. I delivered him into my uncle Yannis's care.'

At the village, they had to walk the last quarter-mile to his uncle's house, up a steep and stony path between trees twisted by the storms sweeping in from the sea – Frances with the hood of her waterproof coat up, Dimitri bravely ignoring the rain on his bare head.

They had been taken upstairs in the old whitewashed house: downstairs was reserved for the animals – a donkey, two goats and several flapping chickens. Dimitri and Yannis had engaged in a furious conversation that did nothing to quell the trepidation rising within Frances. Where was David?

Then Dimitri turned to her again with his soothing smile. 'Do not worry, madam. Your son is safe. He has gone on an expedition, that is all. But he is with a guide – an old man who knows these mountains well. And,' he made a small flourish with his hand, as though this fact clinched David's safety completely, 'he has a donkey.'

'They will not have been able to climb Mount Saos in this storm, but the old man will have found shelter.'

Far from reassured, Frances felt totally bewildered. She had been travelling for more than three days now, and when she hadn't been on the move or actively searching for David, or horribly seasick, she had been lying awake worrying about him. Now her shoulders sagged forward, and she looked very pale.

Dimitri was master of the situation. He stepped across to her, put his hand under her arm firmly, and spoke. 'There is nothing more we can do. Soon it will be dark. You must be tired. I will take you home now, and tomorrow we will return here at first light. Then we will find your son.'

Exhaustion finally overcame anxiety and Frances slept

soundly. She awoke refreshed the next morning, before Dimitri's knock on her door, and dressed hurriedly in walking boots and trousers of heavy denim. She found her waterproof in the kitchen, dried in the heat from the stove. She ate a quick breakfast of honey and almonds, and goat's-milk yoghurt; and then Dimitri was revving his engine downstairs.

Improbably, the sky was a clear blue, and the countryside looked fresh-washed in the aftermath of the storm. Frances saw organic lumps of rock, petrified mushrooms washed round and stained black; and beyond that, the steep rise to the central mountains, a pale pink rock with the strata broken and folded, jagged peaks rising against the skyline.

The storm was not over yet. By the time they had reached Paleopolis, the clouds had returned, and a few drops of rain had fallen. Frances listened with rising anxiety to another noisy, quick-fire conversation between Dimitri and his uncle. Then the younger man translated the essence of it, with reassuring gestures. 'Your son is very close now. He came down last night to the temple, and sent the guide away. The old man told Yannis that he seemed very angry. It is a short walk. Come, I am quite certain that we will find him there.'

Full of hope, almost running, Frances had set off up the path to the dig with Dimitri silent by her side. It was a narrow stony track, buffetted by winds that carried an incongruously peaceful and domestic scent of wild thyme and oregano. Once she slipped on the stony path, and Dimitri's strong hand came out to support her.

It was less than a mile, and it took even less time to find the place the guide had described as the site of David's tent.

It was empty . . . there was no one there. The marks of the tent-pegs remained, but David had gone.

Frances felt the waves of misgiving and frustration again. For once, Dimitri seemed at loss for an answer. They must go back to the village, he said. They would send search parties out.

Frances took control. 'Not yet, Dimitri. You go to the village, and wait for me there.' She needed to be alone, to think things through – to try and put herself in David's position, and to imagine where he would have gone.

His tent had been pitched on a high corner of the site. Frances looked out at the squalls sweeping in over the sea. The wind was biting cold. Then, through the trees, she glimpsed a stone structure – the remnants of a column. It must be the temple, she thought, and even though she knew there were only ruins, she started walking towards it. Perhaps there would be shelter there among the broken bits of the ancient mysteries.

The silent stones had a peace of their own. More than two thousand years of history exerted a powerful effect on Frances, as it had on so many people before her, and with the cold wind howling round the old stonework it was impossible not to feel her own insignificance. As though she was being told to be patient, that her questions would all be answered in time. Either that, or they would cease to be important to her.

Then her eye caught on an incongruous colour – a piece of bright yellow, flapping in the wind. At first she thought it was a piece of garbage. Then she looked again, and though she could only see a corner of it, she could discern that the object had shape. Whatever it was, was just out of her line of sight in the rough shelter of some broken columns and a half-shattered wall. Frances walked towards it.

Her footsteps quickened as she drew closer. At first, it looked like a discarded bundle of clothes. Then she turned a corner in some time-worn marble steps, rounded by the tread of centuries, and could see more clearly. It was the body of a man, huddled for shelter, motionless, turned away from her.

Fear gripped her, and she paused for a moment. What if it were a dead body? What would she do then?

Then she caught a glimpse of a strand of blonde hair, blown by the wind, and she broke into a run.

It was David.

Frances fell to her knees beside the jumbled form. Frantically, she shook his shoulder. He was asleep, but shivering with cold. He woke with a shock, looking dazed and confused. When he recognized Frances, his expression changed. Then his fine features crumpled, and he hung his head.

'Fran,' he said. 'I have done a terrible thing. I have done something that can never be undone.'

After a wild night on the mountainside, he was obviously in a state of exhaustion. He tried to talk on, but was unable to finish any sentence for the sobs that he couldn't control. His agony tore at Frances as though it was her own.

'Not now, David. Tell me later. Now we must get you warm and dry.'

CHAPTER TWENTY-NINE

Frances heard the engines lower their pitch at the same time as the aircraft changed its altitude in the sky. A second later came the calm voice over the speakers: 'Ladies and Gentlemen, we have started our descent towards John F Kennedy airport. We will be landing in approximately twenty minutes.'

Frances shifted in her seat. God, she had spent too much time in aircraft. It would have to stop.

What a long way she'd been, she thought. So many miles. And how far she had come. A journey from an old life to a new, from the past into the future. And now the final segment of the journey, the last flight, the last final approach, the last landing, was soon to be behind her.

The return to New York had started walking beside a donkey, carrying her luggage down to a lonely jetty. Then came a frightening voyage on stormy seas; followed by the first of the aircraft rides, to Athens; next stop New York.

She thought back to the storm-lashed hillside on Samothraki. Now it seemed to her that finding David had been the turning point for her – not the damage to PS-21. She remembered how frightened David had looked, and how she had soothed his anguish, taking him in her arms like a child.

They had left his rucksack to be collected later, and Frances had helped him down the stony path to Paleopolis. There, Dimitri had taken over, and two hours afterwards, after bathing in water heated over the fire, and eating ravenously – dipping hunks of bread in olive oil, and dealing with a pile of scrambled eggs, David had recovered enough to talk. He sat opposite Frances, wrapped in a blanket, gazing at his fourth small cup of the strong, sweet Greek coffee. 'Now, David, you must tell me everything,' said Frances.

The story came out piece by piece, David speaking in a matter-of-fact voice, quietly and steadily. Most of the time he looked into the fire; now and then he would glance across and meet Frances's eyes.

'It was all my fault, Frances,' he began. 'Because of myself, because of my weakness.' Frances flinched as he told her of Xavier, of how they had become friends, and then lovers. Then he had revealed the train of events as it had happened to him – Xavier's fake uncle, Xavier's drug addiction, and Xavier's betrayal.

Frances's emotions were too confused for her to react. Overwhelmingly she felt relief, that David had been used in the same way that she had been used, innocent of any real crime. Like herself, he too was a scapegoat rather than villain.

But there was an overlay of growing discontent that – although she now knew some of the details that had been worrying her – she was still no closer to the real truth of the conspiracy.

David's guilt was different. It concerned not only the collapse of PS-21, but his own broken promise to his mother. After the episode with Milton's photograph, he had made a vow to her and himself that he would never again expose her to risk in this way. Instead, he had fallen for the first pretty boy that had come along.

'Fran,' he said piteously at the end. 'Can you ever forgive me?'

She thought for a while. 'I can forgive you, David, yes. You were caught up in things beyond your control. But I can never forgive myself. The security was my responsibility, and it wasn't good enough.

'But David, who is behind it. It is obviously the same people who are supplying Xavier with his drugs. Who was that?'

'They all came through a man called Geek. That's all Xavier knew – and he only found that out because one of the men he was dealing with in Paris let his name slip. The dealer was also a heroin addict, and once he and Xavier shot up together. It slipped out then.'

'Xavier is a very sick boy, you know, David. Tragically sick. He needs help. Gray found him at the airport. That's how we were sure where you'd gone.'

At the mention of his friend, David's face collapsed. 'I shouldn't have left him,' he wailed.

'My God – you should have,' retorted Frances. 'You really should have. And a damn long time ago. For Chrissakes, David, why didn't you tell me before?'

And then Frances had forced herself to stop the anger. It was too late for that.

While they were talking, the howling of the wind outside deepened in pitch, and the gaps between the squalls grew shorter. Then Dimitri came in with more coffee and a plate of sweetmeats with almonds and honey.

'Very bad,' he said. 'The storm is only beginning now. Samothraki is known as an island of storms. Now you will know why. Sometimes they can last for a week or more. So rough! There will be no ferries landing here for many days. Luckily, we have everything we need.'

'But that means we are trapped,' said Frances, her mind flying quickly to her commitments in Paris and New York. 'Is there no way off? What about an aircraft?'

Dimitri laughed. 'We have no flat land for an airstrip,' he said. 'Besides – how could you find one? The storm has broken the

341

cable lines; we have no way of communicating with the mainland until the storm has blown itself out.'

There comes a point, thought Frances, when control has been lost irrevocably. She would fight harder than anybody to stay in command up until then; but after that, even she knew the futility of even trying.

That point had been reached right then, and as she settled back into the aircraft seat cushions, she recalled that the relief at the unburdening had been enormous.

Sudden clarity. No deadlines, no pressure. No decisions. They'd been taken out of her hands. It was inevitable she would miss the Cranston board meeting. At a time when her division – the whole Cranston Group – was facing the biggest crisis in its history – a plight of her making – she had left it all behind, and become stranded on a remote island halfway around the world. Maxwell would have no option but to fire her. The storm had left both of them with no choice.

She was half-sitting on the bed in her room – a rough blanket round her shoulders, her knees drawn up to her chest. She wouldn't sleep much that night, she knew. Her mind was too full. But there would be plenty of time to sleep later.

A quiet knock on the door had roused her. It was David, equally sleepless. 'Fran? You awake?' And they had talked, late into the night, about everything under the sun except for PS-21. David had spoken with eager, shining eyes about the archaeological research on the island.

'I'm going to join the dig here if I can,' he said. 'Where you got to me, was the temple where they found the winged statue of Nike,' he said. 'But the current research is into something much older. They still haven't found out just when this place was first recognized as a mystical spot, and they've gone back more than two thousand years already. Fran, I'm going to stay on here. The team leader is in Athens, but he's coming back soon. I hope he'll let me join the dig.'

Frances smiled as she remembered the conversation. The aircraft banked slightly now, making the first of its course adjustments that would bring it in to its final approach. It had been like going back in time to David's late childhood. They had talked about everything and nothing, and it was as though they were starting their relationship with a clean plate.

In this way, they had seen out the storm. In her reflective mood, Frances now realized that this had been figuratively as well as literally true. She and David had ridden out their own emotional storm, undergoing death and rebirth while the tempest raged outside.

It had lasted another three days, before the howling gales began to moderate in intensity. Together, Frances and David had relapsed into the island pace of life, sleeping long hours, then taking bracing walks along the sea-shore, where the angry breakers rolled in. Her impatience forcibly suppressed, Frances loved their time together. The Board meeting was the next day, and there was no way she could even inform Maxwell of her whereabouts.

But she felt enormous relief when Dimitri had brought the news that the port authorities would be taking a launch to the mainland the following day, if the weather broke as predicted. They had agreed to take her as a passenger.

That night was the last she was to spend in companionship with David. 'I will be sorry to go,' said Frances. 'I have so enjoyed these past three days. It's the first time we've been alone together for years.' She didn't add what she was thinking; that Samothraki, in its elemental fury, and because of the truths they had both had to confront, had taken them both through a spiritual experience, and that she felt cleansed, even purged.

'What about you David? Why don't you come home for a while?'

'No, Frances. I'm not ready. I can't come home yet.'

'You'll need some money then?'

David had agreed and she had given him the one thousand dollars she had on her in cash. 'I'll send more through the bank.'

343

It was the first time he had willingly accepted anything from her in years, she realized. *It really is as though we have begun again.*

'How long will you stay on this island?'

'I don't know. I guess not more than six months. I need space and time, then I'll go back and start up again. This time, I'll make it work.'

'Where?' asked Frances, hoping he would say New York.

'London,' he replied. 'With Gaby, if she'll come. This time I'll make that work too. I've written her a note. Will you post it for me? What about you, Fran? Will you have to find another job?'

'Probably.' The tone was dry.

'It'll be tough.'

'No. The tough part is trying to find myself.'

David didn't pursue the theme. It led to Gray Barnard, and the South African was one subject that had been taboo, in spite of all the other barriers that had been broken down in the past days. 'Maybe it's a good chance to start again?' he said.

'Right from scratch.' Frances laughed.

'Are you afraid, Fran?'

'Yes.'

'You'll be okay.'

'Yes, I know that. But it will never be the same again.'

'Anyway, maybe that's not such a bad thing.'

The next morning, as they waited together in the café-bar by the quayside for the powerful launch that was to carry her to Alexandropoulis, she turned and faced him. 'David, we've avoided it up until now. But we must talk about Gray Barnard.'

He looked away. 'Okay.'

'I love him, David. In fact, he is the only force that is pulling me in any direction from this island. And Stacey, of course. I miss that little girl so much. It's as though . . . ' But then her voice choked with emotion, and the tears sprang quickly to her eyes. She had to wait a while, and wipe her nose, before she could go on.

'And Dad?' David's voice was gentle, not accusing.

'Dad will cope. He always does. He loves me, and I love him too. But I cannot compromise myself any longer. So I have decided that I must go with Gray. I need to be with him. If I don't, this PS-21 disaster will drag me down. You understand that, don't you David? There is nothing left for me to go back to.'

'Will you go and live in . . . ?' David paused, as though the words 'South Africa' were too uncomfortable for him to speak.

'We haven't worked that out yet, but I doubt it. Besides, I cannot abandon Stacey. A woman can give up a lot. Even her self-respect. But not a child – never a child.'

At this, her eyes filled with tears again, and she clung to David tightly, and he to her.

He was the first to speak. 'You'll be okay, Fran. And so will I.'

'Yes,' she said. 'You're right. We're both okay, and we're both off the merry-go-round. And this time we can decide for ourselves when and where we want to hop on. Did I ever tell you about Professor Rocher?' The image of the old man had appeared before her, smiling his wise, gentle smile.

'He told me once that big corporations were like hosts that eventually ate their own parasites. I remember his words – he spoke of a great beast, and how people leapt onto its back like fleas, eagerly sucking its blood. But then, as time passes, the beast itself starts sucking the blood of the flea, until only a tired-out, worthless husk is left. How sad and how amused he would be about the saga of PS-21. It proved how right he was.'

'Frances, if you start up again, if you ever need me . . . '

'Do you want to come back now?'

He shook his head firmly. 'No.'

'Then you come back when you are ready. I'll be looking forward to it.'

'Sure,' he said. 'I'll be back soon.'

They sat in silence for a while. Then he spoke again.

'You know, Fran – it's strange. But I feel as though the fog has lifted. For the first time, I see things clearly.'

'I understand,' she said. And then Dimitri had come into the room to summon her to the launch. And they had clung together for the last time, before she turned and walked firmly away.

The journey to Athens had been something Frances had tried to forget even as it was happening. Normally, the powerful launch would have made the trip to Alexandropoulis in a little over two hours. Against the heavy seas, it took them almost four, most of which Frances spent huddled miserably in a corner of the cabin, the oily diesel fumes making her more nauseous still.

She had managed to get on the midday flight to Athens, and by early afternoon she was comfortably in a hotel. But before even drawing the long hot bath that she wanted so badly, the first thing she did was to telephone Gray.

It was Sunday noon now. He had promised to wait until Friday. She wondered if he would still be in Paris, but the concierge at the hotel told her he had checked out on Saturday morning, and gone to the airport directly.

Fingers trembling, she dialled the number of *Goedgeluk*. The line clicked and buzzed, and then she heard it ringing. She could imagine the sound bouncing off the polished yellowwood floors, and wondered if there was any answering footfall echoing along the corridor.

Then relief flooded over her as she heard Gray's voice.

'Franci,' he said, his voice overjoyed. 'I've been so scared, so worried. I thought I had lost you.'

'Gray,' she spoke urgently. 'I am going to New York from here. Can you meet me there?'

'Of course. I'll take tonight's flight. What's your flight number?' And then a small pause. 'Franci, are you sure? If I come to New York, it will be for keeps. I mean, you and me.'

'Yes, Gray. For keeps.'

Now she was almost there. She wondered whether Gray would

be waiting. And she suddenly missed David acutely, and thought of him back on Samothraki.

This was so final.

She had spent the whole journey lost in her thoughts. What was going on in New York? It was Monday afternoon. She wondered what was happening at the Cranston Group. Perhaps they were still waiting for her. Perhaps Maxwell had put her past track record above the present disaster. Maybe he'd managed to save her job. She smiled – it seemed unlikely.

Then, as she mused, her eye caught a headline on a copy of the *Herald Tribune*. It was on the fold in the middle of the front page. The half-concealed word in the headline was 'Cranston'. She stood, and leaned forward to take the paper from the rack.

Ultracor's boardroom offered a commanding view over Central Park. In the autumn light Cranston Towers was clearly visible a little further along Fifth Avenue. Three men looked out from the boardroom, with a gleam of proprietorship in their eyes.

They were Art Millard, Chairman of Ultracor, Fritz Clements, lawyer to Jim Farnsworth and to Ultracor, and Tab Brooks, executive assistant to the Chairman. All three were in a jubilant mood.

Across the table, unable to see the building but trying hard to join in the good spirits, sat Gerry Rule – only his eyes giving away his anxiety behind his thick glasses.

'Well worth all the effort, wasn't it?' said Rule, giving an ingratiating smile.

The Chairman beamed at them all. 'We saved more than two hundred million dollars compared with the old price, and we bought when they were rock bottom. Another day, and we'd have been on the losing end again. Instead, we are now the largest diversified group in America.'

Brooks turned to his boss. 'Are you quite sure there won't be any trouble from the anti-trust people?'

Again Millard beamed. 'How many times must I tell you? The

347

whole point of going for Cranston was that it was both big enough to be interesting, and different enough not to lead us into conflict with the Justice Department. Anyway, I can tell you now – I squared it with them beforehand.'

Gerry spoke into the silence that followed. 'I take it, er, Number One, that I start first thing tomorrow?'

The Chairman looked surprised. 'No, my dear boy. Your job is over. We're grateful of course, but there's no more in it for you.' He grinned ferociously.

Rule stood, almost knocking his chair over. He looked aghast, nervously scratching his head. 'But . . . but I was promised. A top job. Tell him, Brooks, tell him!'

There was no response.

'Jesus! I set the whole thing up for you. I drove her on. I involved the Frenchy faggot, I set the whole connection with Geek. The whole Goddamn sabotage would have fallen to bits if it hadn't been for me.'

Now it was Brooks who spoke. 'Hold it right there, Gerry. We planned it all, remember. You were only taking orders. And if I remember back to our first briefing, you also said it wouldn't work.'

'I only said I didn't think you could create enough noise to cause the share values to drop so dramatically.'

'And you were wrong, weren't you? The shares dropped twenty-three per cent in a week. And you also said that Kline couldn't get it big enough to make the kind of impact we needed. You said the rejuvenation product wouldn't catch on.'

There was a pause.

'Didn't you?' Brooks's voice was hard-edged now.

'Well, I . . . yes.' Rule fished a Maalox tablet from his jacket pocket, and crunched it between his teeth, without being aware of what he was doing. 'But you pushed for it . . . you used your muscle with those media hot-shots . . . you made sure it worked, then you tore it apart.'

'That's so – part of the plan, my boy.' The Chairman seemed to be enjoying himself.

'But I played my part,' Gerry went on. 'I invented the whole scenario of the Japanese competition. Goddammit, that was dangerous for me. If she'd have checked, I'd have been finished.'

'But she trusted you, Gerry. That's why we used you. In any event, she had to move fast. The Cranston Board gave her an ultimatum.'

'Yes,' said Gerry. 'But you weren't to have known that would happen.'

Brooks and Art Millard exchanged smiles. 'Gerry, friend. You'd be surprised at how much we knew . . . and just how small a part you played. We knew about the ultimatum before she did. Don't forget that Milton Rae was very close to Jim Farnsworth. And Farnsworth told Fritz Clements here everything. We could have done it all without you, you know.'

'How about the boy?' Gerry was screaming now.

'Ah, yes – you did help us with the boy. But when we arranged it for that big job for his agency, and then for it to be taken away suddenly, human nature did the rest. We knew he'd turn to mummy, and we knew she would pick him up by giving him the PS-21 contract.'

Rule shook his head at the elaborate cunning of the plot he'd been involved in. 'Frigging clever,' he said. 'Frigging good timing.'

'You mustn't get the wrong idea, Gerry. That was one thing you did for us, and there were others. And we're grateful.' He took an envelope from his jacket pocket. 'This is for you. It's a token of our appreciation.'

Rule seized the envelope. He tore it open with frenzied fingers. It was stuffed with single dollar bills. Disbelievingly, he looked at it. 'What is this?' he shouted.

Now the Chairman spoke again, in honeyed tones. 'It's a thousand bucks, Gerry. For services rendered. Now your time with Ultracor has come to an end.'

Rule tossed the money to the floor. His cheeks were trembling, a vein was throbbing in his temple. 'A thousand lousy bucks! Christ, Brooks. You promised me a top job. I might as well have kept my face clean. They offered me Kline's job last week. But no, I turned it down. And now I've got nothing! Christ . . . ' He was beginning to babble now, flecks of spittle flying from his mouth and landing on the desk.

The Chairman looked at him without emotion. 'There's no job for you at Cranston either.' Then he looked across to Brooks, who gave a brief nod, and thumbed the buzzer under the desk. In seconds, a burly security man was in the room, and had seized Gerry Rule by the arms. As he kicked and struggled, the dollar bills were sent flying all over the room. Helpless, he was carried to the door. There, he managed to stand his ground for one last minute. 'You bastards. You can't do this to me. I'm one of you.' He looked directly at Brooks.

Millard answered him at once. 'Oh no, my dear boy. Out of the question. We could never have you as one of us. Not after what you did to Frances Kline. How could we ever trust you?'

In the silence that followed, the Chairman smiled smoothly. It was as though nothing had happened. 'Is that cable organized, Brooks?' he asked.

'Of course. She should have it any moment. I arranged for it to be delivered as the aircraft begins its final approach to New York. It's one of the benefits of owning your own airline.'

'She's a good woman that,' said the Chairman. 'She's got balls. Real woman, too. Went after her boy when he was in trouble, even though she had a lot to lose.'

Clements nodded. 'And she's lost it, too.'

'Not yet. I'm looking forward to her reaction to the cable. I can hardly wait. She's got one of the best marketing minds in the business. When the paperwork is done and we move into Cranston, I want her in the top team.'

'I wouldn't count on her coming,' said Clements. 'She's a fiercely independent lady, and PS-21 meant a lot to her.'

'When she finds out that you used her – built her and the

rejuvenation thing up and then destroyed it only to get at Cranston – she'll be mighty pissed off.'

'Yes,' said Millard. 'I know all that. But she's also ambitious. Much too ambitious to miss a chance like this. And with Milton Rae out of the way, she knows she can achieve almost anything. Status, wealth, power. She won't knock that in a hurry.'

Clements had an answer. 'She's also got a man.'

'So, who hasn't?'

'She won't be the same after this,' put in Brooks.

'No,' said the Chairman. 'She'll be better – tougher. You wait and see.'

'Poor old Milton Rae,' said Clements. 'Do you think he really could have screwed up our plans and found a way to block Kline? I'm not so sure I'll miss him, poor bastard.'

'It was justice, Fritz,' said Millard. 'Simple justice. Farnsworth had a right to know about Milton and his son, and you had a duty to tell him. Rae deserved to die.'

Frances sat stunned into silence. The Cranston Group had been taken over, she had read in the newspaper, in a dramatic market coup. What did it mean. What did it all have to do with PS-21? What monstrous conspiracy had this all been?

She smiled at the irony of her wondering whether she still had a job with Cranston. Now all the presidents must be wondering the same thing. Oh, God. Poor old Maxwell, she thought with amused sympathy. He must be sweating. He never did like it when things didn't move perfectly smoothly. This sort of upheaval would make him want to run and hide.

She was still too stupefied to piece together all the details in her mind. Then the stewardess came from the pilot's cabin, walking with an urgency in her step, and stopped at Frances' seat. 'Mrs Kline, this is an important message for you.'

She took the folded paper and opened it out. It was a hand-written radio message, short and to the point.

'WE HAVE INTERESTING PROPOSAL FOR YOU

STOP CAN WE MEET THREE PM OUR HEAD OFFICE TOMORROW STOP' It was signed: ART MILLARD – CHAIRMAN ULTRACOR.

Gray was waiting for her on the other side of the barrier. Their greeting was almost subdued. So much to say that neither knew where to begin. But there was no restraint in the way they hugged one another. Then they fell naturally into step and walked towards the exit, their luggage piled high on one trolley, Gray pushing.

As they set off, she noticed that she still had the Ultracor cable crushed in her pocket. She took it out, screwed it up, and threw it towards a waste-bin.

The paper bounced on the rim, and then fell out onto the floor. It caught the corner of Gray's eye, and suddenly they were both looking at it, a little crumpled ball on the shining floortiles.

'What is that?' asked Gray stopping. 'Something important?'

'Oh, nothing that can't wait until tomorrow,' said Frances, smiling up at him.

Then, arm in arm, they walked to the sidewalk to hail a cab.